GAME CHANGER

Also by Neal Shusterman

Novels
Bruiser
Challenger Deep
Chasing Forgiveness
The Dark Side of Nowhere
Dissidents
Downsiders
The Eyes of Kid Midas
Full Tilt
The Shadow Club
The Shadow Club Rising
Speeding Bullet

The Arc of a Scythe Trilogy
Scythe
Thunderhead
The Toll

The Accelerati Trilogy
(with Eric Elfman)
Tesla's Attic
Edison's Alley
Hawking's Hallway

The Antsy Bonano Series
The Schwa Was Here
Antsy Does Time
Ship Out of Luck

The Unwind Dystology
Unwind
UnWholly
UnSouled
UnDivided
UnBound

The Skinjacker Trilogy
Everlost
Everwild
Everfound

The Star Shards Chronicles
Scorpion Shards
Thief of Souls
Shattered Sky

The Dark Fusion Series
Dread Locks
Red Rider's Hood
Duckling Ugly

Story Collections
Darkness Creeping
MindQuakes
MindStorms

GAME CHANGER

NEAL SHUSTERMAN

Quill Tree Books
An Imprint of HarperCollinsPublishers

Quill Tree Books is an imprint of HarperCollins Publishers.

Game Changer
Copyright © 2021 by Neal Shusterman
All rights reserved. Printed in the United States of America.
No part of this book may be used or reproduced in any manner whatsoever without
written permission except in the case of brief quotations embodied in critical articles
and reviews. For information address HarperCollins Children's Books, a division of
HarperCollins Publishers, 195 Broadway, New York, NY 10007.
www.epicreads.com

Library of Congress Control Number: 2020945269
ISBN 978-0-06-199867-6 (trade bdg.) — ISBN 978-0-06-309480-2 (special edition)

Typography by Joel Tippie
20 21 22 23 24 PC/LSCH 10 9 8 7 6 5 4 3 2 1

First Edition

Ronnie Antonio Paris, 3. Jeremy Mardis, 6. Kameron Prescott, 6. Aiyana Mo'Nay Stanley-Jones, 7. Gabriel Fernandez, 8. Anthony Avalos, 10. Noah Cuarto, 4. Juwan Bymon, 6. Desiree Bymon, 7. Ponda Davis, 28. Lisa Bymon, 26. Stanley Almodovar III, 23. Amanda Alvear, 25. Mercedez Marisol Flores, 26. Oscar A. Aracena-Montero, 26. Simon A. Carrillo Fernandez, 31. Rodolfo Ayala-Ayala, 33. Alejandro Barrios Martinez, 21. Martin Benitez Torres, 33. Antonio D. Brown, 29. Darryl R. Burt II, 29. Angel L. Candelario-Padro, 28. Juan Chevez-Martinez, 25. Tevin E. Crosby, 25. Franky J. Dejesus Velazquez, 50. Deonka D. Drayton, 32. Peter O. Gonzalez-Cruz, 22. Paul T. Henry, 41. Frank Hernandez, 27. Miguel A. Honorato, 30. Javier Jorge-Reyes, 40. Jason B. Josaphat, 19. Eddie J. Justice, 30. Anthony L. Laureano Disla, 25. Christopher A. Leinonen, 32. Juan R. Guerrero, 22. Brenda L. Marquez McCool, 49. Jean C. Mendez Perez, 35. Akyra Monet Murray, 18. Kimberly Morris, 37. Jean C. Nieves Rodriguez, 27. Luis O. Ocasio-Capo, 20. Geraldo A. Ortiz-Jimenez,

Dedicated to the many victims of the cockroaches of ignorance and intolerance.

25. Eric Ivan Ortiz-Rivera, 36. Joel Rayon Paniagua, 31. Enrique L. Rios Jr., 25. Juan P. Rivera Velazquez, 37. Luis D. Conde, 39. Yilmary Rodriguez Solivan, 24. Jonathan A. Camuy Vega, 24. Christopher J. Sanfeliz, 24. Xavier Emmanuel Serrano Rosado, 35. Gilberto Ramon Silva Menendez, 25. Edward Sotomayor Jr., 34. Shane E. Tomlinson, 33. Leroy Valentin Fernandez, 25. Luis S. Vielma, 22. Luis Daniel Wilson-Leon, 37. Jerald A. Wright, 31. Cory J. Connell, 21. Rev. Clementa Pinckney, 41. George Floyd, 46. Cynthia Marie Graham Hurd, 54. Ethel Lee Lance, 70. Rev. DePayne Middleton-Doctor, 49. Tywanza Sanders, 26. Rev. Daniel L. Simmons, 74. Rev. Sharonda Coleman-Singleton, 45. Myra Thompson, 59. Lonette Keehner, 56. Timothy Caughman, 66. Jimmy Smith-Kramer, 20. Balbir Singh Sodhi, 51. Anita "Nicki" Gordon, 63. Anil Thakur, 31. Sandeep Patel, 25. Ji-ye Sun, 34. Thao "Tony" Pham, 27. Garry Lee, 22. Srinivas Kuchibhotla, 32. Waqar Hasan, 46. Vasudev Patel, 49. Paramjit Kaur, 41. Satwant Singh Kaleka, 65. Prakash Singh, 39. Sita Singh, 41. Ranjit Singh, 49. Suveg Singh, 84. Stephen Tyrone Johns, 39. James Craig Anderson, 47. Larnell Bruce Jr., 19. Maurice E. Stallard, 69. Vickie Lee Jones, 67. DeLois Bailey, 53. Sam Cockrell, 46. Micky Fitzgerald, 45. Lynette McCall, 47. Charlie I. Miller, 58. Thomas Willis, 57. John Crawford III, 22. Breonna Taylor, 26. Aura Rosser, 40. Jamarion Robinson, 26. Eleanor Bumpurs, 66. Jaquavion Slaton, 20. Kwame "K.K." Jones, 17. Jimmy Atchison, 21. Kendra James, 21. Kayla Moore, 41. Jordan Edwards, 15. Ukea Davis, 18. Stephanie Thomas, 19. Felicia Moreno, 25. Serena Angelique Velazquez Ramos, 32. Layla Pelaez Sanchez, 21. Alexa Negron Luciano, 26. Yampi Mendez Arocho, 19. Jordan Anchondo, 24. Andre Anchondo, 23. Arturo Benavides, 60. Leonard Cipeda Campos, 41. Maribel Hernandez, 56. Raul Flores, 77. Maria Flores, 77. Jorge Calvillo Garcia, 61. Adolfo Cerros Hernandez, 68. Sara Esther Regalado, 66. Alexander Gerhard Hoffman, 66. David Alvah Johnson, 63. Luis Alfonzo Juarez, 90. Maria Eugina Legarreta Rothe, 58. Elsa Mendoza Marquez, 57. Ivan Hilierto Manzano, 46. Gloria Irma Marquez, 61. Margie Reckard, 63. Javier Amir Rodriguez, 15. Teresa Sanchez de Freitas, 82. Angelina Englisbee, 86. Juan Velazquez, 77. Guillermo "Memo" Garcia, 36. Greg McKendry, 60. Linda Kraeger, 61. Ricky John Best, 53. Taliesin Myrddin Namkai-Meche, 23. Blaze Bernstein, 19. John Freddy, 43. Sukhjit "Sammy" Khajala, 50. Mohammad Zafer, 60. Mohammed Alamgir, 38. Albert Kotlyar, 32. Mohammed Abdul Nasser Ali, 54. Imam Maulama Akonjee, 55. Thara Uddin, 43. Khalid Jabara, 37. Abdisamad Sheikh-Hussein, 15. Deah Barakat, 23. Yusor Abu-Salha, 21. Razan Abu-Salha, 19. Hassan Alawsi, 46. Atatiana Jefferson, 28. Stephon Clark, 22. Botham Jean, 26. Philando Castile, 32. Alton Sterling, 37. Michelle Cusseaux, 50. Freddie Gray, 25. Janisha Fonville, 20. Eric Garner, 43. Akai Gurley, 28. Tamir Rice, 12. Tyre King, 13. Jesus M. Huesca, 25. Michael Brown Jr., 18. Tanisha Anderson, 37. Trayvon Martin, 17. Sean Monterrosa, 22. Jamel Floyd, 35. Danny Overstreet, 43. Fred Martinez, 16. Gwen Amber Rose Araujo, 17. Terrianne Summers, 51. Guin "Richie" Phillips, 36. Sakia Gunn, 15. Ruth "Ruthie" George, 19. Tiarah Poyau, 22. Mollie Tibbetts, 20. Nazma Khanam, 60. Janese Talton-Jackson, 29. Cherica Adams, 24. Jessica Hampton, 25. Mary Spears, 27. Nova Henry, 24. Ava Henry, 10 months. LaVena Johnson, 19. April Jace, 40. Julia Martin, 27. George Chen, 19. Cheng Yuan Hong, 20. Weihan Wang, 20. Katherine Cooper, 22. Christopher Ross Michaels-Martinez, 20. Veronika Weiss, 19. Lori Gilbert-Kaye, 60. Joyce Fienberg, 75. Richard Gottfried, 65. Rose Mallinger, 97. Jerry Rabinowitz, 66. Cecil Rosenthal, 59. David Rosenthal, 54. Bernice Simon, 84. Sylvan Simon, 86. Daniel Stein, 71. Melvin Wax, 88. Irving Younger, 69. Ruth Milton, 95. Dominique "Rem'Mie" Fells, 27. Vanessa Guillen, 20. Kaysera Stops Pretty Places, 18. Henna Harris, 21. Roderica Ribboning, 15. Elijah McClain, 23. Savanna LaFontaine-Greywind, 22. Ahmaud Arbery, 25. Andre Alexander Green, 15. Cameron Tillman, 14. Ciara Meyer, 12. John Albers, 16. Laquan McDonald, 17. Logan Simpson, 16. Giovanni Melton, 14. Zachary Bearheels, 29. Loreal Tsingine, 27. Benjamin Whitesheild, 34. Paul Castaway, 35. Jason Pero, 14. Malena Loonakin, 26. Nireah Johnson, 17. Brandie Coleman, 18. Emonie Spaulding, 25. Andrew Anthon, 79. Cornel Young Jr., 29. Patrick M. Dorismond, 26. John Adams, 61. Alfred "Abuka" Sanders, 23. Christopher Arnold, 23. Djibril Diol, 29. Adja Diol, 23. Khadija Diol, 2. Hassan Diol, 6 months. Zaria Jenkins Burgess, 19. Everardo Torres, 24. Dawn Rae Nelson, 39. Jeanne Taylor, 50. Bruce James Wiegel, 41. Michael Pleasance, 23. Osamane Zongo, 43. Alberto Spruill, 57. Kenneth Walker, 39. Salmon John-Akbar Perez, 26. Michael Bell Jr., 21. Bounmy Ouza, 29. Joseph Rosenbaum, 36. Anthony Huber, 26. Kelly Thomas, 37. Daniel Prude, 41. Oluwatoyin Salau, 19. Nina Pop, 28. Amanda Reyes, 29. Amanda Dubrowski, 31. Mackenzie Lueck, 23. Miles Hall, 23. Ricardo Muñoz, 27. Brandon Roberts, 20. Darius J. Tarver, 23. William Howard Green, 43. Jaquyn O'Neill Light, 20. Manuel Ellis, 33. Donnie Sanders, 47. Etienne T. Tauqette, 38. Tommie Dale McGlothen Jr., 44. Kanisha Necole Fuller, 43. Steven Demarco Taylor, 33. Joel Acevedo, 25. Dijon Kizzee, 29. Simmie Williams Jr., 17. Latisha King, 15. Daniel "Dano" Petty, 39.

Come as you were,
Not as you'll be,
Remember to bring back
the best part of me.
Take what you find,
Leave what you lost,
Light the way burning
the bridges you crossed . . .

— Konniption, "Come As You Were"

1

FULL STOP

You're not going to believe me.

You'll say I've lost my mind, or that I've suffered one too many concussions. Or maybe you'll convince yourself that I'm conning you, and that you're the butt of some elaborate practical joke. That's okay. Believe whatever you want if it helps you sleep. That's what we do, isn't it? Build ourselves a comfy web of reality like busy little spiders, and cling to it so we can get through the worst of days.

We've had plenty of troubled days, haven't we? All of us. The ground shifts, and the world changes, and we go tumbling. It can happen in the time it takes for a traveler to step off an international flight and sneeze. Or the time it takes for a man with a crushed windpipe to stop breathing.

I've seen all that, just like you . . . but I've known other things. The kind of world-bending events that can't be tracked by the news or by scientists. Changes that no one else on Earth will ever know.

But like I said, you don't have to buy into anything I say. In fact, it's better for you if you don't. Tell yourself it's only a story. Stay in the middle of your web. Catch a few flies. Live the dream.

My name is Ash. With all the things that have changed, my name hasn't. It's a constant around which the rest of my universe revolves, and I'm grateful for that.

Less-than-interesting fact: Ash is short for Ashley—which, as my grandmother repeatedly says, was once "a very masculine name." It was her brother's name. Apparently he was named after some guy in *Gone With the Wind*, because he had the bad luck to be born in 1939, when the movie came out—and long before people were willing to admit how racist it was. He had a twin brother named Rhett, who eventually died of polio. And here's the funny thing—the guy who played Ashley Wilkes in the movie? His real name was *Leslie* Howard. Dude couldn't get a break, even fictionally.

My name only became an issue once a year on the first day of school, when clueless teachers called it out, looking for a girl. Anyone who was stupid enough to make an obnoxious comment basically got their liver handed to them by yours truly, so classmates learned to just let it go. Anyway, Ash always worked for me. And only my aforementioned grandmother calls me Ashley.

Although this story begins and ends with football, it's the stuff in between that matters. The mystery meat in the sandwich you've already been warned you won't be able to swallow, much less digest. Drink milk, it'll calm your stomach.

It would be a stretch to say that football was my life—but a lot of my life revolved around it. I played since I was little, and was a starter on my high school team—the Tibbetsville Tsunamis. Don't start. It's not my fault. The school used to be "the Blue Demons" but years ago a holier-than-thou type on the school board raised a big stink, claiming it was "unwholesome," and made the school change it. So our mascot went from a grinning blue demon that never hurt anybody to a snarling blue wave that killed 800,000 people in Southeast Asia, and made sushi radioactive in Japan. Somehow that's less offensive. At least we have cool helmets.

The sport might have been my life if I was a running back, or a wide receiver, or, that dream of dreams, a quarterback. But I'm not fast. I'm not graceful. I'm not "poetry in motion." I'm more like a poetry slam. You could say I'm sturdy. Not fat, but solid. Like an oak. It's part of what makes me a fantastic defensive tackle.

Tackles and linebackers—we do the dirty work and get no glory—but we're always, *always* the reason for victories and losses. See, the quarterback is like the lead singer of a band whose head swells so big, he goes solo, and demands only blue M&M's in his dressing room. The running backs and wide receivers, they're guitar and bass. But the linemen? We're the rhythm. The drummers who hold the beat, but are always in the background.

That's okay, though. I was never in it for the attention. I loved the raw energy of it. I loved the way it felt to smash through an offensive line. And I loved the feel and the sound of crashing helmets. Remember that, because it's going to come back.

I was known for my tackles. My hits. Rarely were there flags on my tackles, and I prided myself on that. I did it right, and I did it well. To the best of my knowledge, I never caused a concussion—but I bruised and got bruised. Sometimes pretty badly, but I never complained. "Walk it off" was our family motto.

"Enjoy it now," my father once told me. "Because it's over sooner than you think."

My dad also played high school football. He was counting on a college scholarship but never got one. Instead he went to work for my uncle, managing auto parts distribution. He walked it off. Between that and what Mom earned as a nutritionist, we scraped by okay. Thank God for fast food; it drove people to my mom like a cattle chute.

That's how things were. It's what doctors call "baseline." The reading by which everything else is measured. It was the normal before everything went to some place way past hell.

There are choices we make, choices that are made for us, and things we ignore long enough until all choices have fallen away. I've been plenty guilty of ignoring stuff I don't want to deal with until it doesn't matter anymore, or it's too screwed up to bother fixing. Like the time I put off registering for the PSAT until it was too late. My mom was furious, but I didn't care. She was enrolling me in an SAT prep class, so what was the point of wasting a perfectly good Saturday on a practice test I'd be taking half a dozen times anyway? Besides, I was hoping for the scholarship Dad never got.

"That's what Jay next door thought," my mom had pointed out. "He hung everything on a scholarship he never got, and didn't get in anywhere."

"There's always community college," my father chimed in, always taking whatever side my mother didn't. "It's less expensive, and he can transfer to a university in two years that won't bankrupt us."

It made me think of my friend Leo Johnson, who was already being courted by major schools. I was happy for him, and it would bring recruiters to our games, but I knew none of them would be looking at me. I can't deny that I envied the options Leo would have—but I had to trust that I'd have choices, too.

So where was my choice, then, that took me down the path to the tweaked places I ended up? It couldn't have been the choice to play ball that day. I mean, who in their right mind chooses not to play their sport without a good reason—such as death or dismemberment. Few things would keep me away from the field. I had an obligation to my team. There wasn't even a premonition that first day. There was nothing to indicate that something was beginning that couldn't be undone.

Maybe it was the choice to play football in the first place all those years ago that set things in motion. But was that really a choice? Football was my father's love. It was the way he and I connected, so I loved it, too. Sometimes it's like that when you're a kid. You eat up whatever your parents put on your life's plate.

So let me set the table for you, before I heap on the crazy-ass casserole. It's Friday, September 8. It's the first game of the season. I'd come back from summer vacation with a growth spurt, and had hit hell week hard. I was ready. As it was still almost two months before daylight savings kicked in, the game would begin in late-afternoon sun, but would end under the stark halogen lights that could turn the ordinary into a spectacle.

The locker room was all wild energy that the coach had to harness into a "wall and a wedge." That's how he wanted us to see it. The Tsunami defense was a wall of water that nothing could get through. The offense was a whitewater wedge, surging through everything in its path.

As soon as I suited up, I went over to Leo. He and I had been best friends for as long as I could remember. We'd been playing football together since we were little kids in the Pop Warner league, where the padding made us so top-heavy we could be tackled by a stiff breeze. Leo was an amazing wide receiver. It was like he had tractor beams in his fingertips that could suck a football out of the sky. He was Black, like about a third of our team. Actually, our team was a good representation of the school demographic. A fair balance between white, Black, and Latinx, with one Asian kid everyone called Kamikaze, even though he was Korean, not Japanese.

I was friends with just about all of them, and we would always give each other good-natured shit.

"If you were any whiter, I could wave you to stop a war," my friend Mateo Zuñiga once told me, after trying and failing to teach me Spanish pronunciation. Mateo was the best field-goal kicker in the county. He might not have helped my pronunciation, but he did a pretty good job of educating my taste buds, since his mother's cooking was a religious experience—including the miracle of late-night *pozole*.

At the time, I thought having a diverse group of friends checked my box of social responsibility. Like there was nothing more for me to do than have some brown at the table. "Color shouldn't matter" I was always taught—and always believed. But there's a big difference between "shouldn't" and "doesn't." Privilege is all about not seeing that gap.

While Mateo and Kamikaze and everyone else in the locker room were whooping themselves into a frenzy, Leo always got quiet before a game. Focusing. "If I'm gonna make it to the end zone, I gotta already be there in my head," he once told me. But today, I knew there was more to it.

"Ready to make the Wildebeests an endangered species?" I asked him, hoping to get him into the spirit of things. (Yes, we were playing the Wharton Wildebeests—they made the Tsunamis sound good.)

Leo grinned. "They're already endangered," he said. "I hear they only breed in captivity."

It was good to get a smile out of him. I knew this was the first game he was playing since his girlfriend moved to Michigan—which might as well have been Mars. In the weeks before the

7

move, Leo was all about applying to Michigan State, convinced that what the two of them had would stand the test of time. Then she sent him a break-up text. From the plane. That had to be a first, getting dumped from 37,000 feet. A long way to fall.

"She did the right thing," Leo said after it happened. "Senior year shouldn't be about waiting for someone you might never see again. And sometimes it's best to pull the Band-Aid off fast." Although it seemed to me it was more like a full chest waxing.

I sat down next to him on the bench. "You do know that all the girls in the stands are gonna have their eyes on you now, right?"

"I know it," he said. "But I'm not there yet. A few more weeks."

I had to hand it to him. Other guys might rebound into the next pair of open arms, but not Leo. He had his priorities straight.

"Well, then," I said, "maybe you can deflect some of those eyes in my direction."

"Will do," he said, then his grin took on the slightest slant. "Problem is, it'll only work for the ones who need glasses."

I laughed, and he laughed harder, and I laughed harder still. That's the way it was with us. The way I thought it would always be.

The first five minutes of the game were high energy, because we were so excited to be back on the field before cheering spectators. The Wildebeests were a competent but uninspired team. A good team to cut our teeth on in the beginning of the season. No score by the start of the second quarter, but we were confident of the win. Then Layton Vandenboom, our quarterback, made a bad pass that was intercepted. While he beat himself up over it (something he would continue to do for a whole week, whether we won or lost), the defensive squad took the field. That meant me, if you haven't been paying attention.

The Wildebeests had a weasel of a quarterback, known for complaining to the refs about every little thing. Taking down the whining Wildebeest weasel would be a very satisfying thing.

So both teams got into position on the line of scrimmage, and the play began. The ball was snapped, and I sprang into action. You're supposed to engage by the shoulders. Helmet crunches, while not strictly forbidden, are not advised, but sometimes can't be avoided. Things happen. And, as I've always loved that head-banging feeling, I never minded when it happened. Like I said, my power hit was my trademark. It was the thing that could maybe get me the scholarships that my father never got.

But this time, the hit was different.

You know how sometimes when you're startled by a loud sound, your brain misfires so you see a phantom flash along with the sound? Well, this was like a sudden surge of phantom cold. Not a blast of air or a feverish chill—it was more like my blood had been replaced by ice water, but only for an instant. Then the feeling was gone and I was on the ground, and I had tackled the Wildebeest weasel, ball still in hand, and the crowd was cheering.

I didn't even remember the time between hitting the lineman

and getting to the quarterback. It was like I teleported there.

Twelve-yard loss for the Wildebeests. The weasel was whining that there should have been a flag on the play, but of course there was none, because there was no infraction. Nothing unusual about the play . . . except for the cold that I could no longer feel, but that had been very real. What the hell *was* that?

High fives, butt slaps, knuckle punches, and back to the line. Only now I had something like a headache. Not really a headache, but something *like* one. It felt like an electric hum that you feel instead of hear. Walk it off, right? I did, and didn't think about it for the rest of the game.

We won twenty-four to fourteen, and in our post-game high, the memory of that icebolt was almost lost. It wasn't until much later that I remembered it.

After the game, a bunch of us went out for burgers at the Tibbetsville Towne Centre—one of those pretentious anti-malls with misplaced *e*'s that's all about Fridaye and Saturdaye nights. Movie theaters, bowling, and restaurants, as well as a fast-food court for those who just wanted to scarf down something quick and cheap. As the best football team in a town that mainlined the sport, the Tsunamis basically owned the food court on Friday nights.

Layton had his girlfriend, Katie, with him. His arm hung around her shoulders like a slab of beef weighing her down. When you think of a quarterback and his popular girlfriend, these are the two you picture. Layton was an all-American, white-bread kid who probably dreamed of being Captain America. Katie was a cheerleader who had a lot more going for her that Layton didn't notice. He had trouble seeing past her pom-poms.

You know how some people see a stereotype, and just become it? The path is there, it's wide, and it's well trod. It's easier to follow that path than to defy it. Some people follow that path all the way into the box that's waiting for them at the end, where the sermon is rote and the flowers are plastic. And so it is and ever shall be, the quarterback and the cheerleader, in every school, in every town, now and forever, amen.

I don't think Katie was really a cheerleader by choice. In the spring she played tennis, and clearly her heart was in that—but her mother had been a cheerleader, and her sister had been, and she had been encouraged in it since she was little. Like I said, we eat from the plate our parents set before us. I must confess here that Katie and I had a history, although not the kind you're thinking. We buried a body together. But I'll get to that later.

Norris, an offensive lineman (and "offensive" has multiple meanings here), was also with us. He was there on his own, because his on-again/off-again relationship with his girlfriend was currently in the off position and seemed likely to stay that way. Norris seemed to like the *idea* of a relationship rather than the actual thing. Or maybe they kept breaking up because of Norris's chronic douchiness, and comments that rarely appeared to have a brain tethered to the other end. I'm sure you know a guy like Norris. Everyone does. Constantly making stupid decisions and saying all the wrong things at all the wrong times, like maybe he was taking a dump when God was handing out common sense. One time he made a bunch of Mexican jokes that nobody wanted to hear, which made Mateo come over and punch his lights out.

You put up with the Norrises of the world because A) He was your friend long before you realized he was an asshole, and B) He's like a sponge for all your bad thoughts about yourself, because no matter how crappy a day you're having, at least you're not Norris.

And, of course Leo was there, with his sister, Angela, who'd taken it upon herself to fill in socially for Leo, now that his ex-girlfriend was a Martian. Angela was a year younger than us, but most people took her and Leo to be twins, since she always hung out with an older crowd. I cannot deny that she was hot. I might have asked her out, but that would have been problematic on several levels. First of all, you don't want to date your best friend's sister because it never ends well on any front. Secondly, although I'm ashamed to admit it, dating a Black girl would have given my grandpa a second heart attack. I wouldn't call my grandfather racist. Okay, well, actually I *would* call him racist, just not to his face.

"It's a generational thing," my mom always said, too embarrassed by it to address it in any meaningful way. Grandpa didn't have a problem with Leo, but I did once catch him hitting the lock button on his car when Leo came over. It's not like he thought Leo would steal it, but seeing a Black kid reminded him to lock it. Old people, right? Leo never made a big deal of it, so it never occurred to me that maybe it bothered him more than he let on.

I got into a fight with Leo only once about race—over two years back, when I made an asinine comment about affirmative action in social studies. I pointed out that Leo had better grades than just about anyone in class—and definitely better than anyone on the football team, which, to the simple sophomore I was at the time, was proof that no one needs to get preferential treatment because of race. Then he smacked me down with talk about all the kids who weren't as lucky as he'd been—who didn't have the opportunities he'd had, and found all the doors shut before they got there. "When you gotta spend all your time just kicking down the door, you're already exhausted, and miles behind the ones who get to prance right through," he had said. "Do you really think that's fair?"

I hadn't thought of it that way, so I apologized and told him I didn't mean anything by it, but I guess you can't backpedal when you say something stupid that you hadn't really thought out. Definitely not one of my shining moments. But at least I'm not Norris.

"This country is filled with the well-intentioned ignorant," Leo told me. "It's a freaking plague, and you're a carrier."

The upshot was that Leo and I didn't talk for about a week. Then it passed, and things were okay. I mean, he was my best friend—we couldn't let a little thing like racial tension get between us. And then I went out to protest police brutality with him, standing with a hand-painted sign and a fist in the air. I thought that was enough to show him I was on the right side of history. I have a different perspective now.

So anyway, six of us were eating burgers. Us guys were still pumped from our victory, and high on the adrenaline that makes any competitive sport so addictive—yet underneath it all, I could feel a strange current of uneasiness. This wasn't a premonition, but an aftershock—because it wasn't about something that was going to happen. It already *had* happened; I just didn't know it yet. A sense of something being "wrong." Was the feeling inside me, or around me? Was it both? In the moment, my body could only translate the feeling into that weird buzzing headache.

"I can't believe I threw such a bad pass," Layton lamented.

"Dude, give it a break," Norris said. "We beat the Wilde-freaks, that's all that matters."

But the look on Layton's face said otherwise. Right about then, Katie shifted beneath his arm and began to eat one french fry after another—so quickly that Layton had to counter by removing his arm from her shoulder and using that hand to grab some fries for himself before they were all gone.

I grinned because I realized that was exactly why she had done it. Not because she wanted the fries, but because she had to motivate Layton to remove his arm, freeing her from the weight. Katie threw me a brief, guilty glance, knowing that I had seen this, and I gave her a quick wink to let her know that her secret was safe with me. She looked away, but then I could see her suppressing a smile. I remember wondering if it was disloyal of me to look forward to the time she and Layton broke up, so I could have my chance with her—a chance I should have taken a while ago, but never had the guts to do. I wouldn't let my mind go down that path too soon, though. I just kept it on a mental back burner. I was never the kind of guy to make moves on someone else's girlfriend. There were rumors, though, that Layton didn't exactly treat her right. At the time, I didn't think it was any of my business—but all the more reason for me to think their 'ship was sinking before the end of football season.

We talked more football as we ate, and Angela became bored. "Don't you guys have any other interests?"

"Food," said Norris. "And sex."

"In that order, for Norris," I added.

"If you didn't want to hear football talk," Leo asked, "why did you come?"

"So that Katie wouldn't have to fight toxic male culture alone."

"We're not toxic," I told her. "Just because we're football players doesn't mean we're unenlightened, and stuff."

"And stuff," she mocked. "I will concede that current toxicity levels are in the green, but if they start to rise, I'll let you know."

A dozen yards away, a server dropped a tray. Since the place served everything in red plastic baskets, nothing broke—there were just a few impotent thuds and the clattering of silverware. It made my head jerk around, though, and my brain spun like one of those dashboard compasses. I took a deep breath, and splayed my hands out on the table, as if feeling a solid, stable surface under my palms and fingertips could reassure me that gravity was still pulling in the same basic direction. Norris had begun the obligatory applause at the food dump, and everyone was looking over in the direction of the hapless waiter scrambling to clean it up before the manager came out. It was Katie who noticed me, the way I had noticed her.

"You okay, Ash?"

"Yeah, fine," I told her. "Just got dizzy for a sec."

Layton then looked at Katie, followed her gaze to me, and raised his eyebrows. "Where'd your blood go, man? Into your toes? You look morgue-ready. Are you gonna hurl?"

"No, I don't think so."

Katie pushed her water glass toward me. "Maybe you're dehydrated," she said.

"Thanks." I took a few gulps, and Layton told me to keep the glass—just in case I was contagious.

The dizziness faded, although it came back whenever I turned my head too fast. Was this a concussion? I'd had concussions before—minor ones—but this was different. You know how, when people get transplants, the body will reject the organ, and they have to take meds to stop it? Well that's the closest I can come to describing the feeling. My body wasn't rejecting my brain, but the stuff inside it. As if my own mind was an invader. It didn't make sense at the time, but later it was weird how accurate that thought was. In the moment, however, I just wanted to deny and dismiss it. I would walk it off, damn it! I would walk it off.

♦ ♦ ♦

I drove Norris home that night because he had yet to pass his driving test. Last time he made it all the way to the end, then honked at an old lady in a crosswalk.

"The guy from the DMV had it out for me," Norris lamented. "I'll bet that old lady was a plant."

"Just add it to your conspiracy theories," I told him, of which he had many.

"Don't laugh," he said. "The truth will out!"

That's when I almost killed us.

Things that change your life—things that change your world—rarely come with a warning. They broadside you like an eighteen-wheeler at an intersection. In football that's called clipping. It's highly illegal. A substantial penalty. But the universe plays by no rules, or at least none that make sense to those of us bound by time and physics.

The truck in question barreled into the intersection after my car clearly had possession. Its horn blared, and I knew slamming on the brakes would guarantee a bloody T-boning, so I punched the accelerator instead, to get far enough in front of it. The truck never slowed down as it flew through the intersection. It missed us by inches.

Now I slammed on the brakes. By the time we came to a stop, we were twenty yards down the street, and the truck had gone its unmerry way. Even though we were at a complete standstill now, I was still gripping the steering wheel in white-knuckle mode, trying to confirm that we were still, indeed, alive.

"Jeez, Ash, what the hell is wrong with you?" Norris blurted, now that it was over. "Are you trying to get us killed?"

"Just you," I told him. "Fail." I hoped a little snark might bring us back to a normal headspace, but it didn't.

And then Norris said, "You totally ran that stop sign."

"No, I didn't. There wasn't one."

But when I looked behind us, I saw the backside of a familiar octagonal sign. I thought back to driving class. Our instructor told us that most accidents are human error. Today *I* was the human error.

I looked around to see who else had witnessed my profoundly bad driving. The only person on the street was a skinny guy on a skateboard. He rolled past, oblivious of the near miss. Turns out that skater was not oblivious at all, but I didn't know that yet. For the time being he was just a dude on a skateboard. Easy to ignore. Easy to forget. For now.

I eased onto the accelerator and resumed our trip, driving much more cautiously than before. Yet in spite of how carefully I was driving, I almost missed the next stop sign as well. I leaned on the brakes—not enough to alert Norris to the fact that I almost ran a stop sign again, but enough to make the stuff on the back seat slide forward to the floor. And that's when I noticed it. The thing I hadn't noticed at the previous intersection, because *that* stop sign was already behind me when I looked; all I had seen was the stainless steel back of it.

See, there are some things about driving that become automatic. You don't think about checking in your mirror and glancing over your shoulder when you change lanes; you just do it. It becomes second nature. And it's second nature to brake when you see a stop sign. There are three mental triggers to a stop sign. They do that on purpose, I guess, to make sure you don't miss it. First there's the shape. Then there's the word "STOP" itself. Then there's the color. If any one of them is missing, you might not consciously notice, but you also might not hit your brakes.

"What's up with that?" I asked Norris, pointing out the sign.

"What's up with what?" he said, completely oblivious.

I pointed to the stop sign again. "It's blue."

Then he looked at me like he was waiting for the punch line of a joke. Finally he said, "Your point?"

So I spelled it out to him, as if to a moron. "I almost didn't see the stop sign because it's blue. Who ever heard of a blue stop sign?"

Again, there was that punch line look from him. "What are you talking about?" he said. "Stop signs are always blue."

The color of a sign is a little thing. Unimportant in the bigger picture. Inconsequential. Like the color of a person's house. If I were to ask you the color of your next-door neighbor's house, I'll bet you wouldn't even be able to tell me for sure, because it's not on your radar—and shouldn't be. You have more important things to think about. The color of stop signs shouldn't matter.

Except that it does.

My parents had both been at the game, but came straight

home after congratulating me on the win. Now Mom was posting embarrassing pictures about it, and Dad was watching his latest binge TV series when I arrived.

"Mom," I asked, trying to choose my words carefully. "What would you say is the exact color of a stop sign?"

She looked up from her laptop, and, just like Norris, she had that look on her face like it was some sort of trick question.

"Blue," she said. "Just . . . regular blue."

"So, no shades of any other color?" I prompted. "Like maybe . . . red?"

She furrowed her eyebrows and took a deep breath, like she sensed the coming of a storm. She closed her computer. "Are you feeling all right, Ash?"

"I'm fine," I snapped. "I just asked a question. Why do you have to go and think something's wrong just because I ask a question?"

She kept her cool, even though I hadn't. "Because it's a strange question," she said.

I opened my mouth to argue how unstrange this question was, but realized it was no use. The more I tried to defend it, the stranger it would seem.

"Never mind," I told her, "it was just a question." And I went to my room giving her no explanation, because there was no explanation to be had. I kept trying to tell myself how unimportant this was, and how ridiculous I was being, but there was a deeper truth here. Even the tiniest loose thread in the fabric of your world cannot be tolerated. Either everything works, or nothing works.

My odd headache never entirely went away, and now it reached that threshold where I noticed it again. I thought I might take some Advil, but was too focused on this loose thread. I went to my computer and did a search on stop sign images. Needless to say, they were all blue. I shouldn't have been shocked, but I was. And it wasn't just signs. Stoplights had three colors. Green, yellow, and blue—which I hadn't noticed while driving because I must have had all green lights.

And here's the thing that was strangest of all: the more I looked at it, the more normal it seemed. The more I considered it, the more memories I had that verified what the images were showing me. But right beside those memories were red signs and red lights—and trying to imagine them both at once made my head resonate like it does when someone squeaks a balloon. I gave up and hurled myself on my bed. I was tired, that's all. Tired and wired from a long day. It would all make sense tomorrow. It would pass. And in the morning, I'd realize that everyone was right. Stop signs had always been blue, and I must have been seriously tweaked to think otherwise.

2

SIDEWAYS

Red is the color of blood. The color of danger. Which means, if there's such a thing as intuition, I should have been seeing red everywhere.

I spent my lunch on Monday in the school library, looking up the history of road signs. I was obsessed now. It would have been easy to just let it go, and treat it like "one of those things," but I'm too much of a pit bull for my own good.

The history of road signs is much more interesting than you might think. Apparently, the color blue was chosen over red for two reasons. First, because of concerns over red-green color blindness. Second, because red invokes anger in mammals. It's the reason why matadors flash red capes in front of bulls. It doesn't make them stop; it makes them charge. Red lights and signs, it was reasoned, would make for angry drivers. So, in 1954 the *American Manual on Uniform Traffic Control Devices* adopted blue as the universal color of "halt." The only place I could find stop signs that were actually red was Hawaii—and only on roads that were privately owned—because by Hawaiian law, the official blue signs are allowed only on public roads.

It all seemed to make sense, and had an internal logic. It's just that its internal logic seemed to exclude me, and the world I thought I knew.

Katie caught me researching during lunch. I told her I was doing a report on road signs.

"Fun," she said with "meh" kind of sarcasm. "What class?"

I was almost stumped by that, and rather than giving her a dumb I-really-haven't-thought-this-out look, I said, "Math," proving that I really hadn't thought this out.

"Road signs for math?"

"I'm . . . uh . . . crunching traffic accident statistics, and how they relate to signage," I said. Kudos to me for pulling something coherent out of my ass.

"Sounds more interesting than algebra," she said.

And suddenly I had an overwhelming urge to confide in her. Maybe that was because she and I already shared a secret, albeit a stupid one.

Long story short, when I was in fifth grade, on the way to school, I ran over a squirrel on my bike. How the hell a squirrel could be slow enough to get caught under a bicycle tire is beyond me, but it did. I skidded to a halt and went back to it, not yet realizing that the roadkill writing was already on the wall. When I picked it up, it was still alive. It opened its mouth and closed it twice, like it was underwater, gasping for air. Then it shivered and died right there in my hands. You might be thinking "Big effing deal, critters die every day." But when was the last time something died on you? And don't talk to me about hunting, because that's different; you know when you go out that it's your intent to kill. But when something unexpectedly dies in your hands and it's looking at you with those what-the-fuck-did-I-ever-do-to-you kind of eyes, it hits you in unpredictable ways. I suddenly burst into tears, talking to the thing like it could still hear me. "I'm sorry, I'm sorry," I whimpered. "I didn't mean it!" Then I look up, and there's Katie watching the whole thing.

I thought she'd say something mean, like "What kind of monster kills a squirrel?" Or maybe she'd laugh at me for my very uncool waterworks. But instead she said, "We should bury it."

Not "*you*," but "*we*." With one word she turned a sad, solitary accident into a cover-up conspiracy.

We buried the squirrel in an unmarked grave in a nearby yard where we knew the owners didn't have a dog that might dig it up. Neither of us spoke of it again, but ever since then, I kind of felt an odd connection with her. And all because she caught me crying over a dead rodent, and never told anyone.

So maybe she wouldn't tell anyone about this, either. And maybe the "I" could become a "we" again, so I wouldn't feel so entirely alone in this.

I pulled up a slew of blue stop sign images for her. "Funny, but I always thought that stop signs were red," I said in an off-hand kind of way.

She looked at me for a moment—not stumped or confused, but pensive. Then she nudged me aside and got on the computer, doing a search of her own. In a few seconds a picture of a dress popped up.

"A while back there was a big controversy over the colors of this dress. What do they look like to you?"

It was pretty obvious. I wondered if it was some kind of trick.

"It's white with gold stripes," I told her. "Duh."

She shook her head. "That's not what I see. When I look at that same picture, I see a blue dress with black stripes."

I looked at it again. "That's crazy. You're kidding me, right?"

"Nope. And it's not just me. Thirty percent of people see the dress like I do, and seventy percent see it the way you do. The point is, different people see the world in different ways . . . so who's to say if your red is everyone else's blue?"

It was the most comforting explanation yet. I wanted to thank her for it, but felt it would get awkward really quickly if I expressed the level of emotion I was actually feeling, so I just said, "That makes sense."

She smiled and left, satisfied to have solved my little dilemma. I watched as she walked away, then looked around to see if anyone else was watching me watch. Then I took a deep breath, let it out, and made the conscious decision to let the whole thing go. I had better things to do than get stuck in a mental riddle that I knew I'd never be able to solve. Katie's explanation made sense.

Or at least sense enough to cling to.

But before I left the library, I stopped a passing student. "Hey," I said. "What color is your shirt?"

He looked at it. "It's red."

Which is exactly how I saw it, too.

Practice that day was hard. It always was—but even as hard as our practices were, games have a certain energy level that practices don't reach. See, practice is just that. It's a projection into the future. It's about being strong enough and skilled enough to compete. But in a game, you're living in the moment; everything is sharper and every second comes at you harder. In other words, while I might hit hard in practice, the hits on game day have a completely different feel. A *world*-changing feel.

So on Monday, there was no repeat of that power hit. No ice in my veins, no lost time. It was just a normal exhausting practice. But it cleared my mind for a while, which was a good thing. I didn't have to worry whether or not I had some weird undiagnosed color blindness, or if I was losing my mind from too much brain-rattling.

Then, when I got home, new drama.

I discovered that my brother, Hunter, had erased my game file for WarMonger 3 to create a new file for himself.

"I didn't mean to," he pleaded. "It didn't tell me it was saving over your file until it was too late."

This might seem microscopically unimportant in the grand scheme of things, but at the moment, I wasn't about grand schemes—and in the minor scheme of me, it was a big deal. WarMonger 3, as I'm sure you know, is one of those games you wait years for, and is so complex, you spend maybe six months trying to beat it. I was well into my fifth month.

The game has three "save" slots, two of which were already hogged by other campaigns that Hunter was running. When you try to save over an existing file, the game asks, "Are you sure you want to obliterate this file?" and if you click "Yes," it flashes a big red stop sign, which I suppose is now blue, and says in all caps, "WARNING! IF YOU ERASE THIS FILE, IT CANNOT BE UNDONE." So basically only a total idiot could accidentally erase it. And in spite of the fact that I would often call him one, Hunter was *not* a total idiot. Which meant he might have done this on purpose.

"I always click too fast, without reading," Hunter blurted. "You always say that." His face was flushed as he spoke, he kept his distance, and he stayed on the balls of his feet in case I lunged at him, and he had to make a quick escape. I couldn't tell whether the redness in his face was from him being upset with himself, or if he was trying to make me *think* he was upset with himself.

My first instinct was to pound him, but I had to restrain myself. Hunter was three years younger than me. Exactly so— we both have the same birthday, which neither of us liked, since neither of us was big on sharing. I had hit my growth spurt, but he hadn't, and I was so much bigger than him now, hitting him could do some real damage.

My second instinct was to erase all of *his* files, but then I realized he would have anticipated this, and maybe didn't care. It was quite possible that he was done with the game, which meant that my retaliation would have no effect at all. He'd win, and would secretly gloat that he had completely duped and manipulated me.

At this point, you may feel I was overthinking this—but if you do, then you've never experienced the mind-boggling actions of a passive-aggressive sibling.

Case in point: three months ago.

A bunch of friends and I were going to see the band Konniption in concert. They actually broke up the day after the gig, so it would be the last time anyone would ever see Konniption perform.

And I lost my ticket.

Usually that wouldn't be a problem. You just print out a new one, right? But one of the band's eccentricities was that you had to actually go down to the stadium and wait in a physical line, to get physical tickets, as an intentional throwback to the early days of rock and roll. And my ticket had vanished.

"Your room's such a mess; how can you find anything?" my mother had pointed out. This was true, but if it was a mess before, that was nothing compared to the debris field left behind after I tore through my room like a tornado searching for that stupid piece of paper.

Ticketless, I went with my friends anyway to plead my case at the entrance, but, of course, no one at the gate cared, or even believed me. I ended up spending the whole night sitting in the car, listening to my Konniption playlist, and pretending I was inside hearing them live.

It didn't occur to me until a week later that maybe I didn't lose that ticket at all.

One night while Hunter was off at a friend's house, I did a much less destructive search of his room for my ticket, on a hunch. I found it—it was in his top desk drawer beneath some old homework. He hadn't even hidden it well.

I was furious, but by the time he got home, my anger had turned to sad bewilderment.

"Why?" I asked him. "Why would you do that?"

At first he claimed he found it after the concert, but even he knew that story had no wings to fly. Finally he got red and teary-eyed and said, "You could have gotten me a ticket, but you didn't even think to ask me, did you? I would have paid with my own money, too."

"So you made sure that I couldn't go out of spite?"

"I was gonna give it back to you," he insisted. "I just wanted to freak you out for a while."

"So why didn't you give it back?"

He looked down. "Remember when I came to talk to you while you were tearing apart your room? 'Maybe you're looking in the wrong place,' I said. And I asked if I could help."

I did remember that. I was already so worked up that I told him to get the hell away from me. And when he wouldn't go, I chucked a moldy sandwich at him. So he left.

"I was gonna drop it behind your desk, then pull the desk out, and let you find it," he told me. "But you didn't want my help. So you didn't get it."

Of course none of that excused what he had done. "I swear, Hunter, sometimes it's like I don't even know you," I told him. His answer to that still makes me shiver.

"You don't," he said. "You've never even tried."

I didn't tell Mom and Dad about the ticket. These kinds of things are between brothers. Instead I installed a better lock on my door—one with a code that no one knew but me. Which made my parents suspicious about what I might be doing in there, but then, if your parents aren't a little paranoid, you're not doing your job.

The thing is, no one ever fully trusts their siblings—that's normal—but you do trust them to have your back when it really counts. Hunter and I didn't even have that.

So did Hunter erase my WarMonger 3 file on purpose? You tell me.

"You can use one of my files," he offered, never actually saying the words "I'm sorry" throughout his whole apology. "I wasn't as far as you on any of them, but it's better than nothing."

At the moment I was still reeling from the loss, thinking about all that wasted time that I'd now have to waste all over again. But I thought about Hunter, and the way he was playing me. It was the same way he played checkers when he was little; stealing pieces off the board when I wasn't looking. The only way to win was to walk away and deny him the victory. So I took a deep breath and swallowed my anger.

"No worries," I told him. "I didn't really like that game anyway."

He was expecting a storm from me; my response threw him off. "But . . . but you said WarMonger 3 was better than the first two combined."

I shrugged. "Did I? I don't remember." Then I left the room and didn't look back at him, for fear that he might read some true feelings in my face.

How did you get this way, Hunter? I wanted to ask him, but never did. Maybe he got it from Dad, who always seemed to take pleasure in selling people auto parts that they didn't need, at inflated prices. Or maybe from Mom, and the way she was so thrilled by the Christmas blizzard last year, because it meant that our neighbors' big expensive Caribbean vacation—the kind that we could never afford—was now a big expensive series of canceled flights.

Not that I'm perfect—I'm sure I have plenty of my parents' bad traits—but taking pleasure in the misfortune of others is not one of them. Unless you count humiliating an opposing team.

Although losing a virtual game world was unimportant, it still stung. What I needed was something to ground me a little more firmly in my real world. Some comfort food for the soul—and for the stomach, too.

There was a standing rule that any time Leo's mom made her

famous lobster mac and cheese, I was invited. I never felt guilty eating a lot of it, because, according to Mrs. Johnson, it wasn't as fancy as it sounded. A bag of frozen Costco lobster meat went a long way, so feeding a family of four, plus one hungry free-loader, cost less than fast food.

"Did you know that lobster used to be what poor people ate in the Northeast?" Leo said as we ate. "Then somebody got the bright idea to market it to New York socialites, and suddenly it became rich-people food."

"It's all about perception," his father said. Mr. Johnson was an exec at a marketing company, so he knew what he was talking about. "You could sell bird turd on toast if the right people were seen eating it."

"Dad," complained Angela, "you're not helping our appe-tites."

"I'm just saying."

"A little less saying, a little more eating," Mrs. Johnson said. "Leftovers are not our friend today—one more piece of Tupper-ware, and we'll lose our latest game of refrigerator Tetris."

After dinner Leo and I went down to the basement, where they had a decent man cave, although Angela always said she resented the implied exclusion, threatening to paint the place pink.

"You hate pink," Leo had reminded her.

"Some points are worth a little suffering," she had responded.

Monday night's game had already started—the Colts versus the Jaguars. I claimed a recliner and sank into it. I thought I'd be able to settle into my comfort zone here, but some things find you wherever you try to hide.

"Wait—what team is that?" I asked, pointing at the TV, where a team in purple was getting ready for the next play.

"The Colts, who else?"

"But the Colts are blue. Blue and white."

Leo looked at me funny. "No, the Jets are blue and white."

"They're *green* and white!"

"You're thinking of the Vikings."

I launched myself out of the recliner. "No! *They're* the ones who are purple!"

I found myself getting light-headed as I stood there, and realized I was hyperventilating. I shut my mouth, and shut my eyes even tighter, and sat back down, burying my head in my hands. When I opened my eyes again, Leo was staring at me.

"Ash, are you okay?"

I wasn't okay, but I couldn't get into this with Leo. Our friendship was like an island of normalcy in a rising sea. I needed that normalcy and didn't want to drag him into the waves. Meanwhile, he was looking at me like I had some serious insult to the brain. That's what doctors call a bad concussion—an "insult"—like maybe the brain might be fine if it just had a really good comeback line.

"This is not what you're thinking," I told him. "It's not something . . . physical."

"I never said that it was," he said, with a calm that felt forced—so I forced myself to seem calm, too.

"I'm fine," I said. "I just got confused, is all. One person's green is another person's purple, right?"

He still stared at me like he was going to ask what the hell I was talking about, but he backed down, and we both returned our attention to the game. But not really. Well, at least the Jaguars were still teal and gold, but the cat on their helmets was facing the wrong way. Then, when it went to commercial, Leo lowered the volume.

"Do you remember a couple of years ago, when Angela came down with meningitis?" he asked, entirely out of the blue.

"Yeah . . ."

"It shook us all up pretty bad. Even after she was all better, my parents were on edge, and I couldn't sleep. I kept thinking the strangest things. Every rainstorm was a hurricane. Whenever the wind blew, it was a tornado. I kept bracing for the worst, and even though it never came, I still kept bracing. We all did. Crazy, right?"

"Wow . . . ," I said. "I'm sorry, Leo. I didn't know."

"Anyway, we went to see this talk doctor. She said we had PTSD. And she helped us get through it. Best thing we ever did."

The game was back on, but he kept the volume down. "Ash, if there's something messing with your head, it's okay to talk about it. And if you can't talk about it with me, that's fine, I get it. So if you want, I can give you her number."

I looked back at the TV, unable to hold eye contact with him. "Thanks, Leo," I said. "After the game, maybe." Yet even as I said it, I knew all the talk in the world wasn't going to fix this.

"But for now, do you think you could maybe . . . just . . . turn the colors off? Just make everything old-school black-and-white?"

He looked at me, and for a moment I thought he might push for an explanation. But then finally he picked up the remote. "I can do that."

He tapped a few buttons, and I watched as the colors faded and were gone. And although it didn't calm me entirely, it narrowed the bandwidth of my stress to simple light and shadow.

"There you go," Leo said. "Black-and-white. Just like the old days."

The rest of that week was so unremarkably normal, I was lulled into a false sense of security. People talk about "the elephant in the room," but this thing with colors, I beat it down until it was more like a mouse in the corner. One tiny blip of weirdness in an otherwise rational world. And if I was apprehensive about our next game, I was in denial about that, too.

There was no reason to think that what happened last Friday would repeat. And for three whole quarters, it didn't. But the fourth quarter was an entirely different story.

Less than five minutes to go in the game. It was third down for the opposing team, first and goal. We were down by six, and the other team's quarterback was throwing passes like guided missiles. I knew I had to take him down before he could throw the ball for the touchdown.

It began like a normal play—and perhaps for everyone else it was. The ball was snapped, I engaged the offensive linemen, getting past them like a greased pig, and headed straight for the quarterback, feeling as fast and powerful as a locomotive.

This time it happened the moment I sacked the quarterback.

I felt the impact. Felt the instant of ice—and this time I actually sensed myself sliding sideways, but just like the chill, it only lasted an instant. And then I was running off the field with the rest of the defensive team. I didn't remember hitting the ground, or getting up. I must have tackled the quarterback, because the other team was punting. I must have lost at least five seconds, maybe ten, and that weird scrambling in my head—the ache-less headache—was back.

I told myself it was nothing. I had a game to play and couldn't let something like this get in the way. Whatever it was, whatever it meant, it could wait. For all I knew everything was now back to normal, and this was the end of it.

We won in sudden death, making our claim of an undefeated season more legit, because we had two victories under our belts now. It wasn't until I got to the locker room that things started to really go sideways. It began when I looked at my helmet. Yes, I had been seeing our helmet on other teammates continually for the last twenty minutes, but there are things you don't notice until you really take the time to look at them. On my helmet—on all of the helmets—instead of a snarling blue wave, there was a grinning blue demon.

I swallowed. Hard. I didn't say anything. I didn't ask anyone about it. The locker room suddenly felt humid, and more sweaty than usual. I showered, dressed, and got out into the fresh air as quickly as I could. *Well,* I thought, *at least it's still blue.*

I waited for the others in the parking lot. The plan was to go to the usual place, with the usual people, and eat the usual food. I had been hungry. I wasn't anymore.

"I'll ride with Layton," Norris said when he saw me waiting. "Because I don't feel like risking my life again."

Layton laughed, and squeezed Katie a little closer. "Yeah, I heard about that. What a waste it would have been if you actually got hit," he said. "Not you guys—I mean the car."

I gave him the obligatory sneer. Katie, I noticed, was wearing her makeup a little heavy today. Actually, I had noticed it before. Some girls do that. Cupcake face. It's like the way some guys wear too much cologne. Stenchies. Usually the Cupcakes and the Stenchies find each other and discover spackled, pungent bliss. But Katie had always been a less-is-more kind of girl. Not that she was fully slathered in the stuff now, but more and more often she looked like she had been professionally made up for a glamour shoot. A little much for football and the food court, even for a cheerleader.

I might have given it more thought, but at the moment, I was seeing blue demons everywhere—stickers on cars, T-shirts, the scoreboard in the field. I just wanted to get out of there. That's when I clicked the button on my remote to find my car, because I couldn't see it in the lot.

My car was an old Dodge that had seen better days. But that wasn't the car that responded to my remote. I thought it was just coincidence, so I did it again, only to see the same car flash and beep.

"Ha!" I said. "That Beemer has the same frequency as my piece of crap. Maybe I oughta take it."

"Dude," said Norris, shaking his head. "That *is* your car."

The crystalline form of solid water is less dense than the liquid. That's why ice floats. But it's only *slightly* less dense. That's why we say things like "the tip of the iceberg," because they float low, and from above appear much smaller than they actually are.

Our altered school mascot was just the tip of today's iceberg, and when it came to density, I was feeling far denser than anything in the universe at the moment.

I stared at the sleek, shiny black BMW, and kept hitting the lock button, watching the car flash and beep, flash and beep, still thinking there must be some mistake. Leo took the keys from me. Gave me a twisty grin and hit the unlock button. The locks *thunked* up.

"Duh," he said in a voice that was slightly off-key.

"Right," I said. "I don't know where my head was at." Which was true. Leo looked at me for just a moment longer, and let it go.

Now that I saw it—now that I knew the car was mine, the memory of it broke the surface. I remembered being inside it. I remembered driving it. And the memory of the near accident from last week? Now I remembered it in *this* car. My old Dodge was still there in my mind, too, but it had been shuffled lower in the deck.

Now I was feeling a rolling in my stomach. I thought I might be sick. Stupid, right? If this was an '80s movie, I'm sure I'd be happy as a clam, and race around town with Marty McFly riding shotgun, and Ferris Bueller reclining in the back, breaking the fourth wall. But when weird crap happens in the real world, it's not popcorn-friendly. It's pretty damn terrifying.

"Hey, listen, I'm kind of zonked," I told my friends. "I think maybe I'm coming down with something. I'm just gonna go home."

I said my goodbyes and left in a car that could do zero to sixty in 3.1 seconds.

The stop sign at the first corner was blue. That hadn't changed. Oddly, that was comforting. Still, my hands were shaking and my stomach still seizing, so I put on some music. My playlists were all the same as they had been, but now they sounded much better on the car's high-quality sound system. I came to a full stop at the next stop sign, closed my eyes, and took a moment to balance myself atop the iceberg.

Either something was very wrong with me, or something was very wrong with the world. Believe it or not, I could deal with something being wrong with *me* far better than the alternative—and if there was an explanation for this, like Katie's color-shifting dress, or even a bad concussion—I would have gleefully jumped on it. But I suspected there was no simple explanation. I did my best to shut down my higher brain functions and stop thinking about it. I focused on driving. The ride was smooth. The leather seats comfortable. But when I got to my street, I didn't turn onto it. Part of me said to turn, but a more *present* part of me knew it was a mistake. I understood why.

A seventeen-year-old who drives a BMW doesn't live in a small, fifty-year-old tract home. But where did I live, if not here?

A car behind me honked, so I pulled off to the side of the road. I could sense that if I put my brain on autopilot, I would make all the correct turns, and it would get me home, wherever that was—but I didn't want to do that. I wanted to know where I was going before I got there. I was quickly discovering, however, that my brain didn't work that way.

It was the skaters that got me moving. Two of them. Twins. One of them knocked on my window, startling me. I rolled it down. "Yeah, what do you want?"

"Hey, could you help us?" one of them said. "We're kind of lost."

I sighed. "What street are you looking for?"

"Cabrera Drive," the other one said.

The name struck home. Literally. "I . . . I live on Cabrera Drive," I told them. Prior to that moment, I had never even heard of it. And yet I knew that I lived there.

"Cool," said one of the twins, "we must be neighbors."

And since we were going to the same place, I offered to give them a ride.

One sat shotgun, the other in the back. They weren't exactly Ferris Bueller and Marty McFly, but now that they were here, I realized that I was glad for the company. My own head had become a treacherous place.

They were pale and a little too thin, and I had a sense that I had seen them before, but couldn't place where.

"Hey, I got a joke," said the first one. "Knock, knock."

"Who's there?" I obliged.

"Depends on which door you open."

The one in the back snickered. I didn't get it. I hated when I didn't get jokes.

The twin next to me rapped me on the shoulder. "Don't you see? It's like 'The Lady or the Tiger.'"

"Oh yeah, I read that story." As I recalled, we never find out what's behind the door the guy was told to choose—a man-eating tiger, or the beautiful girl—because the story ends just as he opens it. I remember wanting to reach through the pages and wring the author's neck.

"But if it's the tiger," said the twin in the back, "you've gotta ask yourself . . . is it alive, or is it dead?"

"If it's Schrödinger's tiger, then it's both," said the twin next to me.

"Yeah," I said, catching on, and proud of myself for it. "But only until you open the door. And if it's not dead, then you are."

Schrödinger, if you didn't know, was a scientist who mathematically proved that a cat inside a box is both dead and alive at the same time, until you open the box. I had argued in class that Schrödinger was wrong—because if the box started to smell like dead cat, you didn't have to open it to know.

I drove into a neighborhood where the streets wove and meandered like they had all the time in the world to get where they were going. Lawns were huge, and trees were lush. I remembered each house I passed, but only once I saw it. That's the way it seemed to work—memories had to be triggered. Then we came to a guard gate, marking the entrance to a gated community.

"Bet you live on the other side of the gate," one of the twins said to me.

"Yeah, I do," I told him, knowing for a fact that I did, but still unable to picture the house itself.

"You can just drop us off here," the one next to me said. So I pulled over and they got out.

"We'll see you around," said one.

"Yeah. Thanks, Ash," said the other, then they hopped on their boards and rode off.

Only much later did I realize that I had never told them my name.

3

COKE AND CRAYOLAS

Here's what I know:

We live in a huge house in a fancy gated neighborhood. That's because my father got a full football scholarship to Notre Dame, then was drafted by the Dallas Cowboys and was a lineman for six years, before a busted hip ended his career. He never quite became a household name, but he made a lot of money in those six years, which he used to start a successful chain of vitamin shops. Now, instead of selling automotive parts that people don't need at inflated prices, he sells vitamin supplements that people don't need at inflated prices, and makes a whole lot more money doing it.

He became a pillar of the community when he returned to his hometown, and was even elected to the school board. Then, when the holier-than-thou board member tried to do away with the high school mascot, my father punted him halfway to the next county. I can't quite say the Tsunamis were now history, because to be history, you have to have actually existed. No one but me remembers our mascot Tsammy Tsunami, the Angry Wave. Mom is still a nutritionist—that hasn't changed—only now she's published books and creates the proprietary formulas for our family's chain of shops.

I wrote all this down, but it really wasn't necessary, because once I remembered it, I couldn't unremember it. It was kind of like that big box-o-crap in your garage. You have no idea what's inside until you open it. Then, once you do—once you see the contents—you remember every single object. So now I had a brainful of new memories—yet I still remembered the world where we weren't rich, and the world before that, where red was the color of stop.

I think the weirdest part was the moment I pulled up to our house. Even though I didn't know where I was going, I knew once I got there. I quickly noticed that mine wasn't the only car that was different. Instead of Mom's questionable Kia, and Dad's dinged-up Honda, our driveway was now a study in German engineering. A second BMW, and a Mercedes. All the cars had the same personalized license plates as they had before. My mother's was EATRYT, and my father's was PGSKN♥R (which I always thought was marginally creepy), and of course mine, QBSACKR.

It's hard to describe what I felt as I got out of my car and approached the front door. You know how before a tsunami, the ocean pulls out and leaves an eerie calm of flopping fish for a hundred yards out? I know all about that, because "the calm before the wave" was always our team cheer before we took the field. Hundreds of people shushing, a few seconds of silence, and then violent screams of death and destruction as the team ran out. Well, my fish were all flopping as I stepped up to the front door—and although I kept waiting for the surge of devastation, it didn't come. I was just left with that lingering void. A numbness like I was having an out-of-body experience while still in my body.

"Hi, Ash!" said Hunter cheerfully as I stepped into the kitchen. He was scarfing guacamole and chips while standing at the granite-topped island in the middle, because what else do you do with all that space, but have a granite-topped island? "How was the game?"

"We won," I told him. He put up his fist for a knuckle punch. It took a moment for me to oblige, because Hunter and I never shared gestures like that. Then he pushed the guacamole bowl in my direction. The Hunter I knew would have either finished or hidden the guacamole before I entered the room. But to be fair, I might have done the same to him. I dipped a chip in. Mom's guac tasted exactly the same, low sodium, and full of mystery spices.

On a hunch, I did some digging in my mental sand, and found that beneath the flopping fish was a memory of the Konniption concert. Not only had I gone, but I had gotten a ticket for Hunter. We sang along to "Come As You Were" on the way home. Suddenly I knew, without even having to check, that my WarMonger 3 file had never been erased.

Hunter glanced at me and his eyebrows furrowed a bit. "You're looking kinda pale. You okay?"

"Yeah, yeah," I said unconvincingly. "I just took a hard hit today, is all."

"Let's check your vision," he said. "How many fingers am I holding up?" And he flipped me the bird.

"Two," I told him. "Thanks for the peace sign."

He laughed, I grinned. It felt brotherly. That was a feeling Hunter and I had never shared before.

"Seriously, if you feel that rattled, tell Mom," Hunter said. "She'll overreact, but hey, better safe than sorry, right?" Then he sauntered off to do whatever an alternate reality brother does.

The wave finally rolled in after I had gone upstairs and locked myself in my room. Once I was there, I screamed into my pillow until I nearly lost my voice. Then, after I exhausted every freaked-out brain cell, I rolled over, looked up at the ceiling, and forced my throbbing brain to do some serious thinking.

Granted, I was only accessing the first layer of memories in this place, but as best as I could tell, I was no happier in this existence. But then I seemed no *less* happy either. I mean, before today I never felt entirely content. Who ever does, really, except for Buddhist monks who have surrendered all earthly possessions and levitate their penniless asses for fun? Yet even levitating monks long for something—even if it's just the longing for a state of nonexistence. As for me, I suppose I still had the same basic wants, the same frustrations. It was all just in a flashier frame.

So, all else being equal, was this—whatever it was—such a bad thing?

My new life had a pool and a pool table. It had an eight-seat home theater in the basement. It had a designer wardrobe without a single pair of Wrangler jeans or Target T-shirts in the bunch. Why was I fighting this? Maybe I needed to take a chill pill as my dad embarrassingly says, and go with the alternate flow. What choice did I have? And it's not like I really missed my old life. Everything here was new and improved, from my socioeconomic status to my relationship with my brother. Hey, what if that other reality was the wrong one? Maybe *this* was the life I was supposed to be living, and the universe, or God, or whatever, decided to fix it.

It's amazing how a simple shift in one's point of view can make things better. *I can live with this,* I told myself. In fact, I could live with it forever. It's like Leo's dad had said—it's all about perception.

Hunter came gently knocking on my door somewhere around ten thirty. He was dressed to go out.

"What, no curfew?" I asked him.

He shrugged. "They won't know I'm gone. And if they do, I'll deal with it."

I suppose it was easier to go unnoticed in a house this big.

"I'll cover for you," I told him, actually glad that he had a social life—something that was iffy before.

"Thanks," he said. "So listen, do you think you could hook me up? I promised my friends."

"Huh?"

"Just a few X, and maybe a gram of the good stuff."

I just stared at him, blocking out the part of me that knew exactly what he was talking about. I found myself looking at my desk—particularly the second drawer down. I reached over and pulled it open, then moved aside a notebook to reveal a kitchen storage container—the kind that snaps on all four sides. Inside were little Ziploc bags containing pills and powders and weed. The new memories washed over me. The second wave of the evening.

"I can pay you on Monday. C'mon, Ash—you know I'm good for it."

Hunter was getting impatient. I was not prepared to deal with this now, so I closed the drawer and said, "Not tonight, Hunter."

He looked at me like I had just slapped him in the face. "You can't be serious!"

"I'm running low on everything," I told him, and I couldn't help but add, "besides, it's not my job to get freshmen high."

"Since when?"

"Since right now."

He glared at me, waiting for me to change my mind, but I wasn't going to. "Listen," I told him, giving him some real and true brotherly advice. "You need to separate out your real friends from the ones who are just using you."

"I already promised them!" he insisted.

"Tell them . . . tell them that your brother is an asshole."

He glared at me. "Fine," he said. "That's *exactly* what I'll tell them." And he stormed out.

Here's how it happened. Here's how it worked. Here's how I made myself believe it was okay.

It started when one of Dad's supplement suppliers sold me some steroid powder on the side. I figured it was a business opportunity—just like those cheap sunglasses I sold at school last year. Selling that steroid powder opened the door to . . . well . . . *other* things. Each week, a variety of stuff showed up in a two-gallon protein powder container in the back room of Dad's local store. I would take whatever was inside and replace it with the cash I made from last week's stash, keeping 20 percent for myself. Then I would break the new supply down into smaller packets, which I would sell at parties, and in school hallways, and out back of various local hangouts. I did it because it was easy. I did it because I could. I did it because I was pissed at my father for making me work at his store part-time, and paying me no more than any of his other employees.

My classmates who do drugs were gonna get it somewhere, I reasoned. Why not from me? And with more and more stuff being legalized in more and more places, how bad was it, really? *I'm a good guy,* I had told myself in this world. I charged fair prices, and I never sold to anyone who I suspected had a serious drug problem. Hell, I even supplied coke to Mr. Gilbreath, my

English teacher, who was an old hippie. If a teacher was okay with it, how could it be bad? As for the digital lock on my bedroom door? It wasn't to keep my brother out. In this world, it was to keep my parents from finding my under-the-counter pharmacy. Not that they ever would. Dad was rarely home, since he traveled the country opening new stores, and Mom, after her nightly bottle of merlot, wouldn't care if a pallet of heroin was airdropped through our living room ceiling. Not that I dealt that stuff. I stayed completely away from heroin and meth. That's part of what made me a good guy. I wasn't a drug dealer—I was a *recreational entrepreneur.*

The half of me who had lived this life thought this all made perfect sense. The other half was ready to beat the shit out of the first half. How do you come to terms with a seedy secret life you didn't even know you had? I felt like Jekyll discovering the exploits of Hyde. *Bizarro Ash is not me!* I kept trying to tell myself. But I knew it wasn't that simple. If this had been my life. If this had been the environment I grew up in . . . then, yes, this *would* be me. Still, the fact that I could reject it gave me hope. It meant that the original me was stronger. That my core was intact.

But would it stay that way? Because, as it turned out, there were a lot more jack-in-the-box memories ready to spring out at me.

The next day I found out what kids who drive late-model BMWs and sell drugs do on Saturday mornings. We watch sports in our pajamas, then complain that we're bored and there's nothing to do. Like the speed of light, some things are constants in all universes.

I sat with Hunter in relative silence, except for the occasional comment on the game. Then, at halftime, Hunter turned to me.

"So about last night," he said. "You were right. I found out who my friends really are."

"I'm sorry."

"No, it's good," he said. Although he didn't sound all that thrilled about it.

"If it makes you feel any better, I'm giving up selling the stuff completely."

Hunter looked dubious. "You always say that."

"Yeah, well this time I mean it."

"You always say that, too."

It frustrated me, because I realized he was right. "It's not . . . who I am," I tried to tell him.

He shrugged. "I know. It's just something you do."

"Did," I said. "Past tense."

"All right then," he said, just to end the conversation. I knew he still didn't believe me. That's okay. Actions speak louder than words. He'd see that I meant it soon enough.

Later that morning, Katie called me. Keep in mind that, in spite of the dead rodent we shared, she had never called me before in any reality. She would occasionally text to ask me if I knew where Layton was, but that was the extent of it. I picked up just before it went to voice mail.

"Hey," she said. "I've been thinking about the stop sign thing."

"Wait," I said, fumbling a bowl of potato chip crumbs and getting them all over the couch, "you remember that?"

"Of course. Why wouldn't I?"

I wasn't quite sure why it surprised me. Maybe it was because *this* me was so far removed from *that* me, my dueling memories were muddled. I had no idea for sure what I did last week in this world.

"There's more going on than just the stop signs," I said.

"Like what?"

"Like I'd rather not talk about it over the phone." Actually, I didn't want to talk about it at all, but maybe with Katie, I might open up. Then she could call the men with white coats, or whatever color they wear these days, and have me taken away for my own protection, because God knows I needed protection from myself in the worst way.

"Can you come over?" she asked. "There's something I need to show you."

I had only been to Katie's house once before, for a party. As I recall, in my old life, I had some beer at that party. In this life I had some beer and sold drugs to her cousins. Katie didn't know that about my current reality. Something to be thankful for.

Her house was a bit nicer than my old one, but not by all that much. Katie, and probably all my friends, saw me as "the rich kid." Maybe the only one in my gated community who didn't go to some private school—because my dad believed in staying loyal to his alma mater. And because they named the new gym after him.

"I'm sure I wouldn't have noticed this if we hadn't talked about it," Katie said, leading me to the kitchen. "But once I saw it, I couldn't get it out of my head."

We sat down at the table and she opened up a little kiddie coloring book, full of thick black lines around fully clothed animals. She turned to a page that featured a comical traffic accident, if such a thing is possible. An angry duck was yelling at a sheepish sheep, while a panda policeman tried to keep the peace. The page was only partially completed, without much attention to detail. The sheep was the color of urine, the duck the color of puke, the sky was a scribble of cornflower blue, and none of the colors stayed within the lines.

"This is my brother's," she told me. "He's five." Then she pushed the book closer to me. "Tell me: What's wrong with this picture?"

As it was an intersection, there was a stoplight. The bottom light was colored lime green, the middle light was the same urine yellow as the sheep, and the top light was purple.

"Why purple?" I asked.

"Look closer," she said.

I looked at the page again, and now I could see it wasn't purple at all. Her brother had filled in that top light with red—but then had gone over it again with blue. The colors had just blended.

"His first instinct had been to make it red," Katie said. "But once he saw his mistake, he fixed it."

"Did you ask him about it?"

"I did, but he just shrugged."

I looked at it again, then flipped to other pages, but there was neither a stoplight nor a stop sign anywhere else in the book.

"You have to admit it's a weird coincidence," Katie said. "Right?"

It was more than weird, which meant it might not have been coincidence at all. I was simultaneously relieved to think that I might not be alone, and terrified to think that this might be bigger than just me.

Katie was looking at me as if I'd give her a satisfactory answer to this mystery, or at least lay out a course of action. And as I looked at her, I couldn't help but notice that she wasn't looking all glamour girl today.

"So where's Layton?" I asked. "I thought you guys were joined at the hip?"

She looked away. "He's off on a fishing trip this weekend."

I nodded. "Well, that explains it," I said. I had meant to only think it, but it came burbling out under my breath.

Katie looked at me with that slightly narrowed kind of gaze that meant a cold front might be rolling in. "Explains what?"

I knew I couldn't backpedal or make something up. I had said it; I needed to own it.

"It explains why you're looking more like yourself today," I told her. And when her eyes didn't un-narrow, I sighed and said, "You know, without all the makeup. I mean, I know it's not my business, but you don't need it."

That did nothing to stall the cold front. She glared at me. "Oh really? Well, I'm wearing makeup right now, so maybe you're not as observant as you think."

"Not as much," I said. "Not nearly as much. But you're right—it's not my business. I'm sorry I said anything."

"You should be."

"I am."

Well, at least this means the makeup wasn't to hide bruises, I thought—and this time I actually thought it instead of saying it out loud. I had always just assumed that Layton was drawn to girls with intense cosmetic precision. Now I realized that he demanded it, whether they were like that or not. It made me angry, because why would Katie, who certainly was her own person, allow that to happen? Why would she let Layton dictate the terms of her own appearance?

Katie's gaze didn't quite soften. It just relented. Like the chill of it had gotten to her as well. "Don't think you know everything," Katie said firmly. "Because you don't."

And because she was absolutely right, I changed the subject.

"Here's something I *do* know," I said. "Yesterday I lived in a small tract home with mold problems on the south side of town."

The non sequitur caught her by surprise. "What are you even talking about?"

"My father sold auto parts and never played professional football, and I didn't drive a BMW," I told her. "I drove a car that we all called the Dread Dodge of Embarrassment."

She didn't respond at first, clearly waiting for me to break into laughter. When I didn't, she looked back at her brother's drawing.

"And that was yesterday?" she asked.

I nodded.

She thought about it for a few moments, never looking up from the coloring book. "Was Layton the same yesterday?" she finally asked.

"Pretty much," I told her. "Yeah, he was."

She didn't say anything to that . . . but I could tell from the look on her face what she was thinking. That maybe there was a world where he was different.

4

HORROR/COMEDY, BUT MOSTLY HORROR

On Sunday night, I had a few friends over for a movie in our home theater. Reclining seats, an old-fashioned popcorn machine with actual movie theater buckets. Everything but the bored zit-faced dude taking your ticket.

Tonight, however, the movie was a study in torture, for reasons that will become clear.

The evening's cast of characters included Leo and Angela; Norris, who wasn't invited, but showed up on a regular basis like a cold sore; Kendra, Norris's date, who I didn't know all that well; and Paul, a classmate who tutored me in math, and deserved all the perks he could get from that thankless job. I invited Katie, but she pointed out that I couldn't invite just her. Layton was part of the package, and they already had other plans. I asked what those plans were, but she told me in no uncertain terms that it was none of my business.

Norris arrived first with Kendra, who, of course, drove. We have this big unnecessary circular driveway, and Kendra parked close to the edge to make room for other cars. That would have been fine, but when Norris got out, he stomped all over my mother's hydrangeas, like it was his own personal flower petal path.

"Horror!" Norris proclaimed. "Kendra wants horror."

And although Kendra's "horror" box was already checked by her choice of date, I refrained from pointing that out.

"Actually," said Kendra, "I said comedy."

"Okay then, a classic horror/comedy, like *Zombieland* or something."

Kendra shrugged, accepting the compromise, so I added it to the list of possible movies.

Paul arrived with a bucket of chicken. "I wasn't sure if I was supposed to bring food or not, so here's a donation of grease and carcinogens."

"Not necessary, but always appreciated," I told him.

As I waited for Leo and Angela to arrive, I was a little bit wary—because Leo had been treating me like a delicate flower all week, since my football jersey meltdown. But then I remembered that was a whole other world ago. Did I have the same meltdown here? My memories said maybe, which is the most useless thing a memory can say.

When Leo and Angela arrived, he didn't give me that are-you-okay-since-the-last-time-I-saw-you look. Instead, he seemed to be in a mood of his own.

"What's wrong with him?" I asked Angela.

"New guard at the gate," she told me.

That shouldn't have been a problem—all my friends have permanent guest passes to get them through the gate. It would have been fine if the gate was automated, but there was a human involved, which can be far more problematic than technology.

"Do you wanna know what he said?" Leo snarled. "Do you?" Leo stormed across the foyer and back. "He took one look at us and said, 'Work hours are over at six.'"

"So did you tell him where to stick it?"

"I'm sure if I had, the damn rent-a-cop woulda Tased me, or worse."

I shook my head. "Dude, you're driving a pickup with tons of crap in the back. He probably thought you were a contractor, or something."

"Are you really that naïve?"

Angela came between us. "Let's save the drama for the movie," she said, but Leo wasn't done.

"You're like a horse with blinders," he told me. "You never see anyone's point of view but your own."

I'm ashamed to admit it, but I remember thinking why would I ever want to see things from his point of view, if it meant I'd always be pissed off?

Although we didn't talk about it anymore, Leo's mood took a long time to lighten. It just went from angry to brooding, like he was obsessing over all the things he wished he would have said to the gate guard.

We decided to play some pool and polish off the chicken before starting the movie—the choice of which was still in debate. I proposed a three-team tournament; the first team to win two games would get to pick the movie. We chose teams by the type of movie we wanted. Kendra split from Norris and joined Paul, who also wanted a comedy. That just made Paul awkward. Leo and Norris were the horror team, and Angela and I were team sci-fi.

In the first game, Norris sank the eight ball halfway through the game, giving the victory to Kendra and Paul.

"My hands were too greasy from the chicken," Norris complained. "And that eight ball had a mind of its own."

Angela and I took on Paul and Kendra, with team horror heckling from the sidelines. Pool was not Angela's thing. She was more about getting volleyballs over nets than billiard balls into pockets.

"You're never gonna sink a ball if you hold the cue like that," Leo told her.

"Will you shut up? Losers don't get to give advice," she told him.

"It's not how she's holding the cue," I offered, then turned to her. "You're just not lining up your eye. Here, I'll show you."

I put my arm around her to help her line up the shot, and the instant I came in contact with her, it was like I got zapped with an electric shock that only I could feel. I pulled away suddenly . . .

. . . Because I knew.

Beyond a shadow of a doubt, I knew. And all from that brief moment of contact. Angela looked at me funny. "What's up with you?"

"Nothing," I said. "I just . . . I gotta use the bathroom," I said, and I bailed out of there, nearly tackling Norris on the way out.

"Hey, I'm standin' here!" Norris yelled after me.

I locked the door to the bathroom. I splashed cold water on my face, again and again, not caring that it soaked my shirt.

In the world where I came from—in the world where I belonged—Angela, being Leo's younger sister, made her like a sister to me. I would *never* put moves on her. But in *this* world, we had secretly hooked up last spring. And we were the only ones who knew.

Who are we, really? Science would tell us that we are nothing more than the sum of our experiences. Faith would tell us that we are a spark that exists separate from the drama of our lives. I've never thought about these things much. On those late nights when friends would get all metaphysical and would start talking about how the universe might be just a crushed bug on the floor of a much bigger universe, I never got involved. The way I always saw it, the stuff that's impossible to figure out was pointless to think about. That attitude left me at a distinct disadvantage now that I was smack in the middle of a metaphysical crisis.

I thought that all possible versions of myself would still be me. But they're not. It was a cold and very rude awakening to discover that the *me* of this world was not a guy I liked at all. Not that I was anything close to perfect before. I've cheated on tests, and lied my way out of bad behavior plenty of times. But the me that *I* knew wouldn't deal drugs, and would never, ever, in a million years, hook up with his best friend's sister behind his back.

But that's not entirely true, is it? There's this thing called "nature versus nurture." How much of us is inborn, and how much comes from our environment? If circumstances had been different—if my father got his scholarship all those years ago—yes, I would be doing those things. Which meant it was part of my nature—or at least my nature wasn't strong enough to stop it. It was both humbling and horrifying to see what I *could* be under certain circumstances. With the old me still alive and kicking, I could fight it—make positive adjustments—so that I could live with myself. But even so, I now knew that I had the capacity to be an industrial sack of shit. It was nauseating. Like biting into a peach to discover it was full of maggots after you've swallowed.

Time out in bathroom solitary did not help. I didn't know how I could go back out there and look any of them in the face. Still I knew I couldn't stay in the bathroom all night. Finally there was a knock on the door.

"I'll be out in a second," I yelled.

"It's Paul. You okay in there? I brought you some ginger ale. Stuff's supposed to settle your stomach."

I opened the door. He looked at me, noting I was all wet and disheveled. "You hurl?" he asked.

"Naah, I'll be okay," I told him. "I think it was the chicken."

He nodded and handed me the ginger ale. Then he looked around to make sure none of the others were in earshot, and asked quietly, "Is . . . uh . . . something going on between you and Leo's sister?"

Leave it to my math tutor to do the math. I could have denied it, but if ever I needed to confess something to an objective third party, it was now. I took a deep breath. "It was months ago. It was only once. But tonight, I had . . . sort of a flashback."

Paul nodded, thought about it, and said, "You know what, the chicken's making me feel queasy, too. I'll tell everyone that's what it is. Come out when you're feeling a little better."

So I took a couple of minutes. I let my shirt dry a little bit, forced myself to meet my own reflection without balking, and then finally rejoined the others.

The game of pool was where we had left it, but no one seemed much interested in playing anymore. Norris was pacing. "So the chicken was tainted?" he said. "I had like five pieces. Should I induce vomiting?"

"You already do," said Leo, which made Kendra laugh. Not exactly the response you'd want from a date.

"If you're not feeling it already, you're probably fine," said Paul. "Ash and I must have gotten the bad pieces."

I couldn't meet Angela's eyes, and so I suggested we go into the theater and start a movie. Any movie. Because being in a darkened room, where no one would see all the crap written on my face, was the best place to be. Under the circumstances, we agreed to put on a dumb comedy, because it was less likely to make anyone hurl. For the life of me, I can't remember what movie it was or tell you anything that happened in it.

When it was over, I tried to wrap up the evening quickly. I was the first one out of my seat, and I did my best to make small talk as I tried to herd everyone toward the door. But even my small talk now had larger implications.

"So Paul—since you're like Mr. STEM—what do you know about alternate universes?"

"Is this a video game question?" he asked. "Because I kick ass on Death Parallax. I can school you in multiple universes, free of charge."

"No, it's a real-world question."

"Hmm," he said. I wasn't quite sure what the "hmm" meant. Maybe he was impressed, or just surprised that I would ask such a question. "Well, according to string theory, there are either ten, eleven, or twenty-six dimensions. But sometimes I think Nobel Prize winners pick random numbers just to piss off the other Nobel Prize winners."

Then Norris said something about there being a black hole in Uranus, and that was the note that ended the evening.

I took a moment at the door to give a heartfelt thanks to Paul. "Y'know—for the chicken," I told him.

"No problem," he said, catching my meaning. "I hope you feel better."

Norris left with Kendra leading the way, and I could already tell they wouldn't be going on another date in any universe.

Leo and Angela were the last to go. I can't deny that I was awkward in my goodbyes to them. That could be easily attributable to my heaving stomach—which really was heaving, just not because of the chicken. But less than a minute after they left, I saw Angela's purse next to the pool table, just as the doorbell rang. I grabbed it, to hand it to her at the door, but the purse, like the bad chicken, was just a ruse. She had left it on purpose.

"What is going on with you, Ash?" she asked as we stood in the foyer, me holding her purse, and her refusing to take it until she had an answer. "And don't you dare tell me it's something you ate."

There was truth, and there was TRUTH. The bigger truth was not something I could share, but the smaller one—the personal one—I could speak to, even though every instinct for self-preservation told me to shut down and say nothing.

"It just kind of hit me when I put my arm around you before . . ." I began. "It's about what happened last May. It never should have happened, and I'm sorry."

She looked at me, a little incredulous. "You're kidding me, right?"

"No . . . no, I'm serious."

She rolled her eyes. "I can't believe we're doing this," she said. "Ash, don't treat me like I was some damsel in distress. It was my idea, remember? It wasn't like you forced it. And although I wouldn't exactly call you a gentleman most of the time, you certainly were that night."

But all I could do was shake my head, trying to make the whole episode go away.

"I should have stopped it before it started," I insisted. "I'm the older one—"

"Yeah, by eleven months," she pointed out, more and more annoyed with every word I said. "And between the two of us, I'm a hell of a lot more mature than you."

"I'm sorry, I just—"

"Enough!" she said, throwing up her hands. "Ash, it happened. And you know what? It wasn't bad . . . but it wasn't all that good either. It just . . . *was*. I let it go; why can't you?"

"Because . . . I thought I was a better person."

She shrugged. "You're not. But that's okay. And hey, maybe you're better now."

"If you're fine with it . . . then I guess I am, too."

Angela breathed a sigh of relief. "Good. Because I'm sure the last thing you want is for Leo to find out."

"Find out what?" said Leo, who was right there, standing at the door behind her.

You rarely stop to think about how life hinges on the smallest events. Things so small you can't even really call them events. Looking right instead of left, and missing the person who could have been the love of your life. Picking the package of meat in the supermarket right next to the one contaminated with E. coli. Arriving at a door just in time to hear something you weren't supposed to hear.

Angela and I were caught red-handed, or blue-handed, I suppose, and there was nothing either of us could say. Leo let it linger for a moment, then he became deadly serious. "What, you think I don't know about the two of you after that party?"

It was the last thing either of us expected to hear.

"You knew?" I asked, stunned.

"Of course I knew—do you think I'm an idiot?"

"How come you never said anything?"

"What the hell was I supposed to say? Don't bang my sister?" Leo stared me down, then turned a gentler gaze to Angela. "Your business is your business," he told her. "I respect you enough to let you make your own decisions. Even the really stupid ones."

That was a backhanded compliment if ever there was one, and Angela responded appropriately. "Thank you, Leo," she said. "But you're an asshole." Then she grabbed her purse from me and stormed out, leaving Leo and me in a standoff.

"Leo—"

"Just shut up, okay, because nothing you say is gonna help your case."

But I couldn't just leave it there. Even if every word dug me a deeper grave, I had to say something. "Leo . . . if I could undo it, I would."

He shifted his shoulders. Not a shrug—more like an uncomfortable rolling, like you do when you feel a fever coming on. "I'll live with it," he said. "I *have* been living with it."

"I wouldn't blame you if you hate me."

His expression didn't soften. He held the same hard gaze. "Did it go beyond that one time?"

"No," I told him. "It didn't."

He nodded. "That's what I thought." I felt the tension ease, but only the slightest bit. "She had a crush on you for years; you know that, don't you? The way I see it, she got it out of her system. Turns out she wasn't all that into you. She was just Ash-curious, and now she's not anymore. She can move on."

I still didn't feel that I deserved to be let off the hook, but both Leo and Angela were bigger than that.

"If you had broken her heart, or hurt her in any way, that'd be different," he said. "I'd have ripped you a new one. And if it had gone the other way, and you ended up as a couple? Yeah, I think I'd be okay with that, because at least I know you'd treat her right."

"I would, Leo. You *know* I would."

"But I've got to be honest, seeing you all contrite and miserable like this gives me the warm fuzzies." Then he rapped me in the arm just lightly enough to be friendly, but just hard enough to hurt. "So go suffer some more, and I'll see you Monday."

5

EXIT STRATEGY

I used to have an issue with heights, so I did what I always do when faced with a challenge. I beat it. We were on vacation years ago, in what must have been the rich-me world, because it was at a fancy resort that we could never afford where I used to come from. So on this vacation, there was a zip line between the two hotel towers. It was the absolute last, most horrifying thing I could ever imagine doing. So I signed up for it, and, as they say, broke my foot off in fear's ass.

I screamed like a little kid the entire way across, convinced every second of the way that I was going to die, and since the most god-awful thing I could imagine doing was looking down, I made myself look down. The stupid part of my brain could not believe the thinking part, which said that the cable and harness were time-tested and relatively safe, in spite of the liability release my father had to sign.

That stupid part of our brains used to be the most valuable thing we had. It kept our paleo-whatever ancestors from getting eaten by saber-toothed tigers and putting their hands in fire. Now it mostly just messes with us and gets us into trouble on a regular basis because it's so damn stupid.

Well, before school started on Monday, my idiot brain kicked in and kept trying to convince me that I was going to die. That the universe was done with me, and it wouldn't even wait until Friday's game. Long before then, it would use my own school to kill me by splitting my skull with a falling air vent, or choking me with a cafeteria hot dog, or blowing me up in a science experiment gone terribly wrong. I was totally, irrationally, bracing for the worst—just like Leo had talked about in his basement that day.

But I did what I had to do. I pretended like I wasn't screaming on the inside, and went to school, like it was an ordinary Monday.

And you know what? It *was* an ordinary Monday. It was almost disappointing how ordinary it was. I gave a weak excuse for a late English paper; I got a B on a math quiz, thanks to being tutored; and I ate lunch with the usual crowd, and did not choke. If I didn't know any better, I'd think everything was fine.

And that night, I did what I do every Monday night in this world. Hint: it wasn't watching Monday Night Football. It was dealing drugs. I was a drug dealer. Even now, saying those words, it just doesn't sound real. Like a line from someone else's miserable life.

Because of Monday Night Football, it was the only night I knew that my dad wouldn't turn up at the store unexpected. Because when I wasn't selling at parties and school hallways, I had my customers come to me, in our supplement store, once seven o'clock rolled around, and I was the only employee on duty.

My first customer was a kid my age, but not from my school, who came in at seven on the dot. "Hey, Ash," he said, handing me a big wad of bills that was mostly singles. "The usual. Count it if you want."

"Sure thing, Alex." I hadn't known his face until I saw him. I didn't know his name until I spoke it. And I didn't know what his usual was, until muscle memory made me reach beneath the counter and pull out a bottle of vitamin C, which I suddenly remembered contained a baggie with a gram of coke. "I don't have to count it," I told him. "I trust you."

"Thanks, man."

I pocketed the cash, the little bell above the door jingled as he left, and I felt a whole new level of disgust for what I had just done—at furious odds with the part of me that saw this as business as usual.

The rest of the evening was a mix of normal customers and "special" customers. And it wasn't like you could pick these people out of a lineup. There was one lawyer-looking guy who asked for two bottles of my "special vitamin C," which was a top seller. A woman my mother's age in a tennis outfit, who had her kids wait in the car while she bought our proprietary blend of echinacea. Echinacea = ecstasy. And there was an old lady who was sweet, but slow, and very tired, who asked how my family was, then requested a bottle of our best ornithine. Ornithine = oxycodone. There were some customers my alt-me knew better than others, but no one was new to this ball game.

I found that the only way to deal with this was to fold in on myself, becoming an observer in my own flesh. I knew what to do without having to think, so I did my best to shut down all my higher brain functions. I told myself I was just a passenger on a screwed-up ride. The ride would end, but where would it leave me? What was my next destination? The stop signs were all still blue, which meant the worlds didn't cancel each other out—instead they *built* on one another. It probably meant in the next one, my family would still be rich, and I'd still be dealing drugs.

Maybe, I thought, this might be the end of it. I'd be stuck here in this reality, and would have to figure out how to make the best of it. If I could wash away the sleazy part of this life, and stop dealing, I'd be okay. The thing is, sleaziness is like an oil stain on your driveway. No matter how many times you wash it, it just keeps seeping back up through the concrete.

On Wednesday my drug cache was replenished by the delivery-man for Nutro-Quest Supplements—a guy named Ralston. He would leave my private container hiding just behind the other protein jugs. You'd have to restock an awful lot of protein to find it, so it was never disturbed. Sometimes things are remarkably easy to hide in plain sight.

I usually didn't work Wednesday evenings, but this week I made an exception and switched shifts with one of the other employees, then waited for Ralston to show up. He hadn't started unloading his delivery yet. I found him out by the service door in the back, smoking an e-cig.. It was this sickly sweet sour-apple flavor. Who vapes sour apple? What was this world coming to?

"Well, if it isn't the man himself," he said, offering a friendly handshake. We got through the niceties of greeting, and then I cleared my throat and launched into this whole preamble that I needed breadcrumbs to find my way out of.

"I've given it a lot of thought," I told him, "and I know I've been at this for a year and I'll admit the money is good—that's not what this is about—but I think it's time I considered the possibility of ending our private business relationship."

He looked at me, puffed, and got lost behind a candy-apple cloud. When he emerged from the cloud, he said, "So you want out?"

"Yeah, I want out."

He nodded. "Okay," he said. "What's your exit strategy?"

"Exit strategy," I repeated, deadpan and dull.

"Exit strategy," he said again.

"Well . . . I just figured I'd . . . stop?"

He laughed. It wasn't an actual laugh; it was the kind of laugh that announced the coming of a condescending lecture.

"Let me explain how these things work," Ralston said. "There's you. Then there's me. Then there's the guy I work for.

Then there's the guy he works for, and the guy who *that* guy works for, and at least one more guy on top of that. The top guy is someone I don't know, and don't want to know—but I can guarantee you that he's big and he's bad. The guy right beneath him, who I also don't know, is not quite so big, and not quite so bad, and so on and so on, until it gets to me, who's a pretty nice guy, and you, who are a decent, upstanding kid." He paused to make sure I got it all. "Now when the upstanding kid tells the pretty nice guy that he doesn't want to sell anymore, what do you think happens?"

I didn't answer him; I just wanted him to get to the point. With no response from me, he continued.

"The nice guy (me) has to tell the not-quite-as-nice guy he works for, who then tells the guy *he* works for, who's a real creep, and so on and so on, all the way up the chain."

I knew where this was going, and it was pissing me off. "Are you threatening me?"

"No," he said. "You're not hearing me. I told you I'm a nice guy. I'm not going to hurt you. But the guy above me? If I tell him this, he'll send someone to rough you up pretty bad. Why? Because the guy above him might break his nose. Why? Because the guy above *him* might break his legs. Why? Because the guy above *him* might put a bullet in his brain. Why? Because the guy at the top might take out his entire family. And all because you want out. So to prevent this very unpleasant and senseless chain of events, it's in everyone's best interests for you to have a viable exit strategy."

"Maybe I'll just go to the police and tell them you're supplying drugs to kids."

He grimaced. "See, you really don't want to do that because if I get arrested, suddenly the guy all the way at the top knows you exist. Trust me, you don't want him to know you exist. Whoever he is."

That shut me up. Suddenly I felt intimidated. I never feel intimidated, but this scrawny, sleazy guy now had me under his thumb.

"So here's what you're going to do," he said, putting his arm over my shoulder like a buddy. "You're going to continue accepting and paying for my deliveries until you find someone else equally capable, but a little more eager than you to do the job. You teach him all you know about how to do it. Then he steps in, you step out, and voilà. Exit strategy."

"You want me to turn one of my friends into a drug dealer?"

"Right," he said. "Simple as that."

Only it wasn't simple at all.

After Ralston left, I felt like I was stuck in quicksand. Any move I made would pull me deeper, and the only escape was to climb out over someone else's back.

As I went into the shop, I started to run through my mind everyone I knew, and who among them might be greedy enough, stupid enough, and naïve enough to take over for me. After all, I had been all three of those things—at least in this reality— surely there had to be other idiots out there. But here's the thing: like it or not, my conscience came along with me from my non-drug-dealing reality. Now that I knew how screwed up this was, how could I foist that upon someone I knew and liked? I suppose I could have foisted it upon someone I *didn't* like, but that was dangerous, because if the feeling was mutual, they might just turn me in.

I believed Ralston was telling the truth about the consequences if I didn't find a replacement—he wasn't just blowing steam. If I disrupted the flow, I'd get my ass kicked, or worse, from people even sleazier than Ralston—who, by the way, is not the "nice guy" he thinks he is.

It was just past nine when I locked up. Then, as I headed for my car, I heard the sound of polyurethane wheels on pavement, and turned to see none other than the twin skaters heading my way. Being as dense as I can sometimes be, I didn't think anything of it. It's not that big of a town. You always run into the same people.

"Hey, Ash!" one of them said brightly, like we were old friends. He hopped off his board and kicked it under his arm in a single smooth motion, and the other did the same.

"Hey," I said half-heartedly. I didn't know their names, nor, at the time, did I care to.

"Aw, you're closed," said the second twin. "We were hoping to get some glucosamine. Good for the knees, y'know?"

I looked back to the store. The register was shut down, and our useless point-of-sale software would take ten minutes to reload if I turned it on. I did not feel like extending this day by a single second.

"Sorry, guys. Can't reopen once everything's shut down."

"No worries, we'll come back."

And yet they didn't skate off, they just lingered. Watching me.

"You need a ride again?" I asked.

"Naah, we're good," one of them said. "How's your headache?"

That caught me by surprise. "How do you know I have a headache?"

He shrugged. "You took a pretty bad hit in the game on Friday, right?"

"Yeah, you told us about how your head hurt when you drove us home," said the other.

"I did?"

"Sure. How else would we know?"

With two sets of memories fighting for higher ground in my head, it was totally possible that I forgot, so I accepted their explanation. Still, I didn't want to talk about it with a couple of losers, so even though my head still felt funny, I just said, "It's okay now."

"Really? Okay?"

Now they were just being annoying. "Why do you even care? And how do you even know me? I never told you my name."

"We're football fans," one of them said with a smile. "We know the names of all the players on the Tsunamis."

"Right. Well, I gotta go."

I turned away from them, but one of them—the more talkative one—grabbed me by the arm, and said, in a voice that was just slightly above a whisper, "Take a few bottles of potassium pills. Grind them up with a whole bunch of eggshells, and a bottle of mint extract. Then add it to a hot bath. It's an old family cure. I guarantee it'll help the kind of headache you've got."

Then they skated off together in perfect unison. I remember thinking at the time there was something strange about how they skated. It was like they weren't really moving at all. Instead the rest of the world was moving beneath the two of them, while they stood still.

I'm generally not a bath kind of guy, but I decided to take their suggestion. We always had a supply of mineral supplements at the house, so the potassium was easy. I had to buy the rest. At the market, the checker looked at me funny when I came to the register with four dozen eggs and a bottle of mint extract.

I wasn't sure why I believed a random skater dude when it came to how to relieve a headache—especially a headache as nontraditional as mine. I guess I was so desperate I was willing to try anything. So when I got home, I cracked the eggs into a container, figuring someone could use them for something, then pulverized the shells and the potassium in a food processor.

The potassium dissolved in the hot bathwater, but the eggshells stayed like a fine sand on the bottom of the tub. The mint—which made the entire bathroom reek—tinged the water the slightest bit green, and smelled much stronger than I thought it would. After ten minutes in the bath, I had to admit my head felt a little less tightly packed. Still, there was something bouncing around my brain like an old-fashioned pinball, ricocheting off of my overtaxed gray matter, until finally it dropped.

"We know the names of all the players on the Tsunamis."

Have you ever gotten a sudden chill while you're in a hot bath? It's not a pleasant thing. I leapt up so quickly I think half the bath splashed out; I lost my balance and fell to the floor with a heavy thud. I yelled and cursed, not just because of the fall, but because it had taken me so long to realize. The Tsunamis didn't exist in this world! Here, we were still the Blue Demons, just like they were when my father played. *Who the hell are these skaters?*

As I left the bathroom, towel-wrapped, but still dripping wet, my mother intercepted me.

"What was that I heard? Did you fall?"

"I'm fine."

She looked into the bathroom, took a whiff, and said, "What's going on in here? It smells like you killed a Christmas elf."

"New cologne," I told her. "It's called Blitzen." And I quickly hurried to my room, closing out any conversation.

Once in my room, I immediately grabbed my phone. I hadn't spoken to Katie since the weekend, but she was the only person I could share this with who wouldn't think I was out of my mind.

New development, I texted, then I got dressed, and worked on a game plan without patience to wait for a response.

I bounded out of my room, about to head downstairs and out

the door, but I passed Hunter's room, and what I heard gave me pause. He was in his room playing electric guitar. Hunter didn't have a guitar, or the skill to even play one in our original world. Neither of us had been musically inclined. He looked up and saw me.

"Hey, listen to this," he said, and played a complicated riff. When he looked up at me for validation, he saw I was wearing multiple layers of confusion along with a jacket. "What's up? Going somewhere?"

In my previous life, I would have told him it was none of his business—but then, *that* Hunter wouldn't have cared enough to ask. I hesitated, then offered him an entry into my world. "If I told you, you'd think I was nuts."

"And how would that be different from any other day?"

I looked at my phone. Katie hadn't responded. Maybe she had changed her mind and decided I was ten-foot-pole material. Or maybe she was with Layton and wasn't free to text me. Either way, I couldn't wait on this; I had to move now. I didn't tell Hunter what was up. Instead, I just said, "Wanna come with?"

"Sure," he said. "It's dead around here."

He put down his guitar and grabbed a hoodie. The fact that he'd come with me without even knowing what I was up to said a lot about him. It said a lot about us as brothers. This reality was not all roses and puppies—but if there was one thing that tipped the scale and made me think that this might be the better place to be, it was Hunter. Not the money, not the car, not the home theater, but having a brother who felt like a brother. Used to be we tolerated each other, and only barely. A textbook case of "I love you but that doesn't mean I have to like you," which I think he once actually said to me when we were younger, and our mother forced us to hug it out after a fight.

"So where are we going?" he asked as we got into my car. "Do you need me to navigate?"

"The skate park," I told him.

"You? The skate park? You don't even own a skateboard."

Which was true in all realities. Throwing people off balance was my forte. My own balance was questionable—or at least it was on wheels.

"We're looking for someone," I told him. "Actually two some-ones. Two skaters."

"Okay—what do they look like?"

"Each other," I told him. "They're twins."

"What do you need them for? They owe you money?"

I glanced over to him. He probably thought this had to do with my little side business. It bothered me that he would think that. "Not money," I told him. "They owe me an explanation."

The skate park is down by the community center, the only part of the center that's open until midnight. The idea was that if you could keep the town's sketchy kids congregated in a single well-lit place, there'd be less sketchy activity in the unlit places. What they didn't realize is that the town's sketchiest kids could find darkness anywhere.

I asked kids I knew, and ones I didn't know. No one had

seen twin skaters. No one knew them. If they lived here, and they skated, someone had to know them, right? And here's the weirdest thing. Every time someone asked me to describe them, I couldn't. What color was their hair? Was it short or long? Did they have acne? Braces? Any distinguishing marks? I didn't know. I couldn't even be sure of their ethnicity.

There's this thing I heard about. Prosopagnosia. It's an inability to recognize faces. Your own mother could walk into a room, and you wouldn't know it was her until you heard her voice. That's how I felt with the twins. Their faces left no memory.

"Well, if you can't describe them, I can't help you," the skate park manager told me, and walked away.

Hunter, who had been working the far side of the skate park, came back. No surprise that he had no luck either.

"Maybe these guys aren't from here," Hunter said.

I pulled out my phone, hoping that Katie had responded, but she hadn't. More than anything, I wanted to tell her about this. But I wouldn't text her again.

"Why are they so important?" Hunter asked. "And why don't you know what they look like?"

Those were the million-dollar questions, weren't they?

"Forget it," I told him. "It's not important."

I turned to go, but he grabbed me hard enough to make me turn back to him. "But it *is* important, isn't it?" he said. "I don't know why . . . but it *feels* like this is really important. Because . . . because . . ."

Whatever he was trying to say, he was having a hard time with it. I could see his Adam's apple bouncing, fighting to keep the words from coming out. ". . . because something's . . . *wrong* . . . isn't it?"

So Hunter felt it. This was another development.

I could have told him that, yes, something was very wrong, but I wasn't ready to do that. I played my cards tight. For his own sanity as well as mine. "How do you mean?" I asked, trying to sound as oblivious as possible.

"I don't know," he said. I could tell he was getting frustrated with himself. It's hard to fight all those parts of yourself that tell you you're being ridiculous. "It's just a feeling. And the weird thing is . . . I only feel it when I'm around you."

I looked at him, watching him struggle to make sense of a feeling that made no sense at all. He wanted an answer, but I couldn't give him one. All I could give him were more questions that would scramble his brain even more. But maybe he didn't need an answer right now. Maybe he just needed comfort.

"It's not your imagination," I told him, but offered him no more than that. Even so, he heaved a breath of intense relief.

And it made me realize something. They say that misery loves company. That never rang true for me. But I do know that when you're facing a vast unknown, company is the only thing that makes it bearable.

6

HOSTILE TERRITORY

There are people who live in a constant state of stress because they spend their time obsessing about what might be. All the things that could go wrong. All the terrible tomorrows that, by and large, never arrive.

Then there are those whose thoughts are trapped in yesterday. Woulda-shoulda-coulda. All the regrets about missed opportunities and bad decisions that they can't live down. All that effort and energy spent reliving things that can't be changed.

And then there are people like me. I try to live in the moment. Isn't that what we're supposed to do? Experience life as it happens? Get the most out of every second of every day? But there's a downside to that, too. Because when you live like that, you don't think much.

There are these gurus who say thinking is the enemy. One self-help dude said he sat under a tree in a park for two years and did nothing but try to not think—like he'd rather be a bush than human. I guess thinking is the enemy if you're spiraling into regrets, or imagining nasty futures, but otherwise thinking is the most important thing we do. It's what sets us apart from shrubs and slugs.

Thought is what we're all about, whether the shrubbery-men like it or not. We just have to use it, and not let *it* use *us*. But when it comes to my life—or the way I lived before the game totally changed—I was a man of action rather than a man of thought, so my brain was definitely not prepared to be handling dimensions beyond the standard three.

Accosting Katie in the hallway before first period was not the most effective way to approach her, but after a sleepless night, I was desperate for answers, or at least someone who understood the question.

"I got your text," she said. "What's up?"

"I need to show you something, and I need you to tell me if you recognize it."

She glanced around, then looked at me dubiously, as if she half expected me to flash my junk. "Uh, sure, okay."

I'm not an artist—not by a long shot—but that morning I did my best to sketch Tsammy, the snarling wave that used to be the mascot of the Tibbetsville Tsunamis.

"Does this mean anything to you?" I unfolded the paper and

held it in front of her, carefully gauging her reaction—and for a moment, just for a moment, there was something in her eyes. Something bordering on confusion. "No . . . Wait . . . No," she finally decided. "No, I don't recognize that. It looks like an angry wizard," she said, pointing to the crest of the wave, which she had mistaken for a wizard's hat. Like I said, I am not an artist.

"But for a second you looked like you weren't sure . . ."

Katie met my gaze, maybe a little bit bothered that I could read her so easily. "It was nothing," she said. "Just déjà vu or something."

"Or something," I repeated. "'Déjà vu' translates to mean 'already seen,' right? It's Latin."

"French," she corrected. "But yeah."

"And you *have* already seen this. Because this is—"

"A mascot!" she blurted. "It's the mascot of one of the other schools we play, right? And it's not a wizard, it's a . . . it's a . . ."

I waited for it. And she said—

"It's a . . . tree?"

"It's a wave," I finally told her. "It's blue! It's a wave."

And she grinned. "Are you sure it's not red?"

I had to give her a point for that. "Well, then it would be the Crimson Tide, and not the Tibbetsville Tsunamis." Although the Crimson Tide's mascot is an elephant. In what universe does that make sense?

"Tibbetsville?" she said.

I nodded and let her piece it together, hoping that this time she'd do better than "tree."

"*Our* mascot?"

I nodded again. "Last week."

She looked at the image, then to me, then to the image again. "Normally I would tell you that you've taken one too many hits, but every time I look back at it, for like a tenth of a second, I remember something about it."

She grabbed it away from me. "Like this—" And she pointed to the hands I drew on the wave. Don't ask me why a tsunami has hands, but it does. "You drew four fingers, but it only has three. Isn't that right?"

And yes, she was right.

"Can I keep this?"

"Sure."

She folded it and stuck it in her locker, and that's when Layton appeared like a stealth bomber, putting his five-fingered hand around her waist. "What's going on here?" he asked jovially. "Something I should be worried about?"

Katie didn't miss a beat. "Ash was just asking if I knew where you were."

He pulled her closer in a bone-crush of affection. "I'm right here."

"So . . . I was wondering if I could borrow your notes for science," I told him, pulling the fiction out of thin air just as deftly as Katie had. "My notebook fell in our Jacuzzi."

"I thought your Toughbook was waterproof," he said. "You're always bragging about it."

"Oh, right. No, I meant the paper kind."

He scoffed at the idea of me using a paper notebook. In my old life I didn't have any waterproof electronics. Just an old iPhone with a perpetually cracked screen, and a "fair condition" eBay Mac with memory issues.

"Why don't you ask that brainy kid, Peter, that you hang out with?"

"It's Paul," I told him.

"Yeah, ask him—his notes'll be way better than mine."

Then he sauntered off to class with Katie in his proprietary grip. Katie didn't turn back to look at me or say goodbye. Maybe because she knew Layton would notice or maybe because the near headlock he had her in restricted her motion.

Mission two of that morning: identify the twin skaters. I started by charming the school secretary before class with small talk and mild flattery, noticing how cool it was that her earrings matched her nail polish. Then, before it got weird, I asked her the big question.

"Do you think maybe you could help me? I'm doing a genetics report and I need to interview all the identical twins at our school."

There were only two sets of twins that I knew: the Tomassini sisters, who had diverged to opposite poles. Bronwyn had buzz-cut hair, tattoos, and so many piercings it looked like she'd been attacked by a BeDazzler. Her sister, Beth, had a perpetual perm, liked unicorns, and wore a charm bracelet that looked like the custodian's keychain. Then there were the Hudson brothers, who looked exactly alike, except that Ethan was a nice guy and Mark was a dickwad. You could only tell them apart when they opened their mouths: if every third word was an f-bomb, then you knew it was Mark.

The secretary knew without even looking at her computer that those were the only identical twins at our school.

"How about graduates?" I asked. "Or ones who dropped out?"

"Honey," she said, "they don't pay me enough to dig that deep, and even if they did, I don't have access to the archives."

Fail. I expected as much.

I hadn't seen much of Leo or Angela since Sunday night. I didn't avoid them intentionally, but it wasn't entirely unintentional either. I saw Leo at practice, and I had a few classes with him, but neither of us engaged. There was a distance that hadn't been there before. Like we were in the same classroom, but at completely different schools.

On Thursday, Angela came over to sit with me during lunch. Until then, I had chosen to sit alone—something I never did, but things change.

"My brother wants me to tell you that your penance is served, and you're out of the doghouse," Angela said.

"How about you?" I asked.

"You were never in the doghouse with me," she said, then thought about it and said, "Can I rephrase that?"

I gave her an obligatory laugh that felt more awkward than helpful.

"Anyway," said Angela, "that's not what I really came over to talk about. I hear you've been talking to Katie."

I sighed. Why is it that everyone always knows everyone else's business in this town? "Yeah, I'm worried about her," I told Angela.

"So am I. She says everything's fine, but I have a hard time believing it. Layton is . . . controlling."

"That's a nice way of putting it."

"What has Katie told you?"

I shook my head. "Nothing but to mind my own business."

Angela dropped her shoulders, disappointed. "She's in love with him, and she's scared of him. That's a bad combination."

"I don't think he's hurting her. Physically, I mean."

"Not yet, anyway. But there are other ways to bruise a person, you know?"

And that made me think about the way Layton looked at Katie. It was the way he might look at a treasured painting that he felt was just a little crooked on the wall, so he was constantly, endlessly adjusting it.

"If you ask me, she'd be better off with *anyone* else," I told Angela. "Hell, she'd even be better off with Norris."

Angela laughed at that. Katie with Norris would be a local production of *Beauty and the Beast*. Except at the end, the beast just transforms into a turd.

Angela tapped her fingertips against her lips—as if what she was thinking had just come to mind—which clearly it hadn't. "If anybody would be better . . . how about you?" she suggested.

The last thing I needed at the moment was Angela playing matchmaker. "That," I said, "would not help the situation."

"Well at the very least, you should have a talk with Layton."

"And say what?" I glanced over to the table where Katie sat with Layton and a few of their friends, who were couples. They seemed happy enough. "Seemed" was the operative word here. Layton himself was never actually happy. In his world, there was always something to find fault with.

"We'll watch," I suggested. "We'll keep an eye on the situation."

But Angela wasn't too happy with that approach. "Why is it that guys just want to sit around and watch until something awful happens?"

She stormed off before I could have any sort of comeback. I wanted to tell her that it wasn't like that. That sometimes you have to see where things are going in order to plan an effective strategy. That making vague accusations against our star quarterback could backfire—because there were way too many people who believed he could do no wrong. It would be different if Katie broke up with him. I would totally stand behind her— even in front of her—to protect her. But that wasn't the train she was currently on. She, like the rest of our school, was on the Layton Vandenboom Express, and it wasn't slowing down enough for her to get off.

Leo and I spoke after practice that night, for the first time since the revelation about me and his sister. Technically, it was only a revelation for me, because Leo already knew. But now I knew he knew, which was awkward. I longed for the time when nobody knew anything.

We talked sports first to break the ice. Leo reminded me that tomorrow's game was an away game, and how the other team's field had lousy turf. Slippery and hard on the bones.

"You know we're okay, right?" he finally said.

"You're sure?"

That annoyed him. "What is it with you, that you need constant reassurance now?"

"Because if it was the other way around, I might not be okay with it."

"See, Ash, that's the difference between you and me," he said. "Me, I'm all magnanimous and shit, because I see the big picture. But you can't see much of anything because you got your head up your ass."

That actually made me smile. "Sometimes it's the safest place to be."

"Safe is overrated," he said. "Can't we just go back to the way things were before?"

That was just what I needed to hear. Things going back to normal. I just wished more things could. "So we're still friends, right?"

"For better or for worse, that's a given," he said.

But things that are given can also be taken away.

This week's game was on hostile territory. We had a crowd on the visitors' side, but nowhere near as big as the home crowd. The other team's mascot was the Phoenix, which probably seemed a good idea at the time, until someone realized the plural of "Phoenix" was Phoenices. And when the loudspeaker proudly announced, "The Phoenices are on the field!" none of us could keep a straight face. Maybe that was part of their psychological tactics. Weaken us through laughter.

All joking aside, they were a tough team. We're hard to beat, but I guess you could say the Phoenices rose to the occasion.

By the beginning of the fourth quarter, we were down twenty to fourteen. Layton was furious at himself for allowing such a thing to happen, while at the same time blaming everyone else. I knew I was holding back, not playing as hard as I usually do, because my fear of going sideways again muted all my responses. Which meant if we lost, I would be a part of the reason.

The truth is, I shouldn't have been there at all. I should have retired my jersey while it was still blue and lived a tackle-free life. Because this world, as twisted as it was, was fixable. It wouldn't be easy, but it could be done. I could be the old me in the new digs. If I knew what was coming, that's what I would have done. But I was foolish. I was arrogant. Like Leo said, my head was lodged in a place where the sun, moon, and stars don't shine.

With eight minutes left to play, the ball changed hands, and I took the field with the rest of the defensive team, determined to make these next few plays count.

I got into position, the ball was snapped, and I lunged forward like a freight train. The opposing lineman misjudged, engaging me off balance. I pushed past him, making him spin like a turnstile. The QB was fading back, looking for a receiver to pass to. His eyes kept darting. I could tell he couldn't throw a clear pass, and he was going to make a run for it. I could see, almost feel, his center of gravity shifting, and I knew which direction he was going to run an instant before he made the move. I surged toward him, knowing if I took him down it would be a major loss of yardage for the Phoenices. I hit him hard.

And the moment I made contact, it happened again.

This time it was different. The instant of cold wasn't just an instant. It was like being submerged in ice water. Like the people leaping from the *Titanic* must have felt the second they hit the frigid Atlantic. And I was moving. I wasn't falling, I was sliding. Not backward or forward, not up or down, or even sideways. I was sliding in a direction that doesn't exist. I instinctively knew that this was much worse than before. The air was sucked out of my lungs, and I thought, This is it. This is what I feared. The zip line cable snapping. The plunge to oblivion.

And then I gasped. Not just gasped but sucked two whole lungfuls of air. In spite of feeling like I had just returned from a trip to deep space, I got to my feet, trying to catch my breath, not sure how long I had been lying there. It must not have been long, because no one seemed to notice. Everyone was just getting ready for the next play.

Everything seemed normal. Almost. Everything seemed fine. But not really. Because my head was still feeling the resonance of that place between. The phantom headache had an entire new dimension. There had been a colossal shift, but here, in the middle of a football field, I couldn't see it yet.

So I did what I was supposed to do. I did my job. I took to the line. I didn't take down the quarterback again, but my previous power tackle made him timidly toss away the next two passes, and then the Phoenices punted. I was off the field as our offensive team took their places.

Once I was on the sidelines, I started to become aware of things. First were the names on the jerseys of the kids around me. Out on the field, I didn't notice—I mean, we're all suited up, with helmets and mouth guards that distort our features behind the face masks. Only now, when helmets were off, did I realize that I didn't know some of these kids. And yet I did. To the real me, at least half the faces and half the names were completely unfamiliar. But once I connected a name to a face, the memories from this new reality kicked in with a painful mental resonance that made me wince.

"You okay, man?" asked a teammate whose jersey said "Jenkins," a kid who wasn't on the team ten minutes ago. "That was one helluva sack out there."

"Yeah, thanks," I told him, trying not to wince at the vibrations twanking in my head.

Out on the field, Layton took the snap, and the play came to life. Leo went long. Layton passed. Leo caught the ball, to the roar of our fans and teammates. No one was near him. He took it all the way down for a touchdown!

It was only when he came back from the end zone that I

realized something was very wrong with this triumphant picture.

"Damn," said Jenkins, "he's fast as a s'equal on payday!"

"Fast as a *what?*" But Jenkins didn't even hear me—he was whooping and whistling and giving Leo the adulation he deserved.

Only here's the thing . . .

It wasn't Leo.

The name on his jersey said "Easley" and when he took off his helmet, it was this ginger dude, with skin about a million shades lighter than Leo's. In fact, as I looked around me, there was an uneasy *sameness* to the team.

White. They were all white. This, on a team that is about as ethnically diverse as a team can get. But all the brown kids were nowhere to be seen. I looked up to the stands and saw this crazy sea of pale on both sides of the field. And I knew the sickness I now felt in my gut was only going to get worse.

7

MY SUNSCREEN IGNORANCE

Here's what I know:

Back in the 1950s there was this Supreme Court case called *Brown v. Board of Education*. It wasn't just one case, but five cases combined into one. I know this because it was a question on a social studies test. I'm embarrassed to say that something so important—so monumental—had, until now, been reduced to an index card in my head.

The case was all about segregation, which was legal back then. In a big part of the country, white kids went to white schools, and Black kids went to Black schools that were supposed to be "separate but equal," but of course there was nothing equal about them.

The Supreme Court unanimously decided that segregation was unconstitutional, and therefore illegal. It took a while for them to get to that decision unanimously, but they did, and the law changed.

There was pushback, of course, from people who liked things the way they were, and who resisted. The governor of Alabama stood in a school doorway to prevent two Black students from going in. A county in Virginia actually closed all of its public schools for five years rather than integrate them. Really. I'm not making this up—this crap went down in *my* reality. My *original* reality. But in spite of resistance, the Supreme Court decision that struck down segregation was an important victory in a never-ending battle.

So what happened here to screw that up?

I didn't know it at the time, but in *this* new world, that Supreme Court decision wasn't unanimous. In fact, it went the other way. Three to five. Five Supreme Court justices upheld segregation.

That decision changed everything.

History forked in a different direction. Segregation remained the law of the land. And that expression, "s'equal"? Turns out it's a derogatory term for anyone from "those" schools in "those" neighborhoods. It's short for "separate-but-equal."

I'm a strong guy, but just thinking about it made me crumble. The America I knew was already battling a dark age where Miss Liberty's light flickered like a bulb ready to be changed. But in *this* America, her torch had already been completely and utterly doused.

◆ ◆ ◆

After the game, I went out to the Towne Centre like I always do, on autopilot. I was too stunned to be anything but habitual. I knew there'd be memories of who I was in this world. They were waiting for me if I dug too deep, and I wasn't ready to know. So I did my best to skate on the surface until I had the courage to take the deep dive.

But even the Towne Centre had changed. Different restaurants, alternate-universe movies. And the seating area of the food court was divided. Here's where I really started to get a sense of what this world was all about. Because the food court had a white side, and a nonwhite side.

"Over here, Ash!" called that redheaded receiver who had taken Leo's place on the team. Josh Easley. A hint of a memory told me he was my best friend in this world. He was sitting with Norris and a few others, some of whom were there before, others who were specific to this world. Maybe they had existed before, but they certainly weren't on the team.

"I'm gonna get food," I shouted, to stall having to sit on the "white side."

I wish I could tell you that I left. I wish I could tell you that I refused to play in this segregated sandbox. But in the end, I got my burger and planted my ass where I was expected to plant it.

Josh Easley, my best friend who I didn't actually know, made room for me. I resented that. I resented *him*, because Leo and Angela's absence was eating at my guts like an alien. I kept looking over to the other side, to see if maybe they might be there, but no such luck.

Layton was at our table, too. With Katie. She was like an oasis in this desert—but was she still the same Katie? I simply didn't know.

Layton was nursing the loss of tonight's game in his own personal cone of misery that he was happy to extend over us. "I can't believe we lost to the stinking Phoenices!" Layton said, which made Norris snicker. Any adjective with the word "phoenices" made him snicker. "What, you think it's funny?" snapped Layton. "Maybe if the rest of you played a little harder, we'd be celebrating instead of kicking ourselves."

He grabbed his burger and bit into it with such angry force, half of it squirted out the other side. He cursed and complained that their buns were too small. Which also made Norris snicker.

I looked at Katie, but she wouldn't make eye contact.

"Dude," said the Easley kid, "they're a strong team. We knew it would be rough."

"That's right, just make excuses," growled Layton. And then he looked over at Katie, who was doing her best not to join his pity party. "Are you really gonna eat that whole basket of onion rings?" he asked her—but it was more of an accusation than a question, and it really rankled me. "How many have you had already? Do you know how many calories are in those things?"

"You ordered them!" she countered.

"Layton, c'mon, leave her alone," said Easley, "it's not her you're mad at."

Layton pursed his lips and let out a long slow breath through his nose. "Fine," he said. "It's just that . . ."

But with all of us looking at him and wondering how he was going to justify food-shaming Katie, he had nothing.

"Never mind," he grumbled, then he turned to Katie. "Eat whatever you want, I don't care."

But she pushed the onion rings away. "I've lost my appetite." Then she got up and stormed toward the bathroom.

Once she was gone, Layton looked at us with a smirk and shook his head. "Girls, right?"

"I hear ya," said Norris, because Norris had always idolized Layton. In Norris's mind, Layton defined what it meant to be a man, and it made me boil, because as far as role models go, Layton was no quarterback. Hell, he didn't even deserve to be on the field.

"Got anything else you want to take out on her?" I dared to ask. "Maybe a bad grade you got on a test? Or that ketchup stain on your shirt?"

"Watch yourself, Ash," Layton threatened.

"Then I'd be just like you," I said. "I'd be watching myself all day."

I left the table, claiming the last word—but I didn't go the same direction as Katie, because I didn't want to create any more grief for her—and if Layton saw me going in that direction, there would definitely be grief by the bushel. I did need to talk to her—to make sure she was okay, and also to make sure she was still the same Katie—but I wouldn't make her the object of a pissing contest between me and Layton. That was just one more way of disrespecting her.

I strode around the food court, too ashamed to make eye contact with anyone in the "other-than-white" section. Then I noticed that there was a third section, smaller than the other two, and tucked away, as to be less obvious. This third section looked a little more like my world. Some white families, some brown. An oasis of normal in the pit of despair.

"Ash," I heard someone call. I turned to see Paul Fisher, my math tutor friend. He was with his parents in this unsegregated section. The Fishers are white, but they were choosing to sit here. Suddenly I liked Paul a whole lot more.

"You're standing like you forgot where you were going."

"Yeah," I told him. "Problem is, I wasn't really going anywhere."

"If you're hungry, why don't you join us," Paul's mother said. "We ordered way too much."

I was far from hungry, but I sat with them anyway, because this table was the first inviting thing I'd seen in this world. We made small talk, and I was grateful for it. Paul told his parents about my home theater, I told them it was nothing special. His little sister complained that her burrito had no flavor. Which didn't surprise me—the Mexican place that this world had vomited forth didn't have anyone behind the counter who looked remotely Mexican.

I realized I had no Latinx friends in this world. The word didn't even exist here. Then I pinged on a memory: how an eerily identical President Trump had triumphantly claimed that decades of our closed-door policy had kept COVID out of the US. Until nearly a million Americans died, while the rest of the continent stayed clean. Turns out our closed-door policy kept the virus in, not out. My grandpa Duncan died of it in this world. The racist one. But before then, he must have thrived in this place, like yeast in fresh dough.

Shaking off the memory, I glanced over to the bathrooms, my thoughts going back to Katie. She'd come out, and now Layton was there, talking to her earnestly. I didn't need to hear the conversation to know the gist of it. Layton was wearing Katie down with an apology. Finally she accepted it, and they left together with his arm around her. Maybe Layton actually believed that his apology was from the bottom of his heart, but when you're the type of guy who treats girls the way Layton does, how deep can your heart really go? It doesn't take much to reach the bottom of it.

The only good thing about Layton's momentary remorse was that he'd be good to Katie for the rest of the day, maybe even the whole weekend. It would give me time to figure out what to do about it—because now I realized that Angela, wherever she was, was right. I couldn't just sit and watch.

"First time in the Alt?" Paul asked.

"The what?"

"You know—the alternative dining area."

"Oh, right. Yeah," I told him, "but I think I might make it a regular thing, you know?"

"Good for you!" said his mom. "Someone from a family as prominent as yours sitting in the alternative section will be a statement. Really ruffle some feathers!"

"Just trying to be a decent person," I said.

"Doesn't your school have a de-seg club?" his mom asked. "You should join."

I turned to Paul. "Are you in it?" I asked.

"Not yet," he said, a little sheepish about it, "but I'll join if you do."

And so I agreed to join the desegregation club. I didn't know what a bunch of white kids in a white school could do against a hurricane of people not giving a shit, but if the choice was either that or do nothing, I'd rather scream into the storm.

None of my football buds asked for a ride home that night. Maybe they sensed that there was something different about me from the Ash they knew, or maybe they didn't want to step into the "alternative" section. Not even Norris, who always asked for a ride, came near me. I'm sure he was trying to distance himself from me, considering how I disrespected Layton, our all-American golden boy. Did you know that "all-American" is often a code word for "white"? Leo had told me that. I didn't believe it at the time; I thought it was just Leo being Leo—but I was now giving everything he had ever told me a whole lot more credibility. "Your ignorance is like a layer of stupid-ass sunscreen I gotta scrape off just to expose you to the light," Leo had once told me. So where the hell was he?

I drove home alone, relieved to be in a protective steel shell. I didn't want to know anything more about this place—but mostly

I didn't want to know who *I* was in this world.

"Tough game," Hunter said when I got home. "You played okay, though; you took down the quarterback so hard, I didn't think he'd get back up."

Then, from the family room, I heard my father say, "Shoulda made sure he *didn't* get back up. Then maybe you might have won."

At first I thought he was joking, but then I realized he wasn't. Not something my real dad would say. Cruelty must have come holding hands with racism.

At least I was able to take some comfort from the fact that my relationship with Hunter was still a good one.

He challenged me to a game of pool before bed. But halfway through, I dared to ask a question I dreaded having to ask.

"Hunter," I said, "do we know Leo and Angela Johnson?"

He thought about it, and, just like when I showed Katie that bad drawing of Tsammy Tsunami, there was a moment of hesitation, recognition maybe, but the spark of that recognition quickly went out. "I don't think so," he said. "Why?"

"They're Black," I prompted.

"Oh," he said. "Who do they work for?"

I gritted my teeth, trying not to be angry with him. *This version of Hunter is a product of this world,* I told myself.

"They don't work for anybody," I told him. "They're friends."

He raised an eyebrow. Not in any sort of disapproval, but out of surprise. "I didn't know you had any black friends."

"Do you have any?" I asked.

"Not lately." But then he considered it. I realized that he was questioning himself about it, once more sensing that something was wrong, but not being able to put his finger on it.

That's when my brain suddenly zeroed in on the right frequency, and more memories began to broadcast themselves into consciousness. It felt like a crack in a dam oozing rank river sludge through the breach, bringing on a surge of that strange headache. I brought my hands to my head as if it was the only way to hold the two halves of my skull together.

I closed my eyes, trying to process the memories forcing their way in. I knew who I was in this world now. And here's the terrible, horrible truth.

I wasn't all that different.

Aside from having no Black or Latinx friends here, I was the same as I was in the previous worlds. I thought this version of me—this product of segregation—would be some terrible fun house distortion. But I wasn't any more clueless or insensitive than before . . . because I was already clueless and insensitive. The plague of ignorance, the stupid-ass sunscreen—all the ways Leo had tried to open my eyes—had never really worked. Because they only saw what they wanted to see. What was *easy* to see. What was convenient.

So how far was this world from mine? Not nearly as far as it should be.

"Headache again?" Hunter asked.

I nodded. "Worst of the worst."

"Well maybe this will take your mind off it," he said. "Because

I think I found those twin skaters you were looking for. Only they're not twins," he said. "They're triplets."

I'll get back to the skaters in a bit—but first let me try to give you a brief vision of this world. Stagnant is the best way to describe it. You know how a stagnant pond festers? It starts to reek, and fill with diseased mosquitoes? Not that my original world was a raging river of justice, but at least there was pressure on the floodgates. But there was none of that here. The rot was evident everywhere—from that brutal border policy that had kept out anyone seeking a better life, to a failed economy, because without migrant farmworkers, the entire American agricultural industry had collapsed.

It trickled down in weird, unexpected ways. Like music. Apparently, my favorite band, Konniption, didn't exist in this world. A search for them revealed that they had released a self-produced single that no one bought. The band had fizzled and was never heard of again. Their music was "too hard on the ear," reviews said. But where I come from, that's a prerequisite for rock and roll stardom.

In this world, my playlist had bands I had never heard of in my old world, and that probably didn't even exist there. And for good reason. Their music was bland and soulless—*tepid*, that's the word. Like stuff you'd hear playing in the background while the dentist drills on your molars. It had no passion—no forward momentum. It just spun in uninspired circles.

I found some "Black radio stations" but it seemed like rap

and hip-hop never made an appearance here. Instead, it all felt stuck in the past. Just rehashed soul riffs that hadn't evolved in fifty years.

I quickly came to realize that what passed for mainstream American culture here had no bite, no flavor. Mayonnaise blandness on all fronts. So, added to my shock was pity. I pitied the people who called this world home. People who couldn't conceive of anything better.

I spent Saturday morning online, searching for Leo, terrified that I might not find him. That maybe he didn't even exist. It was a pain that he had such a common name because there were hundreds of Leo Johnsons on social media. A lot of them showed no location on their profile, and could have been anywhere. It took hours of searching, but I finally did find him. I was relieved, but also troubled.

Leo still lived here in T-ville, and he worked at a supermarket. That much was on his profile. Finding which market he worked at took some legwork. Turns out it was a Publix on the white side of town. His family wasn't supposed to shop there, but he could work there.

That afternoon, I went to find him.

I knew the Publix—it was one of the stores my family shopped at. Like everything else, it looked just a little bit different. I circled the block at least half a dozen times, building up the courage to actually park and go inside. Meanwhile, my current playlist featured a band called Amber Wave, which really should have been called Pea Green Hurl, because they were that bad. Finally I turned off the music and pulled into the lot to park. Even so, getting out of my car was like jumping off a high dive. I had to build up courage just to open the door and take the leap.

Once in the market, I saw Leo right away. He was the checker on register three. My heart sank to see him there, because I knew this wasn't just a part-time job. His profile didn't list a school.

I grabbed a cart and threw some random things into it, because it would be weird to get in his line with nothing. A Gatorade. A box of cookies stacked in a display. An overpriced orange from an atrophied produce section the size of a bookcase. Then I realized that the more items I had, the longer I'd be able to talk to him, so I went down a few aisles, grabbing a cartful of unrelated items. Then I finally got in his line. Someone tried to call me over to an empty line, but I would not budge. I loaded my things onto the belt, and when the customer before me left, Leo began to ring my items up.

"Hi, Leo," I said.

"Hello, sir," he said absently and with a respect I didn't deserve. He probably figured I knew his name from his name tag. He continued ringing things up. Baked beans, a bag of rice, peanut butter.

"Working here long?" I asked.

He glanced at me, but if he made eye contact, it was so brief I missed it. "Going on two years, now," he said, and scanned the next item. It didn't scan, so he entered the number by hand.

Keep in mind, this was a guy who was looking at scholarships to any number of universities. I had been jealous of the opportunities he had ahead of him.

"How's your sister?" I asked. "Still playing volleyball?"

He stopped in mid-scan. This time he looked at me. And the look on his face was suspicion, and maybe something a little bit worse. Something bitter that I couldn't place.

"I'd rather not talk about my sister, if you don't mind," he said, then scanned my last item. "Did you find everything you need, sir?"

"What? Oh yeah, yeah, I found everything." Which was true, since the only thing I was looking for was him. "You really don't know who I am?" I asked, desperate for my best friend to at least have that brief moment of uncertainty like Katie and Hunter had. But he didn't. Because he didn't see *me* when he looked at me. He saw what I represented. What I stood for in this world.

"Oh, I know who you are," he said coolly. "Everyone in this town knows the Bowmans."

"We know each other more than that, Leo," I said, grabbing his arm. "We do—you just don't remember."

He shook my arm off. "I don't know what you're talking about—all I know is that there's a line behind you, and people are getting impatient!"

"But your sister—"

"You don't talk about my sister!" he said, his voice getting a little too loud. He looked around, maybe to see if his manager was watching. Then Leo leaned closer and spoke quietly.

"I don't know what business she is of yours, but I'd be much obliged if people could let her memory rest."

"Memory?"

And then he leveled a terrible truth at me. "Angela died of spinal meningitis over a year ago."

8

THE MEMORY OF MEMORIES

We are so limited. As a species. As individuals. Not only can't we see the future, we can't even see the present for what it is. We're too clouded by the things we want and the things we fear. But worse than any other blindness is that we can't see the consequences of our actions.

I had wanted a world where that night between Angela and me never happened. And I ended up with a world in which it didn't. I was envious of everything Leo had going for him. Did my envy play a part in landing us here, and stealing it all away from him?

They say be careful what you wish for, but you know what? No matter how careful we are, it's not enough. We should know by now that *anything* we desire, and *anything* we achieve, comes at a cost, and with consequences we didn't care enough to consider.

I stood there in the line at Publix, knowing what I heard, but refusing to believe Leo said it. I just stared at him, shaking my head.

"If you got a club card, you should scan it," he said.

Angela was dead. She was dead. No! I wouldn't accept that. I wouldn't allow it to be true!

"Oh God, I'm sorry, Leo. I'm so, so sorry . . ."

"A lot of people are. You should pay now."

And then I went out on a limb, because I had to. I just had to.

"What time do you get off?" I asked him. "There are things I need to talk to you about."

"With all due respect, you and I got nothing to discuss."

"It's important!"

And then he held my gaze with such fire, it nearly made me stumble backward against the candy rack.

"You think I don't know what you do? What you *sell?* And do you think I don't know how guys like you treat girls like my sister? I want nothing to do with you, now or ever. Nothing!"

Now more and more people were taking notice. Not just shoppers but other cashiers. His manager was coming over and I worried that I might get him fired, and I thought, *So what? This job sucks. He'll get a better one.* But what if he couldn't? What if the things Leo had going for him didn't mean a damn thing in this place?

"Please, Leo," I said. Now I was begging. "Whatever you think I'm gonna say to you, you're wrong."

Maybe he finally read the sincerity in my voice. And maybe I was starting to tear up. Okay, not maybe, *definitely*. And he saw it. Tears for Angela, tears for him, tears for everything that had been lost. His glare softened. He was about to say something—but then I heard a voice behind me.

"C'mon," the guy behind me in line said, "some of us have places to be!"

I could have taken him out at that moment. Just put all my emotions behind a fist, and knocked that guy halfway to next week's specials. But who the hell knew what next week would be? Instead, I controlled myself. I wiped my eyes before the tears rolled down my face. I fumbled with my wallet and shoved my card into the reader.

Then Leo said, "I get off when I get off. If you're still waiting outside when my shift is over, I'll talk to you. Now leave."

That was the best I was going to get, and it was good enough. I took my pointless groceries, and I went to my car. I waited there for hours. Long past sunset, listening to music I didn't like, in a car I shouldn't own.

I almost missed Leo when he came out. He certainly wasn't looking for me. To Leo, I was just a weird blip in his day that probably got him a scolding from his manager. A nuisance best forgotten. He was halfway across the parking lot by the time I spotted him. It was dark now. I got out of my car and called to him. He turned, acknowledging that he heard me, but just kept on walking. I caught up with him at a bus stop. He was sitting, waiting for a bus, and actively ignoring me. I didn't sit down—I felt like I needed to earn the right to intrude on his airspace—although, to be honest, I was already a pretty uninvited intrusion.

"So you stayed all day waiting for me to get off work?"

"I did," I told him. "I would have waited longer. I would have waited all night if I had to." I had hoped that would impress upon him how legitimate I was—how important this was to both of us. Instead it just came off as weird.

"Either you're not right in the head, or there's something seriously wrong with you," he said. It made me laugh, because that was something Leo would say back in the world where we were friends.

"Sit down," he invited. "You're making me nervous."

So I did. I sat next to him.

"Tell me why you're here," he said, "and if there's anything I don't like about it, I walk."

"I thought you were taking a bus."

Normally Leo would call me a smartass for that, but instead he just said, "Point taken."

I drew a deep breath. For hours I had been running through my aching mind all the things I was going to say—but now none of them felt right. They all seemed like things that would literally make him walk—or more likely run—than wait for the bus. So I reached in and pulled something out of my brain that I didn't even know was there.

"When you were a baby you burned your left hand on an oven door," I said. I knew that burn had carried over into this world because I could see his scarred palm. "You always felt like it was a little gift from God, because it roughed up your palm just enough to make it a little bit easier to catch a pass."

He was unimpressed. "There's a thousand ways you coulda known that. You coulda talked to people who know me. Hell, you coulda read the interview a school reporter did. It's old news," he said. "Older still, because I dropped out before it could mean anything anyway."

I tried to hide the pain I felt at hearing that. I knew that to reach him, I had to dig deeper.

"When you were eight," I told him, noticing the small scar on his left cheek, "you got hit by a drunk driver while you were on your bike. Hit and run. You broke a few ribs, and it left you with that scar. The guy would have gotten away with it, but you remembered the last three digits of the license plate. For more than a year you would go out riding everywhere in town until you finally found the right car. The guy was convicted and went to jail for it."

Leo tried to act unimpressed again, but I could tell that it was getting to him. I could tell by the way he rolled his shoulders, like he had a kink in his neck. It's what he always did when trying to hide the fact that something was working on his nerves.

"You got that wrong," he said. "I found the guy, but he never went to jail. He pleaded it out, and they gave him community service." Leo spat out a breath. "Can you believe that? Community service for hitting a kid on a bike and taking off. I don't know why I even bothered."

"Well, he went to jail where I come from."

That made him look at me. "Exactly where do you come from?"

I chose not to answer that. Not yet, anyway. I decided to try to reach him one more time. I had to come up with something I couldn't find out elsewhere. Something he never spoke about to anyone. Anyone but me. It came to me in a flash, and I smiled as I remembered—I could only hope it happened in this world, too.

"You shaved your head in seventh grade," I told him. "Because you thought it would make you look cool."

Now he turned to me with suspicion, and maybe a little bit of fear. But I wasn't done.

"You hated the way it looked, though, so for a month you wore a baseball cap until your hair started to grow back in."

Now I could tell he was slightly freaked out—but I still wasn't done. Now I went in for the kill.

"That's when you found a lump on the back of your shaved head—a little off center. You didn't tell your parents about it, but until it went away, you were convinced it was a brain tumor."

Now Leo looked angry.

"How the hell do you know that?"

"Because you confided in your best friend, and your best friend told you that little lump wasn't a tumor, it was your entire brain, and you punched him so hard it left a bruise on his arm for like a week." My eyes were moist now. So were his.

"I never told anyone," he insisted. "Not my friends, not anyone—and definitely not you!"

"But you remember it a little, don't you? Like maybe you did—"

"I'm remembering a dream, that's all. Maybe I dreamed I told someone."

"How would I know something you dreamed?"

He had no answer to that. None at all.

"What the fuck are you?"

The fact that he said "what" instead of "who" was a good sign. It was a sign that he realized this was bigger than just him and me. That this was a *thing*. A thing that had to be reckoned with. So I went all in, and decided to answer his previous question.

"I'm from a place where you and I are best friends, and you don't work as a cashier at Publix, and you still play football, with your eye on USC. Where I come from, your life is going places I could only dream mine would go."

That made him disappear into himself for a long moment. A bus came. The door opened. The driver looked at Leo for a second, and Leo waved him off. The door closed, and the bus pulled out, the noisy drone of its engines fading into the normal buzz of late-night traffic and the rustling of leaves that were already starting to yellow.

"You don't make any sense," Leo said, wiping away what might have been a tear. It didn't linger long enough for me to be sure. "USC might as well be the moon."

"Guion Bluford—the first African American in space." I wondered if it was true in this world. I wanted to believe it was, but doubted it. "Not quite the moon, but close." And then I added, "You taught me that."

Leo shook his head. "'African American,'" he said. "Here, it's just black, or negro, or s'equal, or worse."

I wanted to tell him I was sorry about that. About everything—all the shitty cards he got dealt, and the fact that his entire deck was now stacked with shitty cards. But the *other* Leo would remind me that the cards in my world weren't all that much better. That segregation and stolen opportunities still happened in sneaky, and not-so-sneaky, ways.

"This is all crazy, you know that, right?" Leo said.

I shrugged. "But you're still listening."

"Maybe because I'm just as crazy as you."

Then he bit his lip. "And in this place you say you come from . . . What happened to my sister?"

I chose my words carefully. Spoke slowly. "She's still here, Leo," I told him. "She had meningitis but survived it. Better doctors, I guess. She's a junior at Tibbetsville High—made varsity volleyball."

His tears flowed freely now; he didn't even try to hide them, but through them he still let out a rueful laugh. "T-ville High? Now I know you're making shit up."

"It's integrated, Leo. All schools are. Or at least they're supposed to be."

He took a moment, then dismissed it as too much to swallow. "Right, and we got a black president, and everyone's got their own pet dragons."

"We did have a Black president," I told him. "For eight years. No dragons, though."

Leo let it all brew for a bit, and then he surprised me. "You know what?" he said. "As crazy as you sound, it's just late enough, and I'm just tired enough, that I believe you."

But I knew it was a little more than that. I knew from how Katie and Hunter had reacted around me. There was still the memory of memories there. I thought about an old cassette tape my dad played for me. A "mix tape" from the '80s, long before playlists were a thing. In between songs you could hear the hint of older music—music that had been recorded over. I had turned up the volume all the way to see if I could recognize the song underneath, but never could.

"So if everything you're saying is true," Leo asked, "what are we supposed to do about it?"

"I don't know, Leo. I just don't know."

"Then why the hell did you come here?" he said, getting angry. "Why the hell are you giving me useless stories about a world I can't be a part of?"

"Because maybe you could help me make it real again."

And that hung heavy in the air between us for a long time.

We didn't talk much after that. He didn't ask me any more questions. In the end I gave him my phone number—and he guessed the last two digits before I said them. More proof for him. More hidden tones in the silence between songs.

When the next bus came, he got up.

"Don't expect me to call you," he said. "Ever."

But I knew he would. Because I knew Leo. I'd know him in any world.

I said I'd get back to the skaters. Here's where they reenter in their strange elliptical orbit. As I was walking back to my car in the Publix parking lot, which was mostly empty now, I heard the unmistakable high rumble of polyurethane wheels on asphalt. Turns out I didn't have to go looking for the skaters; instead, they found me.

As Hunter had said, they weren't twins, they were triplets. Identical triplets. The instance of identical triplets is one in 60,000 births. I know this because it was a *Jeopardy!* answer that got stuck in my head like a piece of toilet paper on my shoe. Random useless facts plague me.

I have to admit I was relieved to see them. I didn't know what their connection to these reality shifts was, but I knew they were connected. After all, they remembered the Tsunamis, which meant that maybe they could give me some answers.

The trio of identical skaters began to circle me—and I noticed pretty quickly that their boards were like perpetual motion machines. That is to say, they never had to put a foot down to push themselves. It was as if, no matter where they were, every direction was downhill. I never found out their names, so to make things easier, let's just call them Ed, Edd, and Eddy, in honor of my misspent Cartoon Network childhood.

"You screwed up big this time, didn't you, Ash?" Ed said.

"What do you know about it?" I asked—and I wasn't just

matching his attitude, it was a legitimate question.

"We know what we know," said Edd.

"Which is a lot less than what we don't know," said Eddy.

They were moving around me fast enough to make me dizzy when I tried to focus on any one of them. "Why don't you start by telling me who the hell you are."

"Just your typical neighborhood skater bros," said Ed, with a smirk.

"Ask anyone who knows us," added Edd.

"Oh, wait, no one knows us," concluded Eddy.

I was starting to understand their dynamic. Ed was the alpha sibling, as he always seemed to answer first. Edd followed with a snide comment, and Eddy was the closer. "Are you here just to mess with me, or are you going to help me?"

And then they started talking in a very literal round-robin that made me even more dizzy.

"We haven't been 'messing with you.'"

"We were testing you."

"To see how quick you were."

"Not very."

"But he caught on quicker than some."

"True, but I'm not impressed."

"Me neither."

"It could be worse."

I wanted to grab one of them, pull him off his skateboard, and shake something helpful out of him, but I knew that would be counterproductive. Impulse control was key here. Instead I took a deep breath and tried to find my happy place. Or at least my less-miserable place.

"Look, I know something's broken, and I know I broke it. If you can help me fix it, then I'm all ears."

Then the three stopped circling. They hopped off their boards in unison, kicking them up into their arms, and stood there. Somehow, though, it still seemed like the world was spinning around me. Optical illusion. I'll go with that.

"All ears," Edd said without the slightest bit of irony. "If you're not careful, you might be."

I released a shuddering breath. He was dead serious.

"What the hell is going on?" I asked, trying to meet each of their identical gazes. "Don't you think I deserve to know?"

They were silent for a moment, studying me. Two of them looked to the leader, who stepped forward. Ed held my gaze a moment more, and sighed. "The best way to explain your circumstance is probably the worst thing we could tell a human being."

"Understood," I said, bracing myself. "Tell me anyway."

Ed looked to the other two, to make sure they were all in agreement. They seemed to be, although reluctantly. Then Ed turned to me, and said:

"You, Ashley Bowman, have become the center of the universe."

9

ALL THE THINGS THAT NEVER HAPPENED

The center of the universe. I suppose we all imagine ourselves in that position. Even though most of us know we're not, we can't help but feel, on some subconscious level, that we are. When we're babies, we can't tell the difference between the world and ourselves. The whole of creation is just a part of us; just another uncooperative appendage to go along with our legs that can't walk, and hands that can barely grasp. Then, as we're learning to walk and talk, we recognize the foreignness of things outside of our bodies, but still feel that we're at the center of it all. Some of us never grow past that, but most of us do move on to adulthood. Once we're adults, we've learned to pretend that we don't think we're the center of the universe. But deep down, a part of us will always believe that we are. If you need proof, look at all the people who buy lottery tickets, enter sweepstakes, or go to Las Vegas. People who believe fortunes will fall their way in spite of all logic and proven mathematical odds, because when you secretly think you're the center of the universe, you feel outrageously lucky.

And now I was told that I was, indeed, the center of the universe. So why didn't I feel like I won the lottery?

Maybe because being the center of the universe is like being an only child in a family with extremely high expectations. Nothing you do will ever be good enough.

That's where the skaters come in.

They're not skaters, if you haven't figured that much out. They told me, and I quote: "We are multidimensional beings that project into your world in this unobtrusive, camouflaged form."

No one seems to have told them that being skater triplets is not exactly unobtrusive camouflage.

"Our purpose is to quell disturbances," Ed told me.

"So you're like God's therapists?" I suggested.

"If there's a God—and we're not saying that there is," said Edd, "he/she/they would not need therapy."

"And if there is no God—and we're not saying that there isn't," said Eddy, "then the universe would be an *it* rather than a he/she/they, and wouldn't need therapy either."

"We quell disturbances, let's just leave it at that," said Ed. "Now follow us and don't get lost on the way."

There was an abandoned Toys "R" Us up on Oldchurch Road that never got repurposed when the company went belly-up. It just sat there behind a chain-link fence, presiding over a weed-filled parking lot like a horror movie waiting to happen. This was where the Edwards led me.

"Leave your car," they told me, and pointed. "There's a hole in the fence down there that you can climb through." They, however, did not use the hole. They just walked through the fence. Not like ghosts, more like Play-Doh, pressing through the links. That killed any doubts I might have had about them. They definitely were not from around here.

Ed turned back and saw the look on my face. "It's not a big deal," he said. "It's a three-dimensional fence. In spite of what it looked like, we just walked around it in a different dimension. If you'd like, we could show you how," he offered.

"Uh . . . thanks, but no," I told him, still not ready to follow them.

"Don't worry," said Ed. "We won't do anything to hurt you. We couldn't hurt you even if we wanted to; it's not in our nature."

And although I wanted to turn and run, I swallowed my highly rational terror of this highly irrational reality, walked a dozen yards down, and climbed through the hole in the fence.

There is nothing cheerful about the inside of a dead toy mega-store. The space had been stripped of everything that wasn't built in, which left tons of empty, brightly colored displays, barely visible in the scant lighting the Edwards had set up. Aside from a few forlorn stuffed animals, and the occasional Barbie head, there was nothing else to see . . . until we got to a space that had once been the Lego pavilion. Instead of a quaint Lego city, the Edwards had set up a makeshift living space.

Furniture. A television. A refrigerator. All the appliances were fully operational with no visible source of power.

"If you're not human, why do you need all this?" I asked.

"When in Rome," Ed said, which is the first half of an expression I don't actually know the rest of.

Their lair was not the cleanest of places—fast-food wrappers were everywhere. Edd saw me noticing the mess and glared at me.

"Is there a problem?" he asked.

"No. But how are you supposed to clean up the universe if you can't pick up your own trash?"

"It's not trash," Edd grumbled. "It just projects into this universe as trash." Even so, he began to clean it up.

Meanwhile, Eddy turned on the TV, settled in on the sofa, grabbed what looked like a game controller, and began to play a video game that they told me was not actually a video game. It was their quantum interdimensional research tool (QuIRT).

"It's the QuIRT that identified you as the current center of the universe," Ed told me. "Technically, it's called being the *Subjective Locus*. Sub-loc for short. While you're the sub-loc, you redefine reality, bouncing what *is* into a variation of what *isn't*. Or at least what *wasn't* until you made it so."

"So . . . when I have a power tackle, it's like hitting a universal remote. Literally."

"Yes," said Edd. "Your brutish concussive jolts are the mechanism. The method of change is different for every sub-loc, depending on their 'skill sets.'" He said it as if my "skill set" wasn't much of one. Of the three, Edd was quickly becoming my least favorite.

Eddy tapped on his game controller and it brought up a dizzying stream of illegible data flying across the screen.

"Basically," said Ed, "all the things that never happened, all the choices never made, and all random possibilities that fizzled away become possible again. It's actually pretty exciting."

But Edd shook his head. "Not when a sub-loc dredges up a world as miserable as this one." And he looked at me as if I had brought about this abomination on purpose.

"He's still untrained," Ed said, coming to my defense. "With our help, his influence can be a positive one."

The two looked at each other. I sensed some unspoken communication between them. Not so much mind reading, as reading between each other's lines. There was more going on here that I wasn't privy to.

So I decided to ask the big question. "Why me?"

Their response was to launch into another one of their hot-potato conversations, as if the question made them nervous.

"Why not you?"

"We think it's random."

"Unless it's not random."

"There's evidence to support both possibilities."

"Yes, the jury's still out."

"There is no jury."

"It's a figure of speech."

"You know that, right?"

"We don't want you thinking there's a jury."

I threw up my hands. "I get it! I know there's no jury. Just . . . just tell me how long I'm going to be this 'subjective locus' thing."

"It varies," Edd said. "Five, maybe six jumps—but once you cease being the sub-loc, the world will be stuck whatever way you've left it."

Then Ed put a hand on my shoulder that was supposed to be comforting, and gave me a brief history of the multiverse, or at least how it pertained to me. "Your situation is not all that unusual," he told me. "This kind of thing is happening all the time. There's always someone somewhere who's the sub-loc."

He told me that the universe tended to center on individuals of sapient species (that is, species capable of intelligent thought), which were scattered throughout the universe—and since most shifts happen millions of light-years away, they don't even affect us here on Earth.

"Since intelligent life appeared on Earth, there have been about forty sub-locs here," Ed told me. "Of course half of those times, it was a dolphin."

Just then Eddy leapt up and shouted so suddenly, it made Edd drop all the trash he had collected.

"I found it!" Eddy said. "I traced the current reality back to its source!"

"I know its source," I told them, feeling, for once, like intelligent life. "I figured it out—it was *Brown versus Board of Education*—when the Supreme Court didn't strike down segregation."

"That was the result," said Eddy. "But the seed came before that. It was the failure of Joe."

"Joe who?" I asked.

"Joe's not a *who*, but a *what*," Eddy explained. "August 29, 1949. In your previous realities, that was the date of the first successful Soviet atomic bomb test. Code name Joe-1. But in this world Joe-1 failed dismally, and it set the Soviet nuclear program back by ten years."

Suddenly I wasn't feeling like intelligent life anymore. "What the hell do Russian nukes have to do with segregation in the United States?"

"Everything's related," Ed told me. "All things are interconnected."

He took the controller, tapped a few keys, and set the QuIRT to English. Then he showed me a list of events that happened in this world, versus ones that happened in the world I came from. As it turns out, in *my* world, the nuclear arms race with the Soviet Union—better known as the Cold War—was putting a lot of pressure on the United States. Our racial inequalities were well known around the world—and once the Soviets developed nukes, it became a mad scramble to make sure we could get as much of the world on our side as possible. But America's racial record was an embarrassment. And so, when the matter of segregation reached the Supreme Court, they decided that racial segregation violated the Fourteenth Amendment. Four of the justices voted to end it because it was the right thing to do. The others were swayed by America's embarrassment factor, and the fear of a nuclear-ready Soviet Union having the moral high ground over us.

But here—in this reality—America hadn't cared how it looked to the rest of the world in 1954, since a nuclear Russia was not yet on the horizon. And without that pressure, the justices fighting for change were overruled by the ones who were happy to keep things exactly the way they were.

Eddy started to move on to the equal rights movement of the '60s, and how that played out here—the failed marches, and the rousing speeches that fell on deaf ears—but before he could paint the whole miserable picture, I took the controller from him and hit the Home button, pausing the display. For once I wished the Home button would actually take me home. It was like someone had set off a hydrogen bomb in my brain, and this one worked. To think that so much of history—the good, and the bad—is influenced by hidden factors that no one even thinks about. Could the fall of the Roman Empire be traced back to the moment some Caesar gave a thumbs-down in the circus, condemning a fallen gladiator to death, instead of a thumbs-up saving his life? And what about now? What about today? What choices are being made, what things are being said by people in high places that might seem so unimportant now, but are laying the groundwork for truly horrible things tomorrow?

"How could I have known any of this?" I blurted out.

"You couldn't have; you were flying blind," said Ed.

"But look," said Eddy, changing the display on the QuIRT to some sort of multidimensional graph, "each of your incursions into Elsewhere was deeper than the ones before."

"Which means he's more dangerous!" said Edd.

"No," said Ed, always the more optimistic one, "it just means he's getting better at it. Now he needs to control it."

That just frustrated Edd even more. "Look at him! Does he look like he can control anything? He's nothing but a weapon!"

"A knife can be a weapon," said Ed, "but it can also be a surgical instrument."

"Maybe," said Edd, "but a bullet has only one purpose."

"Hey!" I shouted, getting between them. "I'm not a scalpel, and I'm not a bullet. I'm a tackle. I've got a mind of my own, which means I can bring things back around to how they were, if you show me how."

The three looked at me, looked at one another, then Edd backed down, striding away. "Fine. If you think you can turn a bludgeon into a boomerang, be my guest."

I took a deep breath. "I can do this," I said, dredging up all the confidence I had.

Ed smiled. "I believe you might be able to."

"He might die in the process . . . ," Eddy warned.

"A risk I'm sure he's willing to take," Ed said, looking to me as if I was going to give him a big *Hell, yeah!*

"About how many sub-locs died trying?" I asked.

"On Earth? About twenty," Ed said.

"Yes," said Eddy, "but half of those were dolphins."

After leaving the Edwards, I sat in my car, trying to process everything they had told me. There was hope, but there was also risk. There were things I couldn't control, but maybe some things I could. I was not entirely alone. And I'm not just talking about the Edwards. Before I had left that day, I had asked them why, if the universe changed, did some people have partial memories—like Katie remembering Tsammy Tsunami. The Edwards were not surprised. In fact, they had a name for it. They had a name for everything.

"It's called the proximity effect," they told me. "The closer someone is to the subjective locus, the more likely they, and even people around them, are to have stray memories from other existences." I wasn't sure whether they meant physical closeness, or emotional, but either way, it explained why Leo, Katie, and even Katie's brother had flashes of memory. Who knows, maybe others would, too.

Before I drove home, I texted Katie. I had to believe that our conversations in those other realities had carried through to this one, the way my conversation with Hunter about the skaters had. It kind of makes my brain spin to think about it, but there was evidence in every world that my jumps were a constant. In other words, even in this reality, stop signs had once been red, and I hadn't always been rich. Which meant that I must have confided to *this* Katie about the jumps as well. At least I hoped that I had. There was only one way to find out.

Hey if the T-ville Tsunamis and red stop signs mean anything 2U text me back becuz I know whats going on now. And if not just ignore this.

Then I waited. It felt like ten minutes of waiting, but to be honest it was probably less than two.

Hi Caitlin no way thats hilarious ROTFL

I texted her back a quick WTF, and her next response made it all fall into place.

Layton says hi.

Okay, so Layton was with her, and she couldn't talk—or text—without him getting suspicious. I wondered if she'd had the foresight to save my phone number as "Caitlin" so that when it popped up on her phone, Layton wouldn't think anything of it. Katie was definitely thinking a few moves ahead. I needed the help of someone like that, because thinking ahead has never been one of my personal strengths. It's why I suck at chess, and in the past had been known to make fun of kids who didn't. It's a time-honored tradition, isn't it? Define yourself by what you're good at, and piss on the things you're not? I'm sure that behavioral flaw goes back to when we were lower mammals.

See you before school Monday, she texted. I left my math book in the gym maybe you could help me find it.

Got it! Code for meet her before school in the gym. I applauded myself for not being a complete imbecile, and sent her a thumbs-up.

By the time I got home, I wanted to put my head in a vise grip just to keep it from exploding.

"You're suffering from memory fatigue," the Edwards had told me. "While everyone else's memories are pretty much replaced, with the sub-loc it's different—you remember everything." Which meant that each shift left me with a whole lifetime of new memories competing for real estate in my brain.

"The good news," the Edwards had explained, "is that the human brain has about two point five petabytes of storage space—a million gigs—most of which isn't used. The bad news is, with each leap, you burn a few hundred thousand gigs of mental storage space."

It meant that I only had a limited number of jumps before my brain reached capacity. After that, I'd have a cerebral meltdown, which would leave me dead, or brain-dead, or worse—although I couldn't imagine what "worse" could be. But in the meantime, they assured me that the eggshell/mint/potassium baths would help. "Mint enhances brain function, potassium gets more oxygen to the brain, and eggshells are practically magical in all dimensions," the Edwards told me.

Once home, I went straight for the kitchen. Not to eat, because I had nothing resembling an appetite, but to get eggshells for an EMP bath. As I was grabbing the eggs, Hunter, who had been waiting for me to come home, popped up out of nowhere, startling me enough to drop a couple on the floor.

"I covered for you," he said.

"What do you mean 'covered'?"

"Your shift," he said.

My heart literally missed a beat. *"You know about the shifts?"*

He looked at me funny. "Yeah, your shift at the store."

"Oh, right." I gave myself an idiot pass for that one.

"I told Dad you were helping the coaches scout out the upcoming crop at a few Pop Warner games. I figured a football excuse might fly with him."

I sighed. "Okay, Hunter, cut the shit and just tell me what you want."

He was taken aback. "I dunno—maybe just to know where the hell you were?"

Only then did it occur to me that *this* Hunter didn't help me because he wanted something in return; he did it because helping was in his nature. I felt embarrassed for thinking otherwise. At the moment, I didn't want to look at him, because I thought I might get a little damp-eyed, so I bent down, mopped up the eggs, and retrieved the broken shells.

"It's probably better if you don't know where I was," I told him—but he wasn't buying that.

"Did you go looking for that Leon kid you were talking about?"

"Leo," I told him. "And yeah, I found him." Then I closed my eyes—not just because of the headache but out of respect for Angela. A moment of silence for her. Still, my grief was a little bit tempered by the thought that I could bring her back. Her death was only as real as this world, and I was determined it wouldn't be real for long.

And then Hunter said something that really got my attention.

"You know," he said, "I've been having these crazy dreams."

"What kind of dreams?"

He shrugged like it was nothing, but clearly it was something. "About a house that we never lived in. Things that we never did, with people we don't know."

I took a deep breath. "Maybe they're not dreams."

"What else could they be?"

I didn't answer him. How could I? He was experiencing the proximity effect, with no frame of reference to make sense of the memories.

"Whatever they are, I'm sure they'll pass."

"Yeah, maybe," he said, but didn't sound too convinced.

I put the eggshells in the blender, and although Hunter gave me an odd look, I didn't feel like volunteering an explanation. I noticed that Mom and Dad were nowhere to be found, but the house was so big, it didn't mean they weren't home. You could go days without seeing each other in this house.

"Thanks, Hunter," I said, realizing that I had never actually thanked him for taking over at the store for me. "I'll pay you whatever I would have made for my shift."

"No worries," he said. Then he added, "I took care of some of your 'special' customers, too."

That stopped me cold.

"You did what?"

"Don't worry, I was careful. And I already knew where you kept stuff—you showed me once, remember?"

I could feel my ears getting hot with anger—not at Hunter, but at myself. My other self. The one who remembered showing him the stash, like it was something to be proud of.

"Don't you ever do that again," I told him. "Do you hear me? Never!"

"It's not a big deal," he insisted. "I'm not gonna butt in on your business or anything." Then he added, "Unless you want me to."

"I don't!" I told him. If I wanted to be away from these worlds before, I couldn't wait to make them not exist. Because even though I couldn't see the future, I suspected that Hunter would eventually be dealing drugs. Just like his older brother.

"Listen to me, Hunter." I set the pulverized eggshells on a counter, and put my hands on his shoulders, forcing myself to make eye contact. "My 'business' was a mistake—probably the worst mistake of my life—and I don't want you to make the same stupid choices I did."

He shrugged out of my grip. "If it's so bad, then why don't you just stop, like you always say you will?"

I thought back to all the things that Ralston had said. The veiled threats that weren't all that veiled. "It's not that easy."

"Yeah it is," Hunter said, still young enough to be painfully naïve. "You just stop. It's not like they're gonna kill you."

10

CHEESEBURGER IN PARALLEL

There used to be a farm next to my school. I'm not sure what grew there because I never paid much attention. But it didn't matter now, because the field was gone, replaced by the Bowman Athletic Center—our school's state-of-the-art sports complex, named, of course, after our family, or more accurately, my father.

I got to school an hour early, not sure when Katie would show. The athletic center was already full of activity. On Tuesdays and Thursdays, the football team had early-morning weight training, but as today was Monday, I had no idea what teams were filling the various spaces. Turns out the expansive double gym was being shared by gymnastics and the girls' volleyball team today. *A team that Angela would have been on,* a woeful part of my mind reminded me.

"Ash! Over here . . ."

I followed the loud whisper to the bleachers, which were empty. Katie was in the space below the retractable bleachers, famous for kids making out and for spider infestations. I went around the side and slipped into the shadows of the steel infrastructure.

"Are you sure this is a good idea," I said with a smirk as I approached her. "If someone hits the button, we could be diced and sliced like those two ninth graders last year."

Katie shrugged. "Secret meetings are dangerous."

Those kids actually didn't get diced and sliced, by the way. It was more like trapped and embarrassed—primarily because they were secretly making out, although they claimed to be looking for rare spiders. I suddenly had to shake off a chill. I was remembering it like it was a real memory. Maybe it was for the rich me with the football star father, but not the *me* me who was really me. I got a little spike of anxiety as I realized there might come a time when I couldn't differentiate between the memories anymore.

"So what did you find out?" Katie asked. "I can't wait to hear." Then she added, "I think."

I hesitated, then realized there was no easy way to couch the news, so I just put it out there.

"We're dealing with multiple parallel dimensions."

"Okay . . . ," she said with doubt in her voice.

"There's this team of . . . Well, they called themselves multi-dimensional beings. On skateboards. Only they're not actually skateboards."

"Okay . . . ," she said, no change in her tone of voice.

"Anyway, they're helping me get things back to the way they're supposed to be."

To her credit she didn't run away screaming. She waited for more, but I knew I had already hurled too much at her. Telling her that I was the current center of the universe might have been too much to swallow.

Now it was time to present her with some evidence she couldn't refute because it would be from her own mind. "Close your eyes," I said.

"Why?"

"Trust me."

And she did. She trusted me. She closed her eyes. That might seem like a very small thing, but to me it was huge.

"I want you to picture someone you don't know," I said.

"How can I do that?"

I didn't answer. Instead, I just said, "Picture Angela Johnson."

Her face scrunched a bit, then relaxed. "She's black, isn't she? And plays a sport at Southside High."

"No, she plays here."

Then she opened her eyes and gave me a seriously deep look. "Our school . . . is supposed to have black students, isn't it?"

I nodded. "It does where we used to come from."

She looked away from me. I waited. It was like she dove into herself for a moment to dig up the resolve she would need. Then she said, "How can I help?"

Knowing that I had her support, her partnership in this, meant the world to me. "I need you to see things before I do," I told her.

She laughed at that. "If I could do that, I never would have started dating Layton." Then seemed to regret having said that.

In the silence that followed that particular revelation, I did something that was a really bad idea, but sometimes when gravity takes over, you have no choice but to fall. I leaned forward and gave her a gentle kiss.

She accepted it—leaned into it, even—but only for a moment before pulling away.

"Don't," she said.

I immediately regretted it. But I don't think I would have been able to undo it in any world. "I'm sorry," I told her. "I wasn't thinking. I won't do it again."

"I didn't say not to do it again," Katie told me, without looking at me. "Just don't do it now." Then she left me to ponder the million parallel universes of what that meant.

The problem with secret meetings in dangerous places—especially dangerous places that have been the subject of lawsuits from the parents of mechanically ensnared kids—is that they are under constant surveillance to prevent future lawsuits.

But I'll get to that.

First I need to tell you about lunchtime. Monday lunch hour was when the SAS Club got together. That's the Students Against Segregation Club. I had told Paul that I would join, and although there are various other ways I screw up, I am always a man of my word. Besides, I was grateful that there was a group of like-minded people in my school unwilling to accept the status quo. I found Paul in the cafeteria, and we went to Mr. DeVaney's room, where the meetings were held.

"I didn't think you'd actually join," Paul said as we left the cafeteria. "I figured you were just saying you'd join to be polite."

"When have you ever known me to be polite?" I asked.

"Good point."

Mr. DeVaney was a popular teacher. He taught woodworking and ceramics, and apparently saw his real job to be molding shapeless high school minds into things of beauty. Or at least things that were marginally useful. There were about twenty kids in the room. Some of them I knew, some I didn't, and some I'm pretty sure didn't exist before last week.

I wanted there to be more members. I had imagined standing room only. I suppose there were more kids who supported desegregation, but didn't support it enough to join a club. It made me wonder how many important causes were crushed not by opposition, but by lukewarm support.

And also by useless measures.

Today's discussion was about a proposed bake sale "to raise money and awareness for desegregation." One girl was planning to make black-and-white cookies, but someone else argued that the very nature of black-and-white cookies reinforced segregation, and that led to a full-on debate about the symbolic nature and unintended messages of desserts.

"Uh . . . excuse me," I said, because no one seemed to notice me raising my hand. "I'm sure the cookies will be delicious regardless of their symbolism—but do you really think a bake sale is the best way to go about this?"

All eyes turned to me, and I realized I had nothing. No ideas, just complaints about theirs.

Mr. DeVaney took control of the situation with practiced calm. "We've been planning this for quite a while, Ash," he said—his way of reminding me that I was a new voice in the room. But as a new voice, maybe I had a fresh perspective.

"What if we did bigger things," I asked the group. "We could . . . I don't know . . . hold a school walkout. Or we could pack a city council meeting and demand justice—you know, something that would get in the news and might convince others to do it, too. I mean, a bake sale's fine if you want to raise money for a dance—but . . ." And since I had nothing past the "but," I shut up.

There was stunned silence. Until someone said, "I think that's a great idea." It was the cookie girl. I was ready to gloat with satisfaction from my impassioned, persuasive speech . . . until the cookie girl said, "We should use the money from the bake sale to have an interracial dance!"

And suddenly everyone was energized with this new idea that they accused me of coming up with.

"Hey," Paul said to me with a shrug, "maybe it'll make the news, like you said, and get other schools to do it, too."

I left the meeting feeling like I'd accomplished a whole lot of nothing.

"Don't be so surprised," Paul said. "Support for desegregation might be miles wide, but around here it's only inches deep."

Considering how little time I'd been spending on schoolwork lately, Paul and I made plans for some much-needed math tutoring, then went our separate ways. It wasn't until after the last bell rang that things took yet another unexpected turn.

"Ash, wait up!"

It was Layton. He came trotting toward me with Katie in tow as I shut my locker at the end of the day.

"Hey," he said. "Glad I caught you before practice. Katie and I need to talk to you."

"We do?" said Katie, clearly not consulted about this encounter.

"Yeah," said Layton, "I thought I told you." Then Layton pulled out his phone. "There's this new app—have you heard about it? It's called Public-i. It lets you access feeds from any public video camera anywhere in the country—and if you report something that actually leads to an arrest, they pay you in Bitcoin."

"That so?" I said, not caring in the least, and too slow on the uptake to know where this conversation was going. But Katie clearly did, and got visibly nervous.

"Yeah," continued Layton. "People are getting rich off of it—and the best thing about it is that it's a public service!"

I idly wondered if this app existed in my old world, or if it was unique to this one. Maybe I didn't want to know.

"Anyway—and this is really cool—look what I caught this morning!"

He pulled up the app, and the second I saw the video, I knew what this was about. He had tapped a surveillance feed in the gym—the one set up so that security guards could shoo away any horny or spider-interested kids who had slipped behind the bleachers. Public-i now showed Katie and me coming out from under the bleachers.

"Isn't this an amazing app!" said Layton with a forced enthusiasm that was too scary for words. "Hey, here's an idea! Why don't you explain to me why you and my girlfriend were hanging out in a known make-out spot."

A suitable response did not present itself to my brain, so Katie took over.

"I can explain," she said with a sigh, then she looked at me with mournful eyes. "I'm sorry, Ash, I just can't do this anymore. Please don't hate me." Then she turned to Layton. "Ash has been having some . . . well . . . pretty serious psychological problems. It could be concussion-related."

Jaws do drop. Not exactly like in cartoons, but they do, because at that moment mine did.

"What kind of problems?" Layton asked.

Katie did not hesitate. "He thinks he's traveling to other universes. He thinks stop signs were red, and that, until last week, our school was integrated. And he thinks there are interdimensional people on skateboards following him around."

I could feel my entire spirit implode from this betrayal. And all I could dredge up to say was "I told you, they're not really skateboards . . ."

Katie forced Layton to look at her instead of me. Or maybe so that *she* didn't have to look at me. "I've been talking to the school counselor about it. We've been trying to figure out a way to get Ash to go in and talk to her on his own." Then finally she turned back to me. "I'm so sorry, Ash. I never meant to hurt you. I just wanted to help you."

Layton seemed to flush with relief. Like a dark cloud had parted and drenched him in sunlight. "So that's why you've been talking to the counselor?"

"Of course," she said. "Why else would I be talking to her?"

Layton relaxed even further, then he put his arm around her in that possessive way he had.

"Dude," he said, invoking bro-talk. "If Katie thinks you need help, then you probably need help—but skip the school counselor—she can't prescribe the meds you probably need."

I didn't know how to respond to this. I felt like a balloon popping in slow motion, shredding and shrinking and losing my insides all at once. And Layton knew it. He seemed to swell even as I withered.

"It's all good," he said, with a jovial smile. Then he leaned closer. "But if I ever catch you talking to Katie again, I don't care who your father is, I'll beat the shit out of you."

Normally I would not have stood for a threat like that. Normally I would have given as good as I got. But to push back, you have to have leverage. You have to be grounded and centered and poised to strike. I had none of those things in that moment. So I just stood there saying nothing as he swept Katie away.

◆ ◆ ◆

Football practice was a drudgery of soul-numbing drills. Punishment for our loss to the Phoenices. That was okay. I needed a little soul-numbing. And running defensive drills meant we didn't even come in contact with the offensive players today. I was far away from Layton, and I was more than fine with that.

Truth be told, he was never actually my friend. He was just a football buddy, and, because he was our quarterback, we had to exhibit loyalty. In general I'm not a hater, but in all honesty, I can't remember a time in my life that I despised another human being as much as I despised Layton. Not just for humiliating me and threatening me, but for how he treated Katie—a girl who, even in betrayal, was only trying to help me.

As soon as practice was done, I left. I didn't even hit the showers, I just wanted to be out of there. I'd shower at home—or more likely take another EMP bath. But as I crossed the parking lot toward my car, Norris came running after me.

"Ash, wait up!"

I figured he wanted a ride home, and I didn't know if I could endure his blathering today. Still, I couldn't just ignore him, so I slowed down and let him catch up with me.

"I'm feeling sick, Norris," I told him. "Best if you stay away; I might have the flu."

He paused for a second, then said, "You're lying. Why are you lying so much all of a sudden?"

I really had no strength to deny it, although I was surprised that Norris's powers of observation could pick it out. "What do you want, Norris?" I asked bluntly.

"Just checking in with you, man," he said. "I mean, Layton says you've been having hallucinations and stuff."

I didn't even know there was a deeper level of hate I could feel toward Layton, but here it was. "Really? Layton said that? What else did he say?"

"Is it true?" Norris asked.

"Yeah," I told him. "I'm seeing flying elephants and a talking mouse. Oh, wait, that's Disneyland."

"I'm being serious."

"You haven't been serious a day in your life, Norris, why start now?"

He backed away. Maybe I shouldn't have snapped at him, but he picked the wrong day to experiment with compassion.

"You wanna lose your friends, just keep it up, Ash," he said, then stormed away.

But the joke was on him. I had already lost my friends a world ago.

After practice, I had my Monday-night shift. The one where I did most of my dealing. But the second I was left alone in the store, I locked up and bailed, leaving a sign on the door that said "Closed for Religious Reasons." Then before I drove off, I checked to see if, by chance, there was a holiday that day. Turns out that it was Yom Kippur—the Jewish day of atonement. The perfect day for my "special customers" to repent from their drug habit.

I had made plans to meet with the Edwards. My first official training session in the art of existential manipulation. They were ready for me—because in a corner that was once the Star Wars area of the old Toys "R" Us was a big white capsule that fit perfectly with the rest of the décor. It kind of looked like a pharaoh's sarcophagus, if ancient Egyptians knew about plastic.

"Interdimensional transport device?" I asked, half joking, half terrified. "Bet you didn't get that from Amazon."

"There's nothing interdimensional about it," Ed said. "It's a sensory deprivation tank."

Edd popped open the lid.

"Get naked and get in."

I had heard about these things. The water inside is body temperature, and loaded with about as much salt as the Dead Sea, so you float high. With no sound or light, there's absolutely no stimulation but what comes loaded in your own mental software. I knew a kid who knew a kid whose hippy-dippy father got high, got in a tank, and became one with the universe. That is to say he had a coronary in there, and went belly-up. Literally.

So, needless to say, I was apprehensive.

"There's nothing to be afraid of," Ed told me. "It's just a good way to get you focused and visualizing."

"Alpha state," I said. "Isn't that what they call it?"

"Call it whatever you like, as long as it gets you in there," said Edd, losing patience. Ed raised a hand to quiet him. "There's no lock on the lid, Ash. You can get out any time you like—but I think once you're in there you won't want to leave."

And I could smell why. From the open lid of the tank a waft of sultry air carried the strong smell of mint. This tank wasn't filled with ordinary salt water—this was the ultimate, fully saturated EMP bath.

So even though getting into a water coffin in a dead Toys "R" Us didn't feel like a good idea in any universe, I agreed. I stripped down, stepped in, then lay faceup in the warm water. When they closed the lid, the darkness was absolute. So was the silence. In a few moments all I could hear was my own heartbeat. Not only that, but within seconds the headache that I always struggled to tune out was gone.

After a few minutes of silence, I heard Ed's voice through an underwater speaker. It actually startled me.

"You should be nice and relaxed now," he said.

"Mmmyeah," I croaked.

"Good. Now I want you to go back to the moment of one of your shifts. Imagine it deeply."

So I tried. And got nothing. The thing is, the jumps were both instantaneous and not. Like being under anesthesia. You know the "after" is different from the "before," but you can't access the in-between.

"This is pointless."

"Just keep trying."

I sighed and moved slightly, feeling the water ripple around my body. I felt myself getting tense, so I forced my limbs to relax again. Then my mind started to ping on something. You know how sometimes you unexpectedly trigger the memory of a dream you had? Not even a recent one, but one you had maybe years ago, but never remembered until that moment? That's what this was like. The in-between was there—I just had to relax into it.

Soon I was there again. The "Elsewhere," as the Edwards called it. I remembered flashes of light and sound. Uneven, like Morse code. There was an indescribable sense of movement. I was moving left and right, back and forth all at once.

"I got something," I rasped. "I got something!"

"Slow it down," Ed said. "Take it in. Let the feeling linger. What's around you?"

But my mind was already drifting, and I was now seeing cheeseburgers in my head, because I was hungry. I told them, and they didn't seem as exasperated as I thought they would be.

"That's how your mind is interpreting the realities," Ed said. "Just go with it. Pick a burger."

"Which one?"

"The best-tasting one."

"How do I know how it tastes before I pick it?"

This is the moment that Obi-Wan Kenobi tells Luke to use the Force. But somehow choosing an imaginary cheeseburger seemed like an absolute waste of a Jedi Master's time.

I chose one. But I didn't get to eat it—because it devoured me first. The moment it was chosen, it enveloped me. Its meat was rancid. Fetid. Disgusting, but it was too late to escape, because I had lost control. Then I realized that I was reliving my arrival in this world. I remembered that sense of foreboding when I snapped back to the field after I tackled the quarterback. I knew it was bad, even before I knew how bad.

I leapt up almost involuntarily, knocked open the lid, and spilled out onto the floor beside the tank, dripping wet and out of breath.

"Well," Ed said. "It looks like you had a breakthrough."

11

NEVERMORE

I couldn't sleep that night. Not because of my headache—my deep-brain EMP float had eased that. It was because I couldn't stop thinking about Leo. To me, he had always been the definition of dignity. But now he had been knocked so far down, every one of his expectations had fallen to the level of simple survival. A place where one's own self-respect had to be sacrificed on a regular basis just to make it through the day.

The idea of basic human dignity being stripped away was way on the edge of my radar. People whose lives were so far removed from mine, they might as well have been on a different planet. It's like the way my parents always change the channel whenever some ad comes on for a charity about starving people in terrible places. It isn't just a case of "not my problem." It's "not my universe."

But what happens when someone's future is stripped away—their entire life hamstrung right in front of you? Someone who, in a sense, you love, although you'd never use that word to describe it—but what is friendship if it isn't some kind of love?

On Tuesday Leo called me. He left a message while I was at school. He was the only person I knew who actually left voice messages—same as the Leo from my world. It was comforting.

"It's Leo Johnson," he said, *"from Publix."* Like he needed to remind me. *"Yeah, so meet me at St. Clair Park at four o'clock today."*

It would mean ditching football practice—an inexcusable offense—but my priorities had shifted.

St. Clair Park was actually St. Clair *Memorial* Park. A cemetery. The place where Angela was buried. Leo was waiting for me when I got there, and led me to her grave.

"I wanted you to see it," Leo said. "I don't know why, I just wanted to show it to you."

Angela's gravestone was pink. Seeing that gravestone made it painfully real. According to the date, she died a year and a half ago. On April Fools' Day, like it was all some cosmic practical joke.

"I'm glad you had me come here," I told him, even though I wasn't, really. But he needed to do this, and I respected that. I could withstand a few nightmares if it eased his. "She would have hated that it was pink," I told him.

Leo laughed. "Got that right. But my parents still saw her as their little princess." Then he got serious again. "I've been getting more memories of things that couldn't have happened," he said. "Not big ones, just little things."

"Like what?"

"Like, did you once break your arm at a birthday party?"

"Ha!" Now there was a memory I'd prefer to forget myself. "Freaking Norris. He was swinging at a piñata and missed."

"Who's Norris?" Leo asked.

"A friend of ours," I told him. "Sort of."

Leo accepted it, but clearly had no memory of him.

"Of course I could have heard about it somewhere. That would be the sensible explanation."

"Yeah," I had to admit, "it would be."

"But here's the thing. You know that scientist guy—Stephen Hawking? Well, right before he died, he published a paper saying that parallel universes probably exist. They say he would've gotten a Nobel Prize for it, but you gotta be alive to get one of those."

"So you're saying you believe me now?"

He took a deep breath. "Let's not go there," he said. "Let's just go with what is. What we know for sure. And what I know for sure is *this*." Then he took out a football from his backpack. "I was thinking maybe we could toss it around."

"Here? In a graveyard?"

"The dead don't mind. And neither do the caretakers. My dad and I come here and toss a ball around sometimes. They know us. They know about Angela. And I'm sure the caretakers won't mind you handling a football here, considering who your father is."

My father. It was an odd thing being in his shadow now, when I had never known him to cast much of a shadow at all.

"I was thinking," said Leo, "that maybe I'd get my GED and go to community college. Maybe get back into football. Some community colleges here have good teams, don't they?"

"Yeah, Leo," I said, trying to keep my eyes from clouding up. "Yeah, they do." I backed up to put a fair throwing distance between us, then we started tossing the ball back and forth over the dead like it was a perfectly natural thing to do. We kept it up until sundown, when the caretakers politely shooed us out and locked the gate for the night. But before I left, I put a hand on Angela's headstone, said a silent prayer, and made her a promise that I would not leave her like this.

"If you need my help with this *thing* that you say is going on," Leo said, "you got my number."

Then we went our separate ways.

I got home just in time for an honest-to-goodness sit-down dinner—something that was rare for our family in this world, although in my original dump of a house, we did it almost every night. Here, no one lived on the same schedule, so most of the time it was takeout, and leftovers from yesterday's takeout.

But tonight, Cara, our housekeeper, had prepared a real meal: a roast with fingerling potatoes, which always sounded vaguely cannibalistic to me. Cara was Black. She tried to serve us, but I insisted on serving myself—and, following my lead, so did Hunter.

"Why don't you go home, Cara," my mom said. "You've had a long day."

To which Cara responded, "Thank you, ma'am. Enjoy the roast."

I hated that she called my mom "ma'am." I hated that she was cooking for us instead of for her own family. I felt uptight and awkward about it even after she had gone. Especially because the me from this world never gave it a second thought. He didn't even know or care if she had a family.

My parents made small talk over dinner, trying to engage Hunter and me, but we were both the princes of one-word answers. How's school? "Good." Doing anything interesting? "Eh." Coach working you too hard? "Naah." Eventually they just resorted to talking to each other. Today's topics of conversation were the Icelandic refugee crisis (which was a unique aspect of this world), and whether or not electrolyte-infused goji berry protein powder was a growing trend in the supplement market.

I, of course, had to open my big mouth about that. "Do goji berries grow in Iceland?" I asked. The question stymied my parents.

"I don't know," my mother said. "Probably not. Why?"

"Because I don't get how you could talk about a country's civil war in the same breath that you talk about some stupid protein powder."

My father gave me one notch beneath a glare. "All these things affect our lives in one way or another."

"Actually, I was thinking that maybe we could take in an

Icelandic refugee family," Mom suggested. "Let them stay in our carriage house."

And my dad said, "I'll look into it. I think it would be . . . a meaningful gesture."

I accessed some memories of my parents here. They were quite the philanthropists—donating time and money to worthy causes. Some causes more than others. But taking in a displaced family seemed a step out of their comfort zone. I didn't think much about it at first.

Hunter ate quickly and excused himself. I was done only seconds after him, but my parents asked me to stay for a moment.

"Why?" I asked. "Is there dessert?"

But the reason had nothing to do with the food, and everything to do with why we were having this meal in the first place. It was to ambush me.

"We heard you've joined a social action club at school," my dad said.

I immediately became suspicious. "Heard from who?"

He just shrugged. "Just around. People talk."

Then my mom chimed in. "We think it's wonderful that you're taking an interest in social issues, Ash. We just want to make sure that this is really something you want to be involved in."

"And that you've thought it through," added my father.

Clearly, they knew what club I had joined. I was not interested in this conversation. "Are we done?" I asked, pushing my chair back to indicate that, even if they weren't, I was.

Dad sighed. "Ash, I'm no fan of segregation. If you ask me,

anyone should be able to go to any school they want. But not everybody feels that way."

"And we need to respect those feelings, too," said Mom, like thunder chasing lightning.

"I *have* no respect for people who feel that way," I told her.

"And that's your prerogative," said my father, "but your actions have ramifications you might not have considered."

"Like what?"

My father went silent for a moment. "I've been considering a run for mayor," he finally said. "And I expect the support I'll be getting will be from people who like things to change much more slowly . . ."

"You mean not at all."

"I mean that you can't change people's minds without first winning them over. There are what? Six states now trying to ban segregation? If they succeed, I'm sure more will follow. In the meantime we have to look at things practically."

There's this old movie where all the real people start getting replaced by pod people, who pop out of giant veiny seeds. They look the same, but you can tell that something's terribly wrong—and if you're not careful you become one of them. That's what my parents were now. Pod people.

"What if I told you that my best friend is a Black kid?" I hurled at them. "A Black kid who dropped out of school and works as a supermarket checker, because he never had the chance to do anything else."

"I'd say that you were lying," said my father. "Because I know all your friends."

"You once knew this one . . . ," I prompted, watching them for that moment of confused recognition—but there was nothing. They were so single-minded with their agenda, and so close-minded in other ways, the proximity effect didn't seem to work on them. Their tunnel vision didn't leave room for anything in the periphery.

"We're glad that you've taken on a cause so admirable," Mom said, getting the conversation back on point.

"But," added Dad, "maybe you can redirect that energy."

And then Mom laid the rest of their cards on the table. "Why don't you help us choose an Icelandic family to take in?"

While I had sympathy for displaced Icelandic people, there was a glaring absurdity to this pod-people solution.

"Are you kidding me? There are families on the other side of town who are struggling, and you want to ignore them and help people from Iceland instead?"

I stood up, and so did my father.

"Ash," he said, "my own son taking a vocal stance right now on such a hot-button issue as segregation is going to make it very difficult for me to run a campaign."

"Well, then," I said, "maybe you need to redirect that energy."

"I heard the whole thing," Hunter said when I passed his room upstairs, a few minutes later. "I want you to know that I think it's pretty cool what you're doing. Even if it does screw things up for Dad."

"Thanks, Hunter."

He took a moment to think about it. "I . . . I'd probably feel a little awkward going to school with black kids at first," he said. "But just because it makes me uncomfortable doesn't mean it shouldn't happen, right? I mean, if we just did things that made us feel comfortable, we'd never leave the couch. Maybe I'll do something to fight segregation, too."

"Start by sitting in the integrated section at the Towne Centre, and other places," I suggested. "See which friends join you, and which ones don't. Then maybe make some new friends."

He grinned. "That easy, huh?"

It reminded me of something else Hunter had said should be easy. And so I made a pact with him. "If you do it, I'll stop selling drugs for good."

He considered that. "Even to me?"

"Especially to you."

He weighed that and nodded. "I can live with that," he said.

I had another sit-down dinner the following night—but thankfully not at my house, and not with my parents. Leo asked me over for dinner.

"Don't make a big deal of it," he told me. "I told my mom we tossed a ball together, and she wouldn't get out of my face until I invited you over. I think she thought I was making it up, and she called my bluff."

I said yes, but I was almost afraid to go. I didn't want to see how he was forced to live in this world. Turns out he lived in the same place as before, but the house—as well as the neighborhood around it—was different. Homes that had once been well kept were in disrepair. Sagging overhangs, peeling paint, yards gone to seed. Someone passing by on their proverbial high horse might turn up their nose and say these people just didn't care—but I knew that couldn't be further from the truth. Of course they cared—but how can you pay for a new roof when you're struggling to put food on the table? How do you paint your house when you're already working two jobs? True in my original world as well, but that didn't mean my privileged ass ever thought about it before today.

If you looked close enough, however, there were plenty of signs that people took pride in every way they could. A small but perfectly manicured flower garden in an otherwise wild yard. A car detailed and polished to a showroom sheen, in absolute defiance of the dent in its side.

In my world, Leo's parents had rebuilt their porch, but here it sagged from the weight of fifty summers. And yet above it, hanging from the awning, were dozens of beautiful wind chimes tinkling and twinkling in the night. Yeah, this was Leo's home.

"Where I come from," I told him, "your mom has a side business making those."

"Yeah, she makes 'em," Leo said. "No business though. She sells them at church bazaars sometimes, but mostly she gives 'em as gifts." Then he added, "Wish she'd give away more—those damn things keep me up all night."

Leo's mom greeted me at the door a bit awkwardly. "Ash Bowman," she said, "pleased to meet you. I hope you like mac and cheese."

"And not the store-bought stuff," Leo was quick to say. "The real thing—from scratch."

I smiled as I shook her hand. "I always love your mac and cheese, Mrs. Johnson." Then I gave a nervous little cough. "I mean . . . I always love homemade, and I'm sure yours is something special."

It was a fair enough save, although Leo gave me a sideways glance.

"Leo tells me you're encouraging him back into football. Good to see a prominent family like yours taking an interest in others."

I wanted to tell her that it wasn't my family, it was just me—but that would have been petty. "Talent deserves attention," I told her instead. "Glad I can give some."

She glanced at Leo, glowing with just enough pride to be below the embarrassment threshold, before going back into the kitchen.

In my world, Mrs. Johnson was the head of human resources at a local hospital. According to Leo, she still worked at the hospital, but here it was in food service, wheeling meals to patients. Minimum wage, which here was single digits. There were pictures of Angela everywhere. She looked the same as I remembered. Except that she was gone. Leo's father was in a lot of pictures, but wasn't present that night. "He works the night shift," Leo told me. I didn't ask doing what.

"The Blue Demons having a good year?" Leo's mom asked as the three of us sat down to dinner.

"I guess," I told her. "Two and one. Still too early to say."

I dug in. There was no lobster in the mac and cheese; it had crawfish instead, which to me tasted exactly the same. Comfort-food perfection. I complimented Mrs. Johnson on it— but then Leo said something that sent me spiraling.

"Hey, maybe your family could use a part-time cook."

I nearly gagged, but instead swallowed so much that it gave me the hiccups. The idea of Mrs. Johnson working for us in our kitchen, having to call my mother Mrs. Bowman, or even worse, "ma'am," made me sick.

The hiccup saved me from having to respond. Leo poured me more lemonade and I took a long draught, not just to quell the hiccups, but to let the subject change, so I didn't have to say what an insult it would be to *her* if she had to work for *us*.

"My hands are full already," Mrs. Johnson said. "I'll send along the recipe." Mercifully the conversation switched to the mundane: movies, sports, and weather.

Then, after dinner, almost on autopilot, I opened the door to the basement.

"What are you doing that for?" Leo asked.

"I dunno. I just thought we'd go downstairs and hang out."

Mrs. Johnson looked at me funny. "The basement? Nothing down there but laundry and bugs gone to Jesus."

I sheepishly closed the door.

Once his mother was out of earshot, Leo gave me a smirk that was as pained as it was amused. "Don't tell me—where you come from, I got a whole rec room down there."

"So you remember?"

"Hell, no! Just why else would you want to go to the basement? I suppose I got a Beemer like you, too."

I shook my head. "No—you have your dad's old Subaru."

He took a moment to weigh it in his mind.

"Subaru . . ." he said, then took a shot in the dark. "Was it . . . green?"

"It was!"

He grinned. "Damn. So you think if I smacked you upside the head hard enough, it'd knock us all back there?"

"It'd have to be really hard," I told him.

He considered it and shook his head. "Naah," he said. "Can't hit a friend like that, 'less he deserves it."

And I smiled. It was good to hear him call me a friend.

"Tell me about it," Leo said. "Tell me about this world you want me to believe in."

Not an easy request. It's like when my great-uncle, who hadn't seen me since I was three, came over and asked, "So what have you been up to?" I mean, where did I begin?

"Well . . . like I said, in my world, you didn't drop out," I told Leo. "In fact, you were waiting for scholarships—and not just football, academic too. You were waiting on USC, but a scout from Clemson—"

"No!" He put up his hand to stop me. He looked away, closed his eyes, grimaced like he was in pain. "Don't do that. I don't want to hear that."

All at once I realized how insensitive it was to keep telling him all the dreams he'd never get to have here.

He put his hand down. Took a moment to let it pass. "I want you to tell me what it was like. A story about you and me. What were *we* like in this wonderland world of yours?"

Wonderland world? Had I really been selling it to him that way? I felt myself sour with shame. They say shame and guilt are useless emotions—because they let you wallow without taking any action. The first step toward action is speaking truth. All at once, I knew what story to tell him. Not the one I wanted to tell, but the one I needed to.

"A while back, you and I went out to join the protests," I said, then I waited for him to ask, "What protests?" but he didn't. He just waited for me to explain. "Because another white cop killed another Black man, and people had had enough."

Leo drew a deep breath, leaned back, and crossed his arms. He still didn't say a thing.

"But the city was too far, and we didn't drive yet," I continued. "Besides, your mom didn't know how bad it would get out there—she was already worked up, and you didn't want to worry her."

"Nothing's changed there," Leo said. "So what'd we do?"

I told him about how we went down to Market Street, T-ville's old downtown—which is just three blocks of outdated buildings trying to convince the world they're quaint. There's a bank that's now a clothing store, some holdout mom-and-pop shops, and a town hall that you'd miss if you blinked. Not the center of anyone's universe.

"There were maybe about a hundred of us," I told him. "We stood on the corners chanting and holding up signs." I had to take a moment before I told him the next part. "But then you got mad. Because it looked like people were having a party—like it was all some sort of pep rally—and no one should be enjoying this. And I said, 'Leo, this is a good thing—every single car that passes is honking in support.' And you said—"

"And I said '*Honk if you hate racism* is not a solution. It's worse than doing nothing.'"

"You remember!"

He paused. He squinted. He sighed. "I did for a second. Now it's gone."

But it wasn't gone. It was still in my head. In my memories. I needed to hold those memories for both of us, until they were his again. I hadn't seen what he saw that night. All I saw were people showing support. But he saw people who thought giving a thumbs-up to protesters was the full extent of their civic responsibility—as if acknowledging that Black lives mattered was all it took to clear their consciences. And later, when the news chose to focus on scenes of mayhem, and fires raging in every major city, I remember thinking, *Is this what Leo wants?* As if there weren't a million choices between honking your horn and burning it all to the ground.

"You were right, Leo. You were right about all of it, but I just didn't get it. And I'm sorry."

My voice was cracking, and my heart felt like it was looking for the nearest hole to hurl itself out of. And Leo was making that really long face you make when you're trying not to cry and you're pissed off that you're not succeeding.

"You were supposed to tell me a story that would cheer me up. About flying cars, and fresh vegetables and shit."

"You deserve to know the truth . . . Where I'm from is no wonderland. Not by a long shot."

Leo looked off, considered it, then returned his gaze to me. "Fair enough—but I'm still down to see it," he said. "I'd rather live in a world where hope's alive but sick, than a world where it's already in the morgue."

Having Leo's support made a world of difference. It was a call to action. I continued "training" with the Edwards each night—but after that first breakthrough, my progress was slow. My mind was so cluttered and distracted, it took forever to focus once I was in the tank. Sometimes I would just fall asleep in the warm, buoyant water. Other times, even when I could access the memory of "Elsewhere," the various versions of reality didn't present themselves in a meaningful way. An array of playing cards that were all facedown. A ball pit where all the balls were gray. And each time I would do nothing more than relive different versions of how I wound up here, in this wretched world.

"You have to move beyond your memory," the Edwards told me. "Make the choice you *didn't* make before."

And I tried. I really tried. But my brain would not cooperate. On Thursday night—my last session before Friday's game—my mind seized on Edgar Allan Poe, because we were studying his poetry in English, and the multiverse presented itself as an infinite flock of ravens, all shouting the same miserable word. I wanted to strangle them all.

I climbed out of the tank, frustrated and mentally exhausted. Ed handed me a towel and offered me a sympathetic sigh, but the other two weren't quite as compassionate.

"I don't know why we're even bothering—he's never going to get it," said Edd. "You can't teach a mule to fly."

"I'm sure there are universes in which they do," Ed said.

But Eddy, who was all about the numbers on the QuIRT, put down his game controller, also ready to accept defeat. "Maybe we should just let this run its course and get out before the correction."

"I agree," said Edd. "It'll be no great loss."

I didn't like the sound of that. "What do you mean by 'correction'?"

"It's nothing for you to worry about," said Edd. But clearly it was, so I turned to Ed, who was always more forthcoming, and I demanded an explanation.

Reluctantly, Ed told me this:

"Sometimes when a sub-loc shoots reality past a critical transdimensional event horizon, the universe will initiate a course correction."

"English, please!" I told him. "For us one-dimensional human beings."

To which Eddy said, "Human beings only *seem* one-dimensional at times. Technically you're three-dimensional."

I ignored him and waited for Ed to respond.

"The universe," said Ed, "will occasionally protect itself by neutralizing the sub-loc, and everything that the sub-loc has affected."

"What do you mean 'neutralize'? What do you mean 'everything'?"

Ed sighed. "Planetary extinction. A complete wipeout—usually by comet or spontaneous black hole."

"A black hole is cleaner," said Eddy, "because it sucks in the entire star system, leaving no trace. Universally motivated comet strikes are messy."

"You've seen this?"

"Nobody sees a black hole," said Edd. "It's when you *don't* see something that you should worry."

"So it's happened before?" I asked. And all three of them became universally defensive.

"Let's not dwell on the past."

"It wasn't our fault."

"We did everything we could."

"But arthropods will be arthropods."

I took a deep breath and closed my eyes, deeply sorry I had asked. I thought about the ravens' dismal proclamation, hoping it wasn't prophetic.

"I'll try it again," I told them with renewed determination. I threw my towel at Edd hard enough to knock him off balance, then slipped back into the tank.

I told them not to guide me through it, but to just leave me alone with my thoughts. I knew what I had to do. Breathe, relax, remember. Breathe, relax, remember. Push out all the other things cluttering my mind. Breathe . . . relax . . . remember.

And there I was again. Elsewhere. The odd flashing, as if light and dark were competing with each other. In a moment, infinite possible realities would present themselves in the form of something dragged from my subconscious. But then I thought—*What if I could direct that, even just a little bit? What if I could represent these worlds in a form I could more easily read?* And just willing it made it so. Suddenly I was visualizing the array of realities as—wait for it—phone emojis.

That might sound annoying and useless, but it was actually helpful. Emojis communicated something. They *meant* something—although what I thought they meant wasn't always their official meaning, but that didn't matter. These were pulled out of *my* subconscious, so they meant exactly what I wanted them to.

I stayed away from the angry ones, the crying ones, the sick ones, and went nowhere near the grinning turd.

I settled on the smiley face with sunglasses—my personal favorite. It felt familiar. Comfortable. I willed myself to slide toward it. It grew. I fell into one of the lenses. And suddenly I felt triumphant. Not like the way you feel when you win a big game—more like the childish joy of tying your shoelaces for the first time.

It was just practice, of course—when the real thing came, I doubted I'd be seeing emojis, but the sense of those other worlds would be the same. I needed to remember that shoelace feeling. Simple, familiar accomplishment. And the joy of coming home.

12

WHO WE ARE

"I just want to wish you good luck."

Katie intercepted me on the way into the locker room before Friday's game. I'm sure Layton had already gone in, otherwise she would never have taken the chance to talk to me. She'd been avoiding me since Monday. Truth be told, I was avoiding her, too.

"We don't need luck," I told her flatly. "The Torkington Storks are the worst team in the league."

"That's not what I'm talking about."

Yeah, I knew that. "Oh, then you mean good luck with my delusions," I said, dripping sarcasm. "I don't need luck there, either. All I need are meds, like Layton said."

She glared at me. "Do you really think I meant what I said the other day, Ash?"

"You sure sounded convincing."

"Of course I did! I had to! Layton can't know any of this—so I gave him a half-truth, because he would have known a full-out lie." Then she took a moment to think about things, and gave me something she never gave Layton. A full-truth.

"I admit that everything you've told me sounds like you've lost touch with reality," she said. "And at first I did think that might be the case . . . But if you've lost touch, then I have, too—because I do remember the Tsunamis, and I do know who Angela Johnson is." Then she pulled out a pencil sketch she had done. It was Angela. The eyes were a little wrong, but not by much. Katie had drawn her entirely from the memory of a memory.

"This is her, isn't it?"

I nodded, speechless.

"Did you find her? I want to talk to her," Katie said. "I want to know if she remembers anything, too."

"You can't talk to her," I told Katie.

"Why not?"

But now was not the time to get into it. Besides, it was just too painful, so I said, "She doesn't live here anymore."

Katie was disappointed but accepted it. "Do you think things are going to change again tonight?" she asked.

I nodded. "I'm counting on it."

"Then promise me that after it happens, you'll tell me what changed. And you'll make me believe it."

Twenty minutes later, we took to the field. Bright lights, cheering crowds. A sea of white faces. All wrong. But only for now.

My parents were there. Hunter. And down front, with a good view, were the Edwards. One of them gave me an encouraging thumbs-up. Must have been Ed.

I was excited and ready, yet terrified and not ready at all. I was already moving in multiple directions at the same time, cycling through emotions like a roulette wheel. I knew what could go wrong. I knew the dangers, even if I didn't know each outcome. I was ready for this. I could never be ready for this.

We stood for the national anthem in a world where no players have ever dared to take a knee. Coin flip. We'd kick, the Storks would receive. Then after the kickoff, the starting defensive squad took the field.

But the coach stopped me before I ran out.

"You're not starting today, Ash," he told me. Then he gestured to a knee-bouncing bench-warmer, just up from JV. "Svec!" he called. "You're nose tackle. Get out there."

Svec hopped up like an oversized puppy and raced to the line.

I was reeling. What the hell was going on? "Are you kidding me? Svec as nose tackle?"

"C'mon, it's the Storks, Ash. We'll wipe the floor with them, and this is the only chance some of our kids will get to play this season."

And although I'm not the most observant person in the world, lately I've been getting better. He was lying through his teeth. And I was pretty sure I knew why. I looked over to Layton. Had he slipped to the whole team and the coaches that I was having issues? That maybe micro-concussions had messed with my brain? *Maybe Ash needs a full checkup,* he would have told them. *Maybe he needs some time on the bench. For his own good.*

I stormed up to Layton on the sidelines. "What did you tell them?" I demanded. "And don't lie to me!"

"I don't know what the hell you're talking about," he said.

I tried to read if he was lying. I was sure he was, but I couldn't sense any tells in his voice or body language.

Then he sneered at me. "Boohoo," he said, "the football star's son doesn't get to start for once. Get over it, Bowman. You're part of a team. Act like it."

I could have hit him, but I didn't. Because something suddenly occurred to me. I looked up to the stands and caught sight of my parents. My father. Sitting there, stoic. Arms crossed. And I knew it wasn't Layton at all.

By halftime we were beating the Storks by twenty to three. Svec did a respectable job on the defensive line. But we didn't need a respectable job. We needed a tackle powerful enough to change the world.

I confronted the coach after his halftime pep talk. Svec was out for the second half, and another newbie was put in instead of me. That only made the truth even clearer to me.

"What did my father tell you?" I asked the coach. "You owe me an answer."

He put up his hands. "Ash, I really don't want to get in the middle of this."

And there it was. Confirmation. "So it *was* my father."

The coach sighed. "He said you've been making some bad choices. I have no idea what he's talking about, but he feels you needed to understand the consequences of your actions."

"The consequences of my actions?" I echoed loudly—which made his voice get even quieter.

"That's what he said. And I owe him, Ash—he got me this job; you know that. What was I supposed to do?"

"You tell him no! You tell him this is your team, and you'll coach it the way you see fit!"

"Do you think I like being put in this position? Whatever's going on, you work it out with your father."

Then he left to get ready for the second half. I wanted to be mad at him, but how could I? This wasn't his fault. He had no idea what was at stake. And as for my father—did this side of him exist in my old world? Manipulative and self-serving? In *my* world his life was all bitter regret. He saw himself as a failure, yet he was a kind man. A good man. A man who was home every night to be with his family. I didn't like the person success had made my father. I much preferred the "failure."

The third quarter saw two more touchdowns for us, and one more field goal for the Storks that bounced off the goalpost in the right direction to give them three sorry points. The score was thirty-four, Demons; six, Storks; zero, me.

I made one final plea to the coach.

"One play, that's all I ask!" I begged. "I've learned my lesson. Please don't humiliate me by not putting me in at all."

"Just sit down and wait," he said. And so I did. I waited

through one more T-ville touchdown. I waited through play after successful play that made Layton look like a god, and the only consolation was that he'd end the game in a good mood and would have nothing to take out on Katie.

Then at the two-minute warning, the coach put me in. Not as nose tackle, but as right end. That was fine with me. It was on the line, and that's all that mattered. I had one chance to do this, and one chance only. I couldn't screw this up.

The ball was snapped. I launched forward with worlds—literally worlds—of determination. I crashed through the Storks' weak offensive line. Their quarterback was fading back for a pass, and I hurled myself at him, screaming. I made contact and—

Wham!

I was sliding. Ice in my arteries. Vertigo making my mind reel.

It was all happening between the smallest fractions of a second, but I stretched it. I made time move sideways instead of forward.

And I saw things I hadn't seen before.

There was a pit. I was skating around it, always on the verge of losing my balance and falling in. Instinctively I knew if I fell in, that would be the end. Either of me, or of everything, or both.

And around me what I was sensing, it wasn't as simple as cheeseburgers or emojis. There were pulsating shapeless things fighting for space, making it clear that these realities, all struggling to exist, were in some way alive.

Some were malevolent. Some were benign. I could sense

familiar ones, but they were being forced out. To reach them I would have to squeeze between others and risk slipping into that pit. And the others, they were grabbing me, clinging to me like octopuses—and the second I imagined that, that's exactly what they became. Millions of octopuses suffocating me, reaching for me, ensnaring me.

Then one reality loomed before me. It was neither bad nor good, light nor dark. It was curious. It desperately wanted to know what it would be like to exist. I could sense that this reality carried with it great and far-reaching change. I didn't know what that change would be, but it was clearly not a boomerang reality. It would take me even further away from the world I knew.

It took hold of me, longing to envelop me, but I would not let that happen. I would not be passively consumed by yet another unknown, opaque world. I would control this. It wouldn't devour me; *I* would devour *it*.

So I threw my arms around it, embracing it. I pulled it in. For a moment I felt like a soldier throwing himself on a grenade. But instead of detonating, it relaxed. It curled in upon itself, settling deep within me, happy to have a place. I felt its contentment. Its relief. Its joy at finally being real.

I opened my eyes.

I was on the turf. The coach was looming over me.

"Ash, look at me," he said. He held out his index finger and slowly moved it back and forth. "Follow my finger," he said. I did. He seemed satisfied. "Can you sit up?"

I did, but the world swirled around me. My brain felt like an angry zit about to pop. I couldn't think clearly, much less access whatever memories filled this world. I took a few moments. The world stopped spinning. I stood up, digging my cleats into the turf. I kept my balance. Bit by bit, I took in the things around me.

The Storks' quarterback was still down. Out cold. They had taken off his helmet. His coach and trainer were kneeling, taking his vitals. I realized I hadn't just taken him down, I had taken him out. Had I killed him? Had I hit him that hard? For a terrible moment I thought that I had—but then he groaned, and his eyes fluttered.

My coach let out a shuddering breath of relief, then he looked to me. "Never seen a sack like that," he told me, but he didn't sound all that pleased. "Damn, Ash—it's the freaking Storks. I'd never tell you not to play your best . . . but was that really necessary?"

They asked the semiconscious quarterback to move his hands, then his feet. They asked him a few questions I couldn't hear, then they finally helped him up and off the field to the obligatory applause.

The coach motioned for me to leave the field, too. "Go see the trainer," he said. "Have him check you out. Concussion protocol. You know the drill." The coach had promised me one play, and that's what I got. The Storks put in their second-string quarterback, and the game resumed.

On the sidelines, the trainer deemed me fit, but told me to

take it easy over the weekend and look for signs of concussion. Like the headache I didn't tell him about. Once he left, I tried to ignore my pulsing head and look for the changes. The inconsistencies. But everything looked exactly the same as it did before. There was still a sea of white faces in the stands. Damn! If something was different, I couldn't see it, but I knew for a fact that something had changed.

I knew because when I looked at the Edwards sitting in the stands, there weren't three of them. Now there were four.

Who we are is defined by a whole lot of things. Our family, our friends, our genetics, all the good things that have happened to us, as well as the traumatic things. And although we're always redefining ourselves, some things are constants. They are part of who we are and don't change. Unless, of course, you're shifting between universes.

I was wary after the game, looking at everyone, trying to decipher what the change was, and relying on what little power of observation I had to pick out the inconsistencies. There was still not a single thing I could see, hear, taste, or smell that was any different from the previous world.

But I could *feel* something was different.

I knew this was not like the other reality shifts. In those I fell into each new world, rather than *it* falling into *me*. My trip through Elsewhere left me feeling fried, and my thoughts were sluggish. It was hard to think, hard to reason, and whenever I tried, I got dizzy. I wouldn't tell the coach about it, or my parents, because it wasn't the kind of concussion that anyone could do anything about. My brain was now crammed with yet another set of latent memories I had not unpacked. I would take it slow, I decided. I'd let the world present itself to me in its own time.

Once more I went home alone, skipping the locker room banter, and this time Norris didn't bother coming after me. I hadn't spoken to him much this week. I hadn't hung out with the usual group of friends at all, because Leo wasn't a part of that group anymore. My best friend in this world, Josh Easley, wondered what was up with me, and yeah, I did have memories of our friendship, but I felt I had to distance myself from them.

When I started my car, that bland music blared at an embarrassing volume. I turned it off. The parking lot was now a crawl of a hundred cars trying to get out the single exit all at the same time. I didn't see the Edwards. They probably scooted off on their "skateboards." Or maybe they were still here looking for me. I wasn't ready to check in with them, because I didn't want them to grill me. I was in no state for a mental barbecue right now—I just wanted my nice hot EMP bath, in my nice quiet bathroom, because as much as I wanted to know what this world had in store, I also didn't want to know. I had failed to move things back toward home, and that was enough to grapple with for now. Maybe I could, for once, just sleep on it. Maybe the world would come to me in a dream and I'd wake up without a headache, knowing all I needed to know to make it through this next week.

My car inched along in the crush of vehicles, crippling my smooth escape. There were some spectators in Storks shirts meandering in front of me, taking their time in getting to their car, like they weren't in the middle of a parking lot. There was a guy in shorts even though it was too chilly for shorts. Nice calves. Probably a speed skater, or some other ballistic sport. Good hair, too. I tapped my horn in a non-rude kind of way to get him and his girlfriend to step aside. I spared a glance at them in the rearview mirror after I inched past just long enough to note that, in spite of the hair and calves, the guy was not much to look at from the front. All zits and Adam's apple.

Once out of the lot, the drive home was grueling. It seems like I hit every single blue light on the way. Then when I was finally home, even before I could go upstairs, the doorbell rang.

I checked the peephole, figuring if it was someone I didn't want to see, I could silently back away and just ignore them. I could pretend I was already in the bath. Turns out it was Paul at the door. Although I really didn't feel like being around anyone right then, I found I was kinda glad to see him. So I opened the door.

"Hey," he said. "Just checking on you. That was one hard hit you took—you okay?"

"I didn't take the hit, I gave it," I reminded him.

"Well, either way, you were almost down for the count." He stepped in and glanced around. "Where is everyone?"

"Not home yet." I figured my parents and Hunter stopped on the way to get takeout.

Paul closed the door behind him. "Good," he said with a smirk. Then he leaned into my airspace like airspace was something we shared, and kept on leaning closer until there was no airspace between us at all.

I'm going to pause here and give you a chance to process this in a way that I could not at the time. Take a moment. Take another moment. Get over it. Now let's continue.

The kiss pretty much laid waste to my brain. It was the master key opening up all the doors of this world at once, and I was overwhelmed. I froze completely, unable to move. A part of me was screaming, *What the Fuck? What the Fuck? I don't want this!* But another, more immediate part of me was screaming, *Hell, yeah, you do want it; in fact, you've been waiting for it all day.*

Memories of this world came surging through, and I knew if I tried to resist them, I'd drown in the floodwaters, like this was the tsunami my school was no longer named for. I found that my arms had come up involuntarily to hold Paul, and I wasn't pulling away.

This is not who I am!

This is *who I am!*

I am not enjoying this!

Oh, man am I enjoying this!

And the part of me that was not into other guys got smaller and weaker, as the part of me who was totally into other guys took over—and both parts realized that the only way to survive a tsunami was to surf it. So I kissed Paul with such force, we both stumbled back against the closed front door.

"What's gotten into you?" he said with a grin. "I gotta catch my breath."

Fair enough. So I let him breathe a little before I went in again.

13

IGNORANCE IS A COCKROACH

Here's what I know:

When I was nine, I had a crush on one of my classmates, but never told him. Actually I had a few crushes in grade school. Never on my friends though. It was always some kid I really didn't know all that well and was a little too scared to get to know. I guess I was too young to put much mental energy into wondering what that was all about—or maybe I did kinda know but chose not to think about it.

When I was twelve, I would sometimes get a hard-on in the locker room. I was good at hiding it though. No one ever noticed, or if they did, they didn't say.

When I was thirteen, I started to get the full picture. I liked guys, which meant I was probably gay. And if I wanted to be like all my friends, I had to pass for straight. It wasn't too hard because I was the kind of masculine gay guy that the previous version of me was too ignorant to know existed. The hetero me thought that being gay meant you acted a certain way and talked a certain way—and since there was plenty of ignorance to go around, I was able to pass for straight all these years—and I naïvely thought that if I pretended long enough, it would become real. That the gayness was just a phase that would go away.

But of course it didn't.

When I was in ninth grade, I made out with a friend the night before he moved away. I think we both felt safe going for it, because if it went wrong, we'd never see each other again anyway. He couldn't out me, and I couldn't out him. We wouldn't have to look at each other in the hallway every day. So by fifteen years old, I was feverishly furnishing that closet I'd be in for the rest of high school.

Then in junior year, Paul started tutoring me in math. After we got to know each other, he took a chance and told me he was gay over a particularly difficult algebra problem. I told him I was cool with that, and we went on to solve the equation. Two weeks later I confided in him that I was, too, and the rest was history. I think he was closer to being out than I was, but he wasn't there yet. Actually, I think he might have come out if it hadn't been for me. I didn't want him to be, because it might out me, too. I know that was selfish. I'm not proud of it. Even though I'm brave in some ways, there are other ways that I'm not. And being an openly gay athlete requires the kind of bravery I didn't have.

I think Paul and I were in love. I say "think" because it's a hard feeling to nail down. Especially because the feeling was so weighted down with other baggage. Fear of what my parents would think; the irrational belief that this gay thing might still go away; anger that I didn't fit the mold I thought I was supposed to; and confusion about what my future would hold. But when Paul and I were together, with no one else around, all that went away. That's why I thought it might have been love.

Even so, I couldn't quite wrap my mind around it. I mean, I couldn't even use the word "boyfriend" in my own head, much less out loud. How messed up is that? The closest I could come was to say that Paul and I were "buds."

And so in this reality, Paul and I found times and places to be together in secret. Places where we could leave the rest of the world out of it and pretend it didn't exist.

So back to the two of us making out in the foyer. In previous worlds, when Paul was just my math tutor, it had never occurred to me that he was kind of hot. Now it was obvious. How could I have missed it? Inside I was feeling maybe every possible human emotion all at once, the good and the bad. I felt like a power plant struck by lightning. All that flaring, buzzing energy shooting down high-tension wires too feeble to handle it. I was melting down.

Then I heard the garage door grinding open. That was perhaps the only sound that could make us stop. I finally broke off the kiss. "I . . . uh . . . gotta take a shower," I told Paul.

"Better make it a cold shower," he joked.

"Very funny."

I went upstairs and heard my parents and Hunter coming in, saying hello to Paul, just as I closed the bathroom door. To them, he was still just my friend and math tutor. I had gone to great pains to make sure they had no reason to think otherwise.

I hadn't brought up any of the ingredients for the EMP bath, but now I didn't want to take one anyway. It would be rude to Paul if I just disappeared upstairs for the better part of an hour. So I did what I said I would do: I took a quick shower, and for the life of me I can't remember whether it was hot, cold, or somewhere in between, because my mind was somewhere else entirely.

I wasn't faced with a world that was different from the previous one, was I? The world, awful as it was, didn't change this time. Instead, it was *me* who was different—and flashing through my life with this new lens wasn't easy. All the lies I had told, all the things I'd pretended to be. And shame. Not shame for being gay, but shame for being unable to embrace it. Too much of a coward to say it out loud.

"Someday you'll be ready," Paul had told me. "You'll come out at your own speed, and that's okay. Everyone has to do it on their own terms." And then he had added, "When you come out, I will, too."

Which just reinforced the fact that I was the one holding him back, even though he didn't see it that way.

When I came downstairs—wearing jeans and a shirt that Paul once said looked good on me—Paul was sitting with Hunter in the family room, watching TV. Some sitcom that I don't think existed in the world I started from, but just as unfunny as most of the ones that did.

"Why are you just standing there?" asked Hunter. "You're freaking me out."

So I sat down next to Paul, obsessively aware of the buffer zone I put between us as we watched bad TV.

There's something to be said about the communal experience of staring at a screen and allowing it to collectively empty your minds. It didn't exactly unscramble my thoughts and emotions, but it numbed them just a little. It was comforting just silently sitting next to my brother and my boyfriend—and yeah, I'll say the B-word now, even though I wouldn't say it then.

"Are you staying over, Paul?" my mother asked, half an hour later. "Should I make up one of the guest rooms?" It was less of an invitation than my mom's polite way of suggesting that it was time to leave.

Paul tossed me a poker-faced glance and said, "Naah, I'd better get home."

Other friends often did avail themselves of the guest room option, but never Paul. Maybe he was always waiting for *me* to make the invitation—but I never had. The thought of him just down the hall would keep me up all night.

As I thought of this, my straight self surfaced for a moment and groaned with mournful nostalgia for the girls I'd dated, or at least fantasized about, and all the desires that had dropped off this new, unfamiliar horizon. I remembered what it felt like, but the actual feeling was gone. It was like I had taken one of those Mberries that totally altered your taste buds, but instead of just your sense of taste, the change went down to your very nature. What used to be bitter was now sweet, and what was once sweet had no flavor at all.

As I saw Paul to the door, he said, "You're still looking kind of off. You sure you're okay?"

"Just tired," I told him. "I'll be fine."

"So . . . math on Sunday?" he asked. "Usual time?"

I offered him a slight grin. In all worlds Paul tutored me on Sundays. Even here, those sessions were actually about math.

"See you then," I told him. We fist-bumped a goodbye but held our knuckles together longer than a fist bump usually lasts. It's amazing how much your knuckles can feel when you really want them to. Then he went to his car and I closed the door behind him, the old part of me relieved, and the new part already missing him.

There are a great many things I don't understand. I'm sure it's the same for you. No matter how smart we think we are, we simply can't know all there is to know—and if you spend all your time thinking about those things, it will drive you crazy.

Mostly, we're okay with the things we don't get. We shrug our shoulders, accept the mystery, and move on.

But not everyone's like that. There are people who are so threatened by things they don't understand that they feel a need to stomp them out. They have to crush them so that each thing killed is one less thing to tax their brain. It's the force behind war, behind genocide, behind the worst things that human beings are capable of.

It's also the cause of the small injustices we come across every single day.

My dad once told me a story about his father. How, when his dad was little, he would naturally pick up crayons with his left hand. But then he had an old-school teacher in first grade, and I mean "old-school" in the true sense. When she caught him putting a crayon in his left hand, she would smack it painfully with a ruler and make him switch to his right hand. Left-handedness was shameful and wrong. Conformity was the solution.

But you know what? He still played sports left-handed. His sport was baseball, and as a baseball player, being a lefty was a highly valued trait. But his handwriting was the worst, and he developed a stutter the same year he was forced to switch hands in school. Don't tell me that those things aren't related.

Did you know that in the Dark Ages, people who used their left hand were considered evil and even satanic? The word "sinister" is Latin for left, the devil is portrayed as left-handed, and in the Dark Ages, southpaws were accused of witchcraft and put to death. Can you imagine a world so ignorant?

Yeah, sadly, you can—because even though the particulars change, ignorance is a cockroach you can't kill no matter how hard you try. It hides in dark, fetid places, then darts out into the open.

Which brings me to the situation I now found myself in.

Intellectually, I thought I knew what being gay meant.

Same-sex attraction. Simple, right? It's part of who you are, like your handedness, or the color of your eyes. But I wasn't seeing the whole picture—the whole *person*—because for so many, it's not a *part* of who you are, it's right there at the core, *defining* who you are. How much more horrifying, then, when someone rejects you at your very core?

And so you end up with two choices. Either you embrace it and demand that people accept you for who you truly are . . . or you live your life in silent desperation, hiding it from the light, or even denying it to yourself. Not a way anyone should have to live. But there are still plenty of witch-burners out there—and some of them are in our own heads.

Back in my old world—my original one—I always considered myself a tolerant person and tried to distance myself from those who weren't—although sometimes I would rationalize the intolerance of friends and look the other way. You know how when a friend says a joke that maybe shouldn't have been said? Rather than calling them out on it, you let it go. Pretend it doesn't matter.

But it does matter. And you know it.

I will admit—and shamefully so—that I would ignore it when a friend smirked about one of the openly gay kids at school, or said something like "That's so gay." I didn't join in, but I didn't discourage it either. I just let it go. And as my memories of this new world flooded me, I realized that I'd done the same thing here—but for a different reason. Here, I was afraid that speaking up would out me. Which meant that in this world, I was one of those people living in silent desperation.

And then there was Katie. How did Katie figure into all of this? My new memories told me that she did figure, but not the way she used to. In this world, we also had that secret conversation beneath the bleachers, but here, I didn't kiss her. Our history in this world was similar, but none of it was sexually charged. I thought of Leo, whose reality was still as screwed up as it was yesterday. Would I somehow relate to him differently now? I would have to feel my way through the nuances of this place piece by piece, person by person.

In the morning I paid a visit to the Edwards. As I said, there was a fourth one now. We'll call him Eduardo.

"I guess our secret's out," Eduardo said. "We're not actually brothers."

"So then what the hell are you?" I asked, although I was beginning to suspect the answer.

"We're the same person," Ed told me. "Just from four different space-time continuums."

Apparently, each shift produced a new Edward, with his own skateboard that wasn't a skateboard, and his own attitude, too, since they all bickered and disagreed on a regular basis.

Eduardo, who knew everything about this world, had been up all night with Eddy, comparing notes, trying to determine how this world was different from the previous one, because it seemed identical. They had no clue until I showed up to tell them. They were tickled by the news.

"Wow! So you absorbed the entire change yourself?"

"Yeah, pretty much."

"And it affected the nature of your sexuality?"

"More than affected it."

"That's incredible!"

"Yeah, tell me about it."

The Edwards were entirely nonsexual beings, so they had limited empathy for my current situation.

"Six of one, half dozen of another," they said. "No big deal."

Eddy and Eduardo went to the QuIRT, and, in light of the new information, did some fresh calculations.

"This is an amazing thing you've done," Eduardo said. "Entirely different from your previous shifts. This time you took complete control!"

The others agreed—even Edd, who said, "I will admit this wasn't an entire disaster."

"It's a major step in the right direction," Ed said. "If you had allowed it to pass around you, rather than into you, there's a good chance the sexual orientation of all humanity would have flipped."

"That would've been interesting," Eddy said.

Edd furrowed his brow. "It's normal for up to ten percent of an evolved population to have primary same-sex attraction—if it wasn't a natural thing, it wouldn't exist—but flip that, and you have only ten percent or less of the population attracted to the opposite sex. Major ramifications there."

"Life always finds a way," Eduardo pointed out.

"True," said Edd, "but it would be a very different social dynamic."

"Well," said Eddy, "I would've liked to have seen it."

I was losing patience quickly. "Maybe another lifetime," I told them. "But right now, let's focus on the reason why we're all here: getting everything back to the way it was. Including me."

Eduardo took a long look at me. "Personal changes are hard to undo," he said. "If you were able to get the world back to the way it started, but you remained this way, would that be acceptable to you?"

Part of me screamed *yes*, part of me screamed *no*, so I sidestepped the question. "What matters most is that everything *else* gets undone."

"That's very noble of you," said Ed. "Putting the needs of the world before your own."

I didn't feel all that noble. I just felt lost. "I . . . I don't know how to navigate this world," I confided. "The thought of going back to school on Monday . . . I can't even imagine what it will be like."

Ed put a comforting hand on my shoulder. "Hey, don't forget that you have all the memories of this world, Ash. You just need to integrate who you are now into who you were. But in the end, you're still you."

"You've just had a makeover," suggested Eduardo.

"More like a make-under," Eddy said.

"Don't hide from it," said Ed. "Experience it. Experiencing your lives is the most important thing you can do."

14

HERE'S THE THING...

"Did it happen? I've been texting you since last night."

Katie called just as I was driving away from the Edwards'. It wasn't that I was avoiding talking to her, it's just that I was avoiding talking to her.

"I had my phone off," I told her, which was true. It was off because I knew she'd be trying to reach me.

"So something *did* happen!"

"Sort of."

She took that as a yes. "Okay—meet me at the public library at noon."

"Why there?"

"Because it's the one place in town where I know I won't run into Layton."

◆ ◆ ◆

The library had a nonsegregation policy. Anyone could sit any-where they wanted. Unfortunately people tended to bring their predispositions with them, so tables often seemed to divide by race, regardless of policy. Something that often happened in my world, too. When I got there, I was surprised to see that it wasn't just Katie. Leo was also there. Katie had managed to find him on her own.

"Sit down, Ash," said Katie.

I sat across from them. Some old guy at another table gave us a glance from behind his newspaper. I couldn't tell whether the glance was judgmental or just a glance. A moment later, he left. I couldn't tell if he left because he didn't approve of the three of us together, or if he just felt it was time to go. That's the maddening thing about racism. Sometimes you just don't know.

"Leo and I have been having a good talk," she said. "About Angela . . . about everything."

"She helped me remember stuff," said Leo. "Like being on the team with you. Playing football with the football star's son."

"Yeah, well my dad wasn't a football star where I come from."

"Too bad," said Leo.

"Not really."

The fact that they had been talking about this without me present was a good thing. Three heads were better than one, and with both of them on board, I didn't feel so alone.

"So how did the world change?" said Katie. "Out with it."

Interesting choice of words. "The *world* didn't exactly change," I told them.

"Bro, it's a yes or no question," Leo said. "Either it did or it didn't."

"Okay, yes. Yes, there was a change."

"And?" prompted Katie.

I took a moment to look at each of them and realized there was just no way around this. So I just told them.

"I'm gay."

Katie continued to look at me, as if there'd be more. "And?"

"There is no 'and.' That's it."

"Ash," she said, with an impish grin, "that's not really a surprise . . ."

Leo, who didn't know me at all in this world, had the wisdom to stay quiet and just let this play out between me and Katie.

"Wait—you already knew?" I asked her.

"I suspected."

I scrolled back through my memories of this world. I thought I had done a pretty good job keeping it on the down-low. "How'd you know?"

"Well . . . maybe because you only dated 'safe' girls. And how, at parties, the way you'd always strike up conversations with good-looking guys."

"I was just being social!" I insisted.

"Right. Anyway, if you're worried about being outed, don't," said Katie. "I'm probably the only one who noticed. Most people are too much into themselves to see things like that."

And then something occurred to me. The reason why Katie was aware, when others weren't. "You noticed because . . . you were interested in me?"

"Maybe," she said. "But that's moot now, isn't it?"

I took a deep breath. "In the other worlds it wouldn't have been moot." And then I told her. "In the last world we kissed."

She took a moment. Maybe she remembered something of that kiss, maybe not, but after thinking about it, she said, "I'm sure that created a whole lot of problems that I'm glad we don't have to deal with right now." And she was absolutely right.

Through all of this, Leo sat back, absorbing. Finally he shook his head and laughed. "So let me get this straight: the big jock football lineman, whose famous father is T-ville's favorite son . . . is gay."

"Yeah," I said, getting defensive. "You got a problem with that?"

Leo put up his hands. "Hell no, I got no problem. I just wanna be at a safe distance, but with a good view, when you come out—because those'll be some kick-ass fireworks."

Which brought Katie to her next question. "Do your parents know?"

"My parents here are very self-absorbed, like those other kids you were talking about. They don't notice much of anything when it comes to me and my brother. Totally oblivious." And it occurred to me that I was one of those oblivious people, too—or at least I had been before the world started changing.

"Parents are rarely as clueless as they seem," Katie advised. It made me a little uncomfortable to think that she might be right.

"Yeah," seconded Leo, "and when it comes to shit about you, they mostly worry A) Are you okay? and B) How does it affect them? But not necessarily in that order."

◆ ◆ ◆

For the next few days, I took the Edwards' advice, and let myself fearlessly experience the make-under.

It started with going to Paul's house on Sunday to work on math. I couldn't deny the excitement I felt simply arriving at his door, but kept it all inside. Although maybe I rang the bell one too many times.

"Hey," he said as he answered the door, much sweatier than I expected him to be. "Tennis with my dad. Just got back."

"Hi, Ash," his dad said from back in the kitchen. He looked much worse than Paul, as he guzzled a glass of ice water.

"Hi, Mr. Fisher. Looks like Paul ran you all over the court," I commented.

"That he did."

Then Paul, taking a step toward the stairs, said, as casually as can be, "Gotta hit the shower. Wanna come with?"

And it's like I imploded. I felt my ears and nose going red hot. "No. Uh . . . No," I stammered. "I'll just . . . uh . . . wait down here." I looked toward the kitchen. Mr. Fisher was no longer in view when Paul said it, but was he in earshot? What about his mom? I hadn't seen her yet. Either of them might have heard it.

Seeing my reaction, Paul stopped and turned around with a long-suffering smirk. "I'm sorry," he said quietly. "It was a joke."

And even more quietly, I said, "It's not a joke if you secretly mean it."

"But it *is* a joke," he argued, "because *you* know that *I* know that there's no universe in which you'd come upstairs with my whole family here."

I didn't even realize I had another nerve to hit. "Universe? What do you mean, *universe*?"

He chuckled, and I realized it was just an innocent figure of speech. "Ash, you are very weird," he said. "And I like it."

And he was gone to take his shower.

The thing is, Paul would often joke like this—in such an offhand way that nobody but me would ever give it a second thought. He liked to see me squirm—but only because he knew I kinda liked squirming a little. Yet as tempted as I was by that dangerous edge, I didn't do well looking over it.

I looked around one more time. No one there. I could hear his father on the phone somewhere else in the house. Paul hadn't come out to his parents, but he was pretty sure they knew. Did that mean they knew about me, too? Indirectly, like the way Katie knew? And if they did, and were okay with it, shouldn't *I* be okay with *them* being okay? Still, just thinking about it made me tense.

"It's like you're always on the field, toeing the line, waiting for the snap," Paul once told me. Then he had hooked his finger on my shorts and snapped the waistband. Right in the school hallway. And I squirmed and got mad and kind of liked it.

Man, these memories! I caught myself grinning, then cringing, then grinning again, as I sat in the living room waiting for Paul to come back down. I was letting in more and more bits and pieces of this world, allowing them to ricochet around my brain. Not just stuff with Paul, but of my whole life here. How it was mostly the same, and yet entirely different. I could remember the same life events, the same parties, but recalled other things about them. All those things that struck me enough to lodge in my long-term memory. A conversation. A look. And I understood how, through everything, I kept myself so protected. That core of who I was. I held it close like a quarterback, terrified I'd fumble. Like fragile china in layers of bubble wrap. No one got to see it, so no one could break it. And Paul? He was the mischievous hand popping those layers one bubble at a time. I wondered what would happen when they were all gone.

This is how the old me and the even older me came to know the new me. While the Edwards kept dividing and separating, I had to do the opposite, and try to blend multiple selves into a singular "I." There were parts that had to be subdued. Quelled. I'm talking about the parts that dealt drugs and treated people like shit. But this part—this *queer* part—I didn't want to silence at all. I mean, I didn't want to go skipping on rainbows with it either, but getting to know it—getting to know *him*—wasn't a bad thing. I was learning to be okay in my own skin. That's more than I could say about the original me.

When Paul came down, we worked on math—and I got it, because Paul was a much better teacher than my actual teacher. Or maybe it was just that everything he said always made sense, regardless of the subject. Afterwards we hung out watching a game with his dad. Whenever we watched a game together, we did this thing where we bumped hands in the chip bowl. First time it was an accident, but now it was like the fist bump. Something we shared that no one could come between.

Later, when his parents went out for dinner, we got closer on the sofa, leaning into each other. And that was it. Just quiet closeness—because between Paul and me, it wasn't just about the obvious stuff you might be thinking in your dirty little mind. More than any of that, it was about connection. It was about being close to someone you wanted to be with.

The straight me didn't have a real handle on the concept of "connection" yet. In my original world, I had dated a lot of girls. Last year I had been with Amy Anders for most of the school year, before she bailed on me and went for the captain of the goddamn debate team. I figured he had won her over with a persuasive argument. But now, I'm thinking maybe it was because I had never really let her in. I never forged that connection. If I ever got back to my old world and returned to my old self, I wanted to take that feeling of connection with me—and maybe I would find it there. Maybe with Katie.

But if that happened, I'd lose what I had with Paul—and even though I never asked for this, the thought of losing it was like an open wound.

Maybe Paul could tell my mind was in troubled places, or maybe my eyes had gotten a little moist, because he shifted to get a better look at me and said, "What are you thinking about?"

The word that came to mind only made sense to me after I said it out loud.

"Home . . . ," I told him.

"You have to go?"

"No," I explained. "Here. With you. Feels like home."

He shifted. Maybe a little uncomfortably. At the time I didn't know why. "Can't live here," he quipped. "Not enough room. Maybe under my bed, though."

I grinned. "Wouldn't fit. Your closet, maybe." It was an implication you could have driven a bus through, and yet I missed it.

But Paul didn't. He laughed, and said, "I'm sure yours has a lot more room—what with your mansion and all."

School on Monday was, like everything else, different and the same. Walking down the hallway at school, I noticed people I had never noticed in my previous incarnations—and found others with whom I'd never had a problem to be vapid and irritating.

My friends in this world were mostly the same as the last one. That had to do with familiarity, but also keeping up appearances. I had some new friends, though. They were guys and girls who I admired. The ones who stood up for things and who weren't afraid to speak their minds. The ones with all the qualities I wish I had. And then there were the friends that were still just plain gone because of the color of their skin, and that was the hardest thing to face . . .

. . . Which brings me to the SAS Club. The meeting during lunch helped to remind me what was at stake beyond just my own wants and desires. So many people have no interest in change unless it directly affects them. I couldn't be one of those people anymore. Besides, after my father's play against me at Friday's game, now more than ever, I wanted to defy him, to stand up for what I knew to be right. See, in my old world, my dad had been knocked down a few notches by life. Maybe he saw himself as a failure, although I never had. But here, his success had given him a nasty arrogance. Here, he was a bully. I wondered if he had been that way when he was my age—but had been humbled, instead of being rewarded for it. It's a fine line between being the hammer and the nail.

Paul was there when I arrived at the meeting. I sat next to him and pulled out my notebook.

"Did I miss anything?" I asked.

"They're arguing about the playlist for the dance."

The integration dance was still being attributed to me. The gym had been reserved for a Wednesday in November, and the administration supported it. It was hard for me to get excited about an event that seemed more about making the club feel good about itself than actually about doing something meaningful. Not only didn't they see the big picture, they didn't even know there was a picture to see.

"You should pick some songs," I suggested to Paul, "or it'll end up being nothing but Amber Wave and Wunderbred."

"I thought you liked Amber Wave?"

I just shrugged and grunted. Yes, I had memories of liking them—but those fell into the *must be quelled* category. I could have given our club leaders one hell of a playlist; unfortunately the songs I'd give didn't exist anywhere but in my head now.

Thinking about that reminded me of the more important list I was making. I flipped my notebook open, tapped my pen for a few seconds, and added some names.

Nadir Williams . . .

Freddie King . . .

Kamisha Hicks . . .

"Who are they?" Paul asked.

"Just people we should invite to the dance."

He looked a little confused. "Do I know any of them?"

I sidestepped the question. "They don't go here," I told him. *But they used to,* I wanted to say.

Lynnell Wilson . . .

Keagan Fry . . .

It was my friends and classmates of color from my original world. I had to believe they were still here, just like Leo was. Maybe he knew them.

Mateo Zuñiga . . .

Roberto Guzman . . .

Luz Delgado . . .

While I might find the Black kids across town, there was little hope of finding the Latinx ones. They had other lives in other places, denied "the American Dream" in a very different way.

Paul didn't ask any more questions or comment further on my list. He wasn't being all that talkative today. At the time I figured he was just listening to the main conversation.

Everyone was put in charge of something. I volunteered to spread the word in the Black community, hoping that Leo might help me. It all felt like play-acting, though, because if the world reset, none of it would happen. Paul was put in charge of finances. Again, he seemed distracted and muted when he accepted the position. Again, I thought nothing of it. But later that day I was blindsided by something that I should have seen coming.

"Ash, can we talk?"

Paul caught me at my locker at the end of the day.

"Yeah, sure," I said, "what about?"

"About us."

I looked around to see if anyone was listening. It was a reflex. There were plenty of others in the hallway. They all seemed to be into their own business, but still . . .

"You want to talk about that here?"

"Yeah," he said, "I do."

And before I could ask him to save it for a more private time and place, he went on. "Yesterday when you said all that about being 'home,' I couldn't stop thinking about it."

"Me neither," I told him.

"But home isn't where the heart is, Ash. It's where you choose to be. How can you ever be home, if you're pretending you're somewhere else?"

"I know what I felt," I said, as quietly as I could. "I know what I *feel*."

He sighed. "Ash, here's the thing . . ."

And that's when I knew. I knew everything he was about to

say. Because no matter who you are, or who you're dating—no matter who you might be in love with—"Here's the thing . . ." is a phrase that has only one outcome.

"Ash, your life is all laid out for you. A big football college like your father, an NFL team like your father—and even if you don't get that far, your life is going in a direction that mine isn't."

"Wh . . . What are you talking about?" I stammered. "You get good grades. Whatever you do, you're gonna be successful."

"That's not what I'm talking about . . ."

And then it hit me what he meant. I had no comeback line for it.

"You're never coming out, Ash," he said. "You know it as well as I do. Your life's gonna be about secret 'buds' and passing for straight. If that's the life you choose, hey, I won't judge, it's your choice to make . . . but it's not what *I* want."

I felt something welling up inside of me. Something powerful. I couldn't remember the last time I felt it. It was loss. The loss of something so important to me, it was unfathomable. Did I say I *thought* I loved Paul? Who was I kidding? I did. I do.

"I'm joining the LGBTQ Alliance," he said. "I'm joining, and I'm coming out. I thought you should know, so you could distance yourself before I did."

Tears were building—I couldn't stop them. "Why would I want to distance myself from you?"

I could tell that my tears were triggering his, but he wiped them away before they could fall. "Be honest with yourself, Ash—at least about that."

And he was right. My brain was already running scenarios and escape routes. All the smoke and mirrors I would use to deflect attention when Paul came out. How I'd act all supportive, because it was the right thing to do—but from a distance.

Paul thought he had me pegged. Maybe he did. On the other hand, maybe not—because what came next erupted from a place in me I didn't even know existed. And maybe it didn't exist before, in any of the worlds I inhabited. Maybe it only came into being because of the way I now straddled the goddamn multiverse.

I turned to look around us. Lockers opening and closing. Crowded hallway. Good.

"Excuse me," I said to the hallway, and when no one turned, I shouted it. *"Excuse me! I have something to say!"*

Paul's eyes went wide. "Ash, what are you doing?"

But if I answered him, I knew I'd lose my nerve.

The crowd was now looking to me curiously, expectantly.

"You all know who I am, right?" I said—because lately, rather than just being some guy on the football team, I've been *the* guy on the football team. I didn't have to say my name, because they all knew it.

I glanced back at Paul. "You don't have to do this," he said quietly. If he really and truly wanted me to stop, I would have . . . but I saw the slightest grin of anticipation on his face. The good squirm.

I looked around, meeting various eyes in the crowd to make sure I had their attention. "I want you all to listen very carefully," I said. And, since actions speak louder than words, I turned to Paul, and planted one on him that was even better than the kiss at my front door.

The crowd around us gasped and tittered and whispered. Someone pulled out a phone and held it up, capturing the moment. Maybe I should have cared, but I didn't. The part of me that wanted to grab the phone and smash it was otherwise occupied.

I broke off the kiss and turned to the astonished onlookers. Some of them were actually applauding. Others were gawking. And yet others were grinning like it was all very amusing.

"Now go," I told them. "Talk amongst yourselves, gossip, tweet, alert the media—do whatever the fuck you want, I won't stop you."

And then, from out of the crowd stepped Norris, looking like he had just witnessed his home disappear into a sinkhole. I hadn't known he was there, but what did it matter? If I had known I would have done it anyway.

"Dude, say it isn't so . . ."

"It's so," I told him. "Either you're good with it, or you can get the hell out of here."

I probably don't have to tell you that he chose the latter. He turned and toddled off, slowly shaking his head like a bull struck by a car.

I looked back to Paul, who was more than a little bit dazed by the total detonation of my big walk-in closet.

"That," he said, smiling, "may have been the dumbest thing you've ever done."

"Yeah, probably," I admitted. I put up my hand for a fist bump, but then opened my fingers at the last second, and intertwined them with his.

And just like that, my world had changed again.

15

COUNTING COWS

I used to rarely skip football practice. It's a cardinal rule that unless you've been abducted by aliens, or have been pronounced dead, you don't skip practice. But I did today. I couldn't deal with the prospect of two dozen Norrises gaping at me in disbelief. Instead I drove Paul home.

"This is not how I expected this day would go," said Paul, as we neared his street.

"Are you sorry?" I asked.

It took a moment for him to answer. "I thought I was losing you today. I'm glad I didn't. More than glad. Even so, this is uncharted territory for me."

"Me, too," I told him. "I guess we'll chart it together."

He smiled and gave me a quick peck as he got out, and I drove home.

I was terrified of what would come next, but maybe a little excited, too, and a little relieved—or at least looking forward to the moment I could actually feel relieved. Mostly what I felt was dread. An abiding sense of impending doom, like when you total your parents' new car that you weren't supposed to be driving. My head was pounding, but it wasn't an interdimensional headache, it was a real one. Of all the situations I ever thought I might be facing in my life, the original me couldn't even have imagined this being one of them.

When I got home, I drew myself an EMP bath, even though I didn't really need one, and waited for the sky to fall.

It only took about an hour.

Through the magic of social media, the news went schoolwide and beyond in minutes. Someone told my parents—probably anonymously—about the video of me and Paul kissing. That video had already been posted and reposted until it was in so many places, it was the first thing that came up on Google when you entered the words "gay locker kiss."

I want to be able to tell you that my parents surprised me with their reaction. That they were accepting and open-minded and we had a group hug and they told me it was all going to be okay. That does happen sometimes. I know it does. But it didn't happen here.

They called me downstairs just after I had gotten out of the bath. Both of them had come home early. They didn't make small talk or beat around the bush. They told me to sit down. I told them I preferred to stand. They asked me to explain the video. I explained it honestly. They asked me if I was serious. I told them I was. They asked me if I was sure. I told them it was a stupid question. After that, my father paced the kitchen and my mother stood at the granite island, looking down into her cup of coffee. Occasionally she would glance up at me with burdened eyes, as if, when she looked at me, all she could see were her unborn grandchildren dying before her eyes.

It turns out my father had a plan of action.

"You're going to fix this," he said. "You're going to tell everyone that the video was a prank."

"It wasn't a prank."

"I don't care. You'll tell people that it was."

"Why would I do that?"

"Do you want the entire school—your entire team—to think you're gay?"

"I *am* gay," I pointed out.

"Stop saying that."

"Just because I don't say it, that doesn't make it any less true."

"I just . . . I just don't want to hear it, okay? Not today. Not right now." But of course what he really meant was "not ever."

Then my mom spoke up. "Honey, you've had a lot of time to come to terms with this," she said to me. "You can't expect us to get there in a single day."

My father's phone vibrated, and he took his frustration out on it, hurling the defenseless iPhone into the family room, where it skidded on the coffee table, right between two porcelain candlesticks, and onto the floor.

"Goal," I said flatly. No one was amused.

"Do you have any idea what this means for you?" my father said.

"I get the feeling you're more worried about what it means for *you*."

"Ash, you're being unfair," said my mother.

I heard a creak, and turned to see Hunter sitting on the stairs, watching. I tried to figure out how much he'd heard, then realized it didn't take much to know the gist of things. He'd already heard all he needed to hear—maybe he had even seen the video, too. My parents demanded he go upstairs to his room. He grumbled, but left.

Once Hunter was gone, Dad sat down, took a long, slow breath, and looked at my mom. *So what do we do now?* said his gaze, but he didn't speak the words. I didn't catch what my mom gazed back. Then she turned to me.

"I want you to stay away from that boy," she said. And here I thought she was being the sympathetic one. It made me furious, but I didn't yell. That would have only made things worse. I had to stay calm and exist within the shell shock of it all.

"That boy has a name," I said. "And it's not like he did this to me—you can't blame Paul."

"You know what?" said my dad. "It doesn't matter anymore. Do whatever the hell you want. Be with whoever the hell you want. Go take a goat to homecoming for all I care."

"Robert, enough!" said my mom.

It was a horrible thing for him to say, but the good thing

about shell shock is that you don't feel things in the moment. You just feel them later. It was then that I made a poignant and important observation.

"No offense, Dad . . . but you're a fucking asshole."

I thought that would set him off, but it didn't. He didn't even deny the charge.

"You've set yourself on a difficult path, Ash," he said. "I hope you're ready for it."

And that was it. At least for now. My parents had nothing more to say to me, and I had nothing to say to them. It could have gone better, but, as bad as it was, it could have gone worse. As I went upstairs, I found myself wondering how the original versions of them would have reacted. Then I remembered that in my original world, we never would have had this conversation. Maybe I should have just told them that we used to be in an alternate universe where I was an all-American vagina-loving straight boy. They would have thought I was nuts, of course, but maybe I could have planted the idea in their heads, the way I had with Katie and Leo. But you know what? I didn't want to give them the satisfaction. It's their job in *all* universes to support me whoever I am, and whatever I'm feeling, no matter who I'm feeling it for. They didn't deserve to know there was a place where things were different.

I passed Hunter's room on my way to mine. He was lying on his bed, looking at the ceiling.

"How many?" he asked me, when he saw me lingering by his door.

"How many what?"

"How many cows did Mom and Dad have? Because I figure if they had enough, we could open a dairy."

That made me laugh. I didn't think anything could make me laugh today. Leave it to new-world Hunter.

"So, are you okay with this?" I asked him.

He sat up. "Are you gonna leave?"

"No—why would I leave?"

"When Zach Tyner's sister came out, she moved to Portland."

"Don't worry, I'm not moving to Portland."

"I'd visit you if you did."

I offered him a slim smile. "You're a good brother, Hunter."

He looked me over. "So, if you're gay, how come you have such bad fashion sense?"

When your world changes in the normal way—and by normal I mean in a way that leaves you in the same universe—there's a sort of numbness that comes over you after the initial shock. It's a protective numbness, I think.

Unlike shifting between universes, when you've had a non-supernatural kind of change, such as outing yourself, everyone knows it—or at least it feels like everyone does. You find yourself acting like you're the center of the universe, even though you're not. You walk through hallways at school, thinking every giggle, every whisper, is about you, and each glance from people you pass is because they know about your Big Change. Your paradigm shift. And everyone who doesn't make eye contact with you must be intentionally ignoring you.

That's how it was for me when I got to school on Tuesday morning—and although part of me knew that a lot of people either were not aware or couldn't care less about my self-outing yesterday, I was incapable of making the paranoid part of me believe it.

There were some people who clearly knew, though—which, in retrospect, was probably about one-third of the people I thought did. Some were kind, some were cruel, and some were in between.

Before I got to my locker a few people came up to me. A girl I knew, but whose name I didn't, said, "That was really brave of you, Ash." I thanked her without giving away the fact that I couldn't remember her name, then made a mental note to find out her name, just because.

Then there were the unpleasant comments. No one said them to me directly, but they were spoken between friends, and loudly enough to make sure I heard.

"He oughta change his football position to tight end," I heard someone say—as if he actually believed that was clever and original.

Another kid who overheard turned to me and said, "Don't waste your energy on them. Losers will be losers."

It was good advice, but it burned me to just let the guy get away with it. I have always tended toward a quick temper. My parents often advised me that I needed to pick my battles— funny because that advice was most useful against them. I realized that today was a pick-your-battle sort of day. So I let the snide comments roll off my back—but I also kept track of who uttered them, because I am not above payback when the opportunity presents itself.

Through all of this, I didn't see Paul. I wondered if he decided to stay home today. I almost did—but I knew my absence would be conspicuous. Besides, if people are gonna talk behind my back, I'd rather they do it in front of my face.

Josh Easley—the wide receiver who had taken Leo's place as my best friend—came up to me while I was at my locker, just before first period.

"So is it true?" he asked. "Or is it a stunt? Because *your* dad told *my* dad it was just a stunt."

It pissed me off that my father was trying to create spin on the situation—but then, maybe he did it before our conversation last night.

"It wasn't a stunt," I told Josh.

He nodded. "I didn't think so." Then he looked at me, with a kind of searching expression on his face. "So . . . are we still friends?"

It struck me as odd that he'd think we weren't. "Yeah," I said. "Of course."

He was relieved. "Okay, good." Then he left before it could become any more awkward than it already was. All this time I had resented him for taking Leo's place in my life—but even here, I had chosen my best friend well. It made me a little sad to think that Josh might not even exist in the world I was trying to get back to.

◆ ◆ ◆

I was called out of third period to go to the school counselor's office. It came over the classroom's PA system. Exactly what you want to do: draw attention to the last guy in class to want attention, for the one thing he doesn't want attention drawn to.

Ms. Metts, our school counselor, sat me down, gave me a look that was supposed to be comforting but just felt creepy, and told me she was aware of what happened yesterday—big surprise. Then she began asking questions that were more annoying than the ones on the history quiz she had pulled me out of. *How do you feel?* Fine. *Do you need to talk?* No. *Have you spoken with your parents about this?* Yes. *Are they being supportive?* I'll get back to you on that.

When it became clear that she'd get nothing of substance out of me, she handed me a bunch of full-color pamphlets with headings like "Embracing YOU!" and sent me back to class.

I knew the big challenge of the day would be lunch. I was dreading it, because more than hallways and classrooms, the cafeteria was all about social dynamics. I didn't even know where I should sit. Should I join my usual group, or would that be too uncomfortable? Should I seek out the LGBTQ clique and sit with them? Or should I sit by myself, as I had been lately, and see who made a point of coming over? Then I saw Paul. Turns out he was late today, avoiding the hallway gauntlet before first period. It looked like Paul had made that last choice of sitting by himself, so I went to sit with him. He didn't seem all that comfortable when I sat down across from him, though.

"You want me to go?" I asked.

"No," he said. "No, of course not." Then he added, "Just...just no public displays of affection today, okay? At least not here."

I wasn't planning on any, but it irked me a bit to hear him say that. "Weren't you the one who wanted to come out?" I reminded him. "Weren't you the one ready to break up with me because you thought I wasn't ready to?"

"Yes," he admitted. "But I didn't think me coming out would be a major public event. Now it's like I'm what's-her-face who married the prince."

"Naah," I said. "I'm no prince. At best I'm like...the Douche of Windsor."

He laughed at that. Someone had to.

"Ash, there's a difference between being out, and being *OUT*. You didn't give me a choice! Just because I was ready to go through that door doesn't mean I wanted you to kick it open."

"So are you mad at me?"

"Yeah, I am," he said, without hesitating. And then he added, "But I'm crazy-proud of you, too. Those two feelings are stuck together now. You and I are going to have to deal with that for a while."

A few people who saw us together came over to give their support, which we accepted graciously—but I could tell that, like me, Paul just wished they would stop. It reminded me of this kid in middle school, who went to a weight loss camp over the summer and came back twenty pounds lighter. Everyone kept going up to him commenting on how good he looked to the point that it was just plain embarrassing.

I spared a glance over at my usual table. Norris and Layton and a few others. I'm sure that Josh was trying to intercede for me there. He didn't have to—I didn't want him to—but I'm sure he was doing it anyway. If this had happened in my old world, Leo would have done the same. But then, this wouldn't have happened in my old world. I shook my head to stop my brain from spiraling into a multidimensional feedback loop.

"Did you get called in by Metts too?" I asked Paul.

He sighed and pulled a crumpled pamphlet out of his pocket. This one was all about STDs and had the heading "Protecting YOU!" It seemed all the pamphlets featured the word "YOU" prominently. I guess just in case you started to feel like this was all happening to someone else.

"She's just doing her job, I guess," Paul said.

I thought we'd get through lunch unscathed, but toward the end, Layton came over with Katie in tow. Layton sat down right next to me like he was suddenly my best friend—because now it was clear that I wasn't competing for Katie's affection. It just made me dislike him even more, which I didn't think was even possible. Katie sat down as well, offering Paul a warm, understanding smile that was a million times more sincere than anything Layton was offering.

"Dudes," he said to both Paul and me. "I just wanted you to know that me and Katie are completely supportive of your relationship. In fact we've started to call the two of you AshPaul. You like that? AshPaul? I think it's kind of nice."

I cringed, Paul looked at me like WTF, and Katie dislodged herself from Layton's grasp. "*We* haven't started calling them anything," Katie declared. "That was all you."

Layton grinned at her. "Do I detect some disapproval?" he said. "I thought you'd want me to be all empathetic."

"If you were really empathetic, you wouldn't be smirking," she said. Then she turned to me. "I'm really happy for you, Ash. I know it was a hard decision, and I want you to know that I'm one hundred percent behind you."

"So's Paul!" said Layton, like a fart out of his mouth.

Katie stormed off in exasperation and Layton went after her. "What? Whadd-I-do?"

Now it was Paul's turn to smirk. "Can you believe I had a crush on him in sixth grade? Until he swallowed a live goldfish and got parasites."

"I think the parasites won," I said. Our hands were close on the table. Paul nudged my pinkie with his, and I linked them. So much for no public displays.

"You okay?" I asked him.

He nodded, but it was a reluctant nod. "I know it'll all get better—I just wish I could sleep through this part."

"I'm down for that," I told him with a wink.

He gave me a semi-disgusted look. "You're as bad as Layton."

Football practice was fun-and-a-half.

Our coach gathered us on the field before practice. "All right," he said, in his outdoor voice, which I think was the only voice he had. "I am aware that we have a situation today. And, rather than let it fester, we're going to talk about it."

I forced myself not to visibly react. Like I said, I was still in a shell of protective numbness. But I did notice there were a few grunts of discomfort from the team.

"Do we gotta?" Norris asked.

"Yeah, we gotta," said the coach, mocking him, then returned his attention to the rest of us. "Your friend and teammate, Ash, has stepped forward with a major identity reveal this week." (*Major identity reveal.* God. I wondered how long he had struggled to come up with that one.) "I'm sure it wasn't easy, and we need to applaud him for doing it."

Then in the silence that followed, someone began a slow clap that was silenced by a glare from the coach. He pointed at the culprit and said, "That is exactly the kind of thing I will not tolerate. Ash is an important member of this team, and anyone—*anyone*—who gives him a hard time, I don't care who it is, is off the team."

I was actually impressed. Not every coach would make that kind of commitment. But I also hated the fact that he thought I needed institutional protection from my fellow meatheads.

Everyone shifted a bit, but kept their thoughts to themselves, both good and bad. Except for one kid. Dave Riggins. He existed in my original world but was cut from the team back when we were freshmen.

"What about the locker room?" he said.

"What about it?" asked the coach. He knew where Riggins

was going but wasn't going to let him get away without actually asking the question.

"I mean, what if I'm in there, and I'm feeling . . . what's the word . . . *objectified*?"

I took it upon myself to answer his question. "Don't worry, Riggins," I said. "I've seen the object you're talking about. Trust me, you don't have to worry."

That got a round of snickers and razzes.

"Yeah, yeah, very funny," Riggins said.

And that was that. The coach had set the ground rules, and the team would live by them. I think they were actually relieved.

Practice that day was the same as always, and then in the locker room nobody bothered me. You'll find this funny, but this new wrinkle in my life took up so much headspace that the bigger issue—the world-shifting one—had been pushed to my mind's back burner. I'd noticed that once I acclimated to a new reality, it became dominant. As if all of the other worlds were receding toward some mental horizon—and the further away a world got, the less real it seemed. There were times that I had to remind myself how many worlds away from home I actually was.

While I don't want to dwell on my grand out-fest any more than I already have, I think it's worth noting how things went that night at home. As I've said, since becoming rich, family dinners were a rare thing. It was the same that night—there was takeout that we all ate in our own bubbles, on our own schedules. But as I grabbed a plate of food from the kitchen, both Mom and Dad were there, and the lack of conversation, while typical on other days, felt conspicuous today. I couldn't stand it.

"Isn't anyone going to say anything?" I asked.

My father turned to me. He didn't seem angry, or judgmental, like I thought he might be; he just looked tired. "What do you want us to do, Ash?" he said. "Get out Hunter's guitar and sing 'Kumbaya'?"

To which I replied, "I . . . I don't even know what that is."

He sighed. "Listen," he said. "This is how things are now, and we'll all get used to it. We'll get used to it, and everything will be fine." Then he asked me if I had read the articles about "other football players like you," which he had forwarded to me. I'd been avoiding email, so I hadn't seen them yet, but I told him I'd read them.

"It's just to show you that you're in good company," he said, with actual enthusiasm.

"One thing's for sure," my mom said. "With something like this, you find out who your friends are . . . and who you wish *weren't* your friends."

I couldn't have said it better myself.

I might have just taken my plate and left after that, but I didn't. It was the way my father said "football players like you." He still couldn't bring himself to say the word "gay."

"I know you're disappointed in me," I told them. "There's nothing I can do about that."

They looked at each other, for a moment unsure of how to respond.

"No, Ash," Dad said. "I'd be disappointed in you if you

flunked out of school. I'd be disappointed in you if you went to a party and drove home drunk. I'd be disappointed if you went back to pretending like this thing you told us yesterday wasn't true."

"You mean like you wanted him to pretend?" my mother reminded him.

My dad sighed. "I needed to come to my senses." Then he added, "I'm still coming to my senses."

"Disappointment isn't about the things a person *is*," my mom said. "It's about the things they *do*."

I immediately thought about the fact that, even in this world, I was a bona fide drug dealer. They would definitely have been disappointed in me if they knew *that*. Which meant that, given the choice, they would rather me be gay than be a drug dealer. There had to be a way for me to take some twisted comfort in that, right? The problem was, in this world, I was both.

"I only have one thing to ask," Dad said. "Just please . . ." he said, "please don't bring Paul over."

I began to protest, but he put up his hand. "For now. For a while. Just give us time to get used to this."

"Will you?" I asked. "Get used to it?"

He took a moment to really weigh his response. "Yes," he said. "Because I won't accept the alternative."

The alternative, as we all knew, was when parents put up an emotional wall between themselves and their gay kid, removing themselves from that kid's life in every way that mattered. I'm glad that, when it came down to it, my parents were against building that wall.

"We'll invite Paul over for Thanksgiving," my mother announced.

My dad looked at her, considered it, then nodded. "Agreed. Thanksgiving."

"Great," said Hunter, who was, as always, listening in. "Can I bring my boyfriend, too?"

Both our parents froze in place until Hunter grinned and said, "Gotcha!" Then he high-fived me and went back upstairs.

I called Leo that night and told him about my two days of drama. He actually wanted to hear, and while I didn't want to talk to anyone else about it, I found myself spilling my guts to him. I'm not sure why. Maybe because he was a best friend I could talk to in another world, or maybe the opposite. Maybe it was because this version of Leo didn't even know me, so there was no history to make it awkward. In all worlds, Leo was a good listener—not just a pretend listener like a lot of people I know.

"I'll be at your game on Friday," he told me. "Even if I have to watch from the other side of the fence."

"You won't," I assured him, although I couldn't be sure. More reason to hit hard enough to get us all home.

I thought I had until Friday to prepare for whatever I might dive into next. I did not expect I'd be facing a Wednesday smackdown.

16

EXPUNGED, EXPELLED, AND OTHERWISE OBLITERATED

I had promised Hunter I would have the guts to stop selling, and I was true to my word. I hadn't sold a single illegal substance for more than a week. Whenever a regular customer came in asking, I said it was no longer available, and gave them a complimentary bottle of vitamins instead. And I had made sure to be at the store last week, when Ralston came by with his usual deliveries of both legitimate and illegitimate goods, so I could refuse the illegal stuff.

"Sorry, man," I told him. "I'm just selling standard supplements now." And I gave him back all the drugs he had left the week before.

"No exit strategy?" he asked.

"You exit," I told him. "That's my strategy."

He took the drugs and left without another word.

But this Wednesday he came back and had company. Two guys who looked like they had once played football but had graduated to a game that didn't involve protective padding.

When it comes to professional intimidators, the stereotype holds. I'm not sure if that's because it's correct, or because the intimidators wear the stereotype like a uniform. Regardless, these bullies-for-hire were parodies of themselves. The first one had an unpleasant smirk to let me know he was going to enjoy this. The other one had a scar on his face and a unibrow. I didn't know their names, and never will, so let's just call them Thing One and Thing Two.

I wasn't scared.

Okay, that's a lie—I *was* scared. I might have been able to take on one of them, but two was a definite problem. Escape would be my best option—and since my forte was breaking through an offensive line, I felt I had a fair shot. I just needed to choose my moment and go for it. We were in the alley behind the shop. I could go left or right. Having two directions doubled my chances of escape.

"Let me guess," I said to Ralston, "your 'associates' would like to have a word with me."

"They're not much for words," Ralston said. "And I want to remind you that this was not my call. It's a Powers-That-Be kind of thing." Then he cocked his head, thoughtfully. "Think of them as nukes. I don't have to light their asses on fire as long as you agree to get back with the program. No questions, and no more trouble."

But that wasn't going to happen, and we all knew it.

When I didn't back down, Ralston sighed. "Fine," he said. "You do realize why this has to go down, right? You have to be made an example of for others. Kind of like a shipwreck that marks where the rocks are."

Then he signaled for the Things to make their move. Now was my chance. I dug in and charged forward, but this was an alley, not turf. I had no cleats, and there was gunk on the ground that made me slip. Rather than barreling through them, I just fell right into them.

In an instant Thing One was holding me, and Thing Two was swinging away. It was all fists—which was good news in a way. If knives or other weapons were involved it would have meant they intended to kill me. Fists meant they just meant to mess me up—although I wasn't stupid enough to think that death wasn't also a possibility.

I struggled against them. I kicked, swung, and elbowed—I didn't make it easy for them—but any damage I did to them was nothing compared to the punishment I received to my gut, my face, even my groin—and that weakened me to the point of being unable to fight back. I was doubled over, and although my knees were buckling from the pain, Thing One kept me on my feet so they could keep on hitting me. Finally Ralston told them to stop, and they did, like he had hit their Pause button.

"One last chance," he said. "This could end right now, everything could go back to the way it was, and we could all be happy campers."

I responded by telling him to perform an act on himself that I once believed was physically impossible, until Norris sent me the link to a video which proved it wasn't.

Ralston took the Things off pause, and they got back to business, slamming me hard against the brick wall.

And the moment I hit that wall, I felt something.

A snap of cold. A sideways vertigo.

And I instantly knew what was happening.

I was shifting again.

A barista from the Starbucks next door found me slumped in the alley, barely conscious. It could have been seconds later, but it felt like much longer.

"My God! Are you all right? What happened to you? I'm calling nine-one-one!"

"No . . . don't . . . ," I muttered. But he had already done it. He urgently asked the operator for help, then brought me into the back room of the coffeehouse.

"Do you know who did this to you?" he asked. "Were you robbed? Was it s'equals?"

I grimaced. Not from the pain, but from that awful epithet. It meant that this unplanned bounce didn't bring me any closer to home.

I hurled, suddenly and completely. I emptied my guts all over the barista and several sacks of coffee beans. I made a note to stay away from this Starbucks for a while.

I felt a little better after throwing up, though. Good enough to get to my feet and bolt out the back door before the paramedics could arrive.

But even before I left the mouth of the alley I was intercepted.

By quintuplets on skateboards.

"Whatever the change was," said Ed, "it was pinpointed, and controlled."

I was sitting in the Edwards' defunct retail den, moving a bag of ice between my eye and my lip, not sure which needed it more.

Teddy, the newest Edwardian iteration, was a bit more Zen than the rest. While most of the others were frenetic, Teddy was content to sit in one of the space's few comfortable chairs, and take it all in. He wasn't frazzled and overstimulated like the others. He was pensive. I'm sure his wheels were turning just as much as the others', but his were deliberate. Like the gears of a clock. I found myself glancing more at him than at the others, because there was a calmness there that I wished I could borrow.

"Control is a good thing," Ed said, as always trying to find a silver lining. "This shows that he doesn't have to be playing football to shift realities. It can be induced."

All the while, Eddy sat on the couch furiously working the QuIRT, searching for the variations between realities, to figure out how this world was different, and Eduardo was off in the corner of the huge space, preparing the isolation tank—because if I was going to remember exactly what had happened in Elsewhere, I'd have to really get inside my head.

"Can you at least tell us what was going on before the shift happened?" Edd asked, already on his last tether of patience.

I sighed and explained the situation. How I was having the shit kicked out of me by Thing One and Thing Two, while the delivery guy supervised. "They threw me against a wall, everything went sideways, and they took off, leaving me there in the alley."

Ed furrowed his brow and turned to Eddy. "Check the name of the guy who delivers to the vitamin shop."

"His name is . . . Gary," Eddy said, after a few clicks.

"No," I corrected, "it's Ralston."

The Edwards looked to one another like surgeons at a botched operation. Teddy leaned back in his chair and smiled like he knew something the others hadn't grasped yet.

"I'll check the previous iteration." Eddy clicked away while the rest of us waited. Shapes and symbols flew across the screen. "Found him!" Teddy finally said. "His full name is Ralston Klingsmith . . ." Then he tapped for a few more seconds. "Uh . . . Ralston Klingsmith," he said again, and then stopped tapping. "Hmm. I'm having trouble finding him in our current thread."

"Interesting . . . ," said Teddy, leaning back in his chair with satisfaction. But the others were more troubled than content with the news. Ed knelt beside me, and moved the ice away from my face, so he could look me in both eyes. "You need to remember it," he said. "Time to take a bath."

◆ ◆ ◆

The EMP solution burned my wounds as bad as salt would have. The sting made it hard to relax, and relaxation is something you can't force. And it wasn't entirely silent, because I could hear Edd on the outside bad-mouthing me while Ed tried to temper his temper. I was unfit, Edd said. I was a disaster. I was the reason they made black holes.

With my eyes open in the darkness, I pushed my thoughts deeper into my aching neurons—a place I didn't want to be, because my head was getting increasingly crowded with conflicting memories. My brain was not a pleasant place anymore. Not that it ever really was, but now it was positively toxic. Still, I forced myself to go there.

I began to remember the feeling the moment I was jarred into Elsewhere by Ralston's goons. Nothing specific yet. Just the feeling. An escape from the pain of the beating. Relief. Then the feeling resolved into other senses. A taste of blood. A smell like rotting garbage. And the pit.

I was skating on a slippery slope on the edge of the pit. I had sensed that pit the last time I shifted. There were unrealized worlds surrounding me, needy, seeking, caressing me, tugging at me. But this time, I wasn't the only one there. Three others were skating at the edge of that pit. It was Ralston and his goons. Then suddenly I wasn't spiraling toward the pit anymore. I had dug in my heels and I held firm. But the other three were still sliding. In the alley, they had all the power, but I was the one who had power here.

I could have reached out to grab them. And now I

remembered—I *did* reach out. But I didn't grab them. Instead, I pushed. I willfully, decisively pushed.

And the three of them went down the drain.

Then I was in the alley again, nauseous and aching, and being helped by the barista.

I let the memory go and brought my thoughts back to the here and now. I slowly climbed out of the tank. "I know what happened," I told the Edwards. "I know what I did."

Ed called it a "localized excision." Eddy called it a "surgical expunging." The five of them bickered over how the event should be labeled, because it was something they'd never come across before. They had no name for it. But I knew what to call it: murder.

"Don't be ridiculous," said Edd, when I pointed that out. "You can't murder people who don't exist."

It only took a little data crunching by Eddy to confirm it. I had gotten rid of all three of my attackers. But, as Edd said, I didn't kill them. No, that would have been too easy.

"So . . . I jumped into a world where the three of them don't even exist?" I asked.

But Eddy shook his head. "More than that. From what I can see, you obliterated every single world where they *could* have existed."

The Edwards were literally and figuratively beside themselves. They paced, throwing around phrases like "unprecedented complication," and "dire ramifications." Until this moment, I always had the sense that they knew what they were doing, even if I didn't. But now they were flying as blind as me.

Through all of it, only the new guy—Teddy—kept his cool, his wheels slowly turning.

In the end, they decided to call it a "pan-dimensional expulsion," PDE, and somehow having a name for it made them feel a little bit better. Again, it made me think of doctors. My aunt had this weird blood thing that gave her unexplained purple spots on her legs. They diagnosed her with ITP: idiopathic thrombocytopenic purpura, which sounds very lofty and professional, until you look it up and find out that it means "unexplained purple spots."

I put my head in my hands, feeling my swollen face against my palms, and wondered why, if I didn't get beaten up in this world, did I still bear the cuts and bruises?

"It's like your memories," Ed said, when I asked him about it. "Some things come with you."

"The current world will find a rational explanation for it," Teddy assured me.

But that didn't erase what I had done. I had committed the perfect crime. Not only no evidence, but no victims.

"If I deleted every world where they could have existed," I said, "what about the world I came from? My original world?"

I tried to remember if Ralston delivered stuff to my dad's store in my original world. Then I remembered my dad didn't even *have* a chain of vitamin stores in my original world—and just remembering that made my head hurt so badly, I couldn't follow through on the thought.

"If you get back to your world," Ed said, "it will be your world minus three people who you never met."

Without Ralston in the world, it turns out I was no longer dealing drugs. Apparently, he was the one who approached me to deal—I wasn't the one who sought it out. There was some comfort in knowing that I was only a drug dealer by opportunity and not by nature. But I still couldn't get past the fact that I had deleted three people. Granted, it was in self-defense, but still . . . if I had a knife would I have stabbed them each through the heart? If I had a gun would I have shot all three of them dead? What actions are justified in self-defense? Is erasing them from all versions of existence fair punishment for being sleazy rat bastards? They were human beings with mothers who loved them. But now, since their mothers never had them, they didn't even have that.

I felt those useless emotions again. Guilt and shame. Like somehow I had pissed in God's teacup, and not even he knew.

17

DOTS, CONNECTED

The next morning I was caught completely unawares by something I should have anticipated but didn't. I came to school, in spite of my bruises, black eye, and swollen lip. People stared at me, and I stared back, belligerent about it.

"Got a problem?"

"No, no, not at all."

Then they would scurry off.

Paul came up to me at my locker. My infamous locker. People passing by probably thought they'd catch us kissing again. Not today. My lip hurt way too much.

"You want to talk about it?" he asked, looking at my face, and doing his best not to grimace.

"No," I told him. "I got jumped out back of the store, that's all."

There was something in the way he looked at me when I said that. Something I didn't get quite yet. But I would soon enough. "Well," he said. "I hope they look even worse than you."

"Yeah," I told him. "I took them out." And then gave an odd little laugh, thinking how much "out" I had taken them.

During second period, Ms. Metts, the counselor, called me into her office again—and this time the principal was there. Never a good sign. They both stood when I entered.

"Mr. Bowman, please have a seat," Principal Benson said.

I didn't want to be there long enough to sit. "What's this all about?"

Still, they waited for me to sit, and when I didn't, they got right down to business, without small talk or mincing words.

"We want to know who did this to you," Benson said

"No one," I told them—which was the truth because those goons weren't anyone anymore. "I got mugged."

Ms. Metts gave me her most sympathetic look. "Ash, I know you don't want to make a big deal out of this, but it *is* a big deal. It's a hate crime, and you can't just let it go."

"*Hate* crime?"

And that's when it finally hit me what they, and Paul, and everyone who saw me this morning was thinking.

"Ash, be honest, at least with yourself," said the principal. "You came out as gay, and the same week, you're attacked. It doesn't take much to connect the dots."

I shook my head, which made every part of my face hurt. "Just because there's dots doesn't mean they connect!"

The two looked at each other, then back to me. Principal Benson crossed his arms. "If you were mugged, then why didn't you go to the police?"

I started to speak, but stopped myself, realizing there were only two reasons I could give, and neither would fly: A) I didn't go to the police because I was beaten up by my drug supplier, or B) I didn't go to the police because my attackers no longer existed, so what would be the point?

"Whoever you're protecting, Ash, they don't deserve your protection," said Ms. Metts, and Benson agreed.

I realized that the more I denied it, the more it would sound like I was in denial. So I shut them down. Shut them out.

"This is my business," I told them. "I'm taking care of it, and I'd appreciate it if you left me [the fuck] alone." I left the profanity implied rather than spoken, since it was the principal, after all. Then I turned and left. For a brief moment I thought I could put it behind me. But the dots were already connected.

During lunch, Katie managed to get away from Layton long enough to bring me to an empty science lab, where she got out her makeup kit.

"Hold still," she said. "I'll try to be gentle." Then she proceeded to cover my bruises.

"This really isn't necessary," I told her, but didn't stop her.

"If you don't want to be the subject of conversation," she said, "you have to make sure you're not drawing attention to yourself."

"And this you know from experience?"

She stopped dabbing my face, but only for a moment. "Why do you keep looking for something that's not there?" she asked.

"Because I see the way Layton talks to you."

"Talk is talk."

"And you're okay with the way he is?"

She pressed a little too hard as she spread the makeup, and I grimaced. "Sorry," she said, then sighed, and took a moment to regain her composure. "Ash, you have your reasons for keeping the peace, and I have mine," Katie said. "Let's leave it at that."

"But this isn't what people think it is," I told her.

Katie went back to dabbing my face and took her time before responding to that. "Even if it's not, it could have been," she told me. "There are plenty of people out there who would have done this to you if they weren't, literally, beaten to the punch."

And I know she was right. I wanted to tell myself that it was just this messed-up world. That in *my* world it wouldn't be the case . . . but that wasn't true. This place did not have a monopoly on intolerance.

This will all blow over, I told myself. But who was I kidding? Now I wasn't just the queer football player, I was the queer football player who got the shit kicked out of him by some homophobic scum. And while me coming out was Instagram-worthy, this new wrinkle was *news*worthy. Before the end of the day, I got a call from a local reporter—God knows how she even got my number. I hung up on her, then turned off my phone. There was no question that I was now in the seat of a catapult that was about to send me places I didn't want to go.

◆ ◆ ◆

I was excused from Thursday's practice. I didn't ask to be excused.

"We all need a day off once in a while," the coach said, even though I'd taken plenty of days off lately.

"You can't pull me out of the game tomorrow! I *have* to play." And he had no idea how much.

He sighed. "I won't pull you out against your will," he said. "If I did, people will put all sorts of spin on that."

It seemed last week's "lesson" imposed by my father had been swept away by this week's revelations. Suddenly being in the SAS Club wasn't the first of his concerns. Seeing the various versions of my father was eye-opening. I learned he was anything but forward-thinking, and tolerant only of the things he already tolerated. But he was starting to stretch in small ways. Even the most inflexible things start to give when you bend them enough. Either that or they break.

By Friday, my phone was blowing up with media requests. As I was still seventeen, and a minor, I'm sure they weren't legally supposed to do that, but it didn't stop them. Because I stood for something now. I wasn't just the center of the universe—I was the center of a controversy. That was something the media could understand. My parents, and even the school, got calls. Everyone wanted a statement, or an interview with me. No one showed up at our door though. I suppose I wasn't newsworthy enough for that. One thing to be grateful for. Even so, we kept our curtains drawn, just in case.

◆ ◆ ◆

On Friday night, my dad decreed that we'd all drive together to the game in one car. That was something we never did, as our busy lives were always moving in conflicting directions.

"We're a family, let's act like one," he said.

"Good," Mom said. "For once we'll get there early enough to get good seats." Usually when Dad made a unilateral decision without consulting with her, she'd push back, but whenever he did something truly admirable, she was happy to let him run with it. I kept wondering whether he had ulterior motives, because the recent versions of my dad were all schemers. Clearly it had rubbed off on the alternate versions of me. Hooking up with Angela behind Leo's back. Selling dope out of the store. You might think your own personal apple has fallen far from the tree, but that tree has roots you don't see until you trip over them.

"Last time we were all in a car together was Grandpa Duncan's funeral," Hunter commented as we drove to the school. Although I never heard Grandpa Duncan say anything, I'd bet he wasn't just racist, but full-on homophobic, too. His funeral was, as all funerals were during the pandemic, weird. It was us and my aunt Denise's family, who had to stand six feet away from us, on the other side of the grave. The pastor mumbled behind a mask, so no one could really hear him. I was never close to Grandpa Duncan. I should probably have felt bad that he was dead, but instead just felt sad that I didn't feel worse about it.

Anyway, I couldn't even imagine introducing him to Paul, and thinking about Paul made me want to reach out to him. I

245

texted Paul to let him know that I'd see him after the game, and asked if he'd be there. He was always at my games, but after this week, I wasn't sure how he'd feel about it.

He texted back a double thumbs-up, and a spade. The spade, if you never noticed, is an upside-down black heart. It was our code, should anyone read our texts. I texted him back with the right-side-up black heart, thought for a moment, then followed up with an in-your-face red one. He closed with the blatantly erect eggplant, which made me laugh.

My mom threw me a glance in the rearview mirror, and although she didn't see our texts, she must have read them in my face, because she said, "Tell Paul he can sit with us."

Dad said nothing. He wasn't the only one who made unilateral decisions in this family.

The parking lot, which was always full by game time, still had plenty of open spaces this early. When we parked, my dad took a moment before turning off the ignition. Then he looked at me.

"You go out there and play like you always play," he said.

"So how do I always play?" I asked.

He seemed taken aback by the question. "Like a star," he said, as if it was obvious. The thing is, being a lineman didn't often make you a star. It was the first time I'd ever known he'd thought of me as one.

I grabbed my gear from the trunk and headed for the locker room, but long before I got there, I saw the news crews hovering near the entrance.

It wasn't strange to have a crew from the local station cover our games, but this was more than just the T-ville affiliate flunkies. There were three crews right there outside the locker room. One of them even had a satellite van, with a dish on its roof. My first thought was that this was about me. My second thought was to smack myself around at how stupid it was to think a bunch of news crews could possibly be about me. But as I approached, the reporters took notice and the cameras turned my way. I had been right the first time.

The instant I was in shouting range, the reporters started yelling out questions like they do at people who actually matter.

"Will you be playing today, Ash?"

"How extensive are your injuries?"

"Do you know who did this to you?"

"Why haven't you come forward?"

"How many of them were there?"

"Do you have anything to say to other gay athletes?"

"Is this the first time you've been attacked for your sexual orientation?"

I wanted to just run into the locker room, but that would look bad. Like I had something to hide. So I paused and looked at them. The questions stopped as soon as they realized I was on the verge of saying something. Problem was, I had no idea what to say.

"I got a game to play," I finally told them. "You got questions, ask me later."

Because maybe, just maybe, I'd soon be in a universe where no one wanted to interview me about anything.

I was still shell-shocked from the paparazzi as I stepped into the locker room. Although it felt like forever ago, it had only been a few days since I had come out, so the team and I were still in relatively new territory—and the sudden media attention wasn't helping.

Some of my teammates were totally cool with me being out. Some just needed time, and told me so. Others were struggling to navigate what they could and couldn't say, like they had just learned a new language. No one was openly belligerent—but there were those who just didn't engage, and probably never would.

Norris was one of the non-engagers. He didn't look at me, but he also didn't move away when I sat down. He just acted like we were strangers on a bus.

And the funny thing was, I didn't care.

He was my friend for the sole reason that he had always been my friend. He came packaged like a cable station you didn't ask for, but got anyway. I realized that I could do without Norris just fine. But it pissed me off that he got to make that decision.

Josh, on the other hand, continued to prove himself as a real friend, and greeted me like he always did. I really do wish he existed somewhere in my original world. He was too good a guy to get stuck out in Elsewhere.

"So are you gonna talk to the reporters?" Josh asked.

"I got nothing to say."

"Anything you say will be something."

He was right, and it just irked me. "Just because I'm gay and got the shit kicked out of me doesn't mean I'm fucking queer Gandhi," I told him. "It's not like I'm the goddamn center of the universe."

And then I realized that, yes indeed, I was. Damn. It made me wonder if this was all part of being the "subjective locus." Did all of us sub-locs get thrust onto the public stage in one way or another during our accidental reign?

Then I heard a low, deep voice behind me.

"If I was you, I'd use it."

I turned to see Jarvis Burke. He was one of the offensive linemen. I barely knew him. You'd think all us guys on the line would be like our own mini fraternity, but it didn't work that way. Offense and defense were like two different teams. As I looked at him, I suddenly got the feeling that Jarvis had his own thing going on. Nothing like mine, but whatever *his* thing was, he was living with it alone.

"Use it how?" I asked.

Jarvis shrugged. "Any ways you want," he said. "You got the spotlight to say sumpin' worth sayin'. Not everybody gets that. So work it."

And then Layton had to come in with his own opinion—like being the quarterback gave him the right to be in everyone's business. "Football should be about football, not about making a statement. Just saying."

I thought about Katie. She'd be out there now cheering us on, putting on a happy face, no matter what she was feeling inside.

"Is there a problem, Bowman?"

I didn't even realize I was staring at Layton until he said that. Glaring actually.

"You undressing me with your eyes or something?" He laughed, hoping to get some chuckles from the team, and when he didn't, he shrugged it off and turned all friendly. "Naah, just messing with you, man. It's all good."

He rapped me on the shoulder on his way out, like we were buddies. He moved too quick for me to push his hand away— by the time I tried, he was already turning the corner, which also left him with the last word. And it occurred to me that the things that made him a good quarterback—unpredictability, pinpoint accuracy, and the ability to control any play—were the same things that allowed him to get away with the things he did.

Our side was roaring as we took the field. I took a glance up into the stands. I wanted to find Paul out there—to see if he did sit with my family after all. I wanted to see if Leo was there, and the Edwards. But I couldn't find anyone in the crowd today.

What I did see—on the home and visitor sides as well—were people waving rainbow flags. Not everyone, but enough to be seen. Enough to make that statement Layton was so much against.

It's hard to explain what I felt seeing those flags. I felt exposed, but uplifted. I felt isolated, yet embraced. Opposing feelings, not side by side, but living within one another. Today's game was not about football, it was about me—or at least what I'd come to represent. It felt awful. It felt great. It felt like getting your chance to play in a league you know you're not ready for.

Maybe that can explain what happened on the field that day.

Our opponents, the Dewey Pythons, were from a school named after a president who never got elected in my old world. We won the coin toss. Chose to receive instead of kick. Layton and our offense did a few unremarkable plays, and then we punted. Me and the rest of the defensive team went out onto the field.

I was on the field every time the Pythons had the ball. I played well. I played great. I sacked their quarterback twice and made him throw the ball away half a dozen times. But those sacks. Those hits. They weren't power hits. They weren't decimating, world-changing tackles. They were competent. They were skilled. They were not what I needed.

By the time we got down to the two-minute warning, I began to panic. There were only going to be a few more plays. I knew what I had to do, and I thought I knew how to do it—but my head was full of so many things now. Not just half a dozen sets of memories, but hopes and fears that were just as conflicted as how I felt when I ran out on the field. All the things I couldn't get out of my mind. I thought about Paul, and how, if I went back to who I was, we'd be done. He'd be my math tutor, nothing more. Was I ready to lose him? If I did, I'd have feelings for Katie again. What did any of my personal crap matter if I couldn't set Leo back on the path he deserved, and bring Angela back from the grave? And those flags waving in the stands? People wanted something from me in *this* reality—people *needed* something.

Was erasing this world cowardly? Was I just running away?

The play began; I lurched through the line. I saw the yellow flag fly from the ref's hands, heard the whistles, but I didn't stop. I barreled full force at the quarterback. He didn't even have the ball yet. It hadn't even been snapped. I didn't care. I barreled right into him, bringing him down as hard as I could.

But the only place it took me was the ground.

18
A WHILE TILL YESTERDAY

"This was not your finest day," the coach said. He was talking to the whole team at our post-game meeting. I wished he'd just go ahead and single me out, and get it over with, but to be honest the whole team sucked on the field today. It wasn't just me.

"You almost lost to the Pythons! We *never* lose to the Pythons." And finally he zeroed in on me. Here it comes. "And you, Bowman, what were you *thinking* out there?"

Of course I couldn't tell him what I was thinking. That would get me a one-way trip to a psychiatric evaluation. "I was distracted" was all I said.

"We were all 'distracted,'" grumbled Norris, not looking at me, but blaming me all the same.

"Whatever's going on in your personal lives, you forget it when you get on the field. All of you."

"Football's about football," said Layton, echoing his asshole opinion from before—but in the current context it lost the asshole quotient and just sounded like he was endorsing the coach.

"Right. Listen to your quarterback," the coach said. "Of all of you, he's the one who was on point today. If it wasn't for his last-minute Hail Mary, we would have lost the game. To the Pythons. Let's all give the man his due."

The team congratulated Layton, applauding him, and he pretended like he didn't want the attention. Pretended to be gracious. I hated the fact that he was the hero of the game.

"Reporters should be talking to *him*," I heard someone grumble.

"Enough of that!" the coach said, shutting him down. "One thing has nothing to do with the other."

As for me, that offside tackle got me yanked from the game, and got us a twenty-yard penalty, giving the Pythons a first down at their forty-yard line. Could have been a disaster if they scored because of it. If they had, no Hail Mary could have saved us. In that case, I wouldn't just be the linebacker who'd lost the game, I'd be the *gay* linebacker who'd lost the game. From now on, I would always be "that gay football player." Why the hell did the world have to be that way? Slapping labels on us, rather than allowing us to just *be* who we are?

"Bowman, hold up, I want to talk to you," the coach said. I figured I was in for more brow-beating for what I did on the field.

"Coach, I'm sorry," I told him.

"I know you are. And I know it wasn't like you to slip up like that. To be honest, though, I should suspend you for at least a week . . . but I won't. You have enough to deal with already."

I appreciated his empathy. I had never considered him much of an empathetic person. But then, I never had a reason to even think about it before. It wasn't a coach's job to feel your pain.

"Those reporters are still out there," he told me. "But if you went out the back way and didn't talk to them, I wouldn't think any less of you."

Well, he might not, but I would.

"It's okay," I said. "Once I give them a couple of good sound bites, they'll move on. I'll be yesterday's news in no time."

He took off his cap, scratched his head, and sighed. "I think it's going to be a while until you drop into yesterday, Ash."

There were plenty of people outside the locker room. The team's families and friends waiting for us to come out. People were hanging around to congratulate us on our nail-biting win. But today there were more there than usual, thanks to the media. Some knew what the news crews were waiting for, others were just curious. Human interest about today's human interest story.

Leo's was the lone brown face in the crowd. Katie was there, but she was already in the grip of Layton's proprietary arm. My brother and some of his friends were there, too, and of course, Paul, who smiled and gave me a thumbs-up that was both hokey and endearing.

My parents were nowhere to be seen. I had told them not to wait for me, and that I'd get a ride home, but I thought they might be there anyway. Moral support and all. Maybe they didn't know there were reporters waiting for me, or maybe my dad didn't want to get pulled into an interview, him being a minor celebrity and all.

I didn't see the Edwards there, either. No reason for them to linger—they knew nothing had happened, because there wasn't a sixth one in their midst. Were they disappointed, confused, troubled by my dimensional fumble? I had no clue what their reaction would be.

The news crews were patient in their impatience. They didn't crowd me; they waited for me to approach them. Layton met my eye just before I engaged with the reporters. Then he turned to leave with Katie in tow before I said a word—making sure that I saw him turn his back on the whole thing. I'll admit I was pretty smug at having upstaged Layton and his game-saving play. No one wanted to talk to him. But I can't forget that look on Katie's face as she left, and that resigned slump of her shoulders beneath the yoke of his arm—as if she had no choice but to leave with him.

But you do have a choice, Katie. Why can't you see that?

The reporters started asking the same questions they had when I first arrived. I told them to stop.

"Will you be willing to give us a full interview?" one of them asked.

"Depends on what you mean by interview," I told them. "I'll answer questions until I don't feel like answering them anymore."

In 2016, nearly fifty people were killed by a gunman armed with semiautomatic weapons at the Pulse gay nightclub in Orlando. In 1998, Matthew Shepard was tortured, beaten, then tied to a fence and left to die, just because he was gay.

You've probably heard about those things. I'd heard about them in my original world—but they got sorted into the big box of "Horrible Shit That's Not My Problem." We've all got that box, whether we want to admit it or not. In this world, though, they weren't just acts against people I didn't know in places I'd never been. They were attacks on me. *I* was tortured. *I* was beaten. *I* was gunned down. It didn't matter that some of it happened before I was born—it was still me. Because when you're gay, every cowardly homophobic act you see is an act against you.

The Pulse nightclub and Matthew Shepard. Yeah, unless you're living under a deeper rock than I was, you've heard of them. But I'll bet you didn't know about Arthur Warren, who was kicked to death. Or Ruby Ordeñana, who was strangled, or August Provost, who was shot then burned, or Blaze Bernstein, who was stabbed more than twenty times, or the thousands upon thousands upon thousands of murders, beatings, and attacks that happen every day of every year in every country on this sorry planet, targeting people because they're gay, or transgender, or queer in any way. But a lot of people don't see those stories, because our news feeds send us things we're more likely to click on.

There are plenty of survivors who speak out, and families

of those who've been murdered who take on the fight—and it's a fight not just for justice, but for our attention. Struggling to make us see—and care—about what's happening right here on our doorstep.

Those people have more to say than I do. They have more of a right, and they are more eloquent.

But the cameras were now on me, and, like Jarvis Burke said, I had to use them. I had, for this one moment, taken the bully pulpit away from the bullies. I couldn't squander it.

The questions they asked were ones they already knew the answers to—but they wanted to hear me say them. Yes, I was attacked in an alley. No, my injuries were not extensive. No, I wouldn't be able to pick out my assailants in a lineup—because they wouldn't be in any lineup in this world, although I didn't tell them that part.

"You made an illegal tackle today," one of them had to mention. "Do you think the attack on you affected your game today?"

"Yeah, I kinda lost my mojo," I admitted. "But really, I was just trying to bounce the guy into another dimension."

And everyone laughed. Like Paul once pointed out, it's easy to speak the truth when everyone thinks you're joking.

Then once again, one of them asked if I had anything to say to other gay athletes—as if suddenly I was the spokesperson for the rainbow league. I hadn't given much thought to that kind of statement, but I did know what I would have said to myself.

"If you're out, then stand strong. If you're not, don't be

ashamed of who you are. If you've made a choice to keep it on the down-low, just know that your choice can and will change when you're ready. You *will* get to be who you are, both inside and out."

They were unimpressed, but to be honest, my own statement left me a little stunned. I had actually said something that didn't sound entirely idiotic. I was almost eloquent.

"What are you going to do now, Ash?" they asked.

Historically, when sports figures are asked that question by reporters, the standard answer is usually, "I'm going to Disneyland." Sorry, that was not gonna happen here.

"I'm going to live my life with no apologies," I told them. "And anyone who has a problem with that can go fuck themselves."

I'm sure that last part got bleeped out on the news. Thus perished my eloquence.

The reporters thanked me. One said they'd use it on a bigger piece on hate crimes, another said it would be available online, but the third crew—the one with the actual news van—said to look for it on Sunday's national evening news.

The crowd began to disperse. Nothing more to see here. Hunter came over to tell me how great it was that I dropped an f-bomb, then left with his friends. Paul and Leo came up to me from different directions, which suddenly made things awkward.

"So what changed this time?" asked Leo. "Because I'm still in a world where everything sucks."

There hadn't been time to think about why I failed to shift. Too much going on. Too many things drawing me out of myself.

Was I no longer the subjective locus? Was it over? Was this where the world would be left?

"So what changed this time?" Leo's question still hung in the air between us, but I couldn't answer him, because Paul was right there.

"Paul, this is Leo. He's a friend of mine."

Leo looked Paul over. "So this your dude?"

"Yeah," I said, "Paul's my boyfriend." I believe that was the first time I said the word "boyfriend" out loud. Even after the big steps, there were still so many small steps to take.

They shook hands, but it was awkward on more dimensions than I care to count. It's a bitch when your secret life meets your *other* secret life.

"So how do you know each other?" Paul asked.

Leo, who was quicker on the uptake than me, said, "Ash heard I used to play football before I dropped out. Been encouraging me to get back into it. Community outreach kind of thing."

I shrugged. "Yeah, I've been trying to build bridges in the Black community," I said, trying to make it seem like just an SAS thing.

Leo took a moment to look us over, and nodded approvingly. "You make a good couple—and what you said to those reporters is gonna move people. It definitely moved me." He slapped me on the back. "We'll talk."

Then he turned to go. As he did, I noticed some people toss suspicious glances his way. It made me want to kick them in the kneecaps, but that wouldn't have been helpful.

Paul drove me home. Turns out he had not accepted the invitation to sit with my family. Maybe because it felt more like a dare than an invitation.

It was in the car, next to Paul, and happy to be there, when I realized the truth. My failure today had nothing to do with whether or not I still had the power of change. Yes, I tackled the quarterback, but even in the moment, I knew I hadn't hit him hard enough to do the job. I hadn't *committed* to it the way I had before.

I failed because I wanted to fail.

I didn't want to lose this version of me. And it infuriated me. How selfish—how irresponsible it was—to put my needs ahead of the world's. Just because I was temporarily the center of the universe didn't mean I had the right to act like I was.

"So what's the deal with Leo?" Paul asked, trying to sound casual about it. "Because there's definitely a story there that you're not telling."

He came to a full stop at a stop sign. A blue one. He had already hit the gas again by the time I remembered what color it used to be. Paul and Leo did know each other in my original world, but only through me. My best friend and my math tutor. But here they didn't fit in the same picture.

"Leo's a checker at Publix," I told Paul. "We had some words, and it got him in trouble. Since it was my fault, I wanted to do something to help him." All of that was true, and the truth of it seemed to satisfy Paul, although I could tell he was worried there was still more to it. The thought that Paul might be jealous of Leo was both horrifying and hilarious at the same time.

"Trust me," I told Paul, "you've got nothing to worry about."

"Who said I was worried?"

I started to wonder if maybe I could bring Paul into this whole thing. If Katie and Leo could believe what was happening, shouldn't I be able to convince Paul as well? And didn't he have a right to know?

He glanced over at me, reading me. His ability to do that is one of the things that drew me to him. But right now it was a liability.

"Something's up with you, and it's not just the reporters," he said, and waited for me to give him an explanation. But how could I even begin to tell him? The proximity effect should have left him sensing bits and pieces of it, but he showed no signs. Paul was analytical—if he was getting inklings, he was probably suppressing them as irrational.

"Something's up? After this week, what isn't up?" I said.

"Is that a dick joke?"

"Actually, no," I told him. "It's been a rough week, and I'm fried, that's all. Aren't you?"

He sighed, and nodded. "Yeah, so am I." He reached over and gently squeezed my knee, accidentally knocking the transmission into neutral for a second. Was that the multiverse trying to tell me that Paul and I weren't going anywhere? Well, the multiverse could go screw itself in an infinite number of ways.

We drove on in silence. I didn't like silence between us. So I tried, in the smallest of ways, to let him in.

"Somewhere," I said, "there's a world where Black and white kids go to the same school. Where your family's got more money than mine, and I didn't get beaten up in the back of an alley."

Paul looked over at me, wondering where this was coming from, and where it might be going. "And in this shining world of unicorns and marshmallows," he said, "are you and I the king and king of homecoming?"

And I realized, right then and there, that the truth was something I couldn't share with him. Because if I did, it would break his heart. It would break mine, too. So I lied to Paul, and that hurt more than anything.

"Of course we are," I told him. "And we look damn good in those crowns."

19

SKATER ON THE ROOF

My head was throbbing when Paul dropped me off that night, but I was fresh out of eggshells for a bath. What did that matter? I knew all the eggshells in the world couldn't ease what I was feeling. There was no question that the jumps were taking a greater and greater toll on me. My brain was now firing on all cylinders, revving high. You do that to a car for too long, and the engine blows. I know about that—my dad makes a lot of his living off of people who blow out their engines. Or he used to. Or he still does in another place. I couldn't even be sure which world that was. It was starting to swirl together like food on an overloaded Thanksgiving plate.

And that made me think of Paul, and whether or not he'd accept my family's Thanksgiving invitation. This would be one Thanksgiving where I wouldn't be stuffing my face, because

I'd be too nervous about things going well. But what was I even thinking? Because if things went according to plan, Paul wouldn't be there for Thanksgiving. Part of me was okay with that, and the other part of me hated that first part for it.

I was in bed, dozing in that uneasy state, when Katie called me. It was close to midnight now.

"I've been dying to call, but I couldn't with Layton. So tell me! What changed?"

"Nothing," I told her, plain and simple. "Nothing happened."

"But . . . but we all saw that tackle . . ."

"Yeah, I'm sure Layton was going on all night about it, and how I almost lost the game for us, and how he saved the day."

She didn't deny it. But she didn't talk about it either.

"You're telling me that things didn't change at all? Not even a little?"

"It was just an ordinary tackle. I didn't hit hard enough to make a difference."

"Then you have to hit harder!"

I wasn't expecting that from her. Katie was a "you'll do better next time" person. It unsettled me.

"Why are you so desperate to get back to a world you don't even remember?" I asked her.

"Because this one is wrong," she said. "I feel it more and more each day. Maybe not as strongly as you do, but I still feel it!"

"Katie . . . the old world isn't any different for you," I told her—and we both knew what I was talking about. "If you want it different, *you* have to be the one to change it."

She was silent for a moment. Then the phone practically grew cold in my hand when she spoke.

"I didn't call you to get a lecture."

She didn't exactly hang up on me, but everything felt stiff after that. Was I crossing a line in trying to get her to kick Layton to the curb? When I was straight, my motivations might have been muddy, but now it was all about what was best for her. Yes, it was her decision to make—but Layton was abusive. Whether or not it was physical, he was definitely abusing her emotionally. The way he treated her. Like she was just an extension of himself. Like she had surrendered her right to be an individual.

What is it that keeps someone in a relationship like that? I remember thinking. *Shouldn't it be easy to just walk?*

I thought my sleep would be troubled, but the one good thing about exhaustion is that it knocks you out. I didn't wake up once during the night. It was a little after eight when I finally opened my eyes. Then I just lay there, with no idea what my course of action should be.

For the last few weeks, the morning after a game had been all about assessing the change and coming to terms with it. There was nothing new today that I wasn't already grappling with yesterday.

Have you ever just laid in bed unable to dredge up the will to get out of it? I was never a man of inaction, but there I was, wanting to hide under the covers until the world ended. I could say that I wasn't myself, but that would be wrong. I *was* myself—only so many different variations of me that I had no clue who I actually was. Everything I felt, every decision I made, had tendrils of motivation from every world I had inhabited. How could I trust anything I said or did anymore?

"Coming to my game?"

It was Hunter, standing there at my open door, who got me moving that morning.

"Of course," I told him. "Don't I always?"

Did I always? Yes. At least in these worlds I did. Hunter had weekend games, and I always went. But in my original world, Hunter and I weren't close, were we? I never went to his games, and he never came to mine. If I managed to get back there, I wondered if that might change or if that groove was too deeply dug.

"Are you sure you want me to come?" I asked.

He was surprised by the question. "Why wouldn't I?"

I shrugged, wishing I hadn't even said it. "I don't want to upstage you or anything. I don't want to be a distraction."

"You won't be," he said. "As long as you don't bring the paparazzi with you."

I sighed. "None of that was my idea."

"I know."

He lingered there. I knew he wanted to say more, but I had no idea what it might be. Whatever it was, it was weighing heavily on him. "Do you ever wanna just play the game and forget about all the crap in the world?" he asked.

"All the time," I told him.

He nodded, then said what he'd been holding back. "There are five of them, you know."

Maybe I'm just dense, but I didn't realize what he was talking about. "Five what?"

"Skaters. Didn't I go out with you looking for twins? And instead there's five. All identical. I saw them at your game."

I chuckled nervously. "What are the odds?"

He lingered there, not coming in, not leaving. The threshold is a funny place. The ultimate spot of noncommittal. And yet they say it's one of the best places to be in an earthquake. Go figure.

"Ash, what's going on?" Hunter asked. "Because I know something is. Something freaky. I want to know if I should be scared."

There were as many ways to answer that as there were universes. So I chose to slide around the question. "You and I talk about stuff, right?" I asked. Because I had memories of it, but also memories of not talking to Hunter about much at all.

"We never talked about you being gay."

"I know, but I mean other stuff."

He shrugged. "Yeah, I come to you when there are things I don't want to talk to Mom and Dad about, if that's what you mean."

"Yeah, it is."

"But you never come to me."

"I know. It's an older brother thing," I told him. "But maybe I will someday. Maybe I'll need to. Just . . . not right now."

"So I shouldn't be scared?" he said, bringing us back to the question I had hoped he had forgotten.

"I'll be scared for both of us," I told him.

He thought about that. Nodded, took a step back, and was out of the threshold. "Kickoff's at noon," he said. Then he left. I almost went after him to tell him the whole thing, but didn't. He did not need the burden of what I knew. I could spare him that.

The morning continued in a dull shade of mundane. I should have appreciated that, but I was still braced, my fight-or-flight response poised on a hair trigger. Dad was already gone by the time I came downstairs—he had a golf game with the movers and shakers of Tibbetsville, as if anyone in our town can move or shake anything. He was a big fish in a very small pond, trying to become an even bigger fish.

Mom was home, but on the clock, in the middle of a Zoom meeting with one of her clients. It made me think that maybe, just maybe, today could be an ordinary day start to finish. Then I went to take out the trash, and I saw someone on the roof of our backhouse.

Our backhouse—which my mom likes to call "the carriage house," as if just having one isn't pretentious enough—is larger than my house in my original world. In my wealthy worlds, we used to rent out the backhouse on Airbnb, until some bozo threw a party while we were out of town and trashed it. So now the place is reserved for friends and relatives—who can also be bozos, but at least we know where they live.

And today, there was an Edward on the roof. He was grinding along the peak, the sound of his board making an unpleasant hiss. He dislodged a roof tile. It went plunging to the ground and thudded in the flower garden.

I knew he saw me, but he didn't wave or call out. He just moved back and forth along the peak of the roof, knowing that, no matter how much I wanted to ignore him, I couldn't. Resigned, I got the key to the backhouse, went in, then climbed up to the roof from the balcony.

"What the hell are you doing up here?" I asked. "Where are the others?"

He stopped skating and kicked his board up into his hands. "It's just me today," he told me. "The others are all crunching data and worrying about what didn't happen last night."

"But not you?"

"Not me."

I wasn't sure which one this was. When they were together, I could tell them apart by the way they interacted.

"Nice view from up here," he said, sitting down. "Of course it would be even better if this hill was higher. But that would take creating a geological event a few hundred million years ago. Give or take an eon."

"Easier to just cut down some of the trees," I pointed out.

"Maybe, maybe not," he said, with an enigmatic little smile— which is what gave him away.

"Teddy!" I said, proud of myself for having figured it out.

"Excuse me?"

"Uh . . . I mean you're number five." Then I told him my little system for naming them, and he laughed.

"We actually do have a name," he said, but he couldn't tell it to me, because, not only was it unpronounceable by human tongues, it had a three-second blast of radiation in the middle. So "the Edwards" would just have to do.

I reached down to move a displaced tile back into position. "Are you here to debrief me after yesterday?"

"Nothing to debrief," he said. "Our best guess is that you were too drained after Wednesday's shift to do anything meaningful last night."

"I figured as much," I said, keeping my thoughts on the matter to myself. "So why are you up here?"

"When it comes to me and the other 'Edwards' we might all be the same person, but we're not always of the same mind," he said. "You know what our purpose is; we're supposed to minimize damage, rein in the jumps, and help guide the sub-loc to the place they started." Then he gave me that smile again. "But once in a while there's a sub-loc who's incredibly good in the position."

The idea that I was actually good at this was not reflected in my long string of fails. "If I'm good, then I'd hate to see the bad ones."

He laughed at that. "You have no idea what you did in your last jump, do you? Most sub-locs just limp from one world to the next. But you soared through Elsewhere like you owned it. In those first few jumps, yeah, you didn't know what you were doing, but these last two? You exerted your will. You controlled the game."

And although I didn't feel like I controlled much of anything, I kind of got what he was saying. Last Friday, I took the change in, rather than letting it roll me. And on Wednesday . . . well, obliterating Ralston and his goons was an act of will. I chose to do it, whether I liked it or not.

"You might be just a lineman on the field," said Teddy, "but from a universal perspective, you're a quarterback."

I wasn't ready to buy it, but I couldn't deny that I liked the way that sounded. "Why do you think that is?"

"My theory? It's all about balance and knowing your center of gravity. Your sport has trained your mind and body to be aware of such things—and that awareness is something you take with you into Elsewhere. You don't stumble when you're in there. That allows you to take decisive action."

He stood up and suddenly tried to push me off the roof.

"Hey!" I shouted. "What the fuck?"

But he only smiled. "You see? I just pushed you as hard as I could. You didn't lose your balance. You didn't even have to move your feet."

He came toward me again and I put up my hands, ready to hurl him off the roof if he tried that again, but he didn't.

He laughed and looked at me with what I could swear was admiration. "You're trying to bring the world back to the way it was, but you have to admit, that world wasn't all that great. What if you could do better?"

Better. Now there was a loaded word. Katie wanted me to do better. Funny, but I thought I was already doing the best that I could.

"You're saying you want me to fix the world?"

"'Fix' is a relative term," he said. "But I'll bet you can find a world where the worst things—the worst people—never happened. You don't have to settle for baseline—you can find a trillion better worlds than that."

For all my balance, I was feeling dizzy at the thought.

"It's all about shifting time," Teddy told me. "Do you know that if there was a planetary time shift of only three seconds, the asteroid that struck this planet and wiped out seventy-five percent of life—including the dinosaurs—would have missed?"

"Yeah, but I can't shift time."

"Just because you haven't doesn't mean you can't."

After he put it out there, he just let it sit, dangerously perched on the tip of the roof. It could fall either way. An absolute no, or a decisive yes.

"How do the others feel about this?"

Then Teddy gave me that wicked little grin once more. "I don't see why we have to involve them at all."

Have you ever tried to make a list of your perfect universe? It's like being that greedy little kid on Santa's lap. "I want a new bike, and a lightsaber, and world peace, and a puppy that shits candy all day long."

Now imagine that you're not just sitting on Santa's lap, but you're Santa as well, and you're sitting on your own lap—which has got to be illegal in most universes or at least certain states. When you're in that kind of power position, you not only know what to ask for, but what you're able to give. Which is all of it.

And what if Santa actually gave you a puppy that shit candy? Would that be amazing, or would it be so scary that you'd need serious therapy for the rest of your life?

I went to Hunter's game, but my head was somewhere else entirely. Each time the crowd roared, I had to refocus to see what had happened on the field. Hunter was a lineman, too, but on the offensive line. He was the center, snapping the ball to the quarterback. It's the most invisible position in the game, because nobody looks at the center. All eyes are on the quarterback, as if the ball shot into his hands out of nowhere.

If I was now a universal quarterback, that would make Teddy my center, putting a ball in my hands—a ball that I couldn't pass. I'd have to take it up the middle on my own.

I made an appearance at the Edwards' that evening, because I was afraid they might all show up on the roof. Most of them looked exhausted. Only Teddy appeared rested and relaxed. He said nothing of our conversation that morning.

"Five jumps and he's not any closer!" Edd ranted, his usual bundle of nerves.

"Untrue," said Ed, always the reasonable one. "He's not dealing drugs anymore. That's a step in the right direction."

Eduardo was drawing an elaborate decision tree on a wall, and a great deal of the final branches ended with a skull and crossbones. And Eddy was, as always, manning the QuIRT like a video game junkie, in an attempt to get a handle on the big picture. He told me the colorful visual on the screen was "a real-time array of vermiform vectors and quantum particulates." I told him to use fire arrows if he wanted to beat the boss.

"We think we're nearing the end of the line," Ed told me in a calm, even-handed way.

"Meaning?"

"We have reason to think we're getting close to a correction."

They had mentioned the idea of a correction before—in which the whole planet gets deemed a bad egg and goes down the cosmic garbage chute.

"Why do you think that?" I asked.

"Oh, no reason," said Edd, dripping multidimensional sarcasm. "Just the dark matter gathering beyond Neptune's orbit. Just a few trillion cosmic strings tangling like a vacuum cleaner cord."

Eduardo added another line to his tree of possibilities. "It does seem like the universe is preparing for something."

"Preparing and actually proceeding are two separate things," said Ed, then he took me aside and explained. "When a sub-loc is truly irritating to the fabric of time and space, it becomes like an itch that the universe needs to scratch."

"More like chafing," offered Eduardo.

"Right," agreed Edd. "You're chafing the universe. Don't chafe the universe!"

"The point is," said Ed, "just because there's a reason to scratch, it doesn't mean that the universe will do it."

Then Teddy came to my defense. "There's nothing to worry about if Ash moves in a more soothing direction."

"Good point," said Ed, "which means that your next jump needs to be a complete about-face. No more half measures, no more fails. This next jump is do or die."

"I think he can handle it," said Teddy, giving me a surreptitious wink. "Why don't you let me work with him this week and get him as prepared as possible."

Meanwhile, Eddy's screen flashed something that looked suspiciously like "game over," and Eduardo sighed, drawing another skull and crossbones.

20

ALL THE EASY ANSWERS

There are things we tell ourselves. Clever snippets of common wisdom that help us find a moral compass. But witticisms rarely hold up to scrutiny.

A penny saved is a penny earned? False. Plenty of people save pennies they never earned. An apple a day keeps the doctor away? Yeah—right until the day it doesn't and you die.

Maybe I'm just jaded, but I've earned the right. Because the following week shattered my faith in wisdom and all of life's easy answers.

Fallacy #1: Don't look a gift horse in the mouth.

Bad advice. Because what might look like a gift could come with complicated strings and snares, and, as the people of Troy found out, a garrison of Greek soldiers.

On Sunday night, the national news spot dropped, and my interview was broadcast into millions of homes. And by Monday morning, a fresh wave of calls was rolling in. More interview requests. Invitations to public speaking engagements. There were even companies wanting me to sponsor their products. I didn't think my life could feel any more surreal, but there it was.

I already felt like a fraud, so I just wanted my fifteen stupid minutes of fame to be done. Since most of the calls came to my parents, I told them to turn down everything.

"Everything?" my father asked. "Aren't there at least some of them you might want to consider?"

That just blew my already overloaded mind to smithereens. My father, who, just a few days ago, wanted me to lie about who I was, was now ready to sell me to the highest bidder.

"All I'm saying is that this situation might have a silver lining for you. An unexpected gift—and I don't just mean money, I mean prestige."

"You're the famous one, Dad," I reminded him. But on the other hand, I never remembered him being in the spotlight when he played for the NFL. Through all that time, he was on the line, like me. All guts, no glory. Which meant that in one week, I had become more famous than him.

"If you play this right, you could probably get yourself some scholarships," he told me.

"There are gay football scholarships?"

"Not per se," he admitted, "but for a forward-thinking school, you'd be a feather in their cap."

"I don't want to be anyone's feather."

"You're missing the point, Ash."

He might have been right about this, but his motives troubled me. Was it my notoriety he wanted to advance, or his own? Was I now to be a feather in *his* cap? Was it suddenly okay with him that I was gay, because he had found a way to use it?

"You have opportunities here, Ash. Don't squander them."

And I realized this was also an opportunity for him. A chance to really connect with me. Would he take that opportunity, or squander it? I needed to find out.

"So is Paul welcome in our house?" I asked.

He seemed taken aback by the question.

"We agreed Thanksgiving. Now you want to move up the time schedule?"

"There's no 'time schedule,'" I told him. "There's just being decent and not being decent."

"Let's not get ahead of ourselves," he said. "Let's stick to the plan."

So much for connecting with me. "Right," I said, and turned to leave. "You want to endorse a breakfast cereal, be my guest."

"It's not me they're asking."

"Exactly," I said, twisting the knife just a little as I left.

Fallacy #2: Familiarity breeds contempt.

Whoever said that never met Paul. I could be around him every minute of every day, and never get tired of him. The only time I was content to do nothing was when we were together.

And the more time I spent, the more I wanted to spend.

At lunchtime on Monday, in our SAS meeting, Paul and I sat together, as usual, but it felt entirely different. It's not like we were holding hands, but we could have if we wanted to, and that made all the difference in the world. Of course we could have before, but not without a fountain show of spit-takes around the room. Now no one would bat an eye. Or at least no one in *this* room.

Right at the start, the meeting took a critical turn.

"I'm truly sorry to have to inform you," Mr. DeVaney began, "that the administration has rescinded their offer of the gym for the dance, until the issue can be addressed by the school board."

The collective shock around the room could have taken out the power grid. I was angry, but not surprised. Racists like to hide in their living rooms behind quiet policy and group inertia. Armchair terrorism. What was true in my original world was just amplified here.

Then, while the others were voicing their justified fury, Paul leaned over and whispered to me, "This might be the best thing that could have happened."

At first, I was confused, but as I looked at him, and at that subversive grin on his face, I knew exactly what he was thinking.

"You're a genius," I told him.

"Spread the word, I need more tutoring jobs."

I stood up to get everyone's attention and spoke loud.

"Do it anyway!" I said. That shut everyone up, and they looked in our direction. "Do it anyway and let them try to stop it."

Mr. DeVaney took off his glasses. "Ash, I don't think—"

But Paul cut him off. "Because they'd have to send the police to keep us out, and then the whole thing will blow up into a huge and highly visible incident. The kind that the media absolutely loves . . ."

"And," I added, "I've got myself some nice media contacts now."

A moment of silence and everyone started buzzing, to Mr. DeVaney's chagrin. Paul and I had no idea if it would happen or not—but in one smooth stroke we had turned the SAS Club from a bake-sale bunch into a den of revolutionaries.

After practice the next afternoon, I went over to Leo's with Paul, to bring him in on the plan.

"I don't know about this," Leo said.

"It's going to get people's attention," Paul pointed out.

"What makes you think we want people's attention?"

We were sitting at Leo's kitchen table, talking about the dance, with him and his girlfriend, Cerise. Cerise—who didn't dump him from 37,000 feet here. She never moved away, because here, her family had nowhere to go. I could say that Cerise and Leo still being together was one good thing, but a dime in a barrel of shit didn't change the nature of the barrel.

"The whole thing does sound a little risky . . . ," Cerise said.

"It's going to be fine," I told them.

"Easy for you to say," said Leo. "You're not the ones gonna get shot at."

I was about to deny the possibility, but I stopped myself.

Even though we were in the same universe, my reality was not Leo's reality. That was something he had always tried to get across to me.

Paul tried to hide his frustration. I put my hand on his and clasped it. I had to remember that Paul was three layers deep in this world. He had even less understanding of what it meant to be Black in America than he would have in my original world.

"We won't put you or any of your friends in danger," I told Leo and Cerise.

"You can't promise that," said Leo.

"No," agreed Paul, "but I can put our decorations budget into hiring security instead." Which he could definitely do, as he was in charge of finances.

"And what about when there are no rent-a-cops, and no witnesses?" Leo asked. "Like the next day, or the day after that?"

"You're right," I said. "The risk is on you, not on us."

"Which is why anything we do needs to be on *our* terms," Leo said. "Not some harebrained scheme cooked up by a bunch of white kids."

And then, in the silence that followed, Cerise tried to temper Leo's harsh judgment. "Of course, I do like a good dance," she said.

He threw her a look. "Girl, how come you never got my back?"

"I do. Sometimes it just needs a nice scratch." She ran her nails up his spine, and that brought him down like a puppy. "We'll ask around," Cerise said. "See if anyone's interested. No promises."

Leo's mom arrived home with groceries, and while Paul and Cerise went to help her, I showed Leo the list of names I'd been making. He checked off the ones he knew. I was relieved by each check mark, and troubled by the ones left blank.

"Is this even gonna happen, Ash?" he asked. "Because if you do that thing you're supposed to do . . ."

"We need a backup plan," I told him. "In case I fuck up."

"Again," Leo added.

"Again," I admitted.

"A whole other world, or a school dance. Not much of a backup plan if you ask me." He turned to glance out the window at Paul, who was coming up the walk with a bag in each hand. "He know?"

I shook my head.

"You love him?"

I nodded.

Leo raised his eyebrows and sighed. "Wouldn't wanna be you right now." Which made two of us.

Later, Paul and I sat on his living room sofa, no TV, no reason to sit there other than to be together. He was leaning into me, and my arm was around him. We were close enough to feel each other's heartbeats, and I was trying to make mine beat in unison with his.

He rubbed a finger gently along my left lower lid. "The swelling is almost gone," he said. Then he leaned forward and gently kissed my eye.

"All better now?" he said.

"Better than better," I told him. Then I was hit by a wave of sorrow. Things were destined to change between us after this next jump. I tried to hold on to the slim hope that what we had wouldn't fizzle. Paul must have seen the anguish in my face.

"I wish I could know where your head is at," he said.

"I'm thinking about you," I told him. A half-truth, and he knew it.

"I'm sure I'm in there somewhere," he said. "But your thoughts are in darker places than usual tonight."

Then his mom came in with drinks. I flinched reflexively, but Paul held my arm, making sure I didn't pull away, because I didn't have to anymore. His mom offered a kind smile when she saw us like that, but didn't comment. Not at all like at my house, where there was a mandatory waiting period before I could even have Paul over.

I wished I could have stayed longer, but I had a training session with an interdimensional being to get to. Still, I stretched the minutes before I had to leave as best I could, trying to be in the moment, before these moments ceased to exist.

Fallacy #3: Practice makes perfect.

Oversimplification. Perfection is overrated. Sometimes it's more important to fail with grace.

Case in point: my training sessions with Teddy that week. I thought I'd be in the isolation tank again, but Teddy had other plans. He worked with me outside, in the weedy, root-ridden parking lot of the crumbling toy store.

"Passively reliving your jumps can only get you so far," Teddy said. "It's time for you to take charge. Agility. Balance. Decisive action. That's the Ash I want to see."

Each night he put me on his skateboard and had me navigate the treacherous lot where the asphalt had buckled and cracked, filling with evil weeds. Skateboarding was never my thing, but riding this board felt oddly familiar. Only a few minutes into it did I realize why. Standing on that board felt like skirting the slippery slope of Elsewhere. My ability to move was entirely based on my will to do so. At first, I was slow and uneasy on the board, but soon I was navigating the hazards of the lot with increasing confidence. I tried to connect that feeling of confidence to Elsewhere. If I could feel this level of control there, that would be half the battle.

"I believe you have at least one more jump left in you, maybe two, so you have to make them count," Teddy told me.

And so I tried to imagine the world I wanted to see. Better than where I came from. A place that was peaceful and just—where equality wasn't something to strive for but something that had already been achieved. And maybe, just maybe, when I saw that world for real, I would recognize it.

And then Teddy blindfolded me.

If you think I could suddenly sense the weeds and uneven asphalt, you're wrong. The whole night was about falling on my ass and getting scraped up. It pissed me off at first, until I realized the point wasn't to navigate blind but to own each wipeout, commit to it, and learn how to hit the ground right, no matter how unfamiliar the terrain. Tonight was all about sticking the fall.

"I know each time you're in Elsewhere, you perceive it differently," Teddy said, "but even so, some things will be consistent. I want you to think about the things that track."

After a particularly skillful wipeout, while nursing my skinned knees, I took a moment to consider what Teddy had said.

"Each time I'm in Elsewhere, I can sense the different realities all around me," I told him. "They feel alive. They feel . . . *needy*. Like they're afraid of being left behind. Does that make sense?" The image that filled my mind this time was a bunch of little kids waiting to get chosen for a choose-up baseball game. Definitely one of the cruelest Darwinian rites of childhood. No one wants to be that last kid chosen.

My response made Teddy chuckle. "You look at life as this binary thing; either something's alive or it's dead. Has it ever occurred to you that there's another state? To 'not exist' is one thing—but to be outside the *possibility* of existing is far worse. It's no surprise you feel the desire of all the things that will never be. You're a pinprick of light in a place that's forgotten the very concept of illumination."

Teddy took back his board, signaling the end of the evening's exercise. "You said that other realities were all around you. What did you mean by that?"

I shrugged. "All around means all around. Left and right, front and back . . ."

"How about above and below?"

I opened my mouth to speak, but realized I had no response for that. I never exactly looked up in Elsewhere, and other than sensing that swirling abyss of death, I didn't look down either.

"I . . . don't know," I said.

Teddy gave his broad mischievous grin. "I'm not surprised. You play your sport on a gridiron. You might live in a three-dimensional world, but gravity makes it a two-dimensional game. You never think about what's beneath the turf or what's miles above your head, do you?"

"It's not part of the game—"

"But what if it was?"

I tried to imagine that. Linemen emerging from the ground to pull the quarterback down. Passes that could foul the engines of airplanes. Flying backs instead of running backs. Quidditch with padding.

"The things above you will be possible futures," Teddy said. "Don't mess with those, because that will definitely trigger a correction. What I'm more interested in is the past. The things beneath your feet."

"I already changed things in the past," I pointed out. "It didn't go well."

But Teddy shook his head. "You managed to alter specific events—that's not the same as a wholesale shift in local time."

"So you want me to somehow reach into the past and stop time?"

"Or speed it up. If you hit the right moment in history, for the proper length of time, you don't just change a single event that ripples into the future—you change *every* event that happened on Earth at that given moment. Not just a ripple, but a wave."

Or a tsunami, I thought. Wasn't our team called that in another life?

"So . . . you're saying that what I've been doing is like pumping gas, when I could actually be striking oil."

"Bingo!" Teddy said.

"So how do I do it?"

His answer was simple. "By not being afraid to look down."

Fallacy #4: Hindsight is twenty-twenty.

False. There's no truth in that at all. What you see in the rearview mirror of your life is never what actually happened. You're just inventing explanations that let you sleep at night. Hindsight, at best, is Coke-bottle glasses, with lenses that distort everything. It's why they say eyewitness accounts at crime scenes are the least accurate kinds of evidence. What you firmly believe you saw is rarely what you actually saw. In that way, we're all creating our own realities.

What Teddy wanted me to do—that was just a meta version of warped hindsight. A dizzying reach down through time with the benefit of all I thought I knew about the world. I would create that all-consuming tsunami, and, like Noah, ride it out, until it brought us to a better world. It wasn't lost on me that the biblical flood involved killing everyone else in the process.

I wanted to tell myself that Teddy was just blowing smoke and that this was bizarre wishful thinking. But the Edwards had a perspective that I couldn't possibly have. Fact: if being the sub-loc meant that I was the center of the universe, then the universe was mine to mess with. And if I did it right, the universe would be grateful, wouldn't it? My grandma would say God was working through me, because that's the way he worked. I wasn't stealing the power of creation, I was channeling it for the greater good.

These were the kinds of thoughts that filled my aching head the whole week. I was sitting in math class, crunching equations, when all the while I'm thinking that I could write a wrong answer, and then make the universe change math itself, so that my answer was right. Would that be an abuse of power?

And the thought of abuse of power made me think of Layton, who was sitting two seats away from me in math. I'd like to say he was a brainless meathead and couldn't do math for his life. But he was good at it. Not sure whether it came naturally, or whether he had to work at it. All I knew was that he got furious at himself when he made simple mistakes that led to wrong answers—and in math, most wrong answers come from simple mistakes. A billion-dollar spaceship once crashed on Mars because the engineers made the simple mistake of forgetting to convert to metric. Simple mistakes; major consequences.

Layton demanded perfection from himself and visited that upon the people in his life. Nothing and no one was ever good enough. Everyone was riddled with faults and subject to harsh judgment. No surprise that Katie was always first in the line of fire.

On Wednesday, I caught another one of their private moments

before class. He didn't like the way her hair was that day. He was "encouraging" her to wear it differently—the way he liked it. He wasn't berating her—it was one step short of that. More like haranguing. Nagging until she caved. He always seemed to know exactly how far he could push her and get away with it.

Katie and I had English together, and Layton didn't. I told her what I saw, and asked her, just as I had in the previous world, why she didn't bail on him.

"Ash, I love Layton," she told me. "But relationships are complicated. You of all people should know that."

And while I knew how relationships can be full of gray areas, I also knew that certain things were black and white. Still, she shut me down, as she always did, and refused to discuss it. It was as if anyone who questioned her about Layton was the enemy. Why she would defend him and subject herself to that kind of treatment was beyond me. It's not beyond me anymore.

21

LARGER THAN INITIALLY REPORTED

Out beyond the orbit of Neptune, there's shit no one knows what to do with. Asteroids, planetoids, comets, and objects that they ridiculously decided to call "centaurs," because they're neither one thing nor another.

Pluto's bouncing around out there. That sorry rock was stripped of planetary status in 2006. But scientists do believe there's an actual ninth planet hiding from us.

Or at least they used to think it was a planet.

A few years back, a theory emerged that planet nine was actually a primordial black hole, left over from the big bang. Seriously, I'm not making this up. We can't see it, of course; we can only guess at its existence from its effect on the orbits of other random stuff. And at the heart of its darkness is a super-dense rock fifteen times the mass of Earth, but only about the size of a baseball.

Astronomers see this as a glorious facet of the universe. But they don't get it. They don't know what it *really* is . . . But I do.

It's the drain at the bottom of the tub.

An article about the above-mentioned celestial oddity popped up on my news feed on Thursday morning, sandwiched between "Three Senators Indicted for Money Laundering," and "Sixteen Adorable Dog Fails." The headline read, "Primordial Black Hole May Be Larger Than Initially Reported." But the article vanished from my feed before I could tap it. You know how that is. Once an article is gone, you can search for it for hours and never find it again.

Primordial black hole may be larger than initially reported. Today it was just clickbait for nerds. Tomorrow it might be the biggest understatement in the history of the world.

I didn't sleep well on Thursday night, knowing how close the clock was ticking to Friday's game. My dreams were vivid and troubled. I can't remember them all, but I do remember one where I had a conversation with Angela. I was standing with her looking at her grave, but the date of her death was left blank.

"You're not the reason I'm down there," she said, "but actually, you are."

I apologized. It was real and heartfelt, but she wasn't having it.

"Don't apologize, Ash," she said, not angry, but firm. "Just do something about it."

And then I was standing with Leo, just a few feet over, at his grave. The date of his death was there, but covered by weeds, and I realized it could be fifty years from now, or next month, or tomorrow.

"Does it ever bother you," he asked, "that you were named after a guy who was named after a guy who was in a movie that glorified the Confederacy?"

The answer was yes, but instead of saying that, I told him what I always told myself. "Ashley Wilkes said he was going to free his slaves if the war didn't happen first." I know this because my grandma made me sit through all four uncomfortable hours of the movie once.

"But he didn't, did he? Instead he went off and fought for the South. All talk, no action."

"I'm not him!" I told Leo.

Then Leo leaned close and whispered, "Prove it."

Then he disappeared, and when I looked around, all the tombstones in the graveyard were gone. But I knew the dead were still down there, their graves unmarked, their names unremembered.

When the dreams had all evaporated, I woke to a gloomy Friday morning full of that mental dream hangover that lingers with you for the rest of the day. Hunter was already in the kitchen when I came downstairs, inhaling a bowl of Frosted Flakes over the sink.

"Hey, check it out," he said, showing me his T-shirt. The shirt had a logo that read "Live Your Life."

"Yeah, so? What's that supposed to mean?"

"They're your words, don't you remember?"

I hadn't until he mentioned it. It was part of what I said to those reporters.

"They were handing them out for free at school yesterday, so I took a couple. You want one?"

"Absolutely not!" The idea of wearing my own quote felt like masturbating to a mirror. "And who's 'they'?"

"I don't know—the LGBTQ club maybe? They want people to wear them to the game tonight. To support you."

I didn't know how to feel about that, so I decided not to feel anything at all.

"Tonight's game is against Slayback High, isn't it?" Hunter asked.

"Yeah, why?"

"They play dirty," he said. "Everyone knows it."

I tried to shrug it off. "Refs'll be watching."

"Refs can only see so much." And then he put his cereal bowl down and looked at me a little too long.

"What?" I asked.

"Nothing," he said. "It's just . . . I don't know . . . You said not to worry, but I can't stop. You're not yourself, lately—and I don't mean the gay thing. It's something else. Something . . . bigger."

Not myself. That made me laugh. He had no idea how right he was. I had no specific "self" anymore. Just versions. Like a human operating system.

"Well, if I'm not myself, then who am I?"

He had no answer. "Just be careful tonight," he said. "I've got a bad feeling about this game."

I took a deep, slow breath. I knew Hunter meant well, but his dark cloud layered over my own blocked out any hint of light.

"There's nothing to worry about," I told him.

"I know, but still . . . wear your lucky underwear or something."

"Anything *that* close to my sweaty junk all day can't be very lucky."

He gave an obligatory chuckle, and we left it at that.

I was in a daze that day. The world went about its business, not knowing the tether it hung on. The Edwards told me this was always going on somewhere. Maybe it was best to live in ignorance of the big picture. How could the world function if it knew the things I knew?

I didn't want to be in class; I couldn't think, couldn't function, and with each hour that passed, the sky outside got darker, as if that black hole was looming just beyond the clouds.

At noon it rained. It didn't just rain, it poured. If it kept on like that, our game would be canceled. Part of me wanted that, so the inevitable would be postponed, but I knew time was not my ally.

And then there was Katie, who filled the gaps between my thoughts about Leo and the end of the world. Katie and Layton weren't in the lunchroom that day, and it troubled me. As seniors, we could go off campus, but the two of them rarely did. Layton seemed more interested in presiding over his cafeteria court.

"Why do you care?" Paul asked. "Don't we have more

important things to do?"

He and I were working on strategies for the integration dance. Making it happen right under the school board's nose was very much like a football draw play—where the quarterback fakes a pass and hands it off to the running back instead. We were now calling it the "disintegration dance," because we were hoping it would cause certain school board members to melt down into the pork and beans they came from.

And although I wanted every minute I could get with Paul before the next change, I had to go look for Layton and Katie, if only to make sure that Katie was all right.

"Fine," said Paul, refusing to join me in my fool's errand. "But I'm eating your Jell-O."

I found Katie and Layton in the north hallway, having words. I kept my distance, trying to stay out of sight. I was too far away to hear what they were saying—but I could clock their tone of voice. Katie was not happy, and Layton was trying to calm her. That was their pattern. He would make some dick move, or say something cruel, Katie would get angry, and then Layton would flip like a coin, becoming all apologies and charm. He wore her down as he always did, until she stopped talking, and just started nodding. His superpower was the ability to turn girls into bobbleheads. Nod and agree. Nod and agree. As long as it got him to shut up.

That's when Katie saw me at the far end of the hall, and her glance made Layton turn my way as well. I strode off pretending I was just passing by, but I knew I hadn't sold it.

♦ ♦ ♦

There's one more great fallacy of life I learned that day. *What goes around comes around.*

That would be nice, wouldn't it? Everyone getting what they deserve? But more often than not, what goes around just keeps going around again and again and again, kicking you in the head each and every time.

Just as school was letting out, I got a call from Leo. I figured he was calling to update me on any progress he was making in recruiting friends for the dance. But like I said, his world and my world were different places.

"This is my one call," he said flatly.

"Why one?" I asked.

"Because that's all they give you."

And when I was too dense to figure it out, he had to tell me that he'd been arrested. He didn't call his mom or his dad, because he knew they'd be heartbroken. He didn't call Cerise, because he didn't want her to know. He didn't call any of the friends he had before I so rudely inserted myself into his alternate life. He called me.

I was supposed to have a final training session with Teddy, and although that might have served Leo better in the long run, I had to go to him. I brought all the money I could dig up from various hiding places around the house, as well as a fake ID, because if you were over eighteen, you were allowed to post bail. Rich me had multiple fake IDs, so they'd never know I was still seventeen. Leo, on the other hand, was a true eighteen, having had his birthday in August—making him an adult in the eyes of the criminal justice system.

Turns out it didn't matter how much money I brought—the court was backed up, and Leo would have to stay a day, maybe two, in jail before a judge set bail. In my world that was supposed to happen much faster. Just like in my world bail was supposed to be reasonable. The only difference between my world and this one was that in mine it was *supposed* to be better, but lots of times it wasn't. Which proved that no matter what world you lived in, injustice was a shitcake of many layers.

There wasn't glass between us like there was in movies, but armed guards eyed us with suspicion from across the room.

"So what happened?" I asked.

"Broke my boss's nose."

"You must have had a reason for hitting him."

"I didn't hit him, I tackled him," Leo said. Then he let out a bitter laugh. "Your tackle changes the world. Mine just screws up my life."

And then he told me the whole story.

"Homeless guy. Seen him before. Something not right about him. Not strung out or anything, just wrong in the head, you know? Next thing I know, there's this woman screaming over by the deli counter. I leave my register, run over, and this guy—he's been cornered by my manager. The guy's got a knife, and he's scared out of his mind. Because my manager's pulled a gun on him. And this guy—you know what he's got under his arm? A goddamn roast chicken! And his knife? It's nothing but a butter knife. The dude just wants food, and my manager's treating him like he just skinned his mother. The guy tries to bolt, and I know—I *know*—from the look on my manager's face that he's gonna pull the trigger. So I take my manager down before he can. I tackle him to the ground, and the gun goes off, shattering the deli case. And the homeless guy gets away. And now there's blood on the ground, and I'm thinking did someone get shot? But no, the bullet at most killed a honey ham. The blood's from my manager's nose. When he hit the ground, it broke. And the way he's looking at me, I knew that if the gun hadn't flown from his hands, he would have used it on me."

Leo took a moment to wipe his eyes and get himself calmed down. "So I think that's the end of it, but when I get back to my register, it's been cleaned out. Somebody waiting in my goddamn line saw the chance, took the money, and ran. But my manager accuses me. 'The whole thing was planned,' he says. Me, the homeless guy, and someone else were working together. And why does he think this? Because we're both Black. He calls me a 'no-account s'equal.'" Then Leo pursed his lips tight. "I would've hit him for that, but his nose was already broken."

"I woulda hit him anyway," I told him. Easy for me to say, because I might have gotten away with it in a way that Leo couldn't.

"So the police show up a few minutes later, and the manager has me arrested."

"He can't do that! He has no proof you did anything but save that homeless guy's life!"

299

"Assault," Leo said. "Broken nose, blood everywhere. He tells the cops I attacked him, and they haul me away in handcuffs."

I wanted to hurt someone. I wanted to hurt everyone who had a part in this. I wanted to burn it all to the ground. "He can't get away with that!"

"No? Then how come I'm the one in here instead of him?"

I couldn't answer because there was no good answer.

"I'm gonna take care of this, Leo. I'm gonna make it right. Better than right."

Then he glared at me, and suddenly I felt like the enemy. Like I was just another part of this fucked-up world.

"Always the same thing. The great white hero's gonna solve all the world's problems. And I was stupid enough to believe it. You had me fooled, Ash. You had me fooled."

"I'm no hero," I told him. "I'm the monster who did this to you. I stole your life and your future. You have every right to hate me." The truth hurt, but I couldn't hide from it. I made this world. All its flaws and injustices. All its brutal, unthinkable realities. Great white hero, my ass. This miserable world was on me.

Leo couldn't hold back the tears anymore. As much as he didn't want me to see them. "Tell me it's different where you come from," he pleaded. "I know your world ain't perfect, but tell me this wouldn't have happened there."

And as much as I wanted to say that was true—as much as I wanted to comfort him—I couldn't. Because it could have happened to him there, just as easily as here. Because as far as we'd like to think we'd come, we've barely moved the ball inches.

Apathy, resistance, and self-interest hold the line, and the fumbles alone are too many to count.

So I didn't answer him, because I couldn't give him the answer he wanted to hear. And I thought about Teddy, who wanted me to reach down into the murky depths, alter all of human history, and make the world better than when I started. How could I not be tempted by the prospect?

"I swear to you, Leo. I will fix what I broke."

"What if you can't? What if broken means broken?"

"If I can't fix it," I told him, "then I'll die trying."

I had a run-in with Layton just before the game. It was ten minutes to kickoff. I was suiting up with the rest of the team, but I was distracted. Staring at my hands, staring at my feet— wondering if I had what it took to make the sweeping kind of change Teddy had been grooming me for. People trained their whole lives for far less important things. I had barely trained at all. When I finally looked up, most everyone else had gone. It was just me and Layton.

"So, did you get an earful this afternoon?" he asked. "You like listening to other people's conversations?"

The last thing I wanted was to get into this now, but I couldn't shake off Layton's taunting. He was baiting me, and against my better judgment, I took the bait.

"Not particularly," I said. Even though I hadn't heard a thing, I didn't tell Layton that. I let him sweat about it. "But some conversations you can't tune out no matter how hard you try."

"Well, Ash, I know sticking your nose where it doesn't belong is kind of your thing, but what goes on between me and Katie? That's none of your business."

"Whose business is it, Layton? You wrap your arm around Katie like you want to protect her, but who's going to protect her from you?"

Then Layton got almost, but not quite, in my face. It wasn't rage, but a calculated, controlled threat. "You had better watch yourself. I don't care who your father is, I swear I'll—"

"You'll what? You'll hit me? Go on, do it. I want you to. Hit me so hard that it knocks me into next Tuesday. Because I know something about next Tuesday that you don't."

"And what would that be?"

Then I whispered in his ear. "Hit me hard enough, and you won't be there."

And in that moment, I would have done it. I would have slipped into Elsewhere and pushed him right into that pit of oblivion to join Ralston and his goons. No trace, no evidence.

He backed off, not sure what to make of that. "You know what? I'm done with you," he said. "And so is Katie. Get it through your thick skull that we love each other, and I will not let you get in the way of that."

"Love? You wouldn't know love if it bit you in the ass."

And to that, he gave a nasty, lascivious smile. The kind that leaves a bad taste in your mouth just looking at it.

"Maybe you're just jealous," he said. "Maybe you just want what she gets."

I think I would have torn him apart if Norris hadn't shown

up at that exact moment.

"Hey, we're all waiting for you out there. Coach is getting impatient—he wants to give his pep talk."

I was so volcanic, I could feel myself shaking, and the angrier I got, the calmer Layton did. "That's good energy, Bowman," Layton said. "Save it for the game." Then he sauntered off, like he was so golden, nothing could touch him.

I punched a locker so hard, it popped a hinge.

"So was that about Katie?" Norris asked, once Layton was gone. The fact that even Norris had eyes on the situation meant that Layton's treatment of her was obvious, even to him.

"What else would it be about?" I snapped, but then took it down a notch. "Someone had to say something." This was the first time Norris had spoken to me in a week. That didn't earn him a reward, but at least I could try to be civil. And then Norris went and ruined it.

"If you ask me, Katie knew what she was getting into," Norris said. "You date a guy like Layton, you get all that comes with it, good and bad. If she's okay with that, maybe you should be, too."

And you know what the most horrible thing about that was? He wasn't just speaking off the cuff. I could tell he had given it plenty of thought before reaching that fucked-up conclusion.

"Norris, when are you gonna realize that the guy you idolize is not who you think he is?"

Norris took a moment before he responded to that.

"*You're* the one I idolized, Ash," he said. "And you're right. He's not."

◆ ◆ ◆

We ran out onto the field a few minutes later to the expected roars from the crowd, and the familiar pump of adrenaline. But today my adrenaline was flowing at cross-purposes to the game. It had been a long time since I was there to play football. My game had much higher stakes.

The stands on both sides were packed with spectators. Standing room only. Our games were always well attended, but never like that. I wanted to believe it was because the Cheatin' Cheetahs, as we called them, were our archrivals, and this was always the most high-profile game of the season. But it was more than that.

In the stands, on both sides, I saw a fair number of rainbow flags, and people were wearing that "Live Your Life" shirt. While a lot of people out there just came to watch football, there was a large contingent who had come specifically to watch me. It made me feel angry rather than supported. Didn't these people know I was just a lineman? Linemen are not supposed to be the center of attention. We don't want to be. That's why we're on the line. And then I thought, maybe this was some sort of communal expression of the proximity effect. Maybe everyone sensed the *significance* of this game, without knowing why. They were rooting for me to deliver.

I know that sounds pretty self-important. Was I full of myself by this point? Maybe. I think the only way to wield a weapon is to first believe you're capable of it. King Arthur never would have reached for that sword if he didn't secretly believe somewhere deep down that the stone would release it for him. And make no doubt about it, being a sub-loc meant wielding a weapon. I had already used that weapon to erase three people. Now I had to redeem myself by using it to carve out a better world.

I caught sight of the Edwards in the stands. All five of them together—which was anything but inconspicuous. They were the subject of curious glances, and neck-wrenching double takes. One of them gave me a thumbs-up. Was it Teddy? I couldn't tell. Did the other Edwards have any clue what I was going to attempt today? What would they do if they knew? If I dredged up a world better than the one where I started, surely they'd feel the end justified the means, wouldn't they?

I couldn't find Paul in the stands. I knew he was there, but in the sea of faces, he was lost—and that bothered me more today than ever before. When I next saw him, who would he be to me? Thinking about that made my heart sink, and I knew I couldn't allow that. I needed to be at my peak if I was going to do this right.

Anthem, coin toss, kickoff, and I took to the field with the rest of our defensive team. Was it my imagination, or were the lights brighter than usual? Everything seemed sharper, and more defined. Hyper-real.

The Cheetahs' QB was better than Layton, although no one on our team would say that out loud. He had an arm like a cannon, and when he ran, he could weave through defenders like they weren't there. But he rarely had to run. He could throw a tea party in the backfield if he wanted to, because their offensive line was impenetrable. But if I was going to do what I needed to do, I had to break through.

All game I tried. I tried harder than I ever had before. But by halftime, I hadn't put a single dent in that human wall.

The score was tied at thirteen—two touchdowns and one successful extra point for each team. Two of their players and one of ours were pulled out of the game for fighting. And yeah, the Cheetahs were nasty. Flag after flag was thrown for everything from backfield in motion to holding, but in spite of all their penalties, they kept the pressure on—and our team's anger at their poor sportsmanship worked against us. Our team didn't want to play football now; we just wanted to beat the crap out of them. The way I had felt about Layton in the locker room.

"Do not let them psych you out!" the coach yelled during his halftime rant. "It's what they want. It's their strategy. Do not let them faze you!"

But since I was playing a different game, I didn't care whether the Cheetahs followed the rules or not. All I cared about was getting through that line. And hitting. Hard. I would have broken their QB's back if that would take me where I needed to go.

The cheerleaders put on a show, Katie all fake smiles, in spite of anything she might be feeling inside. The band marched through a weak rendition of an even weaker song from this world, and the second half began.

I thought I'd be facing the same impenetrable offensive line, but then a few minutes into the third quarter, I saw my opening. Their center—who I faced on the line—slipped when hiking the ball. Not enough to throw him off balance, but enough to rattle his focus. He recovered in an instant, but that instant was all I needed. I hurled myself into him, he went down, and I was through the line! Their quarterback hadn't yet found a receiver to pass to because I had broken through the line so quickly.

I was a freight train in motion. Single-minded. I would take him down for a ten-yard loss—but more than that, I would launch myself into the true field of play. I was ready. I was confident.

And then it all went wrong.

22

POINT SEVEN THREE

Seventy-three hundredths of a second. 0.73. It's the single beat of a resting heart. It's the difference between being killed by a truck barreling through an intersection and having that same truck miss you by inches. Had Norris and I been killed that night after my first shift, the world would not have been a better place—but it wouldn't have been any worse either. Blue would be the color of stop. Would more people die in car accidents because of it? Probably not, but different people, maybe. Likely no one you know would be affected, and even if they were, you'd never know the difference. Unless of course it was you who got killed. But then it wouldn't matter to you anyway, because you'd be dead.

Point seven three seconds. That meant nothing to me. But it was about to mean all the difference in the world.

It wasn't a truck that hit me on the field, it was a Cheetah. I was clipped illegally by the opposing halfback. He had seen how quickly I broke through the line, and rather than letting me take down the quarterback, he hit me from the side, low and hard, beneath my padding. I felt a rib crack. And with that sharp blast of pain came an icy cold, and darkness. I was sliding again. I was Elsewhere.

I was tumbling, off balance in pain. It was different from the pain of being attacked in the alley, because I had braced for that. This left me reeling, out of control. I had to regain control—everything rested on it—but my head was full of so many conflicting things. Leo, and Katie, and Paul, and all the people whose lives would be affected by these impossibly long microseconds.

According to Teddy, everything that I had done to this point was small potatoes, but they hadn't felt small to me, because they had major consequences.

Don't be afraid to look down.

Because beneath my feet would be glorious realities I could scarcely imagine. Farmlands where deserts used to be. Different nations, different languages.

"Reach for the realities that radiate peace," Teddy had said. "You'll feel them. You'll know."

And the worlds—those needy realities that were alive yet not—were awakened by my presence. They sensed that I was in pain, and compromised, and they were emboldened by it.

They were fighting with one another to get to me first. To consume me.

But I would not allow it. In spite of the pain, I would take control. And so with all the determination I could muster I did what I had to do. I looked down.

Beneath me was the abyss, ever present, and waiting for me to plunge into its depths and cease to exist. But if I shut out my fear of it, I could sense the worlds Teddy spoke about. They were wildly different from the ones swarming around me—those were all just variations of what I already knew, but beneath me were truly new worlds!

I could do it! I could reach down deep to the most peaceful, serene expression of reality. I could grasp a better world!

But at that crucial instant I held back. My own fear of the unknown kept me from reaching that far down. Instead I hedged my bet and grasped a world just beneath my feet. Yes, it was a world of change, but far less change than I could have accomplished.

The moment I claimed it, my heart stopped. For a single beat. Then resumed so powerfully, I felt I would burst from the force of it.

And it was done.

Later I would have to remind myself that I chose to take hold of this world. Some part of me must have known what it would bring. Was that part of me an enemy or a friend? To this day, I don't know.

I snapped out of Elsewhere, back onto the bright, noisy field, gasping, wheezing, the wind knocked out of me, and the pain in my side so intense I was seeing stars. My sense of direction was so fouled I couldn't tell up from down. The announcer was talking about a flag on the play. Damn right there was a flag on the play, I was clipped. Brutally. But I felt an odd distance from the action. That's when I realized that I wasn't on the field. I was on the sidelines, and people were standing over me.

"My gosh, are you okay?"

The face was of a girl I didn't know. I couldn't answer because I still couldn't catch my breath.

Then Katie was there. "Just take deep breaths," she said. "Slow, deep breaths."

"Let me through!" I heard a familiar voice shout. Layton. The last person I wanted to see. Suddenly Layton was standing over me, eclipsing the harsh lights of the field. He knelt down.

"Baby, you okay?"

I just stared at him. *What did he just say? What the hell did he just say?*

"Give her space!" Katie demanded.

"That damn Cheetah!" yelled Layton. "I could kill him!"

"Calm down," the coach said to Layton. "We're about to get the ball back, and I need your head in the game."

But I was still grappling with what both Katie and Layton had just said.

"*. . . Baby, you okay?*"

"*. . . Give her space.*"

Katie helped me sit up. My legs were cold. Because I was in a skirt. A cheerleading uniform.

No no no no no no no!

"This can't be it!" I said, in a voice a full octave higher than the voice I knew. "I need to get back on the field." But it hurt too much as I tried to stand up.

"I'll call an ambulance," the cheer coach said, kneeling beside Katie, taking my hand. "It's okay, Ashley," she said, stroking my hair, which was way too freaking long. On the field the game had resumed, because play doesn't stop because of an injured cheerleader.

I took a deep breath. Held it. Took another and held it again. Then I breathed out slowly, getting the pain and my thoughts under control.

"Let me go," I told Katie and the cheer coach. Then I stood up on my own, fought the pain and the dizziness, and the foreignness of my own body. And once I was sure I had my balance and wouldn't fall, I turned to the cheer coach. "Cancel the ambulance," I told her. "I'll walk it off."

23

"I'M SO GLAD YOU'RE MINE"

Here's what I know.

My name is Ashley Bowman. Everybody calls me that, not just my grandmother. I'm on the cheer squad in the fall, and I do competitive cheerleading in winter, and track and field in the spring. My best event is the long jump. I have a younger brother named Hunter—that hasn't changed. My father still used to be an NFL player, and we're still one of the wealthiest families in town, but here, my parents are divorced.

I'm dating Layton Vandenboom, the star quarterback of the Gray Demons. We've been together for almost a year. Our relationship is . . . complicated.

"Someone should be held responsible!" my mother said, as she drove me to the hospital. Even though an ambulance wasn't called, the swelling in my side warranted a trip to the emergency room. I knew I had a broken rib, but I also knew that there was nothing you could do for that but let it heal on its own. Unless, of course, it punctured an organ, but I didn't think it was quite that bad.

"It was nobody's fault," I told her.

In *this* world, one of the Cheetahs' receivers had just caught a pass and was taking it down the sideline, when one of our boys pushed him out of bounds and into me, taking me down hard.

I was protectively numb about my new situation. The moment I had dared to reach down and felt what was no longer there, and what was in its place, my subconscious switched off all emotion and put my brain in a cast. It was necessary. Because thinking about who Layton was in my life now would have caused me to hurl myself out the door into oncoming traffic.

What troubled me most was the nature of the change. I hadn't taken the world into me as I had once before. This, I knew, was a sweeping change, which meant it involved more than just me.

I didn't know it yet—but what I had done was shift time for a single heartbeat, for every living human male. That might seem like nothing—but it was long enough for a different sperm to fertilize my mother's egg.

And it wasn't just me.

That 0.73 seconds was a hiccup for the entire world—like that awkward time lag you get when you're on a phone call to someone in a different country. Everything in human history happened a heartbeat later than it would have. It altered the world in ways that were impossible to tally. Streets and businesses had different names. Even some buildings were altered.

But none of that compared to the human change.

About three in four people looked the same, proving that some destinies had great inertia and took far more effort to change. But one in four had the same sperm/egg issue I had. About half of those people stayed the same sex but looked like their own nonexistent sibling. The other half, however, had an instant biological sex change. In other words, one in eight guys were now girls, and one in eight girls were now guys.

Now go look at yourself in the mirror, because, for all you know, it could be you. But don't worry about it, because even if it was you, you'd never know. Pleasant dreams.

At 9:00 the next morning, the doorbell rang. Not at 8:59, or 9:01, but precisely 9:00. Because my mom once told Layton that ringing a doorbell before 9:00 a.m. was rude. Layton had a very literal worldview. That was part of a much larger problem.

"Ashley's not down yet," I heard my mom say. "You can wait if you like."

"Thank you, Ms. Bowman."

Although my parents here split up ages ago, my mom kept her married name, because the name meant something here in Taylorville. She considered clout to be part of the divorce settlement.

I had just woken up after a medicated sleep courtesy of last night's ER doctor. I wasn't ready to access my memories of

Layton in this world. I would much rather have had the emotionally detached analysis of the Edwards than all the emotionally charged internal data detailing my life as a girl. But honestly, I wasn't ready to face the Edwards either.

It ached to breathe. The doctor had said the bruising would look worse before it looked better. "Rest and time," she had said. I sat up in bed and lifted my pajama top to see the bruise, but my view was obscured by a breast.

Right. I had those now.

I remembered having them, just like I remembered my first period, just like I remembered having a penis, just like I remembered the first time I saw a real live one in this world, and remembered thinking it looked like a wrinkled old man with a big nose. If we guys knew what we girls thought about our junk, we'd be far less impressed with ourselves.

Knowing Layton wouldn't leave, I steeled myself to go downstairs. But there were a few things I needed to do first.

I checked my texts to see who was in my list of friends. There was Katie, and a few girls from cheer. There were also the names of a few classmates I knew in this world, but not in the others. Hunter and my mom were there, but not my dad. The names I was looking for weren't showing up, and anxiety began to blossom. Then finally Paul made an appearance in the list as I scrolled further down.

The last text from him was three weeks ago. Running late, the old text said. I won't charge for any time I miss.

So he was back to being my math tutor. That bruise hurt more than the one in my side, but it was comforting to know that at least he was still here. I had no indication about Leo, though. As I said, Leo was not a texter. Was he still in jail in this world? Was he in this world at all?

One thing at a time, I told myself. I had to put one foot in front of the other, red toenails and all.

I got dressed. My wardrobe reflected who I was here. I was a little bit lacey and a little bit leathery. I had some things that sparkled, but not all that much. I liked pastels over bright colors, but, like Angela, lavender was the closest I got to pink. Each outfit brought back a memory—either of when I bought it or a time I had worn it. This gown I wore to my sweet sixteen. That blouse I wore on my first date with Layton. That skirt—no, I'm not going to think about that skirt. I'm not going to think about it at all.

I shut the closet door and took a few deep cleansing breaths. *I'm a girl. So?* I told myself. If this was it—if this is how I ended up leaving things—I would adapt. Because if there was anything I had learned in my wild interdimensional travels, it was that there was a playbook for everything. Besides, I was less troubled by how this left me than how it left others.

I picked out a panda T-shirt and a pair of jeans with pointlessly small pockets, then went to the toilet, standing there disoriented for a moment before realizing I had better do this sitting down. Then I brushed my teeth, which hadn't changed, and brushed my hair, which had. In addition to being longer, it had far better texture than guy hair. I tossed it, felt it settle, and liked the feeling.

Hunter was in the hallway when I came out. Seeing him was a breath of fresh air, because he was the same as before, although there was an intensity to his expression that wasn't there in earlier versions.

"Mom told me what happened," he said. "A cracked rib sucks, but you'll probably be able to cheerlead again in a week or two."

"Doctor said three."

"Alternating ice and heat, three times a day," Hunter said. "You'll be good to go in two weeks."

I grinned. "Thank you, Dr. Bowman."

"Don't thank me till you see the bill." Then he glanced down the stairs and said, "Hey, do you want me to run interference with Layton? I could tell him you're still sleeping and get him to throw a ball around in the backyard with me. That'll be good for half an hour at least."

"Thanks, Hunter, but this is a ball I've got to run with."

"Hah! Since when does a lineman run with the ball—" Then he stopped himself. I could swear I saw his pupils constrict a little. "Never mind . . ." he said, a bit uneasily. "I don't know what . . . I don't know what I was thinking."

I gently took his arm. "It was a good thought, Hunter," I said. "And thank you for offering to help."

He held my gaze for a moment, and his disquiet faded. He smiled. "No worries." Then he went into the bathroom. I hoped he would forget that moment of confusion. He didn't deserve to be laid low by the proximity effect.

When I came downstairs, Layton was sitting in the kitchen,

talking about the history of weird sports injuries with my mom. He stood up when he saw me.

"There you are!"

"Hi, Layton."

The sight of him brought forth a flood of emotions tethered to memories that were all too complicated to parse.

My mom left the room, giving us privacy, which I really didn't want at the moment.

"I've been texting you since last night," he said once she was gone.

"The doctor gave me something to help me sleep, so I just now saw them." Which was mostly true. I actually didn't read them. I just saw that he had sent nine texts.

He came close and put his hand around my waist, leaning in, clearly wanting to give me a kiss, but I pulled out of his grip before he could.

"Don't, it hurts," I told him. True, although that's not why I pulled away. Ashley would have received the kiss, but Ash was too horrified to allow it. I knew if I was going to survive this, though, I needed to trust Ashley. My actions and my responses had to be directed by who I was now, not who I used to be. She had to guide me, inside and out.

"How bad is it?" Layton asked. "Can I see?"

I hesitated, but in the end, I lifted the side of my T-shirt to show him. I thought he'd be taken aback enough to keep his distance and give me some space, but instead it was the opposite. "Aw, baby," he said, then knelt down, giving my bruised side the softest kiss. "I wish I could make it all better."

I found my hand involuntarily stroking his hair, but stopped abruptly, feeling horrified that I was touching any part of Layton Vandenboom and liking it.

Stop it, Ash, you're not helping, I wanted to say. *Well, Ashley, running your fingers through his hair isn't really helping either, is it?*

"We don't have to go, if you don't want to," Layton said. "We can stay here today."

I was confused for a moment, then remembered that we were supposed to go to the harvest fair today. Tilt-a-Whirls and corn dogs. Not happening.

"I just want to stay home," I told him, and although that statement didn't include him, he assumed that it did.

So we sat in the family room, close as couples do, and watched a movie. In this world the house didn't have a home theater; Dad had moved out before getting that particular idea, and home theaters are more a dad kind of thing. I was grateful, because in a dark theater closed off from the rest of the house, Layton might have wanted to do a little more than snuggle, and I definitely didn't want that today. All versions of me were in agreement there.

His arm felt heavy around me. But it also felt warm. But it also felt restrictive. But it also felt comforting. But it also felt stifling. It was impossible to make sense of all my conflicting emotions, and they kept changing moment to moment, like I was spinning and lurching on the harvest fair Tilt-a-Whirl after all.

"What happened to you last night never should have

happened," he said, then shifted to look at me with soft, soulful eyes. And with a gentle stroke of his hand on my cheek, said, "That's why you should always pay attention to the game."

When I was a guy, I thought Layton was an open-and-shut case. Football Jock Who Abuses His Girlfriend. I mean, so obvious, he could be an action figure villain. But Layton wasn't the kind of monster I thought he was. He was a different kind.

He never punched me, never smacked me across the face—which meant he probably never did that to Katie either. But that didn't mean he was all that much better.

You know who Layton was? He was that little boy who held his Christmas kitten extra tight to show he loved it. And when it squirmed, he held it tighter to keep it from running into the street. And when it scratched, he grabbed its paws, and when it tried to bite, he squeezed its jaw, and when it hissed, he clamped its neck, and when it died in his hands, it wasn't his fault, because he was only trying to teach it right from wrong, but it just couldn't learn. Why couldn't it learn, Daddy, why? Damn shame—but that's okay, son, we'll get you another kitty.

Even if they begin with good intentions, in their heart of hearts abusers believe love is about control. They believe it's about possession. And why shouldn't they? It's the ugly underbelly of every love song ever written. Don't believe me? How many love songs have the words "you're mine" in the core of the lyrics? Or "I'll never let you go," or "you belong to me." For guys like Layton, it's much too easy to take that literally.

As I sat on the couch with him that morning, there were so many memories of "us" that came to me. You want to hear that our relationship was a perpetual nightmare, don't you? It would be so much easier if I could tell you that. But my memories were a confusing mix. Some were actually warm fuzzy things—the kinds of memories that make you smile. But those good memories were riddled by the bullets of the bad ones. Harsh, secret things that are hard to share even with your closest friends.

We want to portray abusers as having no redeeming qualities. We want to believe a guy who can treat a woman like that is evil through and through. In movies and TV, you always know the abuser, because he's BAD with a capital *B*. It's all clear-cut and simple, and we shake our heads at the poor women who are naïve enough to fall for them. Can't they see that capital *B*? What's wrong with them? It makes the rest of us feel good to know we're so much smarter.

But that's not real life.

Because most abusers aren't assholes in wifebeaters who smack their bitch around because "she deserves it." They're guys wearing a T-shirt of your favorite band. They're funny and charming, and genuine and respectful, right until the moment they're not. But by the time those nastier colors bleed through, you're already snared. Because by then, they know you. They know exactly where your buttons are—not just your buttons but your wounds, too. All those soft vulnerable places filled with self-doubt. They find those places, insert themselves deep, and have their way.

If there's one truth I now know from being a woman caught in Layton's kitten-crushing embrace, it's that most abusers don't leave a wide debris field that's easy to spot, and therefore easy to avoid. They're not nukes; they're radiation zones. They're not tornadoes; they're balmy summer skies, where the morning sun makes you forget the thunderstorm that's coming in the afternoon.

And Layton? He firmly believed that he was one of the good guys, because sometimes he was.

"Your mom making breakfast?" he asked as we sat there, but my mom had already left the house. "Never mind, I'll make you something."

Layton got busy in the kitchen. When my mom was around, he acted like a visitor, but when she wasn't, he took over the house like he owned it. He was not a good cook. I used to find it sweet that he tried. Then he started making my portions ridiculously small. "Because I know you're watching your weight." And the cherry on top was how my mother would react to that. "At least he's looking out for you," she would say.

This time he came back with one and a half scrambled eggs, and instead of throwing him out of the house for trying to dictate my diet, I ate them, telling myself I wasn't very hungry anyway.

At precisely 11:00, Layton got up to leave. "I promised my sister I'd take her to the fair. She'll get all tweaked if I don't."

"Go," I told him. "You put in two solid hours of girlfriend

duty." And I immediately regretted saying it, because that would do nothing but make him say—

"I'll stay if you want."

Which was not what I wanted. Ready or not, I had to face the Edwards. I couldn't do that with Layton doting on me.

"Go take your sister to the fair," I told him, wondering if he even had a sister in my original world. "It's okay, I need more sleep anyway."

I saw him to the door. He gave me a kiss, and this time I accepted it, successfully subduing all the versions of myself that wanted to hurl, because that *definitely* would have made him stay. I let the part of me that took comfort from his kiss feel what it wanted to feel—which was already a mix of emotions—because Ashley didn't need Ash's baggage on top of that.

I watched Layton drive away, took a few moments to settle, then got in my car—a shiny turquoise MINI Cooper instead of a shiny black Beemer—and left to face the Edwardian music.

24

CARS HEADING SOUTH

With all the things going through my mind and heart, it was hard for me to concentrate on the road, especially because some of the roads had changed—and not just names; the map itself was different. I needed to ignore older instincts and rely on the twists and turns that came with my memories of this world. Even so, I had to pull over and regain my bearings. I was disoriented and fuzzy, like a bird who had flown into a window, and my head ached with the pressure of seven distinct realities battling for the right to be remembered.

A text came in as I sat there. It was just a single question mark from Katie. I took a few moments to scroll through all the texts that had come in since last night, this time actually reading what they said. I thought there would be a whole lot of people checking to see if I was okay, but there weren't all that many. I didn't have that many close friends in this world. Teammates and acquaintances, but Katie was the only close friend. Everyone else had gradually fallen away.

To the people who asked how I was, I gave the same answer. I'm fine, thanks so much for asking. Nobody replied to my reply, as if their concern was more obligatory than genuine. That made me sad. No, not quite sad. It made me wistful. I was longing for something that had been lost, but I couldn't quite place where, or even what it was.

Besides those texts, and Layton's persistent pings of increasing concern from last night, were Katie's.

So what changed? her first text said. Followed by question marks every few hours to get my attention when I hadn't answered. It made me laugh. How was I supposed to answer that in a text?

Everything, and nothing, I finally answered.

What does that even mean? she responded within seconds, and when I didn't respond right away, she asked, Can you talk?

At the time I thought that was an odd thing to say. Why wouldn't I be able to talk? And then I realized that she was treating *me* the way I used to treat *her*. She thought I couldn't talk because Layton might be with me. But even though I was free to talk, there was too much to sort out for me to have that conversation now.

We'll talk on Monday, I told her.

A long pause, and finally she wrote, OK, I get it.

◆ ◆ ◆

The Toys "R" Us was gone. At first, I thought it had been torn down, but then I realized that it had never even been built. Instead there was a burned-out church in the middle of a field with tall weeds, and the faint memory of a gravel path. It was an old-fashioned clapboard church: narrow with a sharp wedge of a roof, mostly skeletal now, and the steeple, still intact, stood like a tombstone above the ruin. From the charred remains, you could tell it was once painted sky blue. Out front, a faded sign still held the title of its last sermon. A biblical quote.

"Live Thy Life with Unwavering Conviction."
—Bartholomew 5:11

I'm no biblical scholar, but I know that the gospel of Bartholomew wasn't in anyone's Bible before last night.

Although the roof was barely a memory, the walls still stood. So did the front doors, clinging stubbornly to their rusty hinges. I pushed a door open to find that, sure enough, this was the Edwards' new lair. The squeal of the door alerted them to my presence.

"Look who finally decided to show," one of them said. The implied distaste in his voice make it clear that this was Edd.

"It hardly matters anymore," said another —Eduardo, I think.

Ed just offered a weary sigh and a shake of his head, and Eddy ignored me entirely, tapping away single-mindedly on the QuIRT.

Ned—Edward number six, that is—approached me. "You do

realize what you've done, don't you?" And then he explained to me the consequences of my 0.73-second shift. How so many people were radically different versions of themselves, and how that had affected the world.

"The basic thrust of history is mostly the same as your previous world," Ed explained, "but the particulars are different."

After my injury last night, I had been too dazed to notice how many faces around me had changed. My mother was exactly the same. So were Hunter, Katie, and Layton. But as for everyone else, I had no idea.

"How about Leo?" I asked. "Is he changed?"

Ned glanced to Eddy, who worked it out on the QuIRT.

"You'll find his cheekbones higher, and a half-inch increase in height. But otherwise he's mostly the same."

"And still in jail awaiting trial," Edd said, leveling it at me like an accusation. It answered my most pressing question, but it was not the answer I wanted. At least I hadn't made Leo's situation worse, but there was no comfort in that.

"Well, at least *you* haven't changed," Eddy said, sparing a quick glance at me.

"Excuse me, but I used to be a boy," I pointed out.

He took a second glance at me. "Oh, right. My mistake."

"We only see the inner you," Ned said.

Among the sea of identical faces, the one I most wanted to see—and the one I was most ashamed to face—was Teddy. I had failed to create the kind of shift he wanted. He was counting on me for a bull's-eye, and I had completely missed the target. The others saw me looking for the AWOL Edward, and all their gazes turned to Edd, as if he was now the one calling the shots. That did not bode well on any level.

"What's going on?" I asked.

Ed gave me that sad sigh once more. "I have been voted out," he said. "I'm no longer the premier persona."

"Under his leadership, things have gone increasingly awry. You'll no longer be taking direction from him," Edd told me. "I'm in charge now."

"Where's number five?" I asked, because Teddy was still nowhere to be seen.

That made Edd get even colder. "What the two of you conspired to do was dangerous and irresponsible."

"Where is he?" I asked again.

Edd then gestured toward the front of the church. "See for yourself."

Where the pulpit used to be was now just a pit: a splintered floor and a hole that opened on the remains of a basement. Down in the pit, Teddy sat, tied to a chair. He was in bad shape. Bruised, bloody. Much like I looked after being attacked in the alley. He gazed up at me with a forlorn expression, but didn't even struggle to free himself, or speak when he saw me. The fight had been bludgeoned out of him.

Now as I looked at the others, I could see evidence of the struggle. A scratched cheek here, a puffy eye there.

"You beat yourself up? Why would you do that?"

I thought they'd all start talking at once, rattling off excuses, but no one said a thing.

"You have no idea, do you?" Edd finally said, shaking his

head in disgust. "How did we ever think you'd bring anything but disaster?"

Ed hung his head and walked away. Eddy returned to the safety of his device, and Ned just shrugged. It was Eduardo who took it upon himself to share what the others wouldn't.

"You were seeking a calmer, more peaceful world," he said. "Did you sense those worlds there? Did you feel them reaching for you?"

I nodded. "Yes . . . but I lost my nerve. I couldn't follow through."

"And what kind of world is the most peaceful, do you think?"

I thought it was a trick question, because the answer was pretty simple. "A world without war. Without suffering. Without prejudice. Without inhumanity."

"Yes," agreed Eduardo. "Without inhumanity . . . *or* humanity."

It took a moment for that to sink in. "Wait . . . you mean—"

"I mean that the most peaceful versions of Earth are the ones where intelligent life never developed."

"Actually," said Ned, "the ones where life never developed at all would be the most peaceful."

Edd crossed his arms. "So in your naïve stupidity, you almost erased all life from your planet."

It seems obvious to me now, but at the time, the truth was a crushing revelation. I could have killed everything in the blink of an eye. I'd be gone, along with everyone who had ever lived, leaving behind a sterile, silent world. It would be peaceful and serene, because there'd be nothing to stir up trouble but the wind.

"You say you lost your nerve . . . but what you felt wasn't fear," Eduardo said. "It was intuition."

I went back to the hole in the pulpit and looked down at Teddy. "Is all that true?"

And although he wouldn't look me in the eye, he gave me his reluctant answer. "Choosing a lifeless world would have prevented a correction," he said. "And life could evolve again."

"He's right about that," offered Eddy. "The QuIRT says the bacteria we'd leave behind here would evolve. Who's to say you wouldn't be born into a better world a few hundred million years from now?"

Edd looked at me with an arrogant, superior sneer. "Only a self-centered, privileged fool thinks they can single-handedly fix problems it took all of human history to create." He shook his head in disgust. "The best you could have possibly achieved was a reset to where you started, with the hope your species could eventually find wisdom enough to heal its self-inflicted wounds . . . But it's all moot now."

I did not like the sound of that. "Wait, what's that supposed to mean?"

Edd's gaze, as cold as it was, dipped way below zero. "It means that your meddling stops here! You've made your last jump. You are ordered to leave the world just as it is. You'll keep away from others, and stay away from any situation that might trigger a jump until you're no longer the subjective locus. And if you ask me, that moment can't come soon enough."

But after all I'd been through, I refused to be bullied.

"What if I don't want to be a good little girl and follow orders?" I asked Edd with my best sarcastic sneer.

"Don't tempt me, Ashley," said Edd, not backing down. "Because ending life on Earth might be one way to prevent a correction . . . but ending *you* would be the easier option."

That just made me smile with defiance. "You're bluffing," I said. "You already told me you can't kill me. It's not in your nature."

"That's true," Edd said. "But there are eight billion of your own kind out there . . . and it's certainly in their nature."

Do you know what it's like to be manipulated and toyed with? To be given half-truths and outright lies by those who you thought had your best interests at heart, but turned out not to have hearts at all? I was furious at Teddy for deceiving me. And yet as angry as I was, I had to concede that, in a choice between killing the termites or demolishing the house, you kill the termites—and when it comes down to it, that's all we are as far as the Earth is concerned. I felt crushed by Teddy's vote of no confidence. He tricked me because he had no faith in me. So how could I have faith in myself?

I stormed out of the old church. I was done with them. But before I got to my car, Ed came after me.

"Ashley, listen to me," he said.

"Why should I listen to anything any of you say?"

"Because we've been through this before. We know how this goes down. The others are either ready to give up, or have lost interest in you and your world, but I think there's something here worth preserving, if you can bring things back to your starting point."

"Fine," I told him. "I'm listening."

He took a deep breath and looked back toward the old church, to make sure the others hadn't followed him out, then returned his gaze to me. "This far along, the ultimate sacrifice might be called for."

"I already know that."

"I don't think you do," Ed said. "You have to be willing to not just die, Ashley, but to not exist. Your self-negation may be the only thing that stops the correction and brings back the world you know."

"Why would the universe even care?"

"All I know is that sacrifice is a powerful act. It resonates through all possible yesterdays, todays, and tomorrows."

But I also knew that sacrifice can be pointless if nobody's watching. If nobody cares. How could I trust that anyone would, when something deadly was lurking out there, ready to swallow all there is to swallow?

"So one last jump . . . in which I offer myself up as a sacrifice to the multiverse."

Ed nodded.

"And how will I know when we're getting close to the correction?"

"The world will lose coherence," Ed said. "Things will . . . fall apart."

"How?"

"You'll know when you see it," he said enigmatically. "And just before the end, the northern lights will cover the world."

That evening, I searched the news for evidence of the looming correction. A moderate earthquake in Japan. Unusually high tides in the southern hemisphere. Increased volcanic activity in Hawaii and along the Pacific Rim. None of these things were smoking guns, and for all I knew it was coincidental. But what if it wasn't? What if it was gravitational disruption from that distant black hole, which was only distant when measured by puny human standards?

I caught Hunter peering in my door, glancing at my laptop over my shoulder.

"So you're doing that, too?" he asked.

"Doing what?"

"Checking out stuff happening around the world," he said. "I don't know why, but I've been feeling like . . . I don't know . . . like I need to pay *attention*, you know?"

I tried to downplay it. "We should always pay attention to things going on out there," I told him.

"Yeah, I know. But I keep getting bad feelings. Terrible feelings. They keep me awake at night. They make it hard to do anything. I know something awful is going to happen, and I can't make the feeling go away." He sat down on my bed. "I know you said that I shouldn't worry, but I can't stop. I think maybe there's something wrong with me."

I didn't want to dismiss what he was feeling, but I couldn't let him go on thinking it was his problem.

"Hunter, the feeling is real, and it's not just you," I told him. "Don't ever think you need to bear it alone. I promise I will always be here for you."

He took a deep breath and dredged up a smile for me. "Thanks, Ashley. You're a good sister," he said. "I'll always be here for you, too."

I gave him a hug. In previous worlds I never had. Brothers don't hug much. Even though he was three years younger, he was taller than me here. But it wasn't just that. He was leaner, too, with muscles that were more defined. Then I remembered that in this world, he was being groomed to be a quarterback—they even started him a year late in school so he'd be bigger by the time he hit high school. Because he was the only boy in the family, Dad's focus had been entirely on Hunter when it came to football. And to keep Dad's attention, Hunter had to excel.

He got up and turned to go, but before he left, I stopped him. "Hunter . . . someday, you're going to be the best quarterback this town has ever seen."

He smiled again. This time he didn't have to reach for it. "I already am," he said. "They just don't know it yet."

Paul came by on Sunday evening. I should have expected him. In all worlds we had tutoring on Sunday, although in the last couple it was as much chemistry as it was math, so to speak. But not anymore. Today, he was a bit formal, and all business. It was both charming and troubling. My head was too stuffed to cram anything else in, but spending time with him was the best remedy for my woes, even if everything we studied went in one ear and out the other. We sat at our dining room table, in front of big french doors that overlooked the pool. We had actual books instead of digital ones, because our math teacher believed algebra should always have weight.

"Okay, so this first problem isn't all that hard," Paul said. "Two cars are traveling south along a highway. The first is driving at fifty miles per hour, and the second, which leaves ninety minutes later, travels at sixty miles per hour. How long will it take for the second car to catch up with the first?"

"Are they in the same universe?" I asked.

He grinned. "I assume so."

"What color are they?"

"It doesn't matter."

"It does if they're not the same color that they started."

He looked at me, trying to figure out why I was being so obtuse. Then he came around the table and sat next to me. Taking my pencil, he slowly wrote out the equation in front of me. "I think you're letting yourself be distracted by details," he said. "When you strip everything else away, it's a simple equation."

But my eyes weren't on the numbers, they were on his hands. The way his fingers moved so confidently on the page. I could smell the shampoo he had used that morning. Coconut and cherry. I loved the smell of his hair. I had once told him that—but not in this reality. Here, I was nothing to him but money he was saving for college. I knew the schools he had his eyes on. I had my eyes on those schools too, even though I knew, short of a scholarship, my chances of getting into the same schools as Paul were slim. Was that in my original world? No, I don't think so, but that didn't matter to me anymore.

"See?" he said, solving the equation. "Numbers never lie."

I felt my eyes begin to tear up. "They do sometimes."

He didn't know what to make of that. "Hey . . . are you okay?" He took a long look at me, and I couldn't look away from those eyes. Two primordial black holes like portals to every place I wanted to be.

"Listen, if this isn't a good time—"

And then out of nowhere—I mean completely out of nowhere—I leaned in and kissed him. I just couldn't stop myself. I felt so lost, and so . . . fractured. I wanted him to be who he was before this last shift. But it was so stupid of me. Because Paul *was* exactly who he had been. *I* was the one who had changed. I knew it was a mistake the instant I did it, but some things can't be undone.

He pulled away quickly, and immediately began to go red.

"Wow, okay," he said. "That was . . . unexpected."

"I'm sorry!" I told him. "I don't know what I was thinking."

"I mean, I'm flattered and all, but . . . And don't get me wrong, I think you're really pretty . . ."

I couldn't believe the position I had just put him in. I didn't know if he was out in this world, but even if he was, being gay, and having to fend off the advances of a cheerleader you tutor, was beyond awkward on every level.

"I'm not your type. That's okay," I said, desperate to walk this back. "Forget it ever happened. Let's do some math. Two cars heading south, right? A simple equation."

"Uh . . . okay," he said. He looked at the page a moment more. Tapped the pencil a few times, then said, "You know what? I think I should go."

"No, please, Paul, don't go! I didn't mean it! I said I was sorry."

"I know. But, yeah, I should go. No charge for today's session."

And he was out of there faster than I could blink. And then to pour salt in the wound, Layton texted me within seconds of Paul leaving.

Feeling better? Should I come by? I'm coming by.

And it made me realize that if there were indeed nine levels of hell, then I was in an elevator with Layton, stuck between floors.

On Monday morning, I sat with a spread of Sephora cosmetics in front of the mirror. The *vanity* mirror, they call it. Every bit of language is layered with subtle slights. As women, we're expected to paint ourselves to meet some social norm, and yet the very mirror that we use accuses us of being vain. I never thought about it as a guy. I would have said that was ridiculous. That it didn't matter. But it does. And you know—it's not just women, it's everybody. Language secretly pushes and prods every one of us in hundreds of directions we don't see, until the only way to be careful with your words is to never speak.

I stroked on foundation, smoothing it over my pores. Blended it like a fine artist. A touch of blush, then shadow to accent my eyes. My male self observed the ritual, letting my female self dab and stroke, following muscle memory. I don't think my clumsy male hands would have had either the skill or patience to do this. I'd end up looking like a Picasso.

I applied eyeliner. I thickened my lashes. I took a moment to assess my efforts. My makeup was thicker now than it had been before I started dating Layton. Just like Katie's had been in the other worlds. I used to wonder if maybe Katie's makeup was sometimes hiding bruises. But now I knew it wasn't so simple. Because, for me, the makeup was, more than anything, to hide myself.

"You look pretty," Layton would say. Because when it comes to women, that's what society zeroes in on. Our appearance. And "appearance" is all Layton had. Because I was hidden behind my perfect Sephora mask. And the deeper I was behind it, the easier it was to be an accessory on his arm, all shiny and perfect like his knockoff Rolex watch. Because that wasn't me, it was the mask. The skillful knockoff of a girl.

Of course, I'd be lying if I said he didn't leave bruises once in a while, but never on my face. They'd appear on my arm when he'd grab me to stop me from storming away. They'd show up on my waist when things got hot and heavy, and "stop" was a whisper beneath the roar of a freight train with no emergency brake.

He said I needed to take iron. That I must be anemic. Because if you're anemic, you bruise easily, and he couldn't imagine he was to blame.

Only once did he leave a mark on my neck. We had a fight. I accused him of being a self-centered, narcissistic bastard. Losing control of me made him lose control of himself. He grabbed me by the neck and pushed me against the wall.

It was the only time the makeup was to hide something. If someone had asked if he hit me, I would have told them "No." Because technically, grabbing me by the neck wasn't hitting. And I didn't want anyone to know it had happened.

I was ready to end it when Layton did that. Instead of walking it off, I was ready to walk away. I should have. But over the next week I couldn't escape Layton's tearful contrition.

"Baby, I was wrong, I was out of line, and you have every right to hate me, but I love you, so please forgive me, because I love you, and I'll never do it again, never, and you know I mean it, because I love you, and you know me better than anyone, and I don't know what I'll do if you don't forgive me, so please, Ashley, please, I'll do anything, because I love you."

Days and days of pleading and tender, thoughtful romantic gestures, until I became the bobblehead girl. *"Yes, Layton." "I forgive you, Layton." "I'll give you another chance, Layton."* Because as much as I hated him in all the other worlds, I loved him here, even though I hated that I loved him.

And he was true to his word. He had never done that again. But he didn't have to. Because now I knew he was capable of it. Now the threat was implicit.

So day after day I finished my morning ritual and admired my work in the vanity mirror. I hid behind the mask.

But today was the day that it couldn't protect me anymore.

I moved through the hallway on Monday morning before my first class, trying to avoid eye contact with everyone. Not just because my head ached, but because I didn't want to have to unscramble the faces around me. Who was who, who was new, and who had changed. But the second Nora saw me at my locker, she made a beeline to me before I could slip away.

"That was one nasty hit you took on Friday," she said. "I saw it from the stands."

"It wasn't as bad as it looked," I told her. "I'm fine."

Then Katie was there as well—hand in hand with Josh, who looked a little different, but close enough to his previous self for me to know it was him. He and Katie were a couple here. I was happy for her. Josh was a good guy while he existed.

"I honestly thought you weren't getting up," Josh said. "You looked so dazed."

"Like you got bumped out of this world," said Katie, with a wink. I didn't wink back.

"There are worse things," said Nora with a wry smile. "Personally, I'd have loved a wide receiver on top of me." Then she took off after some cute guy who looked like a boy-band reject.

Katie rolled her eyes.

"Nora. Gotta love her," said Josh.

The first bell rang, and he headed off to class, but Katie waited for me.

"You still haven't told me what changed," she said.

So I looked around us at the passing faces, pulling a few out. "Georgia changed. And so did Max and Patty, to name a few."

"Changed how?"

"Well for one, they used to be George, Maxine, and Patrick. And Nora . . . well, I don't even want to go there."

Katie laughed. "Very funny." But then she registered the look on my face. "You're not kidding, are you?"

I took a long look at her, hoping she would remember who I had been, but it wasn't there. And then something else struck me that I hadn't considered before. "Katie . . . if I was a cheerleader in this world, then how do you remember the other shifts? It's not like I got tackled on the sidelines every week . . ."

And suddenly her pupils constricted—just like Hunter's did when he almost remembered me being a lineman. "I . . . don't know. I just know that they did. Isn't that strange?"

But it was more than strange. Ed said that the world was losing coherence. Reality was struggling to make sense of itself. When it could no longer do that, it would correct, and solve the problem by erasing it.

"You were . . . taller before, weren't you?"

"Yeah, I was."

"And you weren't dating Layton."

"No . . . *you* were," I told her.

She backed up and shook her head, as if trying to get out a bug that had lodged in her hair. "No. You're making that up. I'd *never* be with him."

But I knew better. Because however sure you think your footing is, now I knew there were trapdoors in everyone's fun house.

"You know, if you change your mind about him and break up," Katie said, "I'll support you one hundred percent."

"I know," I told her. Then, before she could launch into a speech about how wrong Layton was for me, I changed the subject. "Katie, I'd like you to come with me this afternoon. I want to go see Leo." And I told her where he was—still in jail, because bail had still not been set, and there was no telling when, or if, it would.

Katie was horrified by what happened to him, but apprehensive about going to see him in jail. At first, I thought she was echoing the racism that permeated these last few worlds—but then I realized that wasn't it. We'd be two teenage girls going alone to the county jailhouse. Granted, we were kick-ass girls, but even as a guy it had been intimidating. But that wasn't the source of Katie's concern either.

"If Layton finds out where you went, you'll have to have a good story."

So it was back to Layton again. I began to get angry—although I knew it wasn't Katie I should be angry at. "Just stop, all right? Layton doesn't need to know where I am every minute of every day."

"Does he know that?" Katie asked. "Because I don't think he got the memo."

By the end of the school day, I was furious on more levels than I could count. I think half the things I learned about being a woman in our world can be unpacked from my interactions that day.

First there were the boys who kept interrupting a response I was giving in history class—boys who didn't interrupt one another, but who clearly thought that a girl's thoughts weren't as important as their own—and to make it worse, our teacher, who was a woman, didn't call them out on it. As if their behavior had been so normalized, she didn't even notice.

Then there was the flyer for the school's college fair. It featured two pictures: a boy in a lab in front of test tubes and beakers . . . and a girl in a library reading Jane Austen. It infuriated me, because whoever designed that poster was probably clueless about the implications, never realizing they were the very definition of pride and prejudice.

But the worst was yet to come. I ran into Mr. Metts in the hallway right before lunch. The last thing I wanted was a conversation with the school counselor.

"I heard there was an incident on Friday night," he said. "I just wanted to make sure you were okay."

"I'm fine," I told him. "A little sore, but I'll be okay."

"No," he said, a little more quietly. "I mean that it must have been traumatic. How are you holding up?"

It felt like an odd question—but that was just the reaction of the various male observers in my peanut gallery of identities. Did he assume that, because I was a girl, I was more emotionally fragile?

"I'm fine," I told him, a little more emphatically. The encounter was making me nervous, and I began to fiddle with a necklace that Layton had given me for my birthday. A little heart encrusted in tiny yellow citrines. My birthstone. As a guy, I hadn't even known what my birthstone was, and hadn't cared.

"Well, just as long as you're okay," Metts said, not quite making eye contact. "But if you start to experience anxiety over it, let me know."

Right, I thought. I'm sure he had a pamphlet entitled "Post-Traumatic YOU!"

It was only after he left that I realized in those last moments of the conversation, his gaze had slipped down to my chest.

"No question, he was checking out your tits," Nora said, when I brought it up at lunch. "It's gross and way creepy, but it's what guys do."

"Or," her band-reject boyfriend said, "he could have been glancing at your necklace. You did say you were fiddling with it, right? That could have drawn his attention."

And I found myself getting angry at both of them. Nora for acting like "that's what guys do" excused it, and at Boy Band, because it pissed me off that there was a chance, however small, that he could have been right. And I realized that what makes sexism so infuriating isn't just the obvious things, but the things you're not entirely sure about. Those insidious moments that make you wonder if you're just being paranoid, or if you're entirely right, but being gaslit by people who want you to believe you're crazy. How maddening to live with such uncertainty! To feel diminished by a world that keeps you on such shaky ground!

And *then*, on top of it, to have your own boyfriend kindly and politely suggest that maybe all this pent-up anger is just because it's your time of the month.

Needless to say, when I left school that day, I was ready for a fight. Just the frame of mind to be in when you're about to pay a visit to the county jail.

25

TWO WHITE GIRLS VISITING A BLACK KID IN JAIL

Spoiler alert: it didn't happen. What did happen, though, made me wonder if a "correction" was exactly what this world needed.

The county jail was exactly as it had been before. Only the clerk behind the glass was different. This time the officer was a guy clearly bitter about being the interface between those on the outside and those on the inside. You could see in his face that he believed there were only two kinds of people in the world: those in jail, and those who hadn't been caught yet. Layton, his timing always terrible, texted Hey, just as we approached the clerk. He must have just gotten out of football practice. I texted him back a heart just to shut him up and turned my attention to the jail clerk.

"We're here to see one of your inmates," I said.

"Doesn't work that way," he said.

It had worked that way last week when I was a guy, but I wasn't going to argue. "So how does it work?" I asked.

"Let's start with a name."

"Leo Johnson."

At the mention of Leo's name he suddenly became much more attentive, and twice as suspicious. "You want to see Leo Johnson?"

"Yes, that's what I said."

"And what is your relationship?"

"We're friends of his."

"Friends." The officer spat the word out, flat and dull, like gum into an empty trash can. "Do your parents know the kinds of 'friends' you keep? Nice girls like you? You shouldn't have anything to do with Leo Johnson."

I wanted to hit him for the disdain and disapproval in his voice, but the glass between us prevented that.

Katie must have seen the fury boiling up in me, because she stepped forward and took the lead. "All right, if you must know, we're interns with the *Taylorville Tribune*," she said, impressively convincing in her delivery. "Our editor heard how Mr. Johnson saved that poor homeless man from being shot at the Publix, and sent us to do a story—in his own words."

That made the officer laugh. "First off, it was a homeless woman, so get your story straight. Secondly, the district attorney believes they were accomplices in the robbery, and third, the *Tribune* oughta know better than to send a couple of kids to interview someone so dangerous."

Katie began going off on how he was trampling our First Amendment rights, but something else caught me about this exchange. Something decidedly off. This was a county jail, after all. Inmates came and went on a regular basis. But this man knew Leo by name, as well as the details of his case.

"You said he was dangerous. Dangerous how?" I asked.

"He's a threat to the peace," the officer said. "That whole community down in South Taylorville's got their braids in a bustle over this guy, calling him a 'symbol of oppression.'" He scoffed at the thought, dismissing it with a sneer. "Word on the street is that he and his girlfriend were organizing some sort of action against T-ville High. That boy was planning a riot!"

It took a few seconds for me to realize he meant the dance. Even *that* was being pounded into a weapon to use against Leo.

"If you girls want to do an interview, why don't you talk to the Publix manager who was attacked and write an article that will set people straight on what *really* happened."

I tried to keep my cool, but it was so incredibly hard. "What if he's lying? What if Leo's telling the truth?"

And then, in a voice oozing condescension, this man said the most offensive thing anyone has ever said to me in any world.

"Sweetie," he said, "a lousy s'equal like Leo Johnson wouldn't know the truth if it shot him in the back."

Was there ever a time in our history that we accepted each other as human beings? Was the line between "us" and "them" always a chasm we couldn't bridge?

We vilify the difference in others; we glorify the differences in ourselves. We put "them" in a box, then create our own boxes. To define ourselves so we don't get defined. To find our tribe and defend it from the others. But that basic human need for identity is, and has always been, a double-edged sword. Because the closer to our feet we draw that line in the sand, the more we see everyone else as the enemy.

As for that jail clerk, there's one core box he belongs in. The asshole box. And it's the most nondiscriminatory box there is. It's home to people of every race, creed, party, and orientation. It's big enough to hold presidents, and small enough to sit on your Thanksgiving table between the turkey and your uncle Bob. It's a truly dangerous box, because it can masquerade as many things, so you're never really sure what it is you're fighting.

The problem is, the asshole box nests way too comfortably within the racist box. And when it does, it becomes a well-fed parasite.

Sadly, I believe that bastard jail clerk exists in all worlds. Screaming at him makes no difference. Raging against him might satisfy our fury but won't make him go away. We can refuse to feed the hateful thing within, but it will always find another source of food. I think the only way to fight the parasite in the box within a box is to keep shining a relentless light, so it can find no shadows to hide in. Maybe then it will finally reveal itself for what it really is: a small and sorry creature not even worthy of our attention.

26

BLUNT OBJECT

So the question remained: Should I play the good girl and listen to Edd, lying low and leaving the world in this wretched state, with hopes that the universe would leave us alone? Or should I risk everything—and I truly mean *everything*—to bring my old imperfect world back? Was it selfish to take that risk, knowing the consequence of failure? Or was it the noble choice? I don't know. Like Leo pointed out, it was arrogant of me to think myself some heroine who could step in and solve the problems of a broken society, but didn't I have an obligation to try? Don't we all?

To the Edwards I was no longer an asset capable of restoring order. I was a loose cannon. And with Edd now in charge, I had no support from them.

And I had no way to know how I was about to be clipped.

Because unlike the Edwards, I could not be in more than one place at a time. That left me completely unaware of the scheme being woven behind my back. It began to play out right around the time I was facing that revolting jail clerk. I wasn't there to see it, but I imagine it went down something like this:

Layton is headed to his car after football practice. It's magic time, although there's nothing magic about it in a high school parking lot. The lights above the lot are flickering on and off, only understanding the binary of night and day, completely baffled by the ambivalence of twilight.

He texts me, a quick "Hey," wondering where I am, and why I haven't texted him for a whole two hours. I answer with a heart. He finds it reassuring rather than placating—because he believes I'm too transparent to be anything but sincere. He even believes in his own sincerity, his own virtue, entirely unaware of how self-serving he often is. But I digress. Back to the parking lot.

As he nears his car, he hears the grinding sound of polyurethane wheels on asphalt. He ignores it, figuring it has nothing to do with him, until he hears an unfamiliar voice call his name.

"Layton! Wait up!"

He turns to see a skater heading his way. Layton immediately checks his pockets, thinking maybe he dropped his wallet or something, and this guy saw it and is bringing it to him, to earn some brownie points with the Big Man on Campus. Or more likely, the dude stole it, and is going to pretend like he found it, but empty of all its cash. That's how Layton might think. Always suspicious. But his wallet is in his pocket and his keys and phone are in hand. So what is this about?

The skater rolls up to him, but in truth it doesn't seem like he's moving at all; it's like the world is moving around him. Layton may or may not be observant enough to notice this.

"Can I help you?" he says, although he's thinking *What the hell do you want?*

"No, but I think I can help *you*," the skater says. "I have something you'll want to see."

Layton is wary. The skater senses that and keeps his distance, taking out his phone and holding it up. Then he waits for Layton's curiosity to ignite, thereby powering the rest of their encounter.

The skater brings up a video on his phone. It's a video of me. Not the public one that outed me in a previous reality, but one from *this* reality. It's a very private moment that no one was supposed to see, much less record. It was a moment I wished could be forgotten, but instead it's been memorialized. Because the Edwards were watching. I should have known they'd be watching.

The scene is of me sitting at my dining table, last night. Whoever's taking the video is just outside the window. Paul is next to me, showing me an equation. It's all about math right until the moment I lean over and kiss him.

And Layton's entire brain—his entire identity—detonates when he sees that. His face tightens. He begins to steam. He's like a bull preparing to charge.

353

"Who the hell are you, and where did you get this?"

"Doesn't matter," the skater says. "All that matters is what you see. And what you'll do about it."

"Get the hell out of my sight!" Layton yells.

The skater obliges, slipping away to join a group of other skaters waiting just outside the lot. They leave in unison. Layton might notice that they look remarkably similar, but probably not, because his mind is too clouded by the image of me kissing Paul, playing in an endless loop in his head.

By now all the lights of the lot have come on, but they do nothing to purge the terrifying darkness that has found a home in Layton's soul.

But I didn't know that yet.

I was just trying to make sense of the things I was beginning to see around me. Ed said the world would lose coherence as we got closer to the correction. Now, as I drove with Katie away from the jail, I was seeing evidence of that decay. Fender benders on nearly every corner, as if the rules of the road were different for everyone. Fights beginning to break out on streets as people blamed one another for an uneasy feeling they couldn't explain. And then there were the children. Inconsolable children everywhere, screaming in their mothers' arms.

Everyone sensed that something was wrong, but no one knew what it was, and the collective tension made my hair stand on end, like electricity buzzing through a power line. Like that feeling you get when you walk out of a scary movie and still feel like you're in it.

"Freaky," said Katie.

I glanced over to see her scrolling obsessively on her phone. "What's freaky?"

"Just stuff in the news," she said. "You heard about the tides, right?"

"More flooding?"

"Yeah—but places that were flooding last night now have shorelines that go out for miles. Look at all these beached whales." She flashed me a picture, but I couldn't take my eyes away from the road long enough to see the details.

"Do they know what's causing it?" I asked. I knew the answer but wondered if anyone else did.

Katie shrugged uneasily. "Some are saying climate change, but others say it's something else. Something worse."

"Are the changes in the tide bigger now than they were yesterday?" I asked.

"How should I know?" Then she took a long look at me. "Is there something you're not telling me?"

"Like what?"

"I don't know—like maybe you changed the rotation of the Earth or something."

"Don't be ridiculous."

"If I'm ridiculous then why are your hands shaking?"

I tightened my grip on the wheel to stop the shaking, but now I was all white knuckles.

She looked at me for a moment more, then I think she realized she didn't want to know. She leaned back, putting her phone away. "It's probably just one of those things," she said.

"Like the way hurricanes and earthquakes come in bunches."

"Probably," I said. I had to remind myself that this wasn't a done deal. These were just warning signs. A correction wouldn't happen until it happened. If I didn't change anything else, things might still heal. But not without terrible scars.

"I need to do it again, Katie," I told her. "I need to do it one last time, but I don't know how."

We were on a country road now. A car approached, speeding in the opposite direction. I thought of a math problem. I thought of the moment when two cars moving in opposite directions met. I watched it as it approached, my hands still tight on the wheel, then felt the blast of wind as it passed just a few feet from us. I tracked it in the rearview mirror until it was gone. Finally, I breathed out, not realizing I had been holding my breath.

"Don't do anything stupid," Katie said, knowing what I was thinking even before I did.

"I'll try not to," was the best I could say. Because every door in front of me had a tiger behind it now.

I drove home in silence after I dropped Katie off, but as I pulled up to my house, the silence was pierced by angry metal. Hunter was up in his room, playing his guitar, and it was blasting from his window. Nothing unusual about that . . . until I realized what song he was playing.

Once inside, I went straight up to his room and pushed open his door. His amp was turned up to earsplitting volume, and he was gripping the neck of his guitar with such force as he switched between chords that his fingertips were bleeding. There was something odd about the blood on his fingertips, but I couldn't focus on that right now. I had to focus on Hunter, who was staring off at nothing, and his eyes—they were pinpricks. I could barely see any pupil in there at all.

"Hunter!" I yelled, but still he played. I turned the amp down. "Hunter!"

Finally he looked at me and blinked like he was coming out of a trance—but even with the volume down, his hands kept moving.

"I can't stop playing," he said. "I can't stop playing this song . . ."

"Put down the guitar, Hunter," I told him, like I was talking him off a ledge. I could see that he wanted to, but he kept on tormenting himself with the tune.

"What is it, Ashley? What is this song? Why can't I get it out of my head?"

"It's called 'Come As You Were,'" I told him. "It's by a band called Konniption."

That just made him grimace as if I had stabbed him. "Who are they? I never heard of them."

"You've never heard of them because they don't exist."

Finally I reached out and wrenched the guitar out of his hands. It let off an ugly twang and fell silent. The moment he was free from it, it was as if a spell had been broken. His shoulders slumped and his back hunched. His irises dilated the tiniest bit to let in a little more light.

"It's still in my head . . ."

"It'll be all right."

But it was as if my words were a betrayal rather than an attempt to comfort him. *"It won't be all right. It won't! Stop saying that it will!"* Then he began to sob. "What's wrong with me, Ashley?"

"It's not you, it's the world," I told him. "But I swear to you, there's a way to make this right, and I'm going to find it."

Then the expression on his face changed. I can't even describe the way he looked at me. There are lots of things I wish I could forget—but nothing more than that look of helpless, hopeless anguish on my brother's face.

"What if you're looking in the wrong place?"

There was nothing I could do but wrap my arms around him and hold him. He just about dissolved into my arms, finally letting go, and putting all his trust in his big sister. In that moment, I knew I had to deliver. I had to find a way to knock myself back into Elsewhere and somehow find the long road back to where we started. And I couldn't wait a week to do it, I had to figure this out now. Then once we were there—I would fix that broken relationship between him and me, because I was no longer the crude, blunt object that I had been.

27

WORLD WITHOUT MIRACLES

It was my power hit that always sent reality reeling, but I was no longer a defensive tackle. Even so, being the sub-loc couldn't just be a matter of size and muscle. It was more than mere brute force. Changing the world was about will. *That* was the force that tipped the balance and altered realities. Hurling myself against walls, slamming my hand in drawers did nothing. Believe me, I tried. All it did was leave me more bruised and aching than I already was. I even went the opposite route. I drew myself an EMP bath as hot as I could stand and tried to relax my way into Elsewhere. It didn't even ease my perpetual headache.

It was dark when I got out of my bath, no closer to a solution than when I started. I checked in on Hunter—he had fallen asleep curled-up knees to chest. Fetal position. Whatever dreams he was having, I hoped they were easy ones.

Mom had left a message that she'd be home late. She had a client a couple of towns away, and an accident on the interstate had brought traffic to a standstill. If what I saw earlier was any indication, it was more than just one accident.

Isn't it strange how we take for granted that the universe works? That the gears all fit together? We can't imagine it being any other way, because it's all we know. But when the gears no longer mesh, anything can happen. Murphy's law becomes as true as the law of gravity. All that can go wrong, will, and without question. We think miracles—if we believe in them at all—are few and far between, but what if the true miracles are the millions of near misses we experience every day? What if they're all a key part of that functioning clockwork? Perhaps without those commonplace miracles, every car would crash, every plane would fall from the sky, and every bridge would buckle under the force of a million failed bolts, bringing the world as we know it crashing down in a single roll of catastrophic thunder.

That's what was happening now. The common miracles were failing, not just in the physical world, but in society. The glue that held us together was gone. I turned on the TV to see not just natural disasters, but human ones. Riots and insurrection breaking out all over the world. And it dawned on me that the correction wasn't a punishment—it was self-defense. The universe was protecting itself from a world without miracles.

My phone rang. It was Layton. I did *not* want to speak to him. He was a distraction. A heavy arm pulling me into the mundane.

I almost didn't answer it. There's not a day that I don't wonder what would have happened if I ignored that call. How things might have gone. But in the end, I picked up the phone, and this game the multiverse and I were playing launched into sudden death.

"Hi, Layton."

Nothing on the other end at first. As I listened, I could hear him breathing. A little heavy. A little out of breath.

"Layton?"

"Why did you do it, Ashley?"

It caught me off guard. I scrolled through my mind all the things I had done that I wouldn't want Layton to know about—which was everything.

"I don't know what you're talking about."

"How long has it been going on? How long, Ashley? Since he started tutoring you? Was it even tutoring at all, or was that just a lie?"

The picture was still fuzzy but coming into focus. "Layton, calm down!"

"I SAW!" he screamed. "There was this guy, and he got it on his phone. *I saw the way you kissed Paul!* How could you do this to me? How could you do this to *us*?"

I knew it must have been the Edwards. They watched me twenty-four seven through their interdimensional peephole. This was Edd following through on his threat to take matters into his own hands. I should have known he'd use Layton as his monkey wrench!

"It's not what you think!" I said—which is what you always say when it's exactly what the other person thinks.

"No? Well, I've got your little boytoy tutor right here. He's got something to say. Go on," prompted Layton. "Tell her you're a loser! Tell her what a piece of shit you are!"

I heard the movement of the phone like the rustling of paper, a *thunk* as the phone dropped. I could hear the two of them fighting. Paul must have gotten the upper hand, because he was the one who picked up the phone.

"Don't listen to him, Ashley! He's lost his mind!"

More grappling, more fighting. This time Layton got the phone.

"Meet me by our tree," Layton told me. "I'll be waiting."

But Paul called out in the background. "Don't go, Ashley! He's got a—"

And the phone went dead.

The night was clear as I drove toward the center of town. More than clear. The heavens were full of stars, horizon to horizon, as if the last of the Earth's clouds had boiled away. I imagined the Earth now like a lidless, unblinking eye in space, unable to turn away from the doom that was soon to swallow it.

At first, I had no idea what Layton was talking about. "Our tree." That memory was buried beneath the memories of other worlds and all the things in *this* world that were more important to me.

But then I remembered. A year ago, when we began dating,

we had walked through a park, and he had carved our initials in a tree—like they did in old black-and-white movies. That was the sort of world Layton existed in. Simple and unambiguous. The quarterback and his girl in a world of winners and losers, with nothing in between. He served a personal cult of apple pie, homecoming royalty, and happily ever after. Anything that didn't conform to that singular vision had to be bent, bound, and broken until it did.

Our tree was in a park with benches and a playground, and handy stations stocked with little scented dog shit bags. There was a fountain in the middle of the park, featuring a concrete cherub holding a bowl of endlessly flowing water. Or at least it was endlessly flowing until last year when an early frost froze the pipes and they burst. Now it was a water feature without water, highly skilled in collecting fallen leaves and litter.

Layton was there sitting on the edge of the fountain. There was a baseball bat beside him. In the light of the streetlamps, I could see the bat was smeared with blood and Layton was splattered with it. But there was something very wrong with this picture—even more than what was already wrong. It took me a moment to realize what it was.

The blood was blue.

Just like the blood on Hunter's fingertips.

Was blood supposed to be blue? For the life of me I didn't know the answer.

And where was Paul?

When Layton saw me, he stood up. The bat rolled off the

fountain, clattering on the ground. He was done playing baseball. There was no telling what his next sport would be.

"You came," he said. As he came closer, I could see his face was bruised and swelling. Layton might have had the strength of a quarterback, but Paul was no weakling. He had done plenty of damage. Even so, Layton was here, and Paul wasn't.

I stood by "our tree," keeping my distance. Making him come to me. "What did you do, Layton? Where's Paul?"

But he wasn't hearing me over whatever thoughts were screaming in his own head. Now, I could see that his pupils had closed down to pinpricks worse than Hunter's had been, letting in only the slightest light. I was the focus of his tunnel vision.

"This is all wrong, Ashley. This isn't how it was supposed to be. Can't you see? Can't you feel it? It's supposed to be you and me. How could you ruin that?"

I said nothing. Not yet. I let him rant.

"I was so stupid to trust you! And now look where we are!" He pointed to the tree. I could see our initials within a rough-hewn heart. I remember thinking when he carved that heart that it was lopsided. "I love you, Ashley. Why are you making me do this?"

I could have placated him and told him what he wanted to hear. But I would not do that. If this was indeed the end of the world, I would let my light go out with dignity.

"Goddamn it, Ashley, don't just stand there! Tell me you love me!"

And so I told him the truth, as best as I knew it. I spoke for me. I spoke for Katie. I spoke for every girl who ever found herself yoked under the arm of a Layton.

"There's a part of me that loves you, Layton. But other parts hate you more than you can possibly imagine. You don't get to 'have' me, Layton. Because you don't deserve me. You could win every game, and every trophy there is. You could ride high on the shoulders of every team you're ever on—and you still won't deserve me."

When something rings true, it resonates. Even in someone who doesn't want to hear it. Even in someone whose very identity hinges on it not being true.

He responded the way I knew he would. Beyond anger, beyond fury. He became absolute wrath.

"You take that back!" His words were that of a furious child, but the way he growled them—with bared teeth and spittle flying from his mouth—he was more like a rabid animal. He now knew I would not bend or be bound. I would no longer contort myself to fit within the crushing curve of his arm.

So he found another use for that arm.

I could see in his eyes the moment he decided he would do it. The moment he chose to become *that* kind of monster, owning it. Embracing it. Because he couldn't embrace me.

He brought his arm up across his chest and swung it in a brutal backhanded slam across my face so powerful it spun me around and knocked me to the ground.

For a moment I thought that hit would be enough to hurl me into Elsewhere, but I should have known nothing Layton would ever do could send me anywhere I wanted to go.

That's when I caught sight of the Edwards. They stood at the edge of the park—all six of them. Whether they were in agreement or not, they were all willing to stand by and watch this happen, a dispassionate jury suspending all judgment.

Then Layton pulled out a gun from his jacket. And seeing that gun made me realize he fully intended to use it. I knew that he was ready to take that final step, becoming the next kind of monster.

"This is on *you*, Ashley," he said. "You and me—we were everything. And now we're nothing. Because of you."

In that moment, I saw three worlds unfolding:

The world where he killed me and ran away . . . the world where he put the gun in his own mouth and blew his brains out in front of me . . . and the world where he did both. In that moment any of those realities were possible, and not even the Edwards knew which it would be.

But then a fourth world eclipsed the other three. I didn't see it coming. Neither did Layton.

Paul! I should have known it would take more than the likes of Layton Vandenboom to take Paul out.

As Layton's grip on the trigger tightened, Paul came up behind him, brandishing the bat, and with all the strength he had left, Paul swung it. The bat connected with the nape of Layton's neck. I could hear the vertebrae fracture. Layton crumpled to the ground, dropping the gun, and Paul, still dripping the bluest of blood from his own wounds, kicked it away. Then Paul fell to the ground as well, entirely spent, while Layton twitched beside him, gasping for air.

"It's okay, Ashley," Paul said, and in spite of everything offered me a smile. "It's all gonna be okay."

But he didn't know what I knew. Because high up above, waves of light began to play across the heavens. The aurora borealis was beginning to shroud the world.

28

HAIL MARY

In everyone's life there comes that moment when you have no choice but to throw caution to the wind and bet everything on a long shot. When the only chances are slim and none, and all that you have left is your will to completion. In football they call it a "Hail Mary." A final play beyond which there can be no other. A desperate prayer without as much as a wing to carry it.

Beneath the swimming light of the aurora, I stormed to the Edwards.

"How do I stop it?" I demanded. "Are you just going to stand there and let this happen? *How do I stop it?*"

"I doubt you can now," said Ed.

"If Layton had killed you, it might have stopped," said Edd. "Now it's too late."

"Not much longer now," said Eddy, looking at the sky.

"If it's any consolation," said Eduardo, "it will be quick and painless. Everyone will be gone in the same instant, before the real fireworks begin."

"These things happen," said Teddy.

"I'm sorry we couldn't be of more help," concluded Ned.

Then one by one they turned and disappeared into thin air, leaving me alone. Getting out before the world took its final breath.

I was not giving up. If I was to go into that darkness, I would go kicking and screaming, fighting dirty, with no excuses. I would live my death with no apologies. They had told me that I had to be willing to make the ultimate sacrifice. I *was* willing. But I wasn't being given the chance.

And that's when I saw the truck.

It was speeding down the street on the far side of the park. And I swear to you, and I will always believe this, and there's no way you can change my mind, or prove me wrong. *It was the same truck*. The one that almost took Norris and me out the night of my first shift.

I want to believe the universe is a perfect circle.

I *choose* to believe that.

And it was telling me that *now* was the time for my Hail Mary.

I took off running. My side ached, my face ached, but none of that mattered. There was only one thing now. When everything else was stripped away, it was a simple equation. The truck's speed versus mine, and the angle of my approach. If I misjudged, it would pass, and I'd lose my chance. I forced more speed into my legs, imagining myself ramping up for the long jump. I threw myself over the bushes at the edge of the park, then launched into the road. The driver didn't see me. He didn't slow down as I leapt out directly into the path of that speeding truck, and *wham*!

A jolt of shock.

Pain.

Panic.

And I was no longer in the street, but in the unbearable cold and confusion of Elsewhere.

The realities caught in there with me were as desperate as I was, as if they knew they would be wiped clean by the correction, one and all. With no Earth, there would be no futures—not even a present—only an infinity of pasts fading to nothing, for there would be no one to remember them.

Maybe you're looking in the wrong place . . .

Hunter was right—and there was only one place left to look. All this time I had stayed clear of the pit. But that's where my world had to be: down there somewhere, spiraling away toward oblivion. I had to be willing to sacrifice everything. I had to go down into that extinguishing darkness, and search for the one-in-a-trillion lost world that was my own.

I fought away from the realities trying to take hold of me as I slid deeper. *Take my hand*, they all seemed to say. *I'll save you!* But it was all lies. None of those other worlds would stop the correction. But they didn't care. Because if I chose one of them, it would have its brief sparkling moment of existence before everything was snuffed out. That's all they wanted. Their moment. They would be satisfied by that. But not me.

I fought off what felt like the grip of a million hands. I pushed through and plunged deeper and deeper. Then one world in the depths of that maelstrom caught my attention. It held my focus in a way the others didn't.

Am I the one you're looking for? it seemed to gently say.

I reached out and grabbed it. It felt imperfect and cracked with rough edges and dirty corners that no one could get clean. Its strength was fraught with frailty, its confidence riddled with self-doubt. There was dishonor, and disgrace, but within it a core of hope that was brighter than the sun. And more than anything it felt . . . familiar.

I held on tight to that flawed world, and let the others fall away. I let it pull me in and I gave myself over to its embrace. And as I did, I heard it whisper in my ear.

"Welcome home, Ashley Bowman. Welcome home."

29

RED

Blood cells are too small to be seen by the naked eye. To show up under a microscope, they have to be magnified four hundred times. Yet without them, we couldn't exist.

A red blood cell doesn't know it's part of a larger organism. It only knows the job it's been given: to carry oxygen to the far reaches of its known universe. If it was self-aware, it might long to be part of something larger than itself, never knowing that it already was. It might dream of a greater purpose, never understanding that it served the most noble purpose of all.

We are those traveling cells. We pulse in the artery of a single organ that is one of a billion organs unaware they're part of something even larger. I know that has to be true—because if life exists four hundred times smaller than we can see, it must also exist four hundred times larger than we can see.

We've come up with a lot of names for the grand whole of it all. And although we do good deeds in those names, we also go to war for the names as well. As if we can't be on the inside unless everyone else is out. Basically we're idiots from a universal perspective. Because whatever name we choose to call it, it's the same thing. All those lines come together at the horizon.

We're always trying to see that horizon, striving for wisdom enough to grasp that bigger picture . . . but we're hopelessly limited. At our best, we only see a glimpse of the universal gearwork, and even then, we don't understand what we see.

Some people find that demoralizing—but to me it's comforting. Because if all of existence was something a human mind could comprehend, what a sad, pathetic universe this would be.

I guess my own spark of enlightenment is an acceptance of all the things I'll never know. And I breathe easy because of it. It leaves me content to be a blood cell, bright red with life, carrying oxygen to the brain.

30

A NEW KIND OF BALANCE

Consciousness didn't come in increments. When I opened my eyes, I was awake. Highly medicated, but awake. I had a throbbing headache, but it was a different kind than I had before. Other parts of me hurt as well. My whole body actually. And there was a terrible tingling in my left leg that felt too deep to scratch. I didn't want to take an accounting of the damage. I'm sure someone had already done that.

This wasn't any version of my room. It was generic. Sterile. A hospital room. My parents were asleep in chairs beside me that seemed too uncomfortable for sitting, much less sleeping. My mother's eyes opened and saw that I was watching her. She quickly shook my father.

"Get up, he's awake!"

He.

So I was a "he" again. Truth be told, I would have been equally happy with "she" or "they." Because what mattered most today were "I" and "we." *I* was alive. And *we* were still here.

Here's what I know.

On Monday, October 28, Layton Vandenboom was driving me home from football practice, because my piece-of-crap Dodge Dart had broken down in the school parking lot. A song by Konniption came on the radio. Layton hated the band, saying they were overplayed. He looked down to change the station. When he did, he ran a red light. We were broadsided by a truck.

I was in a coma for several days. The damage was substantial. Subdural hematoma. My head had to be opened up and drained. Lots of internal bleeding elsewhere, a few broken ribs, and the business with my leg. Not pretty. But what struck me—besides the semi—was how clean the universe was in patching its own wounds. Things were coherent again. The clockwork was turning, the gears all fitting with perfect precision. There was a logical cause and effect for every outcome. All things explained.

I had a lot of visitors those first few days, but I was out of it so it all sort of blends together. Here's what I remember.

The Johnsons came to visit. Leo, his parents, and yes, Angela was there, too. I cried when I saw her. I told them it was the medication. That was a real good excuse for telling a whole lot of people that I loved them. Leo included.

"Bro, look at this face," Leo responded, not missing a beat.

"How could you not love me?"

I asked him if he had heard from USC.

"Not until December fifteenth," he told me. "That's the day of their early admission announcements. But Stanford's pounding on my door now. We'll see."

There were so many things I wanted to tell him. But I couldn't clear my thoughts enough to do it. Maybe that was just as well, because words fall short of expressing things you've come to know in your heart. *I get it now,* I wanted to say, but that wasn't true. I would never quite get it. I would never truly be able to see things from his point of view. But at least I was no longer a carrier in the epidemic of ignorance.

He made a point of staying a little longer, after his parents and sister had left. Then, when he was sure we were alone, his cool composure seemed to shift to a foggier place.

"There's something . . . something I'm not quite remembering," he said. "I keep trying, but when I get close, I get this sick feeling right here." He touched his chest. "It has to do with you," he said, making dead-on eye contact, searching for an answer in my face. "Does that make any sense to you?"

I nodded. "It does."

He took a deep breath. I'm not sure what it meant. That he was relieved to know it wasn't just in his head? That he was shocked to know it wasn't? But then he breathed out long and slow.

"Whatever this thing is, I'm gonna let it go," he said.

"I think that's best," I told him. It was my burden to remember, not his.

Then he smiled and it chased away the shadow that had been hanging over the moment. "I'm just being goofy. It's probably just this place. Hospitals creep me out ever since that time Angela got sick."

For a moment the shadow came back again, but it passed like the smallest of clouds on the brightest of days.

My parents brought Hunter to see me. He was a little standoffish. A little awkward. It was how he was in this world. How *we* were.

"Does it hurt?" he asked.

"Sometimes more than others," I told him. "It's okay right now."

"So . . . I'm glad you didn't die," he said.

That actually made me laugh, but not in a bitter way. "Is that the best you can do?" I teased.

He got a bit prickly. "Well, I don't know what I'm supposed to say for something like this. I'm telling the truth—I really *am* glad you didn't die. If you did, I'd be pissed."

I took a long look at him.

"What?" he said, like the look was an accusation. But it was the opposite. It was an invitation. He didn't know it yet. That was okay. I'd get him to open the invitation eventually.

"Nothing," I told him. "I'm just glad you came. I'm happy to see you."

After hanging for a while, he went down to the cafeteria. Once he left, I told my parents that since our birthdays were coming up, I knew exactly what I wanted for mine.

"For my birthday, I want you to get Hunter an electric guitar," I told them. Because then they could put money that they usually had to divide in two into a single gift.

My dad looked at me funny. "He's never asked for one."

"That's just because he doesn't know he wants it," I told him.

There was an ebb and flow of friends, family, teammates. Mostly, though, I just got cards and flowers. Norris sent a Halloween balloon, because it was now two days after Halloween, so it was cheap. He didn't come by, because he had superstitions about hospitals. I can't say I missed him.

And then Paul came to visit.

He didn't come right away. He had been dealing with his own troubles and triumphs. In this reality, Layton hadn't gone after him, but that fight, and the bruises Paul took from it, translated to this world in a different way. On the same night as my accident, he had been attacked. A hate crime. No one knew who did it, but in the aftermath, the school—in fact the entire town—had risen to support him. Rainbow flags and T-shirts with some of Paul's quotes—which were a hell of a lot better than my quotes had been.

"All of a sudden I'm like the Queer Voice of Tibbetsville," he told me, his voice a mixture of irony, amusement, discomfort, and pride.

He caught me smiling at him. I'm not quite sure what he read in that smile, but he asked, "Did you know? I mean, before I started telling people?"

"Never thought about it," I said—because in this world, I hadn't. I wanted so much to take his hand, I almost reached for it. I came so close. The fact was, three-sevenths of me was in love with Paul. But the rest saw him as a friend. Paul deserved a better equation than that. So if a friendship was all we'd have, I was determined it would be a real friendship.

"Hey," I said, "I was thinking—if you're not doing anything, I'd like to have you over for Thanksgiving."

"Thanks," he said, "but I've already got plans. I'll be meeting my boyfriend's parents."

I had to suppress an involuntary flash of jealousy. "Anyone I know?"

"Naah, he goes to a different school. I mean, you might have played against him—he plays football, too. You'd like him. His name's Josh."

I smiled. I guess I shouldn't have been surprised. When the universe is coherent, things tend to fit. "I'll look forward to making his acquaintance."

We played a game of chess, which Paul said was brain football, and would help with my recovery. "A chess board is pretty much the same as a football formation," he pointed out—something obvious that I had never considered before.

We got through two games before I got too tired to play. I lost both, because Paul respected me enough not to go easy on me. When he left, we bumped fists. And maybe I held my knuckles against his a little longer than guys are supposed to. And maybe I'm not sorry about that at all.

There was one missing visitor, though, as I'm sure you've surmised.

"She's been by," my mother said. "Quite a few times, actually. But you've always been asleep."

It was almost understandable, since during that first week, I was asleep most of the time. Even so, it was more than just bad timing. When others came, they waited. They made enough noise to wake me up, or my parents went ahead and woke me up to see them—but Katie wouldn't let them do that. Not once. It was as if she wanted to see me, but didn't want me to see her.

I told my parents to tell me the next time she came—but not to wake me until right after she left. When they did, I told them I was taking a trip down the hall. In fact the doctors were encouraging me to as often as I could. And although my parents wanted to come with me, I insisted on going on my own.

"Just down the hall and back. No biggie."

I found Katie just where I thought I would. She was in Layton's room. While the hospital had transferred me to a step-down unit the day before, Layton was still in intensive care, and would likely be there for quite some time.

When I wheeled myself in, and Katie turned, she wasn't all that surprised to see me. Her eyes immediately went to the bandaged stump where the lower half of my left leg had been. Everyone who has visited me had done that. It was one of those things you couldn't help. But she looked away from it quickly.

"Hi, Ash," she said. "It's good to see you up."

The Edwards had said I had to be willing to make the ultimate sacrifice. I was, but it turns out that the universe didn't require that. Instead it exacted its price in pounds of flesh. Roughly nine pounds, to be exact. The weight of a leg amputated just below the knee.

"How is he?" I asked.

Katie looked over at Layton, who was in a bed that didn't look like a bed. It looked more like a human-shaped cookie cutter. His arms and legs were spread and held in place by foam wedges. And his head was kept immobile by a tight-fitting contraption that looked like it came off a roller coaster seat.

"Stable," Katie said. "He wakes up once in a while, but he's pretty groggy."

I could see his eyes moving beneath the lids. REM sleep

"Does he know?" I asked.

"His parents don't want anyone to tell him until he's stronger. But he knows. How could he not know?"

While I had lost a leg, Layton had suffered a broken neck. His spinal cord was severed at C-5. He could breathe, speak, and swallow on his own, and maybe even have some upper-arm movement. But he'd never be able to walk or use his hands again.

Katie was holding one of those hands. It was puffy and pale. It didn't grip her back and never would. She looked at me for a moment, then looked away.

"Did you do this?" she asked.

"He was the one driving."

"That's not what I mean, and you know it."

I couldn't hold her gaze. In every world Katie knew something had changed, and that I had changed it, but she had no frame of reference to know how things were different.

Did I do this?

I could have put the blame in half a dozen places, all of which would be true. I could even have told her that Layton brought it on himself, which would also be true. But pointing fingers has never helped a situation. Blame is a Band-Aid on a broken neck.

"It's complicated," I told her. And she nodded. That was something she understood.

"So what changed?" she asked.

"Everything," I told her. "We're back where we started."

She looked at me, incredulous at the thought. "If this is where we started, then the world's a pretty messed-up place."

"Yeah," I agreed. "But it could be much, much worse."

Layton's bed, which was on a mechanical gimbal, rotated slightly, tilting him at an angle to vary his blood flow. The motion woke Layton up. He groaned and his eyes opened lazily.

"Who's there?"

"It's me," Katie told him. "Ash is here, too."

I rolled closer and tried to sit a little higher so I was in his limited line of sight.

"You're alive," he said, all weak and woozy. "For a while I thought I'd killed you."

"Still kicking," I said. "Well, kind of."

Then his expression changed. He looked worried. "Katie . . .

how come you guys are holding hands?"

"We're not," she told him. "It's *your* hand I'm holding." And she lifted it up so he could see it more clearly.

"Oh," he said groggily. "Sorry. Dumb mistake."

Then his eyes closed and he was out.

Katie's eyes began to tear up. I gently put my hand on her shoulder, but she gently pulled away.

"I can't," she said. "Not now. You understand, don't you?"

I nodded. No matter how awful your boyfriend is, you don't walk away from him while he's in intensive care. I knew she'd break up with him at the right time, but I also knew that "Not now" meant not ever for her and me. After what happened, all the worlds where Katie and I could be together were lost in Elsewhere.

As I looked at Layton lying there, his body broken, I had to wonder if this was a tragedy or karma. Does a man who would hit a woman deserve to lose the use of those hands, like some sort of biblical judgment—and to suffer months in intensive care for something that took place in an entirely different reality? Layton was clearly capable of that kind of abuse here—but did capable make him culpable? I honestly don't know.

I had one more brush with the vast beyond. It was during the night while I was still at the hospital. The medication kept me fuzzy at night, in and out of dreams, skimming the surface of consciousness. Which is why I can't be certain that it wasn't a dream, but I think it was real.

I opened my eyes to see a figure standing over my bed. At first, I thought it was the nurse coming to check my telemetry. I was always twisting and turning and pulling off the leads in the middle of the night. Although he was dressed in scrubs, it wasn't one of the nurses. It was an Edward.

"Here to smother me with a pillow?" I asked. If he was, he wouldn't have gotten much resistance. I was too weak to fight it.

"You know I can't," he said. "But even if I could, it's not necessary anymore."

"Which one are you?"

"There was only ever one of us," he said. "Just different facets."

"Are you back on Earth to torment another sub-loc?"

He shook his head. "No—the current sub-loc is a sentient virus on the outer rim of Andromeda." He groaned. "Ugh—don't get me started."

"So why are you back here? What do you want?"

"To apologize," he said. "I . . . underestimated you. And because of that your world was almost lost. I want to make it up to you. By offering a gift."

"I don't want anything from you."

"It's not a 'thing,'" he said. "It's information that you might find useful."

I wanted to tell him where he could stick his information, but I had to admit I was curious.

"You won't forget anything that happened," he told me. "You'll retain the experience of all the other worlds. The memories of the many lives you've lived. Those memories will give you a perspective on life that no one else has."

"And headaches," I pointed out.

"And headaches," Edward agreed. "But there's something you should know. In the course of human history, there have been only nine individuals who survived being the subjective locus. You know their names, because they all went on to live extraordinary lives. Each one of them, in their own way, changed the world for the better . . . And you are the tenth."

The idea that my life might be anything but ordinary was laughable. Even when I was the actual center of the universe, I was nobody special.

"Who were the others?" I asked.

To that, Edward gave a sly smile. "Ah," he said. "That's a good question, isn't it? Goodbye, Ash. May you enjoy how your path unfolds."

And then he was gone, dissolving into long shadows cast by a bright moon.

I turned to look at that moon through my window, a swollen gibbous, nearly full to bursting. There was comfort in its familiarity. Knowing it would always be there, waxing and waning. Nothing I did from this moment on would change that. Sure, I suppose that primordial black hole was still out there, but then, it's always been there, like a far-off hornets' nest. If we don't mess with it, it won't mess with us.

Whether or not I'm wiser for the things I've experienced is not for me to judge. I do know that I have been humbled. I have been schooled in my own ignorance. That's not a bad thing. Understanding the depth of what we don't know protects us from the kind of hubris that destroys worlds. Perhaps, in the end, that's the perspective that matters. Only by being humbled can we ever hope to be great.

I also know, like humanity itself, there are parts of my multiple selves that will never be reconciled. Gaps that can't be sealed but can only be bridged—but as any engineer can tell you, it's the tension in the cables that makes a bridge strong. Trusting the tension between the things we can't unite is what protects us from plunging into the canyon between.

The moon slipped behind a cloud, but the room didn't get dark. There's always light somewhere in a hospital room. I closed my eyes. My body ached, but not as much as before. I was getting used to the void where my left leg had been. I would be okay. I would adapt, because that's what we do. We adapt or we die, and I had no intention of dying anytime soon, not when there's this remarkable life I'm supposed to live.

And there it is. Believe it, don't believe it, it's all the same to me.

I know I'll never be on a defensive line again, but that's okay. I think I've graduated to a much more exciting game. I'm ready to tackle whatever the world throws at me.

So bring it on.

ACKNOWLEDGMENTS

By the time this book is published, I'm hoping that our world will be on track in more ways than one. I won't say "back on track" because there are definitely new tracks that need to be found, as much as there are ones to return to.

If anything, the events of 2020 have reminded us of the things and people we take for granted. Gratitude is said to be the most powerful emotion, and there are so many people to whom, and *for* whom, I am grateful.

Game Changer is an idea that began to take shape over ten years ago, but most of the work and rework and deep dives and soul searching happened over the past four years—and all under the brilliant, gentle guidance of my editor, Rosemary Brosnan. More than an editor, she was a sounding board, conscience, friend—and occasionally therapist—throughout every step of the writing process.

Everyone at HarperCollins has been phenomenally supportive, from associate editor Courtney Stevenson, to designer Joel Tippie; production editor Kathryn Silsand as well as Michael D'Angelo and Anna Bernard in marketing and publicity; Sheala Howley and Rachel Horowitz in subsidiary rights; Patty Rosati, the queen of school and library marketing; and, of course, Suzanne Murphy, who presides over this glorious level of reality.

A warm shout-out to fellow writers Alex London and Nic Stone! Thanks, guys—your thoughtful, and insightful notes on my first draft gave me much-needed perspective, and made a huge difference. You really helped shape this book!

Thanks to my literary agent, Andrea Brown, for everything she does, from encouragement to inspiration to giving me a swift but gentle kick when I need one! Thank you, Taryn Fagerness, for handling foreign sales and putting up with my avoidance of paperwork—and while I'm on the subject, a special thanks to all the international publishers who have been bringing my books to the rest of the world!

A multiverse of gratitude to my entertainment industry agents, Steve Fisher and Debbie Deuble-Hill, at APA; my contract attorneys, Shep Rosenman and Caitlin DiMotta; and my stellar managers, Trevor Engelson and Josh McGuire. Without all of you, my career would most certainly be lost in the Elsewhere.

At the time of this writing, *Game Changer* is in development with Netflix, and I can't thank them enough for their support, and for the vision and brilliance of Brian Yorkey, who'll be running the show. No better universe than that!

Thanks to my assistant, Barb Sobel; my research assistant, Symone Powell; my writing-group-gone-rogue, the Fictionaires, who have adapted to distance, both social and geographical; my social media guru, Matt Lurie; and my dear friend and personal marketing genius, Keith Richardson—who reminds me to take care of myself when I'm too busy to remember. And a sorrowful thank-you to my aunt Mildred Altman, who we lost this year. She read every single book I ever wrote and sent me handwritten letters with her comments. She didn't get to read this one. I will miss those letters, but not as much as I will miss her.

Lately, we've all learned that reality can become very surreal—but in the end there's always something that grounds you. For me, it's my kids: Erin, who's just in the next room, and Brendan, who's on the other side of the planet. Jarrod and Sofi, who spend their time between Madrid and Los Angeles, and Joelle and Nathan, who divide their time between Northern and Southern California. Yet no matter the distance, no matter what world events come between us, they're always close. Thank you for reminding me what matters! I love you from the bottom of my heart to the center of the universe.